PRAI

THE IRISH GIRL

"This historical coming-of-age novel follows young Mary Agnes across the ocean as she seeks her place in the world and within her own soul. Sweeney shows the futility of trying to run from that which truly belongs to us, as well as the promise of finding that which does. A beautifully crafted story that will both transport and transfix readers."
—JUDE BERMAN, author of *The Vow*

"*The Irish Girl* is a story of resilience amidst trauma, love amidst loss, self-acceptance amidst rejection. Reminiscent of our immigrant ancestors and the unfathomable hardships they undoubtedly faced, I read this story in one sitting and found myself thinking about this fiercely strong girl long after I finished."
—KELLI ESTES, *USA Today* best-selling author of *The Girl Who Wrote in Silk*

"I fell deeply under the spell of *The Irish Girl*—a heroic yet relatable immigrant's tale of a thirteen-year-old girl sent to America who faces every challenge with steely determination and, ultimately, hope."
—MARTHA CONWAY, author of *The Physician's Daughter*

"Mary Agnes Coyne leaps off the page, lively, troubled, hungry for life and love. *The Irish Girl* is another winner!"
—SUSAN J. TWEIT, author of *Bless the Birds*

"Singing with drama, rooted in history, and rich in action, *The Irish Girl*'s independent and bold protagonist makes her way from Ireland to America at age thirteen in 1886. Pitted against the challenges of poverty, misogyny, and abuse, Mary Agnes Coyne navigates the twisty streets of New York and Chicago and expansive cattle ranches of Colorado and Santa Fe. But her longing for family and home is deep, and her search to find both leads to a gutsy conclusion. Sweeney's fourth winner!"

    —GRETCHEN CHERINGTON, author of *Poetic License*

"With the spunk of the Irish, Mary Agnes wins your heart from the start. With writing as lush as the Connemara countryside, *The Irish Girl* is a powerful story of a young woman's discovery of hidden strengths against all odds—a story emblematic of the resilient American emigrant spirit that keeps the love of home country while embracing, wholeheartedly, the new."

    —DEBRA THOMAS, author of *Luz*

"*The Irish Girl* captured me from the very first page! At times both tragic and hopeful, this sweeping literary drama is ultimately a story of perseverance—one to which we can all relate somewhere in our immigrant past. Brimming with rich historical details and beautiful, lilting prose, this addictive book is a delight!"

    —MICHELLE COX, author of The Henrietta
    and Inspector Howard series

PRAISE FOR
HARDLAND
(2022, SHE WRITES PRESS)

"A stunner . . . The well-crafted story is firmly grounded in the past, but its powerful messages still resonate today."
—TRUE WEST MAGAZINE

"Ashley E. Sweeney minces few words as she unravels Ruby Fortune's fate on the early Arizona frontier. Wild West performer, drug addict, ardent lover, mother, and murderer, Ruby's story is gritty and unabashedly raw. She quickly learns she is sometimes no match for the trials that come her way, but she survives as only she knows how—with her strength, her wit, and her gun. Spellbinding from beginning to end."
—JAN CLEERE, New Mexico-Arizona Book Award winner of *Military Wives in Arizona Territory*

"Sweeney's stunning portrayal of this tough-minded woman is both compelling and memorable. The fast-paced and intense narrative reaches far beyond the classic Western genre for a wide range of readers who value survival, honesty, and love."
—HISTORICAL NOVELS REVIEW

Praise for
Answer Creek
(2020, SHE WRITES PRESS)

"Ada is an impressive heroine who thinks for herself and exhibits moral courage in dire straits. . . . [the novel] succeeds at capturing the endurance of the human spirit."
—*Publishers Weekly*

"The author is a master of vivid descriptions, dragging readers along every wretched mile of the trail, sharing every dashed hope and every dramatic confrontation, with Ada as their guide. Ada is a marvelous creation, twice orphaned and both hopeful and fearful about a new life in California, the promised land. . . . A vivid westward migration tale with an arresting mixture of history and fiction."
—*Kirkus Reviews*

"In *Answer Creek*, Sweeney rescues the story of the Donner Party from its fate as salacious anecdote and delivers a harrowing tale of resilience, folly, loss, and hope."
—Mary Volmer, author of *Reliance, Illinois*

PRAISE FOR
ELIZA WAITE
(2016, SHE WRITES PRESS)

"Ashley Sweeney's first novel, *Eliza Waite*, is a gem."
—JANE KIRKPATRICK, author
of *Beneath the Bending Skies*

"Cast off by her family and living in the shadow of unthinkable tragedy, Eliza Waite finds the courage to leave her remote island home to join the sea of miners, fortune hunters, con men, and prostitutes in the Klondike during the spring of 1898. Ashley Sweeney's exquisite descriptions, electrifying plot twists, and hardy yet vulnerable characters will captivate historical fiction fans and leave them yearning for more. *Eliza Waite* is a stunning debut!"
—KRISTEN HARNISCH, author
of *The Vintner's Daughter*

"Sweeney's debut novel is a beautifully written work of historical fiction tracing one woman's life in the wilds of nineteenth-century America. Readers will be immersed in Eliza's world, which Sweeney has so authentically and skillfully rendered."
—*BOOKLIST*

THE
IRISH
GIRL

THE
IRISH
GIRL

A NOVEL

ASHLEY E. SWEENEY

SHE WRITES PRESS

Published 2024
Printed in the United States of America
Print ISBN: 978-1-64742-776-4
E-ISBN: 978-1-64742-777-1
Library of Congress Control Number: 2024913205

For information, address:
She Writes Press
1569 Solano Ave #546
Berkeley, CA 94707

Interior Design by Tabitha Lahr

She Writes Press is a division of SparkPoint Studio, LLC.

Company and/or product names that are trade names, logos, trademarks, and/or registered trademarks of third parties are the property of their respective owners and are used in this book for purposes of identification and information only under the Fair Use Doctrine.

This is a work of fiction. Names, characters, places, and incidents either are the product of the author's imagination or are used fictitiously. Any resemblance to actual persons, living or dead, is entirely coincidental.

Other works by Ashley E. Sweeney:

Hardland
Answer Creek
Eliza Waite

For the many daughters
of Mary Agnes Coyne

But I, being poor, have only my dreams . . .
—W. B. YEATS

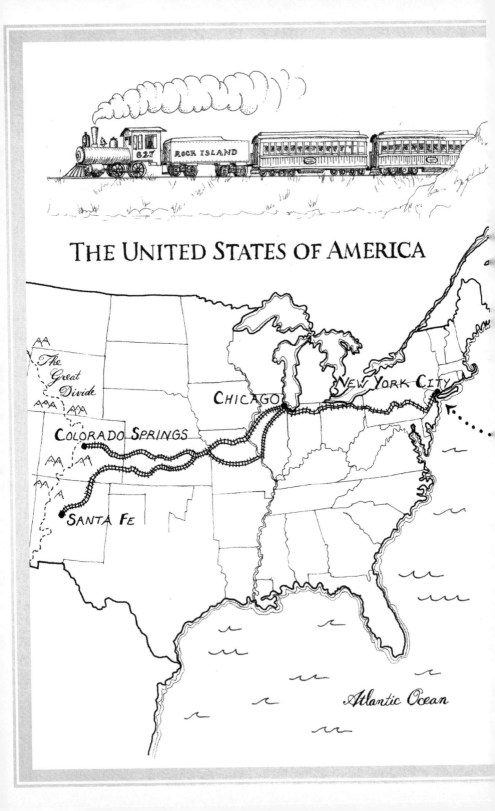

THE UNITED STATES OF AMERICA

The Great Divide

COLORADO SPRINGS

SANTA FE

CHICAGO

NEW YORK CITY

Atlantic Ocean

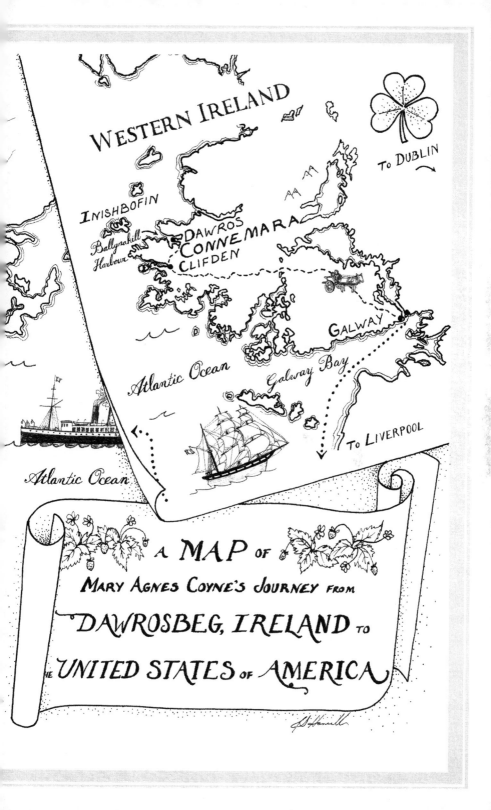

October 1886
Galway City, Ireland

In the dim crease of dawn, Galway's docks clatter with stevedores, sailors, pimps, dogs. The air, laced with coal dust
and smoke, reeks of rotting fish. Mary Agnes Coyne clutches
her granddad's arm as they weave through crowds swarm-
ing the wharfside, the sky leaden, threatening rain. The
hem of Mary Agnes's brown skirt is damp, her worn brown
boots crusted with mud. She wears the new green shawl
her gram knit for her over an ivory cable-knit sweater, her
auburn hair pulled back and covered with a brown wool hat
pulled low. Beyond a tangle of masts and battered hulls, a
constant rumble, as the black River Corrib barrels down the
narrow seaway toward the even-blacker Atlantic.

Am I really leaving Ireland? Going to America? Alone?

At thirteen, Mary Agnes is thinner than most, and not
as tall, with long, thick, dark auburn hair framing a striking
face marked by a prominent widow's peak. Deep-set green

eyes peer over a band of freckles that spans her straight
nose, mirroring her five younger brothers. Unlike her
brothers, though, her teeth are white, and straight.

*The picture of yer mother, everyone says, a beauty she were, that
Laffey girl, when she were young; such a shame what happened to
her, do ya think it could have been her—no, no, best not to say,
best not to say.*

Mary Agnes began her womanhood just last month and
has avoided her fifteen-year-old half-brother Fiach the last
few weeks, especially after—again, best not to say. She still
has deep red scratches on her back from when she fought
him off the first time. Her stomach hasn't settled since and
her heart has turned dark against him, despite the com-
mandment to love one another. Today, her drawers are
stuffed with rags, the bleeding not yet stopped.

Wagons and carts—a steady line of them, some large,
some not so large, merging between people and animals
and cargo on the tight quay—rumble and growl on cobble-
stones slick with grease and dung. Mary Agnes's stomach
rumbles and growls, too. There was no breakfast today.

Feral dogs dart into the narrow thoroughfare, knocking
over bins and scattering debris. When they dash in front of
a small vegetable wagon, its driver tries to avoid a collision.
"For feck's sake," he yells, as dogs nip at his dark roan's
fetlocks and up, up the roan goes on its hind legs, eyes
wild. The teamster yanks the reins and—*one one-thousand,
two one-thousand, three one-thousand,* Mary Agnes counts—the
roan surrenders, its nostrils flaring.

Mary Agnes's heart beats madly, her legs shake. She
leans in toward her granddad, Festus Laffey. As he steers
her toward the doorway of a nearby warehouse, she steps in
a steaming pile of fresh dung. Bile rises in her throat. Will
she risk losing yesterday's late dinner? A weak bowl of fish
chowder and a hard biscuit at a Galway pub? Her granddad

didn't eat, and she noticed. She scrapes muck off her worn boots on uneven cobbles, knowing she's likely only grinding it in deeper. The smell alone is enough to make her retch.

Now under cover and out of the rain, Festus turns to Mary Agnes. "Are ya a-rights, Aggie?" Festus is the only one who calls her Aggie; everyone else calls her Mary A. "Galway is a rough spot for a girl."

Just then, an urchin bumps Festus and reaches for the older man's coat pocket.

"Bogger!" Festus yells. "Ya won't fleece me!" He shakes his fist as the runner darts away, empty-handed.

Mary Agnes tries to get a good look at the boy. *Was he but seven? Or eight? Out scrounging for coin?* She thinks of her five younger brothers. *Will I ever see them again?*

The boy disappears in the throng but, in the looking, Mary Agnes spies the hem of a red dress swishing by. *And what is a fine lady doing out at this hour?* She cranes her neck to follow the hem but can make out only a black shawl, a black hat, a black veil. In less than a minute, the woman is swallowed up by the Spanish Arch at the end of the quay.

Mary Agnes hugs her satchel and keeps up with her granddad's long legs as they walk guardedly through putrefying fish guts in oily puddles. Along the quayside, stout barrels, wooden crates, and cinch-filled sacks wait to be loaded onto ships. Strong stevedores use a crude rope-and-pulley system to hoist crates of sheep over a ship's rail; the animals bleat mournfully as pens *thud* on deck.

All that mutton going to England, as usual, Mary Agnes thinks. *While we starve.*

Down the quay they weave, looking for the ship to Liverpool. *Siren*, it's called, the only ship leaving today. *Leaving. Leaving.* Not that one. No, not that one.

"It'd be here," Festus says. Ahead of them, a barque, in grim need of paint, her faded figurehead jutting from the bow, hair once blonde and breasts exploding from a dull red gown. The ship is perhaps a hundred-fifty feet, give or take as they say, when the answer's in reach, but not yet clear. Heavy lines loop down through rusted hawseholes and tether the ship to large iron rings set into stone at twenty-foot intervals along the dock. Although the ship is bound fast, still she creaks in the raging river.

Two spindly masts pierce low clouds, the rigging a tangle that yaws in the wind and now-pelting rain. Men of every color race up and down masts to harness rigging and bend sails: royals, topgallants, jibs. Two men repair a large gash in the hull, others swarm the deck heaving trunks and provisions. A yell, and then a crash, as something splinters on deck.

A rash of vulgarities then—in both Irish and English—followed quickly by a loud whistle, commotion, and, out of the fray, an enraged ship's master reprimanding the crew in words not meant for thirteen-year-old ears.

Mary Agnes tries to stop up her ears with ungloved hands as she squints to read the ship's badge, hoping against hope this is not the ship. But there it is: *Siren*, carved into rotting wood and devoid of luster. Her heart drops.

Must I board?

But what choice does she have? Today, Mary Agnes is bound for Liverpool, and from there, on another ship to America. It hasn't sunk in yet. It is like she will wake up from a horrid dream and still be in Dawrosbeg, with her grandparents and Jonesy and her brothers. But, her mam. And Fiach. Her stomach lurches. *I cannot have a babe.*

"You could come too, Granda," Mary Agnes says with the steadiest voice she can muster.

"And leave yer Gram? Never. Ireland is my home."

"Aye, it is, but."

Mary Agnes and Festus mill about with other passengers until the ship's master finally lowers the gangway.

Others press in for spots in line to board. Mary Agnes hangs back for as long as she can.

"Last call for Liverpool," the ship's master barks.

Festus presses several folded bills and a letter into Mary Agnes's hand. The envelope bears an unfamiliar address in an unfamiliar handwriting.

"Give this to the good father at the church in New York," Festus says. "It will tell him all he needs to know."

Mary Agnes glances at the envelope. She does not yet know there are more than a hundred churches in New York and finding this particular one will be more difficult than she can imagine. As to the bills, she gasps.

"But Granda—this is a fortune." She fingers six, seven, eight pounds, the sum of a fisherman's yearly wages. What could this amount buy? So many things, clothing and soap and boots and oilskins and eyeglasses and *food*, she thinks, *so much food*.

Festus hugs Mary Agnes and bends to kiss her hair. He holds her in an embrace longer than usual. "'Tis my pleasure, girl. It'll be six pounds alone for yer fare and two to spare. Mind yer purse, but I've no need to say that. Ya've a good head on yer shoulders. And a sight smarter—and prettier—than most, if I don't say so myself. A true Laffey, ya are, Ag."

He turns her face toward his and cups her cheeks. "Don't forget where ya come from."

How can I ever forget? But where is home now?

Festus begins then in Gaelic:

"Go n-éirí an bóthar leat . . ."
May you succeed on the road . . . and until we meet again . . .

"Go gcoinní Dia i mbos A láimhe thú."
May God hold you in the hollow of his hand.

Mary Agnes's eyes tear up.

"Until we meet again. And ya'll see, there'll be an again in it, girl."

I'm not sure of that, Granda. Not sure at all.

"Come along, lass," the ship's master calls. "'Time and tide wait for no man.' Or girl, for that matter."

Mary Agnes peers up at Festus, that rugged face she knows and loves, memorizing it against time. "Goodbye, Granda. I'll miss you . . ."

"God as my witness," he interrupts, touching her cheek, his eyes swelled with tears. "I'll miss ya more than ya'll ever know."

2

Five months earlier
May 1886
Off Dawrosbeg, County Galway, Western Ireland

Mary Agnes holds tight to the sides of her granddad's small fishing boat as they weave through rocky shoals in Ballynakill Harbour toward the wide mouth of the North Atlantic. They're after cod, ling, hake—and not a moment too soon. No fishermen have dared go out during this furious storm that's battered the Irish seaboard for days, "a good stir," Festus calls it, waves that could sink much larger ships. Which means Mary Agnes is desperately hungry by now, five days on; the pain in her stomach throbs like a hammer pounding a nail.

And the storm's not abated yet. Cold salt spray crashes over the tar-covered currach's bow, wave after wave of it, as her granddad rows out with the tide. Rain—*is it ever not raining in Ireland?*—lashes the boat with such vengeance Mary Agnes wonders if God has a special reason for punishing the Irish.

Sure, and there'd be reasons, wet enough to drown the dead, beginning with us Coynes . . .

When they clear Dawrosbeg, Festus heads for the tip of Renvyle Peninsula, four miles northwest, Letter Hill to starboard. Mary Agnes can't quite see the cliff at the end of the peninsula that extends out into the sea, but it's not just because of the rain. She can't see past her hands; everything else is blurry at best.

Mary Agnes's shabby muslin dress, plastered to her shins, is soaked through, despite wearing one of her granddad's oversized woolen sweaters. Her feet, clammy and raw, are stuffed into one-size-too-small boots. She's chilled already, and not a half-hour into their day, with eight, nine hours to go. That she could use an oilskin and a hat like her granddad wears—*and so many other things*—is like conjuring up fairy dreams. There is hardly enough to put food scraps on the table at home. She cannot ask.

A stiff wind skims the skin of the sea as the currach rises and falls in the waves. It's as familiar as her own skin. When she was eight, and every year since, she has taken to the sea with her granddad on Fridays, and it's a relief, getting away from her mam and da and brothers in their overcrowded cottage, unless there's a new little one at home, that is, and then she's pressed into service and misses her Fridays out.

And Mam's due again. More mouths to feed. But feed us what?

Nothing for breakfast again today, for her anyway. The meager slurry her mam scrapes together each morning is for the boys, *and don't ya go grudging it,* her mam says. Mary Agnes's stomach growls, hollow and empty. She's often faint and has trouble concentrating, even on the smallest of tasks. And then there's the constant headache. If it weren't for scant mussels she collects, the family would have even less to eat. And with this recent storm, there's been no mussel gathering for a week.

As she shifts her bottom on the slippery seat, Mary Agnes catches herself before she scrapes already-bruised knees on the ribbed sole of the boat. If only a fish would jump into the currach, she would eat it raw, sink her teeth into the slimy flesh, skin and all, oily innards dripping down her chin. She touches her mouth, as if tasting it.

As they near the point, Mary Agnes sees the faint outline of three familiar islands through patchy fog several miles off the Connemara coast, the largest, *Inis Bo Finne*, dominant. When seas permit, Festus fishes off Inishbofin, that's the English word, and English they're required to speak now, except at home when no one's listening.

But on Fridays, Festus and Mary Agnes fish closer to home off Dawrosbeg. It's their special time. Whether they catch fish or not on Fridays is usually not of issue. Today, however, it's more pressing than usual. Festus hasn't been out for a week due to the weather, and, despite it, he needs fish.

Most of the fish caught in Irish waters is bound for England, and don't think fisherman don't begrudge it, they do. It's as palpable as breath. And not just fish. Cattle, horses, rabbits, and honey—anything exportable—is bound for England to feed the British, leaving the Irish hungry.

It's been this way since before *An Gorta Mór*, the time of great hunger in 1847.

Maybe the famine could have been avoided—or mitigated—but that's an old, tired conversation that loops in pubs and cottages and along the lanes, and the result the same, a million dead, two million moved on, and five million more with nowhere to go, most of them still hungry.

History is in the telling of it, Mary Agnes knows, and this much is true: The famine wasn't the fault of the Irish, none at all, but they're the ones paying the price. That the Irish continue to feed the British, forty years on now, is nothing less than galling. How can someone not begrudge that? She hates the British so much that sometimes her fists clench so hard her jagged nails pierce her palms until they bleed.

Festus whistles as he pulls to the rhythm of the dark, undulating waves with pole-shaped oars—dip, up, dip, up—the sound of wood grating wood as he pulls the oars hard against the oarlocks. He is taller and twice as thin as his kinfolk. In any weather, he wears a worn, ivory cable-knit sweater; suspenders; heavy, dark wool pants; an oilskin; and a tweed flat cap; all he owns except for well-worn mourning clothes. The cap covers his mop of grey hair—what is left of it—and falls low on his weather-withered face. His eyes, green like Mary Agnes's, are filmed over with white.

He clears his throat and begins to sing.

I'm a-rowin' on the ocean
Many miles a-sea . . .

"Join in, Aggie," he says. "It's still a ways off to the point."

Mary Agnes doesn't need to be asked twice, she loves to sing.

And I wonder oh my darlin'
If ya ever think of me.

She is always asked to sing at wakes, songs in the old language. *Demons cower and angels weep*, old folks say when she's finished singing, and everyone nods, *yes, yes, indeed she does, that Coyne girl, she's blessed, what a rare gift she has, that voice, that voice. Like her gram, an angel voice she had, too, when she were young.* And on they go, a drop of whiskey, *and thanks for that*, with the rememberings.

Today, singing keeps Mary Agnes from thinking about cold or hunger—*or about Fiach.*

Festus and Mary Agnes finish all six verses of the shanty—the last verse quite lustily—as her granddad rows and she tends to nets. And then he laughs. Despite years of hardship and heartache and hunger, Festus is almost always merry. Mary Agnes admires that about her granddad. She is not always merry.

They reach the lee of Renvyle Point and tuck into a nook to escape the weather. Here, they ready the hand line. Mary Agnes pulls the bait bucket between her feet while Festus feeds her line. She baits each of the hundred hooks attached to the long line with bits of limpet she collected last week at low tide and kept alive in a bucket of seawater. She's proud how fast she can bait a hook, *faster than any man*, her granddad says. Not today, though. Her fingers are so cold she struggles to work bait onto hooks.

When the lines are ready, Festus rows the boat away from shore and points the bow of the currach into the tidal current. Mary Agnes slowly pays out the line, careful not to let it tangle. She hopes there will be enough fish to sell so Festus can pay his rent. The rest of the fish, well, that's another story. That her gram will only get tails and heads today rankles, but it will be enough for a scanty fish stew, just enough. Mary Agnes's fingers are by now raw, and she curses that she forgot gloves today.

But will she complain? No. If she is to be a fisherwoman, she needs to toughen. So what if she's drenched, cold, famished? She's with her granddad, sheltered and safe.

"GET OFF ME, YOU BRUTE!"

Fiach's hand gropes under Mary Agnes's nightclothes as he pins her to her cot, his fingers cold as dead winter. He smells of dirt and sweat and whiskey. It's May, the rutting season, as he clamps his hand over her mouth, his breath hot and thick. She chokes back a scream and squirms beneath him, distressed she didn't hear him climbing the ladder to the loft where she sleeps on a cot pushed up against the single window.

Fiach is built like Festus, tall and lean. His dark hair hangs around his gaunt face. That he has strength at all may surprise, but he does get breakfast, their mam sees to that. Tonight, his fingers dig deep into her behind after he fumbles with his trousers. If she doesn't act fast, something she dreads more than death might happen nine months from now—all too well she knows about childbearing from her mother. And she is not ready for a child. Especially not now, at thirteen. Mary Agnes bites down hard on Fiach's hand.

"Whore!" he yells. He lurches back, raises his hand, and slaps her face.

She wrenches free of her half-brother's grasp and leaps from the bed, her nightdress drenched with sweat. She grabs a candlestick and raises it above her head.

"One more inch, and I'll bash your face." Her cheek burns from the slap. Her da beats their mam, so this is nothing new in a long line of women in the parish who sport reddened cheeks like rouge. "The weather," they say, or "Clumsy me," or "Walked into the door, that I did." Mary Agnes knows better. She will never marry.

Fiach lunges toward Mary Agnes and she brings the full force of the pewter candleholder down on his arm.

"Damn ya," he yells. He holds his arm and glares at her.

A loud padding from the front room, steps on the ladder. *Da. I thought you'd never come.*

"What the devil?" John Coyne stands at the top of the ladder, his shoulders slumped. Her da is short and stout like many of the Connemara men, built for work. But work is scarce, and he spends his days at the pub. His speech is slurred from drink again tonight.

Fiach grimaces and slinks past his stepfather, not without a cuff to the side of his head. John Coyne stares at Mary Agnes. He does not speak, just remains there, staring.

Does he see me? Does he care?

Mary Agnes breaks the silence, her voice shaky. "He were after me, Da."

Her father grunts. "See as ya don't tempt him."

Tempt him? "How could I tempt him, Da? I were asleep!" "Find a way."

Mary Agnes's eyes blaze. "And how is it I can do that?" He shrugs and turns to leave. "Ask yer mam." "Da!"

He moves away with tired steps.

Ask Mam? Like she knows? Eight children in fifteen years? All those boys like stairsteps, barely a year between them, except the years the tiny white coffins were spirited away and Mam sank into gloom so dark we daren't talk to her? For months?

A wan moon casts weak light through the lone attic window above Mary Agnes's cot. Most nights, she watches the moon, the stars, the clouds, the sea outside her window. Makes up a poem. Sings. But tonight, she doesn't take her eyes off the top of the ladder for the rest of night, short as it is, hoping that a thousand currachs will come to take her away from this place. She pulls her coverlet up to ward off damp and prays under her breath, quiet enough so no one in the cottage will be roused, but loud enough for Mary and the saints to hear.

But the currachs don't come—*and why would I think they would, that's the stuff of folktales.* She will keep a knife under her pillow from now on, a sharp one.

ONE PULL, THEN ANOTHER, AS MARY AGNES and Festus reel in codfish hand over hand onto the sole of the boat. Fish writhe at their feet. Festus takes a club to each to render it still and marks the catch in a small notebook. She pulls hooks from their mouths, disentangles lines, and stuffs silvery fish, eyes now dulled, into worn baskets. Rust-red blood, sea water, and rain pools at her feet and she bails the bottom of the currach with a small bucket.

Mid-afternoon, Festus rows the boat toward a sheltered harbor on an islet called Finishlagh. The cove is protected from wind here, this Mary Agnes can read from the ripples on the water. The rain has eased, "only spitting," Festus calls it. He throws out a small anchor and she unpacks dinner, now cold. They sit, huddled, splitting a small, sliced potato and a piece of pickled cod, washed down with lukewarm tea, each swallow a gift.

When they finish their meal, Festus wipes his mouth with his sleeve, picks up a frayed piece of line, and holds it out toward Mary Agnes. He is missing half of his left forefinger.

"A bowline," he says, as he weaves a knot. "Ya try it."

Mary Agnes stumbles on the first try, but then finds a pattern, weaving a frayed rope up through a loop, around a fixed line, and down through the loop again.

"Now let's race," Festus says. "On your marks, get set, go!"

At the sound of *go*, old fingers and young work the lines, ten seconds on the next try, then eight, and the winning five, Mary Agnes triumphant as she pulls the knot tight. She holds it up for Festus's inspection as the currach bobs in the lagoon, small against the waves, the sea, the world.

"Well done, girl. Now behind yer back. Then we'll try one hand. We'll make a fisherwoman out of ya yet. Maybe take over my operation. Wouldn't that be something, a lass in charge."

Now there's an idea. Take over from Granda. Move to Inishbofin. Live off fish. Mary Agnes can gut a fish as fast as anyone (and maybe faster, her head low to see her hands, and isn't that boning knife sharp and her eyesight not—she has cuts on her knuckles to prove it). *That would solve everything. And I'd be far enough away from Fiach.* Mary Agnes thinks these things as she pulls on a damaged net. She dares to ask the question she's often worried about, seeing as she cannot swim.

"Have you ever fallen over, Granda? Into the sea?"

"One time too few," Festus laughs. Soon his face goes dark. "The sea never gives up, Aggie. Certainly never gives up its dead." His eyes narrow. "I've known too many lost. One day it'll be my turn."

No. Mary Agnes hurries to change the subject. "Do we have time for a story?" Her granddad is known throughout Connemara as one of the best storytellers. He never says no.

Festus checks the sky. "A short one, perhaps. The mad birdman?" He flaps his large arms. "Or the magic salmon?" He motions a fish swimming.

"The magic salmon," she says, and mimics his motion, her hands flying through the air like a salmon swimming upstream.

"Then the magic salmon it is."

And there, amid now choppier waves, wind picking up and seabirds screeching overhead, her granddad begins the story of the boy who caught the world's most elusive salmon and by doing so gained all the knowledge the world has to offer.

Just the word, *fish*, and Mary Agnes's stomach grumbles all the more. It is a curse to even think about food. *Maybe I'll slip one into my dress pocket. Maybe two, when Granda's not looking, and share it with my brothers later at home.*

But then her granddad's numbers would be off and he'd be held accountable, and it's better to be hungry than see her granddad hauled off to prison.

Damn the British, she thinks, *every one of them, sitting at their polished tables eating our food.*

"Can ya imagine it, girl?" Festus asks. "Knowing every-thing? The past and the future?"

Mary Agnes cannot imagine tomorrow, let alone the future. She squints through patches of fog. By now she can't feel her fingers. If only she were in front of a fire, reading. She narrows her eyes again, this time scrunching her whole forehead, eyes slits.

"I cannot see the future," she says. "But I can almost see America from here." Just last week, another family from Dawrosmore emigrated to America. There was an "American Wake" for them: food, music, and Irish blessings. The word *America* conjures so many thoughts. Opportunity. No British rule. Food for every meal. Away from incessant wind and rain.

And far, far away from Fiach.

"Everything's better there, in America, isn't it, Granda?"

Festus pauses and half turns toward her. How Mary Agnes loves his profile, so familiar and comforting. It's as if his very presence undergirds her. She can't imagine life without him.

"I'm not sure of that, girl." Festus shakes his head and looks at her with filmy eyes. "No one who leaves for America ever comes back. A few letters, maybe, and then there's only an empty chair at the table." He sets his shoulders, pulls the oars, and heads back toward Dawrosbeg, the last breath of day limning the horizon with a sliver of light.

Thanks be to God, Festus has a good catch today. The women will be waiting. The children will be waiting. It will be another long night ahead gutting fish, standing in mud to their shins and packing fish into barrels until it's so dark, all they will see is the outline of hands, faces, lives.

As the boat approaches the tip of the Dawros peninsula, Mary Agnes shivers violently. She worries the line in her already-worn pocket, fingering the knot like a rosary.

I'm not sure it's better in America, either, Granda. But I have to get away from Fiach, and soon, before I'm saddled with a babe of my own.

Or I kill him first.

3

May 1886
Dawrosmore, County Galway, Western Ireland

Damp seeps in every crack of the small cottage as Mary Agnes wipes a thin, warped pane with an already-dirtied rag, making small, uneven circles from top to bottom of the glass. Even if her hand rests for a second, her mind never rests. The image of Fiach coming at her is never far from her mind. But he will be going out soon—*thanks be to God*—and won't be expected back until suppertime. She's got a knife under her tick pillow now, it hasn't yet been missed. And if it is, the tinkers will be around soon and her Mam can trade for a new one.

John and Anna Coyne's whitewashed stone cottage sits on a small knoll two hundred yards from the sea at Dawrosmore outside Letterfrack in rural Connemara, a wild and rugged place in the far west of Ireland. Measuring nine feet by fifteen feet, the cottage has three windows, two small rectangular ones framing the worn green door, and another in the attic, above Mary Agnes's cot, facing the sea. A massive fireplace dominates the eastern wall of the earthen-floored cottage.

Inside, the Coynes have cobbled together space for eating: a table and four chairs, rotated between the nine of them; space for sleeping: a curtained area for John and Anna and straw mats lining the walls for the boys; space for gathering: several three-legged stools in front of the smoldering peat fire. It's said the soul flees from the people of a house if the fire goes out, so Mary Agnes, superstitious as she is, makes sure the fire is always fed. Everything smells of smoke.

The sky, a brew of grey and slate and coal, shoulders heavy clouds that loom low over the landscape, obscuring the Twelve Bens beyond. Wind howls down the peninsula's rutted lane and carries with it the breath of the Atlantic. Rain beats against thatch-roofed cottages and age-old stone walls. On rocky knolls, wild thyme, whitethorn, thrift, and stonecrop bloom early after winter, their delicate flowers clinging to life. The sea roars and churns, whitecaps as far as the horizon, out past the outer islands, even, thrusting salt spray in wild lacy bursts up jagged bluffs. Seabirds are no match for the wind today.

Glancing through the window toward the west, beyond the yard, beyond the rain, lies America. Mary Agnes cannot stop thinking about it. Just the saying of it—*America*—has emboldened her.

Maybe I will go there. But going to America is as likely as a deep winter's day in Connemara dawning cornflower blue. *Maybe Galway? Or Dublin? I will never go to England.* She wrestles with where to go, how to stay. *I'll be a fisherwoman, I will, live on Inishbofin, that's how I'll avoid Fiach.* The dilemma consumes her, back, forth, back, forth, *see saw Margery Daw.*

"No breakfast yet?" Fiach Laffey barks at his mother.

"Don't ya be talking to yer mam like that," John Coyne says. He sits at the table slurping tea from a saucer.

"Bastard," Fiach replies.

John Coyne rises and advances toward Fiach, but Fiach's out the cottage door in a flash. John thunders out after him.

You're the bastard, Fiach, Mary Agnes thinks. *For more reasons than one.*

Many an Irish girl gives birth not long after a wedding, and no one mentions it. But her mother? What about that? Didn't anyone suspect? Anna Laffey had Fiach at fourteen, *fourteen, mind you,* unmarried and without the hint of a suitor. Who was his father, then? A local man? The innkeeper? A rogue soldier? The landowner? The priest?

Mary Agnes has often wondered because no one speaks of it. That John Coyne married Anna Laffey soon after Fiach was born might be called laudable, but you don't know John Coyne—and you don't know Fiach Laffey. Fifteen years on, you don't want to be in the same room as the both of them unless you've wagered on it.

"Off with ya, then," Anna Coyne yells. "And stop yer gawking, Mary A." Anna rattles the iron pot over the fire, holding her lumpy stomach like a bag of feed as she stirs contents, weak as the broth is sure to be.

And speaking of weak, was it just last night John Coyne came after Anna Coyne? With a butcher knife? Chased her around the kitchen table? And she with child again? Who does such a thing? It was a good thing John Coyne was on the drink and Anna Coyne faster, despite being heavy with child. All the children witnessed it. They witness plenty. There are always bruises, but never talk of changes.

"Out of my way, will ya?" Anna Coyne swats three-year-old Thomas on the rear. He's small and dark-haired, with merry eyes. Nine-year-old Ferris and five-year old Eamon, both dark-haired and bone thin, scrape chairs up to the table, spoons in hand. Sean and Padraig, eleven and ten, are still out with their da in the barn. None of the children wears shoes or boots, except for Mass.

Mary Agnes motions to Tommy. He scoots up into the window well onto her lap.

"Mammy's sore again," he whispers.

Is her mother ever not in a black mood? Mary Agnes remembers the old Irish saying, "Nothing is worse than a smoking chimney, a scolding woman, and a leaking roof." *We've got all three here, the chimney, the woman, the roof.*

"Shh, now," she says, as she wraps her arms around Tommy's bony frame. He is her favorite, and not just because he is the youngest. Can you feel love through your eyes? This she wonders, because she feels it. Just the way Tommy looks at her thaws her heart. Tommy places his head against her chest, his ribs protruding. She strokes his head, and he settles into her. "Shh," she says again, "lovely boy."

Out the window, the crooked lane in front of the cottage winds down toward the dark Atlantic. If only she could focus clearly, she might be able to identify each of the Jones's lambs in the lower pasture by name, but she can only make out a mass of woolly splotches huddled by the stile. She will have to try to sneak away to see Jonesy later. Thinking about him makes her heart race.

She's known him her whole life, for goodness's sake. When they were but children, they played on grassy knolls, chasing robins and rabbits, digging for buried coin, collecting stones. Their affection grew slowly until recently when they first kissed behind the Jones's barn. Jonesy, a sturdy lad with tousled hair—and hands and feet as large as a man—pulled her close then and stroked her hair. *Tender,* is what she recalls. Now they meet almost daily, away from prying eyes. Only the wind bears witness to it.

Mary Agnes glances outside again, the world blurred and soft around the edges. Unless it's three inches from her face, like a book, she can hardly see. Except for mountains. She can make out the shapes of Letter Hill to the north across the harbor and tall Bengoora to the east, one of the Twelve Bens that surrounds Letterfrack. Because of this, she always knows where she is in relation to the world, north or south or east. West is always the sea. She has always wanted to climb Bengoora. Maybe a miracle would occur there, like miracles in biblical stories, and she would be able to see. But climb the mountain? How? She has to settle for poor eyesight, her da can't afford to buy her eyeglasses, so that is out of the question. It's never talked about, like so many other things.

John Coyne blames everyone and everything for everyone and everything, so what's the use of talking? Blame is always a drink away. Mary Agnes supposes she could blame Jesus, John Coyne does. But how can you blame Jesus for everything that goes wrong? After everything he went through?

Tommy wriggles on her lap. "I'm hun-gy, Ammie A." He can't pronounce Mary yet, let alone Agnes.

"Be still now, Tommy," she whispers back. "Breakfast will be on soon enough." One boiled potato in a slurry, split between all the boys, she means. There's no difference between fasting on a feast-day and eating every day at the Coyne house. Once a month, on a Sunday, Fiach brings in a meager leg of mutton from the neighbors to split nine ways, his wages for a month's work. Her stomach grumbles. She thinks how good mutton will taste this coming week, that rich, dark gravy dribbling down her chin.

This is nothing new, Mary Agnes dreams of food every day. It's a blessing and a curse, dreaming. All at once you are at a banquet, roasts and cakes and wines, and then, just as fast, it all evaporates into thin air and you're left with the wanting of it.

As she shifts Tommy on her lap, Sean and Padraig burst through the cottage door, dripping rain.

"Off with those clothes, all of them," Mam barks.

"But Mam—"

"Quit yer carping. Now."

Soon, a pile of foul, steaming wool and two skinny, naked boys. Mary Agnes doesn't bother to look. Naked boys are all too common with six brothers, although Fiach is the only one with hair.

"Mary A.!" Sean yells. "Look away."

"Not much to look at, Sean."

She hurries Tommy off her lap and pinches Sean on the rear as he hurries to the corner to fetch warm clothes. He turns and smiles, then sticks out his tongue.

At least someone has a sense of humor in this house.

Mary Agnes joins her mother by the fire. "Mam," she begins. "Last night with Da, him coming at you again—"

"Not another word about it. Ya don't understand." Her mam disappears behind the curtain that separates the great room from her bed.

Oh, I understand plenty, Mam. The way Da comes at you every night, stinking drunk and loosening his trousers. But being chased with a knife? Where does this end?

She often wishes she was born into a different family. There would be stories and laugher and maybe, just maybe, enough food.

Mary Agnes gathers drenched clothes and tosses them in the tub. She hastily ties on an old green apron, hoists Tommy to the highchair, and doles out food to her brothers. She'll put up a plate for her da and scrape the blackened pot for her breakfast. And then get to washing up and soaking clothes, making beds and sweeping floors, gathering water and checking for eggs. Not that there'll be any. The hens are so thin. Soon, they'll be in a pot and eggs will be a distant memory.

She stacks chipped plates next to the dry sink overflowing with soiled dishes. Soon, she'll have to go out in torrential rain for water and more turf for the fire and mussels for supper. *And then what? A full day ahead for what purpose? Other than ringing in the hours toward eternity? Will the story ever change?*

She stokes the peat fire, all hiss and smoke, and places a pail under the leak. Water *pings* against metal. And still the rain pounds. How many days has it been? Five? Seven? Five times seven? Mary Agnes has long lost count, and she's good at numbers. She takes a rush broom from its place near the fire and sweeps the dirt floor. When it's dry— *maybe July*, she thinks—she'll haul bucketloads of sand from the beach to spread around the room.

A loud *bang* disturbs her thoughts. Fiach slams the cottage door, scowling, his hair plastered to his face and hands clenched.

Why is he home so soon? The answer cannot be good. Has he been caught stealing? Sacked? *Will there be no mutton this month, then?*

"What're ya staring at?" Fiach hisses.

Mary Agnes glares at him, eyes steady. "The devil himself."

Fiach advances toward her, his large fists clenched. The other boys watch him, eyes wide again.

"Go on, you bastard," she says. "Deck me here, in front of our wee brothers. Set a fine example, why don't you?"

Fiach scowls and aims for her face. She ducks. Sean whoops and Tommy claps his hands. It's a gamble to be a Coyne. You never know what might happen next.

4

The Next Day
May 1886
Dawrosmore, County Galway, Western Ireland

"Ya're nothing but trouble." Her mother's face, ruddy and lined, sneers as she forces shirts through the mangle. In front of them, a large pile of trousers, the last of the drawers.

What have I done now? Mary Agnes thinks.

"Don't talk back at me."

"I didn't say anything!"

"I said, don't talk back." Spittle flies from Anna Coyne's mouth. "Fiach told me everything. How ya lured him into yer bed—"

"I did nothing of the sort, Mam!"

"And then ya attacked him with a candlestick!"

"It should have been a knife."

Anna Coyne drops a wet shirt and rushes her daughter. She slaps her across the mouth.

Mary Agnes stands her ground and wipes blood from her lip with her sleeve. *How many times have I been slapped? And for reasons not of my doing?*

She doesn't break contact with her mother's steely eyes. "You've no call to do that. I did nothing of the sort," she repeats. "I were asleep, Mam. He came at me while I were *asleep*."

"A lie," her mam says. "I won't have a whore under our roof." She throws the now-filthy shirt into the dirty clothes basket.

Whore? When he came at me in the night?

"Remember the Coffey girl? Yer *friend* who got tangled up with the O'Connor boy?" Her mother scowls.

Oh, I remember. Chapter and verse. And not just the O'Connor boy. The whole lot of them in the RIC coming after her.

"Ya'd have to beg the good sisters to take ya in now." She spits at Mary Agnes's feet. "Inviting yer own *brother* into yer bed."

"Mammy! Are you listening?"

"Fiach told me more than what I needed to hear." Her face twists into a scowl. "That it were ya that attacked him."

"It were him that attacked me, Mammy, I swear."

Anna Coyne swipes at the shirt, her face red and contorted. "All that book learning and suddenly ya're too good for the likes of us. Let yer gram and granddad take ya in."

"You're throwing me out? Of my own home?" Mary Agnes flings the now-clean shirt back onto the ground and storms into the cottage. She climbs the ladder to her loft bedroom, rifles through cobwebs and trunks to find a battered satchel, and packs in it her clothes, hair combs, handkerchiefs.

I tell you what I would have enjoyed, Mammy. Knocking Fiach senseless. Running him through with a knife and leaving him there to bleed.

She looks out the attic window, her eye out to the greater world, and takes a moment to memorize the view. Wrapping her brown stole around her shoulders, she steps

rung-by-rung down the ladder, marches past her mother
and younger brothers without a word and slams the door.
In driving rain, she turns right toward her grandparent's
cottage, a mile off at the end of the peninsula. Tommy calls
out after her, but she can't turn around. She won't give her
mother the satisfaction of seeing her cry.

MARY AGNES RUSHES DOWN THE RUTTED lane across the tree-
less peninsula from Dawrosmore to Dawrosbeg. As she
crosses the narrow neck that separates the two, she pulls
her stole closer to avoid the cold cross wind, Ballynakill
Harbour to the north and Barnaderg Bay the south. A mile
on, winding up and over the hill, she passes several iden-
tical cottages before she arrives at her grandparents' small
stone house at the end of Rev. Magee's thirteen holdings
on the claw-shaped point. It's impossible to own land here.
There would never be enough money for that, even if you
weren't Catholic.

She was tempted to go to Jonesy. He would understand, hold her close, shush words into her hair and stroke
her neck. Is there a boy so fine-looking, so kind, within
miles? No. But midday he could be anywhere, in the field,
in the barn, gone into town. She can't wait to be with him
again. Was it just yesterday that they stole kisses behind
the barn? When his hands touch the small of her back, it
sends shivers up her spine. Still, she will have to confess,
every second of it.

Crossing the threshold of her grandparents' cottage,
Mary Agnes runs straight into her grandmother's large
bosom. Grace Laffey winces and then pats Mary Agnes on
the head. "Shh, now, whatever can be the matter?" She
shifts so that Mary Agnes is snuffling into the other side
of her chest. Grace Laffey is a full head shorter than Mary

Agnes, but don't let that fool you. She's as tough as they come with a tongue to prove it.

Low, exposed wooden beams line the ceiling and a peat fire crackles in the hearth. Mary Agnes's feet, caked with mud, streak the wooden floor. Well-worn furniture invites long evenings of stories, old tales that ooze from the cottage every night.

Neighbors don't bother to knock at Festus's door—it is always open. "God save all here," they say as they trundle in, dripping with rain. "God save ya kindly," is always Grace's reply, and a seat and warm mug of tea or a drop of whiskey offered, thank you.

Festus bustles into the cottage smelling of wet wool and love. "What have we got here? More troubles with yer mam, Aggie?"

Mary Agnes nods, wiping snot from her nose.

"She's been sour ever since she married that—"

"Shush yer mutterings, Festus. That's not for the girl to hear."

"The girl knows it already. Her da's a drunk. Thinks he can grace the pub all day, he does. Like rules don't apply to him. And he's no fisherman. Our people are fishermen." He raises his voice.

"Festus! Enough now!" Grace throws a stern look at her husband. "Marriage is a long lane that has no turning."

And don't I know that? Being a Coyne? Mary Agnes thinks.

Festus Laffey hangs his coat on a peg. "Aye, and sometimes that lane is as pleasant as a rose in June." He touches Grace's cheek.

Grace colors like a schoolgirl.

Festus winks at Mary Agnes. "True,'tis." He sits in his familiar chair by the turf fire to pack his pipe. Tobacco in, tamp, tamp, tamp. And then, after lighting the match, he pulls his legs up, one at a time, so his feet rest on the small footstool. He sits, content, exhaling sweet-smelling tobacco. "I've got some good news for ya, girl. We've hired a new tutor for ya. He's coming this very afternoon."

"A tutor? For me?" *How can you afford it, Granda?*

Festus leans back and draws on his pipe again. "A girl needs to know her letters and sums as well as a boy. Maybe even moreso."

"I'm good at sums already, Granda. And letters. Mam says that's enough learning for a girl." *And I can't have you spending all your money on me when the rent's due.*

"There's more, love. Much more." He exhales smoke with his words. "History and Latin. Geography. Poetry."

Poetry, Mary Agnes loves, especially those in the old language, but she is curious about new Irish poets, too. She scribbles poems herself, not very good ones, half-written lines on scraps of paper she saves. A few nights ago, in her attic room at home, she composed a short rhyme.

> *Little window, white and spare,*
> *Give me what you will,*
> *The world itself, rude and bare,*
> *Or birds upon the sill.*

If she works at it, perhaps her poetry will improve. It has to improve.

"But what about fishing?" she asks.

"Ya're welcome anytime."

"Promise?"

"Promise." Festus slurps his tea.

Not long after, a knock.

"Ah, that must be the young lad. Seamus Bourke's the name. From Dublin." Festus lumbers up, crosses the great room, and opens the cottage door. "Come in, young fellow. Get yerself out of this rain. Grace, put on the kettle." He takes the young man's wrap. "Let ya sit down," he says and points to a chair by the fire.

The young man, tall and lanky, wears a disheveled waistcoat and sports a mop of dark, unruly hair under a drenched cap. The hem of his trousers is threadbare and his tie askew. Mary Agnes thinks he looks like he was just run through a mangle and is in dire need of pressing.

Festus stands behind Mary Agnes. "This is yer pupil, Miss Coyne."

"Pardon, but you didn't say it was a . . . girl," the young man says, choking on his words, eyes wide as shillings beneath fogged eyeglasses. He removes his eyeglasses with ink-stained fingers and wipes them with a handkerchief.

"Would ya have come if I did?" Festus asks. He winks at Mary Agnes again.

Mary Agnes sets a teacup on the small table next to the tutor and folds her arms across her chest. "So you know, sir, I'm as good as any boy with letters and sums. I've been to the local school for three grades, until my mam needed me with the littles."

The tutor smiles.

"And that's the truth of it," Festus says. "Smart as a whip, this one. Could go to university anywhere."

"Five times three?" Seamus asks.

"Fifteen," Mary Agnes answers.

"Eight times six?

Mary Agnes shakes her head. "You'll have to make it a bit harder, sir. That's third form."

The tutor suppresses a smile.

Festus ruffles Mary Agnes's hair and turns back to the lanky tutor. "I hope ya find yer lodgings satisfactory. I spoke to Murphy, the barkeep. Said ya'd have one of his finest rooms."

"Hmph. Means the roof don't leak," Grace says.

The young man nods. "The rooms are more than satis-factory, sir. Much better than my rooms at—" He dribbles tea on his stained trousers. "Oh, drat." He smiles at the girl then. "When shall we start?"

"Ya're staying then?" Grace asks.

"Seems I have a promising pupil."

Festus pats the young man on the back. "Well, that's settled then. Come tomorrow at nine. Ya'll work mornings and stay for dinner. But off on Fridays." He puts a large arm around Mary Agnes. "The girl and I have other plans on Fridays."

Through the week, after her morning lessons, Mary Agnes helps her gram with washing up, laundry, stacking wood. Ironing, sweeping, airing out pillows. In peat-smoky evenings, Festus sits court as he spins tales about wild Irish kings and fierce Irish queens. Faeries and warriors. Sea people so beautiful you could be drawn underwater forever and not regret it, the drowning, that is.

Sometimes the Laffey's cottage is so crowded with kinfolk and neighbors and friends (never Mary Agnes's people, they don't come), Mary Agnes wonders if another person could possibly fit, and then the door creaks open and her gram pulls out another hassock or three-legged stool or trunk and everyone crams in, enrapt, as Festus tells stories late into the night.

And then someone is wont to take up a fiddle or flute, a bodhran or penny whistle, and tunes jump up, vibrant and spirited, like something alive, and everyone, young and old, is set to hand clapping and foot stomping as, one by one, old men and young, boys—girls, even—take turns singing old stories to life.

"Come, Aggie," Festus says, and Mary Agnes gets up from where she sits on the floor near her gram and stands by the fire, her auburn hair fanning out from her face and falling below her shoulders to her waist, and, in a simple dress, thin, bare-legged with no shoes, begins the song of Grace O'Malley, the famous Irish pirate queen, and the noise in the cottage swells and her heart swells with it.

"Let's have 'The Walls of Limerick,'" someone yells then, and chairs are pushed back to the edges of the cottage and musicians strike up the lively tune. Men and women, boys and girls, form sets. Up two paces, back two paces, the dance begins, Mary Agnes grasping Jonesy's hand, her face and heart flushed.

It is here, in this tiny cottage at the end of this small peninsula jutting out into the ever-angry sea, Mary Agnes is enfolded in warmth and laughter and love. No raw words. No knives. No rattling ladders. And always music and the promise of Fridays.

She may have worries, what girl of thirteen does not? But she has no fears—none at all—like she does home with her mam and her da and Fiach, a mere mile away. It might as well be half a world away, John and Anne Coyne's cottage, the difference is so pronounced.

After she smoors the peat fire, covering live embers with ashes that will be fanned into flame in the morning, Mary Agnes climbs the stout ladder to her attic room and settles under thick quilts, tired out, but without the hammer pounding in her stomach. She ate today. And she sang tonight. These things fill her as she prays:

Slivered moon, encased by night
Shining like earth's candlelight
Watch me now as I sleep
And til the morning safely keep.

June 1886
Dawrosbeg, County Galway, Western Ireland

"And again, Miss Coyne. We need to tame that brogue of yours if anyone's to understand you outside of Dawrosbeg." The rumpled tutor bends over Mary Agnes as she sits, sums and maps and papers strewn across the Laffey's worn kitchen table. Last night, right here, her gram served her a fish cake held together with stale breadcrumbs and one precious egg. Grace sat with her, not eating.

How many times has Gram gone hungry? To feed me? Mary Agnes thinks.

One might think living by the sea the Irish wouldn't go hungry, but one would be mistaken, every fish accounted for, and all that's left after foraging for scanty shellfish is carragheen, and there's just so much you can do with seaweed, slick and unwieldy, as you're bemoaning the ground that has betrayed you, again, again.

"What do you mean?" Mary Agnes says to her tutor. "Everyone here understands me well enough."

"What if you were to go to Dublin? They'd say, 'she's right off the farm, that one.'"

"As if I am ever going to go to Dublin? Galway City, maybe. They would understand me there."

"Be that as it may, Miss Coyne, I say, let's try again. You never know when you might travel abroad. Why, just yesterday, I scaled Bengoora, and, if it weren't for the fog, I might have been able to see America."

America.

"Can I walk with you the next time?" she asks.

"It mightn't be proper, a young girl going off with her tutor alone."

"I don't care what people think. I want to see for myself."

"That's a conversation for another day," Seamus says, as he holds up a slim volume. "*A Child's Garden of Verses.* Robert Louis Stevenson." He opens the book and begins to read:

> *I should like to rise and go*
> *Where the golden apples grow—*
> *Where below another sky*
> *Parrot islands anchored lie . . .*

Mary Agnes rolls the words around on her tongue: *Abroad. America.*

"Have you ever been to a parrot island?" she interrupts. "The Sandwich Islands? Tahiti, perhaps?"

Seamus looks up, his spectacles askew. "I'm afraid not, Miss Coyne." He rubs his eyes. "Although I would jump at the chance. I've been to Southampton once, saw the tall ships heading out to sea and thought . . . oh, never mind, back to the poem now . . ."

Mary Agnes looks past the trim, unkempt young man to the open window behind him. The mottled clouds have parted and weak sun throws shafts of light into the yard. Chickens scamper and peck for food outside the window, as if they've heard her. Mary Agnes's heart quickens. *Enough of this being cooped up inside. I should be outside today!* She clucks.

"Miss Coyne!" Seamus slams his hand on the table. "You are incorrigible!"

"Sorry, master. It's just . . ."

"Just what, I may ask?" His face darkens.

"My mind tends to wander."

"Since when?"

"Since I was a child. Maybe four. Or before."

"Then we shall have to put an end to that."

"I don't want to put an end to it!" Mary Agnes says. "Didn't Mr. Stevenson say, 'I should like to rise and go?' You just read that. His mind is wandering too. To Tahiti."

The tutor shakes his head. "You've a point there."

"I don't want you to think I'm not listening, I am," Mary Agnes says. "But I don't want to miss anything." She motions toward the window, where the sun has broken brightly after the morning's rain. A rainbow arches over the sea, its red, orange, yellow, giving way to green, blue, dark indigo, violet.

Seamus sighs. "Maybe it's you that's teaching me, then." He puts down the poetry book. "Up now. Let's go outside. Take paper and pen. We'll look about and write it all down until our hands cramp, and then we'll have our tea." He smiles kindly at her.

They sit on the sparsely grassed knoll overlooking the sea, he on a blanket of his own, and she on the ground, her soiled skirt tucked underneath her. She is wearing one of her grandmother's skirts now, a faded green one let out at the hem because of her height. Mary Agnes observes Seamus as he scratches in his notebook. She looks toward the beach and wonders when her granddad will be back.

Every time she sees his lanky form coming up the lane, she breathes a sigh of relief. Another two boats have gone missing in the last week, but thankfully not from Festus's fleet.

"It would kill him," her gram whispered to her when she heard the news. "First the Coombs and now the O'Neills. It'd be the death of your granddad if he lost any of his men."

Mary Agnes looks toward the horizon. No boats coming in yet. She shields her face from the wind and turns to the tutor.

"What is it you're writing?"

"I dabble in poetry."

"So do I. Read to me."

"I couldn't."

"Why not?"

"I'm afraid it's not very good. Not like my friend Yeats. We're at university together."

"What does he write?"

"I've a letter here somewhere." Seamus rustles through his haversack, his stringy hair obscuring his face. "Here it is." He unfolds a piece of yellowing paper. "He's submitting a poem to *The Irish Monthly*. It's called, 'The Stolen Child.'"

"I'd love to hear it."

"'Uh' as in 'luhve,' Miss Coyne, not 'oo' as in 'loove.'"

"I'd 'luhve' to hear it."

Where dips the rocky highland
Of Sleuth Wood in the lake . . .

"What's Sleuth Wood?"

"Listen this once, Miss Coyne. We will discuss it afterward." He continues in his high tenor voice. Mary Agnes wonders if he sings; if he did, he would have such a fine voice for it.

There lies a leafy island
Where flapping herons wake . . .

"I love herons, the way their wings swoop down in layers of grey and—"

"Miss Coyne! Please!" Seamus wipes his face with a handkerchief.

She presses her thin lips together and nods. "I'll listen now."

Come away, O human child!
To the waters and the wild . . .

Seamus drops the letter. "I will never be as good as he is."

Mary Agnes reaches for the parchment. "Let me read. Please."

Seamus hands the crinkled paper to Mary Agnes. She stares at the words for a full minute, her eyes roving down the page. She tilts her head to the side then and reads in a loud voice from the beginning of the stanza.

Come away, O human child!
To the waters and the wild
With faery hand in hand
For the world's more full of weeping than you
can understand.

She scowls. "Whatever might he mean, master, 'the world's more full of weeping'?"

Seamus rubs his eyes. "It means"—he stops, thinks a second, resumes—"two things, the way I see it. To delight in your childhood, as fleeting as it is, lass. You can never get it back once—"

"Once what?"

He clears his throat. "Once the world shows its"—he stumbles for the word—"*underbelly* to you."

"Well. That's already happened to me," she says matter-of-factly.

"And you mean?"

She colors. "I shouldn't say. Not to you." She hands the letter back and doesn't meet his eyes.

Seamus avoids looking at her. "I am pained to hear that, Miss Coyne. You are wiser than most your age. No wonder your granddad has such high hopes for you."

"Does he now? I've got high hopes for myself." She looks at her instructor straight on.

"Marrying well? Like Lady Gregory?"

"Not marrying at all! And not dependent on anyone, much less a man, excuse me for saying, sir."

She stands and then stops. She turns back to Seamus, who looks more unkempt than an hour before, if that is possible. "What is the second meaning of the poem?"

"That's for another day, Miss Coyne. I'm afraid I'm all used up for one day."

6

Late June 1886
Ballynakill Chapel, County Galway, Western Ireland

Sitting on the hard wooden bench at the chapel at Ballynakill between her granddad and her gram, Mary Agnes's feet throb. Her boots are a size too small, her toes crammed. And her ridiculous dress! It may as well be a sack. The air presses in, that slightly moldy, slightly salty tang that pervades the west of Ireland and seeps into homes and pubs and shops and churches. She can feel it, smell it, almost taste it, the sea.

John and Anna Coyne settle in the pew behind her, always in the same row, as if led there by homing pigeons or tradition or stubbornness. Mary Agnes steals a look.

No Fiach. And where is Jonesy, for that matter?

Jonesy's mam and da sit alone today. She stifles thoughts of Jonesy, being in church as she is.

On the far side of the nave—where she dare not look, no, not now, not when her mother is eyeing her—are the rest of the village faithful, led by none other than the O'Connors, despite the troubles with their boy.

Shame on you, Lorcan O'Connor. That you can be sitting here with your mam and da and all those brothers and sisters of yours when Mary Coffey is sent away. Don't think everyone doesn't know, you scoundrel. To deny the babe is yours? When Mary was n'er with another until that night? You will have to live with that for all your days, you and your RIC brothers. Swine.

As far as Mary Agnes has been told, her friend Mary Coffey is at a convent in County Clare now. She will no doubt be back, marked with shame, and no babe. Even her own folk have disowned her.

Where will she live? What will she do? Work the pub? Lift her skirts for other boys?

To take her mind off Lorcan O'Connor, Mary Agnes concentrates on the fourteen wooden plaques that surround the nave, the story of Jesus's last week on earth. In the first scene, Jesus is condemned to death, and in the next, takes up his cross. In the third scene, the one closest to her pew, Jesus falls, his already bloodied knees scraping on rocks and dirt as the story progresses toward Golgotha.

Along the dusty road, Jesus meets his mother, Mary, and then a passerby, Simon of Cyrene. And there, in the next scene, a woman in the crowd steps out to wipe Jesus's now bloodied face. Mary Agnes's hand goes out reflexively to help him.

In the next panel, Jesus stumbles again on the way of suffering. Mary Agnes gasps. Every time. It is as if she is there along the road of sorrows, her hems dusty and crusted, her underarms caked with dirt and sweat. She is thirsty and tired. But no matter what may befall her, she knows she will follow this bruised and bloodied man to his death.

If she turns her head to look to the far side of the nave to see the rest of Jesus's story, it would come with sharp rebuke, *yer mind's a-straying again*, her mother would say, and then the predictable slap. No, Mary Agnes will not look to the right side of the nave, and anyway, no matter how many times she looks, the story never changes. Jesus always dies.

"And he saith to them," Father O'Halloran drones, the only words not uttered in Latin for the last thirty minutes, *and a godsend that is*, Mary Agnes thinks, "Come ye after me, and I will make you to be fishers of men."

Fishers of men!

Mary Agnes pictures the familiar biblical story of the fishermen on the Sea of Galilee. *Fishers. Like us. Simon and Andrew and the sons of Zebedee dee dee dee. And Granda's fleet and all the others . . . oh, the others.* Drowning is the price the sea exacts, she knows. Three wakes in three days. Her voice is near hoarse from all the singing.

Father O'Halloran continues. "And they immediately leaving their nets, followed him."

Festus turns slightly and winks at Mary Agnes.

They laid down their nets! They left their boat to follow him! Mary Agnes tries to think of Jesus here, at Ballynakill Harbour, talking to fishermen. Would Mr. O'Neill and Mr. Coombs—*and Granda*—really drop their nets? Leave everything? Follow him?

A sliver of sunshine penetrates the triptych behind the altar. There, in the center, illuminated now by sunlight, the Blessed Virgin stands, draped in purple robes, her hands extended. Mary Agnes stares at the Holy Mother and wonders if the Purple Mary, Most Holy, Queen of Heaven, Star of the Sea, ever stepped foot in a boat.

What is that I hear? Mary Agnes fidgets on the hard bench and her toes pinch in her boots. There is sure to be blood on her stockings when she gets home. Again, she thinks she hears something. *It must be mam, muttering under her breath.*

With her mother's breath just inches away, and the threat of a slap on the back of her head at any moment, Mary Agnes keeps her head faced forward.

She can't see inside my head now, can she?

And with that, Mary Agnes starts a sonnet in her head, in the well-known pattern she learned at school.

Abaft the wheel, I stand upright, hat low . . .

She thinks about the rhyming pattern and continues.

The squall, southeast, blows full upon my face.

Now for the ending, she thinks, and runs through the alphabet to find rhyming words.

My heart invokes the prayer all fishermen know,
Guide me, wind, time, and tides, back to this . . .

Slap. Mary Agnes snaps back as she's slapped on back of her head. Her face warms. *How does Mam know my mind is wandering?*

Her gram squeezes her hand with her gnarled one.

Mary Agnes is ready to scream but knows the trouble that would bring—*at Mass, no less*—so she takes a deep breath and then another and then entreats the Virgin Herself. *Mary, lead me back to this place, anyplace.*

COME, TAKE MY HAND, THE PURPLE MARY whispers in her ear.

Mary Agnes's eyes dart around the sanctuary. *Did she just speak to me? The Blessed Virgin?*

She doesn't take her eyes off the Purple Mary as she walks forward to receive the Holy Sacrament, step, step, step, her boots echoing on the worn wooden floor. As she approaches the altar, tongue out, she takes the wafer in her mouth, crumbs of Christ dissolving.

What is it that is happening? She's at once dizzy, delirious, disoriented, standing before the priest but disconnected from her body and rising, rising.

She hovers now high above the sanctuary, not an angel, not a girl, not a bird, but a girl-bird weaving in and out of wooden beams, drifting past the triptych. She dips, in and amongst pews, and then up up up again, floating, floating, closer to heaven than she's ever been. She is somewhere outside of herself but wholly herself, not glued to heaven, not glued to earth, but somewhere in between, suspended in time and space. Her mind races, senses heightened.

Back in the pew, shaken, Mary Agnes sits on the hard bench until the sanctuary empties out, family by family, back into sin. Maybe she will volunteer to scrub the scuffed floor, dust the oil panels, change the candles, anything to be here, in this place. *With Mary.* Who knows how long it has been when she hears her gram's voice calling her. She rises and bows to the Purple Mary. The sun crashes through colored glass, the absolute brilliance of it, almost blinding.

"Mary A.!" her gram calls again. "We've got to beat the tide back to Dawros."

Mary Agnes leaves the pew reluctantly. With her back now to the altar, she is tempted to turn around. *What if the Purple Mary has more to say to me?*

Pausing in the vestibule for as long as she can hold off, Mary Agnes counts in her head the days until next Sunday. *Seven.*

It will be a long week until then, waiting. But she will be here, on time, next Sunday at ten sharp, laced into boots too tight and a dress too large, expectant that something will change.

SITTING AT THE EDGE OF HER GRAM'S BED, Mary Agnes kneads her hands in her lap.

"I can't care for ya, Mary A. Not anymore," Grace Laffey says. "I'm not long for this world." She winces as she speaks.

Not long for this world? Not Gram. "What do you mean, Gram?"

"I've got a lump." She points to her breast. "Burns to touch it."

Mary Agnes stares at her grandmother's breast. "I can care for you, Gram."

"Ah, there's a girl. But I wouldn't ask ya to. Ya've got a long life ahead. Ya can't go home to yer mam and da so yer granddad and I have arranged for ya to go to our people, in Chicago. They owe it to yer mother."

"In America?" Her heart quickens. *My chance to get away from Fiach. Live in a grand house. Wear proper dresses and boots . . . but Jonesy!* Her cheeks color. *And how can I leave Gram and Granda? Or Tommy? Sean? The other boys?*

"How soon?" she asks.

"Soon enough. Ya'll go to yer mam's older brother and his wife. They've a girl about yer age, Helen, she's called. She'll be like a sister to ya."

"Mam has an older brother?"

"That she does. He left here before ya were born—had to leave, ya might say, but that's a story long buried."

How many stories are buried, Gram? Every family has them. Why don't we talk about them, ever? Like the babies, carried out and never talked of again. Mary Agnes stares out the wavy panes toward the Atlantic. Her heart drops. "They say no one who goes to America ever comes back."

"It's for the best, Mary A. They'll take good care of ya. They have to. And yer granddad says a girl can go to university in America, right next to the lads. Can ya imagine that? We would be so proud of ya."

"How will I manage? Getting to America? In America?"

"Ya're a quick one, Mary A., bold, independent. I've no doubt ya'll be fine. Now let's make a list." She hands Mary Agnes a pen. "And here, have a look. I'm knitting ya a new shawl. Green, to match your eyes."

Grace puts down the knitting and takes Mary Agnes's face in her gnarled hands. "One word of advice for ya, my love. Watch out for fast lads. They can undo ya in one night."

7

Late August 1886
Off Dawrosbeg, County Galway, Western Ireland

"They say all of Ireland is cursed, but don't ya believe it, Aggie," Festus says, a jaunty smile on his lips.

It's a sultry day, temperature and humidity colliding, only weeks until Mary Agnes's leave taking. Festus and Mary Agnes drift off the inner islands in a lull, their lines down. Mary Agnes wipes her forehead with the back of her hand. She can't believe just two months ago she wished for more layers to keep warm. Today, she yearns for fewer layers, but that would border on obscene. Her shins are already exposed—and her upper arms, her dress rolled up to her shoulder almost—but her granddad doesn't seem to mind, or care.

"Cursed?"

"I say, we're not! What other peoples have wee folk as infamous as giants? Warriors standing side by side with women? Sinners wise as saints? I tell ya, Aggie, we're not cursed. We're made of something different, and don't let anyone tell ya otherwise." He takes off his hat, dips it in the water, and wipes his brow before he puts it back on. "Best in the world, the Irish."

The moon, but a sliver, is visible in the day sky.

"Does the moon really heave the tides, Granda?" Mary Agnes asks. There is so much she wants to know, and little time left to ask.

"Aye, it does, girl. Tides, the ways of the moon and the sea, when and where to fish." He swallows the last of his tea. "In ancient lore, it was thought the sea a living, breathing thing. I don't disagree."

Mary Agnes drains her tea and throws the dregs overboard. "But how does the moon heave the tide? In and out?"

"The moon, she's a powerful force, Aggie. Ya can read her. A moon like that,"—he points to the sickle moon overhead—"is a sign of poor weather. Same when there's a halo around it, especially in winter. We live by the moon, girl. When it waxes, we plant seed crops and slaughter sheep; when it wanes, only woe will come to ya if ya build a stone wall or thatch a roof. And when the moon is at its fullest, tides are highest and life is once again filled with promise. A babe born at the full moon is the luckiest of all."

Mary Agnes looks at the tiny slice of moon and wonders how it holds so much sway.

"I mayn't be able to explain it rightly," Festus says. "But we can count on it, the tides, in, then out, twice a day. The tide can be yer fiercest friend or fiercest foe. Learn to respect it, Aggie." He reaches for Mary Agnes's hand. "Show me yer fingers, girl."

Mary Agnes splays her fingers.

"Ya can count on yer fingers all that's certain in life." He touches the tip of each of her fingers as he lists the reasons. "Tides," he says, as he touches her thumb; "seasons," the pointer finger; "sun rising," the elongated middle one, "moon," her fourth finger. When he gets to her pinky, his eyes close as he says, "And the grave."

The latter she knows. She can't count the wakes she's sung at.

The tide is at its lowest point now, exposing rocks and shoals that foul Ballynakill Harbour. A damp, sour smell pervades the bay. Mary Agnes leans over the side of the currach near a tidal pool filled with prickly sea urchin and flowery anemone, deep-hatted limpet and sleek olive-red carragheen. She runs her hand through cold sea water and watches as a small rock crab scurries into a crevice, until, like her granddad said, the tide begins to turn, slowly, lap by lap, and all—a whole world undersea—is submerged once again.

"Time we get back," Festus says, and Mary Agnes is filled with an overwhelming sense of melancholy, not knowing if she will ever fish with her granddad again.

"Just one more story? I'm keeping them all safe, here, to carry with me." She touches her chest.

Festus looks at Mary Agnes with filmy eyes and reaches for her hand. "How could I ever turn ya down?"

There, amidst gulls and curlews soaring overhead and noisy oystercatchers lining the strand, their long, bright orange beaks piercing the shore, Festus begins another tale.

"The merrow are all about, Aggie, luring sailors and fishermen under." His hands span wide to encompass the sea.

Mary Agnes's eyes grow wide.

"Not the worst way to die, Aggie. It can't be. Ya can hear the merrow at night, their songs rising from the sea. When ya hear them, ya can't row away. Ya don't want to."

"Have you heard them, Granda?"

"That I have, girl, more than once. The first time, off *Inis Bo Finne* I was, I saw the most beautiful woman I had ever seen, God as my witness, fully woman from the waist up . . ." His eyes focus on something beyond the boat, beyond the bay.

"And?" she asks.

He snaps back. "And fish from the waist down."

"Like a mermaid?"

"Aye, with hair the deepest green to match her eyes, like yers they were." Festus pinches her cheek.

"What happened next?" Mary Agnes has not heard this story before. Her spine tingles.

"I was about to take her hand when I was jerked back by a rogue wave. The sea saved me that day, Aggie. But at the time, I wanted nothing more than to follow that sea faery under the waves, live with her for all my days."

"And another time?"

"Not long after that, I went looking for her again."

"Were you married then?"

"No, girl, not yet. I was young and full of drink and thought I'd try my luck with the merrow, see if I could entice one to come and live with me."

"But I thought you said—"

"Yes, I know. But young men have unreasoned thoughts. I thought I could slay the myth. 'If not me, then who?' I would say." He covers his mouth as he coughs.

"Not far from here I saw her,"—he points to a spot south of where they're anchored, near the place they row to Mass on Sundays and Holy Days—"and I heard the most beautiful voice I'd ever heard. And there she was, on the strand, singing me in. It wasn't until I got closer that I realized it was not a sea faery, but yer gram. She sang me home, Aggie. We were married the next Shrovetide and I never heard the merrow again."

From far across the water, weather closes in, quicker than one might think, first a stirring, then a gust, then a deep-throated wind that announces an afternoon squall. Festus takes to his oars and rows the short distance back to Dawrosbeg. There are no fish today, so he pulls the currach deep into the rushes and they walk, granddad and grand-daughter, hand in hand, back up the hill to the cottage.

That night, after the squall has passed and the sun makes its slow descent, Festus spreads a large map on the worn table at the cottage and sits to study it, head close to the parchment.

Mary Agnes watches him, that face she loves. At first she thinks the day will never die, it is light so late this time of year, but when the day finally surrenders, Festus brings the oil lamp close and calls Mary Agnes over. Smoothing the map out with rough hands, all the corners of the earth flat, he points with a stubbed finger to a small peninsula on the far west coast of Ireland.

"Here we are," he says. "Dawrosbeg." He slowly drags his finger across the vast Atlantic Ocean to a large conti-nent. "And here is New York."

"Must I really go, Granda?"

"There's no promise for ya here, girl."

Mary Agnes swallows. "And Chicago?"

Festus points to a spot midway across the North American continent near a series of large lakes. "Right here. Some say there are more Irish in Chicago than all of Ireland by now."

Mary Agnes squints to read: Chicago.

How will I do this? Alone?

"It's a long journey," Festus says, as if to mirror Mary Agnes's thought. "But the die is cast. Ya're off for America and a new life there."

How will I ever manage? Without Gram and Granda?

Festus looks at Mary Agnes with tenderness, as if he can read her mind. "And let me be the first and last to say, I'll miss ya, girl."

AT DINNER THE NEXT DAY, A FISH STEW with soda bread to celebrate Seamus Bourke's forthcoming departure for Dublin,
Mary Agnes plays with her spoon, twirling it in the soup.

"Before Mr. Bourke takes his leave of us, can I climb
Bengoora with him?" she blurts out.

Seamus drops his spoon in his bowl and entreats Festus
like a small boy caught red-handed. "I-I-I didna encourage
this conversation, sir," he says.

"I did," Mary Agnes says. "Mr. Bourke says you can
almost see America from the top."

Festus laughs, deep and booming. "That's a saying,
Aggie. Ya can't see America from anywhere in Ireland. It's
more than five thousand miles to America."

Five thousand miles?

"But, still, I would like to go."

"I find this highly improper, sir," Seamus says. "I
expect you'll refuse."

Festus sits back and rubs his chin. "On the contrary,
young sir. I think it fitting that Aggie here do whatever it
is she likes this last week before she leaves for America. I
climbed Bengoora as a young man just once. I've never
forgotten it, the way ya can see the whole of the countryside like a hawk sees it. And I trust ya, Bourke. What do
ya think, Grace?"

"Heartily. Leave the donkey cart in town with the publican. And mind the weather, ya hear? Be back by dark or
I'll have words with ya, young man."

The following Thursday dawns unusually clear, so
Mary Agnes and Seamus head out early instead of taking
to lessons. The day is fair and cool. Mary Agnes wears her
old boots and her ivory cable-knit sweater over her brown
skirt. Seamus wears sturdy boots, the only thing sturdy
about him. His clothes need washing and pressing. He is
so tall, Mary Agnes often wonders if he could topple over

with just a gust of wind. She also wonders if he ever eats, so thin he is.

Does he have a family? A mother or a sister? A lover in Dublin? She follows him by three paces, wondering these things. Being a university student sounds so intriguing.

They start their trek in dark woods behind the Letterfrack school through thick stands of hawthorn, rowan, oak. It is easy footing here. Grace packed soda bread for them before they set out, so they will eat today. Mary Agnes carries the bread in a kerchief tied in a knot and is cautious lest the bundle tumble to the ground and be water-logged. When she exhales, frosty breath clouds ahead of her.

When they break out of the trees, they're standing in shin-high tufted purple moor grass thick with bell heather and myriad mosses. The ground is hummocked and boggy, with numerous rivulets that surface and disappear as fast.

Picking their way along a meandering sheepherder's path up the constant rise, Seamus points. "Be careful of gullies."

Mary Agnes sidesteps a gully as sun peeks from beneath high, wispy cirrus clouds. After an hour's walk, mostly in silence, Seamus stops at a rocky outcropping and mops his forehead with his handkerchief. Mary Agnes catches up to him and stands beside him. The grade rises sharply from here, crowded with sharp rocks.

"This is as far as we go," Seamus says. "It's quite steep after this. I don't want you to turn an ankle on the rocks."

"But we're not even halfway to the top!"

"We're higher than the trees, lass. Remember we have to account for the journey back down."

"Certainly that will be quicker than the way up."

"It usually is, but we still have to watch our footing."

Mary Agnes kneels in spongy mosses there, a carpet of reddish-brown, golden, and green. She gets down to eye-level with the moss, surprised how intricate each clump is, tiny leaves whorled inward. She runs her hand over the velvety texture as a dragonfly buzzes past. She follows its path until she cannot see it.

Seamus squats near Mary Agnes on the spongy bogland. "You'll be getting damp, kneeling like that," he says.

"I'm used to being damp."

Seamus stands, takes out his field glass, and focuses his sight west.

"Can you see America?" Mary Agnes asks.

"No, lass," he laughs. "But I see Dawros, the shape of it, like a claw." He wipes the lens with a handkerchief and holds the glass to his eye again. "I do believe I can see your granddad's cottage, Miss Coyne. Yes, I'm sure of it. There, at the end. Would you like to see?"

"I'm afraid I can't see past my hands, except if it's large as a mountain." She unties the kerchief and offers her tutor a piece of soda bread.

"Thank you, lass."

"What else can you see?" she asks, as she eats her share of the bread.

He points to the northwest. "Letter Hill, of course."

Mary Agnes squints. She can make out the faint shape of the mountain, but it's blurry.

"And beyond," Seamus says, "the outline of the outer islands."

"Inishbofin? Inishshark? Inishturk?"

"If that be their names."

"Can you see Granda? He's out today." Mary Agnes stands and shields her eyes from the sun. "Be my eyes. Tell me."

Seamus scans the harbor, left to right. "It's a grand soft day, it is. I do see a currach, Miss Coyne. It might be your granddad, but I canna be sure. Yes, wait, I see several of them. More, now that my eye's peeled for them. There's a great many of them, actually, all the way past the point. They look like little blackbirds, they do, bobbing upon the sea."

LATE THAT AFTERNOON, AS AN ALMOST predictable afternoon squall careens across Ballynakill Harbour, Mary Agnes waits on shore with the others for boats to return. It will be a long, wet night fileting fish and packing them in salt barrels. She is tired after the day's walk, but needs must, as her gram says.

One by one the boats come in from the mist offloading their catch. By five-thirty, everyone's eyes are glued to the horizon. All the boats are in except Festus's.

Mary Agnes stands shoulder to shoulder with the others as she guts cod and hake. Her hands are numb and bloodied. There is a rhythm to it, processing fish. Grab by the tail, slice, peel, dump the innards, repeat. The women, usually loud with song (and even louder with gossip), are unusually quiet tonight. Everyone is thinking what no one is saying: *Where is Festus Laffey and his men?*

By nine-thirty, flirting with dark now, women and children peel off toward home. Grace Laffey puts her arm around Mary Agnes. The weather has turned sour, rain in slanting sheets.

"Isn't the first time that man of mine has given me a scare. Come now, child, off to bed. He'll be back, ya'll see. I'll stay up and wait for him."

"It was so nice this morning, when Mr. Bourke and I were walking."

"'Tis Ireland, lass."

Mary Agnes looks up at the night sky as she and her gram walk the rutted lane home. There are no constellations out tonight, no Ursa Major or Ursa Minor, Orion or Cygnus. Not even Polaris, the north star. Polaris cannot lead her granddad home tonight.

At the cottage, Mary Agnes turns to look back at the sea, angry tonight, and black. The wind howls and hurts her ears.

"Dirty weather," Festus would call it.

She looks again to the sky, beseeching all the saints.

Where are you, Granda? Won't you come home?

"THIS, FOR YOU." SEAMUS HANDS Mary Agnes a small gift wrapped in brown paper and twine. They sit at their favorite spot on the knoll behind the Laffey's cottage surrounded by a carpet of tiny wildflowers. She has one eye on Ballynakill Harbour.

Please, Jesus Mary and Joseph, send Granda home.

Mary Agnes swats a midge and turns to the tutor. When she unwraps the package, she clasps it to her chest. A journal. "For me? Thank you, master." Now she can write her poems and keep them in one place, not just on scrap pieces of paper crammed into a book. She can write out Stevenson's poems, too, the ones she's memorized, *Windy Nights*, *The Land of Nod*, *Summer Sun*.

For several minutes, master and student sit side by side without talking.

"He's sure to be back," Seamus says.

"I will count on that," Mary Agnes answers.

"I'm off now."

"To Dublin?"

"Aye." He stands and offers Mary Agnes his hand.

"Thank you again for the walk," she says, and shakes his hand as she's seen men do. "I will remember it always."

"My pleasure, lass. It's good that your gram didn't have to come looking for us. I shudder to think what she would have said had we become lost."

"Do you ever get lost in Dublin?"

"I do. Sometimes I want to."

"What do you mean by that, master?"

He looks at her through smudged eyeglasses. "You'll know one day."

One day?

"Thank you, sir," she says. "For taking a chance on me. I won't soon forget you, either."

"Nor I, you, Miss Coyne. You are a most promising pupil. I have no doubt you will succeed at university in America." He tips his hat and turns to go. "God prosper your day, lass."

Mary Agnes watches as Seamus lumbers down the lane until she cannot see him anymore. It is almost dark now. Her feet sink in peat, leaves and roots and stems and twigs packed down, layer by layer, over tens of thousands of years until the peat is dark and rich, hiding secrets and memories and bones. She ambles down from the knoll toward the cottage, skimming buttercup and dandelion, ribwort and chickweed. She kicks pebbles and dirt along the gravelly lane and answers a loud, fluty thrush in the hedge with faulty bravado. What will she do if her granddad doesn't return for a second night in a row? She will likely have to leave Dawrosbeg even sooner. Like a seesaw, she goes back and forth between wanting to stay and wanting to go.

"I should like to rise and go," she begins, her throaty alto voice putting music to Stevenson's words, "Where golden apples grow—"

A rumble of thunder interrupts her song, the first rain-drop giving way to another and another, and soon she is on the lane in a downpour. She ducks into the broken doorway of an old shed and thinks of Stevenson's poem, *Rain*.

The rain is raining all around,
It falls on field and tree,

It rains on the umbrellas here,
And on the ships at sea.

It is almost dark when she reaches her grandparents' cottage. Her gram is not in, the fire gone nearly cold. She stokes the embers and puts on another bit of turf. Back outside, drenched now, she looks toward the sea.

Where is everyone?

Through thick fog off Dawrosbeg, she cannot see anything on account of poor weather and poor eyesight. Then she hears a shout coming from the strand. Her heart gallops as she heads for the beach. Clutches of men and women and children line the shore, arms waving. Voices shout out: *Festus! Festus!*

Mary Agnes begins to run now, not caring about the rain, her bare feet flying over clods of dirt and weeds as she yells at the top of her lungs: *Granda's home! Granda's home!* She spreads her arms so wide that if she were a bird, she would rise and take flight above Dawros by now, bank left and right over the small peninsula, out past Ballynakill Harbour, out past the point, out past the outer islands, and then circle back above the great ocean itself, singing and squawking, her heart is that happy.

"IT WAS ALL A BOTHER ABOUT NOTHING." Festus sits in his favorite chair by the fire puffing his pipe.

"Well, don't ya go disappearing again anytime soon," Grace says.

"Don't plan to, my love."

"Did you want to get away? Like when you went looking for the merrow?" Mary Agnes sits at her granddad's feet with her head on his knee.

"Not exactly, girl. The wind turned sour and we thought it best to weather the night in the lee of the big island. We pulled the currach far up the strand and turned it upside down. A right little shelter we had there. Out of the wind. Isn't the first time we've done so."

"I told ya he'd be back," her gram says.

"I thought you were lost," Mary Agnes says.

"Nay, girl, not lost."

"My tutor's gone back to Dublin," she says.

"Has he now? I suppose his semester is about to start up."

"He told me you can get lost in Dublin."

"I suppose he's right."

"But he said sometimes he wants to be lost. Whatever does that mean?"

Festus rubs his chin. "Aye, girl, he's right. Sometimes ya just want to disappear in this world. Too many troubles."

Mary Agnes bites her lip, her forehead lined. "Please don't go disappearing again, not before . . ." Her mouth stumbles over the words.

"Shh, now," Festus says. "I've got a story for ya."

Mary Agnes settles at his feet, rests her head on his knee again, and closes her eyes to picture the story.

"Out beyond the islands, as far as eyes can see, and then some," Festus begins, "there lies a Phantom Isle. Some thought it first a whale, and others, a sea monster, but when fishermen approached, it was most certainly land."

Festus takes a long draw on his pipe, and then continues. "But as soon as the fishermen rowed ashore, the island disappeared. The next day, the same fishermen made another attempt, but, again, nothing. The island disappeared into the sea just as they were about to make landfall."

Mary Agnes's mind is filled with images.

"It was on the third day that one of the fishermen— some say it were a woman in disguise—thought to try a new scheme," Festus continues. "She let an arrow fly toward the island, barbed and red-hot with flame, and the arrow landed on the island and stuck."

Mary Agnes opens her eyes and looks up at Festus. "She did that?"

"Aye, she did, girl. With fire, the fiercest of elements. Remember this when ya face something ya think impossible. Take that fire within yer belly and take claim to what's rightfully yers."

8

September 1886
Dawrosbeg, County Galway, Western Ireland

It's a week of lasts.

This morning, Grace collects Tommy and walks him back to the Laffey cottage so Mary Agnes has time with him alone. She is still not allowed at home. *And don't want to be.*

They sit side by side on stools in front of the fire, their heads bent over Mary Agnes's new journal, elbows touching.

"'When I was down beside the sea . . .'" Mary Agnes begins. She pictures the strand at Dawrosbeg, her favorite place to walk, as she starts Stevenson's poem.

Tommy continues with the second line. "'A wooden spade they gave to me to, to, to—'"

"'To dig the sandy shore.' Good, Tommy, you're learning." Mary Agnes squeezes Tommy as she traces her finger over the lines of the now known-by-heart poem written in the journal.

"What's next?" he asks. His freckled face scrunches like it does when he's asking a serious question.

"'My holes were empty—'"

"'Like a cup!'" He claps his hands.

"Yes, like a cup. Now let's say the last line together." She trains her finger over the last line of the verse.

"'In every hole the sea came up, till it could come no more!'"

Mary Agnes beams at Tommy. "We will have to dig holes together, just to see."

But not next summer, or the summer after that, she thinks. *How can I leave you, Tommy?*

"I BEST BE GOING NOW, BEFORE . . ." Mary Agnes and Jonesy are stretched out in one of the empty stalls in the Jones's barn, warm hay beneath them, kissing. They have never gone past kissing before, until today. She initiated it, her hands wandering over his chest, and placing his hand on hers. She thinks *maybe, should we, before I leave?* But *no, no, we can't,* she says over and over to herself. *There aren't enough novenas for that.*

Her breath is ragged. *And I cannot have a babe. Not now.*

He puts his head to her chest. "I c-c-can feel yer heartbeat."

She runs her hands through his dark hair. "Can you now?" Fast she is memorizing every detail about this boy. *The way his hair falls over his eyes just so. His clumsy hands. His stutter. His always-patched trousers. His every kindness. His kisses . . .*

"I'll wait for ya, Mary A."

As she squeezes his hand, her heart squeezes, too. "I fear I won't be coming back, Jonesy."

"Well, Holy Mother of sweet divine suffering, I'll c-c-come after ya then."

"Where would you even start? Granda says there are more Irish in America now than in Ireland. You'd never find me. Plus, you've a farm to run," she says. "Don't go forgetting that. Your people depend on you."

He strokes her face. "I would find ya, Mary A. I swear I would, if I tried. But I'll wait. Ya have my word."

"You'd be best to forget me, Jonesy. It pains me to say it, but there'll be a great black ocean between us and neither of us can swim. And no one from America comes back."

To keep herself from crying, she keeps on talking, something she's good at, although for once she's at a loss for words. She leans in to kiss him again. Afterward, her eyes lock on his and she feels a deep burning in her groin. *No.* She stops herself from doing something she'll regret so she pulls away, sits up, and brushes hay from her skirt.

"Find another lass, Jonesy. One who won't go off and leave you."

MARY AGNES AMBLES DOWN THE LANE in the rain, holding back tears. *Will I never see Jonesy again?* Even though she saw Tommy just this morning, she is leaving tomorrow and feels it only proper to say goodbye to her other brothers. Especially Sean, the only one with a sense of humor. She'll miss him, too. And she might never see him, or any of the others, ever again, either. *Am I really leaving for America? Tomorrow?*

She rounds the edge of her parents' whitewashed cottage and snags her dress on a wild strawberry vine, like she used to do as a girl. Looking up at her old attic window, she has a flash of nostalgia, all the many nights she slept there. Unfortunately, one night blots out all the other nights. The green door to the cottage is closed, so she tries the latch, but it's locked, as if her mam saw her coming and bolted it.

"Mam!" she calls. "I've come to say goodbye." She knocks again, pleads almost. But the door never opens. By now she is drenched, her hair plastered to her face and boots soaked through. Tommy peeks out from the window seat, his hand on the pane. She places her hand on the pane from the outside and tries to smile. "I love you," she mouths through the window. Suddenly, her mam snatches Tommy and he disappears. The window is empty, no Sean or Padraig or Ferris or Eamon, no shadow, just air.

If Mary Agnes has ever been lonelier, she can't think of it. And then she sees Fiach coming up the lane and she runs, runs, but he is all over her, pushing her roughly down on the muddy lane, clamping his hand over her mouth and pinning her down in the muck. His hands are up under her skirt now.

"Stop! You're hurting me!" she screams, and then "Mam! Mam!" but no one comes and this time she can't get away and he's fumbling with her and she retches. When he's done, she knees him in the groin, and he yells as he gets up, leaving her there, covered with mud and sobbing.

"Ya'll pay for this," he hisses.

Mary Agnes limps back to her grandparents' cottage, mute. Festus is out when she arrives, likely in the barn. As if she knows, Grace takes Mary Agnes in her arms and lets her sob. Tears course down Grace's face as she undresses Mary Agnes and works a warm cloth over her face and shoulders and down past her narrow waist. Grace towels Mary Agnes off, helps her pull her nightdress on, and covers her with the new green shawl. Grace rocks Mary Agnes back and forth, back and forth, like a little girl, so long into the night that Mary Agnes wonders if her gram will ever let go.

A loud knock on the door arouses them.

"Open up!" a voice barks from outside the door. "Royal Irish Constabulary."

Mary Agnes freezes. *The RIC? Lorcan O'Connor and his gang? They are out for no good. Could they be coming for me? All of them?*

"Coming," Grace says. She puts her finger to her mouth and moves the rug under the table with her foot to expose the trap door. She opens it and signals for Mary Agnes to climb down into the shallow, damp root cellar.

Mary Agnes clambers down the ladder as noiselessly as she can, her legs shaking. When she gets to the bottom of the short ladder, she nods to her grandmother, who closes the trap door. From her spot cramped in the cellar, Mary Agnes hears her gram nudge the table back and shuffle to the door.

"And ya'd be?" Grace asks. "Ah, Lorcan O'Connor, is it? I recognize ya. What is it that I can do for ya lads tonight?"

It is Lorcan O'Connor. Who undid Mary Coffey.

"We heard the Coyne girl might be here."

"The Coyne girl?"

"Mary Agnes, she's called. Sister of Fiach."

"Why, she would be at home, wouldn't she? At this hour?"

"We've got some business with her but she's slipped away, she has."

"And what business is it that is so important that ya lads are out in this weather? And past ten o'clock?"

Granda!

"Sorry to bother ya, Mrs. Laffey, Captain Laffey."

Mary Agnes hears the door shut, shuffling, the trap door hinging open.

"It's alright, lass," her gram says. "Ya can come up now."

When the night passes away, she is still crumpled on her gram's lap. She wakes to Festus's voice.

"It'll be time for leave taking, girl," he says. "We're off for Gaillimh."

Galway. Fifty long miles away.

After a tearful goodbye to her gram, Mary Agnes sets off down the bumpy lane with Festus, their small wagon pulled by Festus's sure-footed donkey. The sun is long from rising. It will take fifteen hours to get to Galway City via the Clifden Road, the first leg of her long journey to America.

Mary Agnes looks back at Dawrosbeg through bucketing rain, miles of green and ancient stones talking. They pass her mam's and da's cottage, but the windows are dark. As they turn right on the dirt road toward Clifden, she loses sight of the place she's called home for thirteen years. More tears might have come if there were any left after last night, but this morning her eyes—like her heart—are bone dry.

9

October 1886
Aboard the *Siren* from Galway to
Liverpool, United Kingdom

The black shadow of Ireland recedes as Mary Agnes clings to the rail and watches the wide, brooding Atlantic stretch from horizon to horizon. The *Siren* has cleared Galway Bay now and heads south-southwest to round the far reaches of counties Kerry and Cork before it turns eastward toward Britain, wedges through St. George's Channel between Ireland and Wales, and skirts north through the Irish Sea toward Liverpool.

Was it just today that her granddad sent her off with a letter and a year's wages? Leaving everything and everyone at Dawrosbeg? Her gram. Her brothers. Jonesy.

My life.

A flash of memories floods her mind: days and months and years, greening May, lush June, sultry August, barren November. Four, five, six, she is, bare feet and a sack for a dress, plucking tiny flowers in her small hand, catching her sleeve on wild strawberry vines, slurping tea. Always the sea, the sky, the birds. Cormorant. Plover. Gull. Poems and songs. Nights so late your eyes close sitting up. Pipe smoke. Stories. Music. Wind along the lane, always the wind. Eight, nine, ten, hungry or full, happy or not. Limpets. Mussels. Pails of peat. Fishing. Granda and Gram. Her window. The moon. Everything familiar, like the liturgy of every day in a place you'd never think of leaving, famine or feast—for who would want to leave such a place?—until, until . . .

That is why I am standing here on this creaking ship. Nothing has been the same since Fiach. And Mam allowed it. How will I weather it? The leaving? The voyage? Life?

She wonders how many ships have left Ireland's shores since the famine years, leaving everything and everyone behind. Enough to fill a thousand ships? Two thousand? More?

She looks around. *I would know these faces anywhere*, she thinks, wan, sunken, thin, like the washerwoman Mary Casey, or the publican Patrick Gill; the shoemaker Daniel Cregan, or the widow Bridget Doyle. Huddled in clumps, old women bend their heads in conversation. Old men smoke wordlessly, eyes cast down, thinking of failing crops, deaths (and more deaths), no money for rent.

But the real reason everyone is leaving Ireland: *no food, no hope.* Forty years on from the time of great hunger, still Irish leave ruined cottages and ruined furrows and ruined lives (ruined the shared word here).

Why, God? she asks? *Why the Irish?* And underneath it all, *Why me, and not Fiach sent away?*

As the *Siren* slices through dark water away from Galway toward Liverpool, Mary Agnes's face stings with driving rain, tiny needles prickling into her skin. She grasps the wooden ship's rail tighter, as if doing so will keep tears from escaping, and looks down at the surging waves. *Lap slap lap*, they slam against the hull, frothy entrails shoved back at the sea.

Mary Agnes must now navigate Liverpool—and then New York—before she arrives at the Laffey's doorstep in Chicago. "They've a girl your age," her gram had said. *Thirteen*. Mary Agnes wonders what her cousin looks like and if she will like her. She hasn't had a friend to confide in since Mary Coffey was sent away, disgraced. She will never know the friendships now of other Connemara girls, the girls she knew at school, the O'Neill girl and the Buckley girl, growing up and old with them and their husbands and their wee ones. Knowing their thoughts and dreams. The joys of weddings, her voice singing through the day, and the heartaches of wakes, her voice keening for the lost. No, that door is slammed shut with no chance of reopening. She's off for America and won't be back.

She starts a poem in her head to drown out her fears.

Don't forget from whence you came,
You mayn't pass this way again,
The grassy knolls and rocky shore,
Will I see it evermore?
Not until a scrim it seems:
A distant shore in distant dreams . . .

"What're ya dreaming of, Irish?" A young man of Fiach's age comes up next to her on the rail. His coat is threadbare, with holes at the elbows. A mop of dark hair hangs low over his face. He smells of tobacco and whiskey and home as he spits over the rail, yellow bits landing in his stubble.

Squaring her shoulders, the only way she knows to confront impending danger, she narrows her eyes and minces her words. "What do you think, bogger?"

"Bogger, is it now? Like the pot calling the teakettle black, mavourneen. Ya don't smell so good yourself."

Mary Agnes remembers her boots. She will have to

scrape the remaining dung off with her one handkerchief. "And who are you calling mavourneen?"

"Habit, I suppose. Have a passel of sisters. So where ya bound? Boston, perhaps? That's where I'm headed, after Liverpool, that is."

"Maybe." She doesn't want to give out information to a stranger.

As the ship rounds a dark headland silhouetted only by a weak moon, a lighthouse casts lonely beams across the water, flash on, flash off, beware of rocks, beware of shoals, *beware, beware*. Mary Agnes is already homesick. But for what? Not her mam and da. Not Fiach. Not hunger. Not rain.

But.

Her grandparents. Jonesy. Her brothers. The way the sun glinted off the Purple Mary's robe. The rocky knoll outside her grandparents' house where she sat with her tutor. The tang of salt air that permeates everything—*home home home*.

"Mam and Pap sent for ya?"

Mary Agnes's face darkens. "No."

"Grands then?" He sidles closer to Mary Agnes, his back now to the rail.

Granda? Gram? Will I ever see you again?

She takes two steps away from the boy, salt air blasting her face. "No." She keeps her voice measured to belie her true feelings, that's she not sure if this grand journey—*this banishment,* she thinks—is for the best. "There's an uncle and aunt, somewhere in the West. They've a girl my age."

"Which is?"

"None of your business. Old enough. And, if you don't mind me asking, who's asking?"

"Jimmy Scanlon." He makes a mock bow. His vest is threadbare, too, and cap askew over dark curls and piercing green eyes.

"From?"

"Tralee."

"Well, Jimmy Scanlon of Tralee, like I said, it's none of your business."

"They've sent ya alone? Not even a guardian?" he presses. He lifts a flask to his mouth.

"You're an incorrigible one, aren't you? I've a letter. And my wits." *And two pounds, but I won't be telling that to the likes of you.*

"Aren't ya the cheeky one? Ya remind me of my sister, Mary Monica. She's 'round your age. Can't imagine her traveling alone." He turns back to face the sea and shakes his head. Looking straight at Mary Agnes, he says, "When we get to Liverpool, I'll ask at a pub. Say we're brother and sister in need of a cot for the night. Plus, we'll get a hot meal. There'd be no food on this ship unless ya've brought your own."

No food? Still?

Mary Agnes straightens. This trip is going to be more challenging than she thought. "You'll think twice about that, Jimmy Scanlon. Asking me to spend the night with you. Don't act the maggot."

"Don't mean it like that. I've got my pick of girls and if ya don't mind me saying, ya're a bit young for me. I swear on my gram's grave I don't mean ya ill."

"I'm not yet convinced, if you don't mind *me* saying."

"What's *yer* name, then, lass?"

"Mary Agnes Laffey," she lies. "From Galway," she lies again.

"Can I give ya a word of advice, Mary Agnes Laffey of Galway, if ya don't mind?"

She nods.

"Stick to yer own kind, Irish. It's a rough world out there."

CLENCHING HER SATCHEL CLOSE TO HER thigh on the crowded docks at Liverpool, Mary Agnes thinks of all the things she's taking on the journey: Two changes of clothes, rags for her monthlies, a wool hat, a few toilet items, and the slim journal from her tutor, Seamus Bourke. And her fare to America. With Jimmy Scanlon at her side, she dodges rubbish on the filthy quayside. She's decided by now it's safer to travel with him than alone, although she's not yet thoroughly convinced of his motives. She will be wary.

As she looks behind her, she wonders if it's too late to go home. She could take the next ship back to Galway. But her excitement fades. *No, Gram can't care for me anymore. My parents won't have me. And I can't risk seeing Fiach again. I cannot have a babe.*

She clutches her midsection. *I cannot have a babe.*

Jimmy and Mary Agnes avoid baggage runners and dogs. "Sod off!" Jimmy shouts. Mary Agnes's stomach grumbles. *I'll be needing a good meal here. But do I have enough? Better to go hungry. No, better* not *to go hungry. I mayn't keep a thing down on the passage.*

At the corner, they enter a dim pub with a sign long past its prime. The Angler's Arms, she reads, and her heart lurches. *Granda . . . I am already so far away from Dawrosbeg.*

Seated in a cracked red settee surrounded by heavy dark paneling, Mary Agnes and Jimmy order a bowl of hash and a pint of ale each.

"My treat, Irish. To prove to ya I'm above board," Jimmy says. His green eyes smile by themselves.

"All the same, I'll pay my way."

"Not another word," he says. "My gram would box my ears if I didn't offer."

Her eyes adjust to the dark interior as they wait for their fare. The pub, filled with travelers and locals, smells of wet wool and steaming caps. Near the door, older men sit at a long wooden bar, nursing glasses of ale and sadness. Younger men and boys crowd booths and tables and stools, loud in conversation, "America" on their lips. Except for a barmaid, Mary Agnes is one of the only females in the establishment.

Above the booth, filtered sun slices through grimed windows. She instinctively reaches toward the window. Everything is fuzzy around the edges. *Maybe in America, I can afford eyeglasses!* She tries to look forward, to the future instead of the past, but, like her eyesight, everything's hazy.

Mary Agnes and Jimmy linger at the booth, drying out. Before closing time, Jimmy goes to the bar to settle the bill and haggle for a room. He returns, scowling. "There's nothing to be had, so your virtue remains intact, Miss Laffey. We'll have to hunker down somewhere. Maybe an alley. I'll keep watch over ya."

"An alley? What about a graveyard?"

"A boneyard?"

"Who would bother us there?"

"Aye, ya've a point, girl."

They wander through crooked alleyways away from the wharves. Mary Agnes makes a note of their path—Wicker Lane, Boylston Street, St. James Mews—so they will be back to the wharf in time for tomorrow's sailing. Her skirt whips around her legs and she pulls her gram's shawl close. Her satchel bumps her thigh. She notices Jimmy doesn't have a bag.

"Jimmy!" She pulls at Jimmy's arm. "Did you forget your bag at the pub?" She turns to go back from where they came.

"Hold on, Irish. I don't have a bag. Just the clothes I'm wearing, and a knife. Nothing else."

"Nothing else?" *A change of drawers? A letter for a priest? Money?*

"Not a thing. Now, look for a church," he says. "It'll be getting on."

They keep to themselves, avoiding drunks and pimps and street urchins, as they slink from one alley to another near the wharves. Again, Mary Agnes commits to memory their route.

"There!" she points. Just ahead, out of the mist, a spire. Upon closer inspection, she reads the sign: St. Thomas Aquinas. She thinks of little Tommy and her heart stings.

Jimmy pushes open a creaky gate behind the church. It opens to a cloistered cemetery dotted with grey stones, some tilted, others flattened. It is a place long abandoned, dark and overgrown. Rodents scurry in the underbrush and wind whistles through thinning trees. Mary Agnes thinks of the cemetery at Ballynakill. They're long dead, generations of Coynes and Laffeys and the others, Celtic crosses weathered by rain and wind and salt and moss. But their spirits roam at night, this she knows, in shadows on the wall or in the keening of the wind. She pulls her shawl tight. *There are spirits here.*

"Spooky," Jimmy whistles.

"Are you afeard?"

Jimmy stands tall in his worn boots. "Are ya?"

"Not." Mary Agnes turns and begins to sing.

From Liverpool docks we bid adieu
To all the girls and boyos too . . .

"What're ya doing?" Jimmy pulls her sleeve. "Someone might hear ya."

Mary Agnes thinks he looks afraid, although she knows he would never admit it. "There's no one here to listen. My granddad always said, 'When comes the night, it be too long,' and my gram would say, 'Sing to chase it away.' So that's what I'm doing. Chasing away the night." She wipes her mouth on her sleeve and begins again.

The anchor's weighed, the sails unfurl
We're bound across the ocean.

"Ya've a lovely voice," Jimmy says.

"I've been told."

Jimmy continues to scout around the graveyard. He scampers behind slanting gravestones and hoots.

"You won't scare me, Jimmy Scanlon of Tralee. I've seen dead bodies before."

"Aye, haven't we all."

"We'll be needing a place to rest. Not that I think we'll get a wink tonight."

Jimmy points to a large stone with room for two to sit up against. He leans up against the stone, wipes his hands on his dirty trousers, picks at his fingernails. Mary Agnes runs her fingers across the etching: "George Lamphrey. Born 1848 Liverpool. Died 1869 Liverpool. Why, he was just 21." She puts her shawl on the ground to absorb the dampness and pulls her skirt around her bare legs as she sits.

Jimmy sits next to her, not too close. "My brother died at twenty-one, God rest his soul." He makes the sign of the cross. "Accident." His face darkens. "At the mine."

"Sorry for your loss, Jimmy. So young, like poor George Lamphrey here."

They go back and forth then speculating about George Lamphrey's demise. A cart accident. An overdose of opium. Lost at sea.

"No, it were with a woman! He was well able til then!" Jimmy doubles over in laughter.

"That's coarse, Jimmy. I've a mind to leave you right here."

"Don't . . ." He touches her arm.

"I'd keep your hands to yourself, if I were you." She shivers and pulls her arms close to her torso. The bell from the church belfry tolls two times, then three, then four, still hours until dawn and Mary Agnes wide awake in spite of it.

AT DAWN, CLOUDS BLISTER IN, GREY and mauve. Rumpled and damp after a sleepless night, Mary Agnes and Jimmy wend their way back to the wharf and line up with hundreds of passengers to board the steamship *Endeavour* bound for New York. They're jostled as they move up the line in a downpour.

"Did you ever?" Jimmy says, as he covers his head with a castoff newspaper. "Lashing."

"Driving, we say in Connemara." Mary Agnes keeps both hands on her bag. It is all she has from Connemara, except memories.

When they reach the front of the queue, male and female passengers traveling without families are separated. Mary Agnes pries open her purse and pays the fee for a berth in steerage. She loses sight of Jimmy as she's corralled below deck. She looks over her shoulder as she's herded along, but it's no use.

Did he make it aboard? And how did he pay if he has no money? Did he spend the last of it on broth and ale yesterday? And offered to pay my share? And didn't he say he was going to Boston?

Below decks, the stench is overwhelming—vomit, sweat, urine, feces—as if the ship hasn't been swabbed for months. Mary Agnes finds a top bunk in steerage and hefts her satchel up to the bunk to save her place. After changing her bloodied rags and putting them to soak in a pail near her bunk, she bolts for the stairs, gasping.

After taking the air for a half-hour, her hands nearly numb from the cold, she is now back on the top bunk of the small berth she shares with a few dozen other female passengers below decks. The ceiling in steerage is so low, she barely has enough room to fit on the top bunk, her head inches from the creaking wood above her head. Mary Agnes shimmies to her side and takes out her wool purse. She opens the flap and spills out the contents. Just shy of two pounds left after paying her fare. She counts once, and then again, a well-worn bill and the rest in coin. After tucking the money into her purse, Mary Agnes stuffs it beneath her pillow. Pulling the green shawl around her shoulders and upper arms, Mary Agnes burrows into the lumpy mattress. She wishes for a cloak or a blanket.

What is Sean doing now? And the rest of the boys? How is Jonesy? Is Granda back from Inishbofin yet?

Her mind swells with images: Sean acting the man now, Ferris and Eamon hauling water, their thin arms straining against the weight, Tommy shivering, his dark hair slicked down on his head; Jonesy in the barn, hunched over on a stool, milking, whispering to the cow—singing almost; Granda in his brown chair by the fire, looking at Gram with those kind eyes of his . . .

Mary Agnes's stomach rumbles. The hash from yesterday hadn't agreed with her; she heaved up the contents this morning and hasn't been hungry since. *But I know I should eat. Maybe in the morning . . . Or am I with child? Would I know so soon? Who can I ask?*

She turns from side to side, but no matter how much she squirms, she cannot get comfortable. With shaking hands, she pulls her woolen hat lower over her head so that only her eyes and nose and mouth are open to the cold and then pulls the shawl to her chin. She wiggles her toes inside her stinking stockings to get blood moving.

A sour smell pervades the berth as a clutch of rats hugs the wall of the ship and disappears. She shivers. Soon, the berth is filled with night noises—mothers telling familiar stories in hushed tones, soft moans, a gentle snore, interspersed with the wail of a baby. And then, from somewhere, a lullaby. She thinks of Tommy again, tucking him in at night as if he were her own, murmuring songs and pushing his hair back behind his ears before kissing his sweaty forehead.

Closing her eyes, she's transported back to Dawrosbeg. *Ah, Tommy, Eamon, Ferris, Sean. Jonesy. And Granda, shuffling now to place a blanket over Gram as she nods off by the fire. No, I haven't forgotten about you.*

Jimmy Scanlon's offhand comment rattles her brain. "They've sent ya alone?"

Mary Agnes stifles a cry. She doesn't want to disturb the others. But it doesn't mean she couldn't cry a bucketful or scream. She could. Maybe everything in America isn't as grand as she's heard.

Late October 1886
Aboard *Endeavour* from Liverpool,
United Kingdom to New York

Bracing stiff wind and tangy salt air, Mary Agnes zig-zags on the rocking deck toward Jimmy, who stands with another young man leaning on the handrail. The weather has "held off," as her gram used to say, although black clouds scamper across the sky, threatening rain.

"You made it!" she says.

"Aye, and I did."

"How? I thought you were going to Boston."

"I am and I will. Had to jump the first ship going to America." He winks. "Told ya I was lucky. Just can't get caught."

Mary Agnes grasps the rail for balance. "Haven't found my sea legs yet." Enroute now across the Atlantic to New York on the steamship *Endeavour*—twelve or fourteen days, depending on weather—her eyes are rimmed red from lack of sleep. And yes, she's hungry, but that's not the brunt of her worries. She's trying to convince herself she can't be pregnant. With all this blood, she's sure it's her monthly, although she has no one to ask.

"Faith and it's true, she's a beauty," the other boy says, whistling through his teeth. He is about Jimmy's age, and in similar state of dress. He makes a sweeping bow. "Michael O'Hearne's the name, Mick to my friends."

Friends? Mary Agnes looks toward Jimmy, and he nods.

"Thick as thieves, we are," Jimmy says, patting Mick on the shoulder. "Even though we've known each other but a day. Ya can trust him, Irish." He leans over the rail to spit.

"Can I now?"

Mick steadies her elbow.

"Didn't say I were ready to dance a jig," she says, and pulls away.

"Ah, a feisty one." Mick sweeps dark hair from his face and grins. "With that face, though . . . 'a face without freckles is like a sky without stars.'"

"Shut your gob," Mary Agnes says. "Like my little brother, Sean. Always in a scrape, and a mouth on him. I can picture him at twenty, same as you."

"Twenty?!" He throws a hero's smile her way. "Twenty-one next week."

"Yeah, and yer mother's the Blessed Virgin herself," Jimmy says. "We're both eighteen, lass, not a day older. Don't let that braggard tell ya any different."

Mary Agnes looks out at the black ocean and squeezes her hands tightly. Even though she can't see her, the Holy Mother is with her, she knows.

"Do you think I could pass for sixteen?" she asks. She's instantly sorry that she's given out too much information, and to lads, no less.

Jimmy looks at her bosom. "Fourteen, maybe."

"Who's to know?" Mick says. "Say ya're sixteen and how do they prove it? They see a pretty face and ya're hired." He pinches her cheek.

Mary Agnes slaps his hand. "And I'd be keeping your hands to yourself."

Watch out for fast lads. They can undo ya in one night.

She turns away from Mick and entreats Jimmy with her eyes.

"Don't worry, Irish. Mick here already has a girl on the ship. Don't mind him."

"What do you mean, hired?" she asks.

"All the pretty Irish girls are housekeepers," Mick says.

"Not me. I'll be going to school."

Both boys whistle at the same time.

"School, is it?" Mick says. "No shame in hard work. My mam's a housekeeper, and my aunties. And then there's my cousins . . ."

"We don't need to hear about all of Wexford, you noodenaddy," Jimmy says.

"Just telling Mary A. here there's no shame in it."

"That I know, Michael," she says.

"Mick, please."

"And I'm not afraid of it, Michael, Mick. But I'm good at numbers. I'll be at school. Training for"—she thinks before she speaks, hoping she doesn't sound too posh — "university."

"University, now, is it?" Jimmy says. "Head in the clouds, Irish?"

"I mean it, Jimmy." *I am going to university.*

"Ya, well. Good luck to ya."

Mick snorts. "Class horse, this one thinks she is. Outta my league." He turns heel and heads for the mess hall.

Jimmy moves toward Mary Agnes. "Don't mind him. He's from Wexford. I'm famished. Ya?"

Mary Agnes nods. *That too. When have I never been hungry?* "Even if I can't bear the sight of food right now." *Seasickness? Or pregnant?*

They scramble across the rolling deck toward the wide doors of the mess hall. Jimmy bends over and snatches a coin off the deck.

"I'm on the pig's back now!" he says, pocketing the coin. "Luck is always with me." He holds the door for Mary Agnes and she grasps the doorframe for balance.

The mess is unusually empty for this time in the morning. Even Mick has disappeared. *Maybe everyone's feeling off,* Mary Agnes thinks. *Like me.*

But her stomach grumbles and food is offered so she chews deliberately, every morsel strength for her body, strength for the trip. After a breakfast of thin oatmeal, hard biscuit, and weak tea, Mary Agnes excuses herself. She fears she might not stomach this meal, either.

Jimmy holds the door for her. "I'll be looking out for ya, don't worry. At least until New York. Ya could always come to Boston."

"I'm going to . . . let's just say I heard you the first time, Jimmy. I might be four—" she stops herself in the lie.

"I knew it! Same age as my sister, Mary Monica." He slaps his thigh.

"Well, yes, then. Fourteen." *Thirteen, if you really want to know.* The lies she tells are mounting, like her sins. "But I can do this, Jimmy."

I have to do this. Even if I have to do it by myself.

THEY'VE BEEN ON THE SHIP FOR FIVE days now, and Mary Agnes can't keep food down. She's not the only one. Below decks, the ship is filled with Irish refugees from Mayo and Clare, Sligo and Galway, retching in pails. Above deck, to get sea air, she feels a bit better—and doesn't feel alone. A mother there, nursing a wee one, two littles clinging to her skirt.

Lads playing jacks. Children scampering about, wisps of curled red hair peeking from beneath caps. Pretty girls walking two by two, threadbare shawls and battered boots and tattered hems.

It is with girls like this Mary Agnes shares the dank hold, separated into three compartments, one for women and girls; another for men and boys; and the largest reserved for families quartered together. Even though thin sheets separate them, Mary Agnes cannot escape sounds— or smells—from the other sections and often wraps her shawl over her hat to cover her ears and nose and mouth.

From beyond the curtain tonight, in the men's berth, she hears soft uillean pipes and loud swearing over card games and fist fights. Smoke from the men's compartment drifts through the sheets and spills over to the women's compartment. She's seen several of the older women smoke pipes on deck, and she's glad none of them smoke below decks, it's smoky enough as it is, children set to coughing from it.

Mary Agnes is glad to be with single women, although the dichotomies in steerage are as clear here as anywhere in Ireland, whispers and sneers, singing and snores. She is glad she is not in the family hold.

But why? She asks herself. The answer is clear. *I have no family. Except for my brothers.* She shivers then. Will the image of Fiach, and those nasty, greedy, shameful hands, ever go away?

Mary Agnes's berth mate flops down on the bottom bunk, wiping her mouth. "Sorry we haven't met. I've been, oh, never mind. Name's Mary Catherine Reilly. From Donegal. Where are yer people from?" she asks with a yawn.

Mary Agnes leans down over the edge of the top bunk and whispers her answer. "North of Galway." She is stingy with details.

"Ya're a bit young to be traveling alone."

"Aye. Unless I lie about my age."

"Lying is a sin, and ya know it." The girl laughs. "But it hasn't done me any harm." She pats the empty space next to her. "And what's yer name, then?"

Mary Agnes climbs down from the top bunk to sit next to the older girl. "Laffey. Mary Agnes Laffey," she lies again. *Is this what having a sister is like? If so, I shouldn't fib.* "What age are you?" she asks.

"Sixteen next month."

"The truth?"

"Aye, the eighth of November."

"I'm the eighteenth."

"Then we're both Scorpio," Mary Catherine says. Her strawberry-blonde hair is down around her shoulders, blue eyes merry.

"Pardon?"

"Ya ninny. Have ya never heard of the signs of the zodiac?"

"Astrology, you mean? Reading the stars? That's strictly forbidden, and you know it."

Mary Catherine laughs. "Prude, are ya?"

"Am not."

Mary Catherine wiggles her fingers like a scorpion. "Have ya never seen it, Scorpio? It's in the night sky, low on the horizon, in summertime. Other times of the year, it disappears." She pulls her blanket up to shield her face.

Mary Agnes doesn't know if she should delve further into the subject, but she can't help herself. She is curious. "What makes you a Scorpio? Other than talkative." Mary Agnes nudges her berth mate.

"Me?" She nudges Mary Agnes back. "Strong. Motivated to succeed. Secretive," Mary Catherine says with a wink.

"How secretive?"

"That's for me to know."

"And the priest."

Mary Catherine laughs. "I haven't been to confession since—"

"How dare you not?" Mary Agnes's eyes burst wide.

"I'd keep the good father there all day," she laughs.

"You are wicked then," Mary Agnes says, trying to keep a straight face.

"What secrets do ya have, Mary A.?"

Fiach. "None," Mary Agnes lies.

"Ya must have. Everyone does. Resentment. Impatience. Lust."

"If I did, why would I tell you? If I'm a Scorpio?"

"Got me there," Mary Catherine says. "How many girls of—how old are ya anyway?"

Mary Agnes stammers. "Fourteen, soon."

"Aye, so how many girls of *thirteen* do ya see traveling alone?" Mary Catherine sweeps her hands around the berth. "I don't see a one here."

Side by side on the bottom bunk, bunched together under Mary Catherine's blanket (and Mary Agnes wishing for a blanket), they trade stories of families, friends.

"Have a sweetheart?" Mary Catherine asks.

Jonesy. Mary Agnes nods.

"Ya've lain with him, then, before ya left?" Mary Catherine asks.

"Heavens, no." *Is my midsection swelling? Is that why she asked? Maybe I can ask her about it. She'd be likely to know.* Mary Agnes can't keep the images from her mind, Fiach attacking her not once, but twice, as if he could not stop until he bested her, *and then*, she thinks, *how many more times would he have ravaged me? To see me cry?* In the cottage? In the barn? In the lane? On the strand? In back of the neighbor's? She shudders as she tries to thrust Fiach out of her mind.

"Ya've a world to learn then," Mary Catherine says.

"Once ya've been with a lad, ya'll want to be with others. To see what it's like."

No. I do not want to do that ever again. "You've lain with a lad?"

"Lads, Mary A. More than one."

"Aren't you afraid you'll be . . ."

"There's ways to prevent it."

But what if it's already happened? Would I still be bleeding? Mary Agnes wraps her shawl around her shoulders and makes for the upper bunk. "I should be to bed." She resolves to ask Mary Catherine everything she can think of about the facts of life. Maybe tomorrow.

"Here, have a swig." Mary Catherine offers Mary Agnes a small flask.

"I couldn't."

Mary Catherine takes a long swig. "Take the risk or lose the chance, Mary A. I'm off now," she says, and grabs her wrap. "To bed." She hops off the bunk, looks over her shoulder, and blows a kiss as she slips out of the berth and disappears down the companionway.

TAKE THE RISK OR LOSE THE CHANCE?

Mary Agnes wishes she had choices. Where to live. What to do or what to eat. So far in her life, other people have made all the choices for her. Maybe it will be different in America. But first, she will have to get to Chicago, to her people. She doesn't have enough money for anything else so it's ridiculous to think of other choices. *The die is cast, Granda said.*

She reaches under her pillow for her purse. *My purse?* Nothing. Her fingers splay out, groping at the edges of the mattress. *Where is it?* Her heart races as she scrambles down the crude ladder. *What have I done with my purse?*

She ransacks the lower mattress, belonging to her bunkmate. Still nothing. On her hands and knees now, heart
pumping in her throat, she rummages beneath the bunk. A
rat scurries past, its tail skimming her fingers. She shudders.
Through a mass of dust and debris, she thinks she spies the
purse in the far corner. She shimmies on her belly under the
bunk and reaches for it. Out she wriggles and sits with her
back against Mary Catherine's bunk. She brings the purse
to her chest and clenches it, feeling for the clasp. There
isn't one. She brings the purse up in front of her face and
sniffs. There is no mistaking the smell—a long unwashed
woolen sock.

Mary Catherine stumbles into the berth, her legs unsteady.

"Have you seen my purse?" Mary Agnes asks.

The girl pries open her eyes. "What's that ya say?"

"My purse? Have you seen my purse?"

"I haven't any idea about yer purse."

*What will I do now? With no money to my name? Will I have
to steal food to get by? Or face a future like my friend Mary?
Lifting my skirts? No, not that. Never.*

WHY MARY AGNES BOTHERS GETTING UP at all is anyone's guess.
It's the seventh day and she hasn't felt well since the first
night. But many others are in much worse shape than she
is. Mary Catherine, for one.

"My bunkmate, she's ill," Mary Agnes says to Jimmy
at supper. "She hasn't gotten out of bed yet today." They
are sitting on hard benches of the mess, a few feet between
them. Fewer and fewer people come to meals now.

"Ship's fever?"

"Likely."

"What's her name, this bunkmate?" he asks.

"Mary Catherine. Mary Catherine Reilly."

"Christ in the marketplace! She's a fast one. Probably has the clap by now."

What does Jimmy know?

"Remember I said Mick had a girl? That's her. If he doesn't watch out, he'll have the clap, too."

Mary Agnes doesn't know what "the clap" is and doesn't want to ask. The thin stew that passes for supper fills her stomach with little sustenance tonight, three small pieces of brown potato swimming in greasy broth. No carrots, no turnips. Sitting on the worn bench, Mary Agnes slurps weak stew, her lips by now dry and chapped. She tastes blood. Forcing herself to finish, she gags on a bit of gristle. She coughs and then chews slowly. Her mam, never the cook like Mrs. Jones next door (and always trying to prove that she was), could make a stew much heartier and tastier than this. A child could do better.

"I'd best be back to her," Mary Agnes says. "See you tomorrow, Jimmy." She dips her cup into the brine that passes for drinking water and brings it to her cracked lips. She's weak, her stools loose. And always thirsty. She can't help running her tongue along her upper and lower lips, although that won't help with the chapping. But it's a moment's relief—and the last of the salt—and she does it again. She dips the cup another time and takes it with her. She'll return it tomorrow, maybe.

As she makes her way back to the berth, water sloshes over the sides of the cup. When she reaches her bunk, Mary Catherine is still in bed, wan and listless. She has missed all the meals today.

"Mary Catherine! Wake up!" Mary Agnes shakes her bunkmate's shoulder. More water spills out.

Mary Catherine opens her eyes. "I haven't the need." She pulls her blanket under her chin.

Mary Agnes runs her hand over Mary Catherine's forehead. "You're burning up." She grabs the blanket and strips it from Mary Catherine's body.

"Don't!"

"You'll do as I say or you won't survive this journey. Here, drink this." She lifts the cup to Mary Catherine's lips.

"What in God's name is that? Will make me boke. Get me whiskey."

"Who would I ask? And how would I pay? I've lost my purse."

"I don't care what ya do, or how ya do it, just get it for me. I can't get up."

"You've got to get up, Mary Catherine. You've got to pass water at least once per day."

"I don't have to go."

"You've got to try." Mary Agnes helps the older girl to sit.

While Mary Catherine uses the communal chamber pot, Mary Agnes strips the mattress. The sheets are damp and soiled. She'll use her own sheets to remake Mary Catherine's bed and sleep on the raw tick mattress herself. At the head of Mary Catherine's lice-ridden mattress, she sees a familiar item.

What is that? My purse? Mary Agnes reaches for it just as Mary Catherine clambers back into the bunk.

"What are you doing with my purse?" Mary Agnes asks.

"Oh, that. I found it, yesterday."

"Were you going to tell me?" Mary Agnes unclasps the purse and looks inside.

"I was, but—"

"And might you tell my where half my money's gone?"

"Don't know. I told ya I found it."

"Lying is a sin and you know it, Mary Catherine."

"Isn't."

"Isn't what?"

A cough wracks the sick girl's thin frame. "A sin."

"We've no time to debate. What am I supposed to think? You having my purse."

Mary Catherine closes her eyes. "I found it yesterday. On the floor, under here." She points under the cot. "Like ya dropped it. I meant to tell ya, I did. But I forgot . . ." Her eyes close again.

"What have you done with my money?" Mary Agnes shakes the older girl. Mary Catherine doesn't respond. It's like she's slipped into another realm. Mary Agnes has seen this before. Death will come soon. Already there have been twelve deaths since leaving Liverpool; this will be the thirteenth, and she knows she cannot stop it. Although she's filled with rage, she cannot rail against a girl so close to death. *What's done is done. And I'll not get to ask her all the questions I have, but that's sinful, me thinking of myself when she's the one in need.*

Mary Agnes washes Mary Catherine's arms and legs with a cloth, avoiding open sores. She doesn't have soap to wash the girl's hair so she straightens tangles with her fingers. Her own scalp itches and she stops to scratch her head.

As Mary Agnes repeats the Hail Mary over and over again, *pray for us sinners now, and at the hour of our death,* she feels night pressing in, long, and short, depending how she frames it, her thoughts disjointed from lack of sleep. Mary Catherine descends into mumbling as she tosses and turns. At one point, Mary Agnes wonders which breath will be Mary Catherine's last, and when the girl's body lurches and then stills, Mary Agnes sits with her until dawn, the Purple Mary her only companion, *Blessed art thou amongst women.*

Later that morning, as Mary Catherine's shrouded body is lowered overboard into the churning sea, Mary Agnes doesn't know what to believe. She's been betrayed and abandoned, she's alone and scared, but it's a sin to think poorly of the dead so she closes the lid on the subject. She has recovered her purse and has one pound left.

But she's keenly aware she's lost something, too.

And not only my purse. Or the girl who stole it, who I thought was a friend. I've lost my home. My brothers. My grandparents. Jonesy. Life in Ireland.

Mary Agnes stands with Jimmy at the rail longer than anyone else, the taciturn captain included, except for Mick O'Hearne, who stares at the swirling black water as if waiting for Mary Catherine to rise back out of the sea like a siren, a sea goddess, Amphitrite herself. But the sea never gives up its dead. Her granddad told her that.

Late October 1886
New York, New York

As *Endeavour* rounds the southwestern tip of Long Island in dense fog and squeezes through The Narrows into New York Harbor, Mary Agnes stands at the rail with Jimmy Scanlon, desperate to leave the ship alive. Eighteen are now dead, and many close to death. Mary Agnes can feel her ribs protruding and prays to keep just broth and bread down. Standing on solid ground will help.

"Well, do ya see that?" Jimmy whistles.

Mary Agnes squints. "What is it?"

"A statue. I think it's a woman, big as a giant."

"What does she look like?" *Damn I can't see.*

"She's standing on a pedestal. Bright copper, like a penny." He leans over the rail to get a better look through the fog as *Endeavour* makes its way deeper into New York Harbor. "Looks like she's wearing some kind of robe. She's holding a book, or, wait, maybe a tablet, like Moses."

Mary Agnes catches a glimpse of a tall statue and makes out a pointed crown and an arm held aloft.

"What is she holding with her other hand?"

"A torch."

That could be a sign. "Anything else?"

"She's got bare feet."

When they pass the great statue, Mary Agnes turns toward the scene before her and gasps. Even with poor eyesight, she makes out towering masts, tall buildings, smokestacks, pointed spires. Dawrosbeg seems so small and distant, as if it can't exist in the same world as this modern city. She thinks of the Stevenson poem she's committed to memory and sees with her own eyes what wonders the world has to offer, if you rise up and go.

When *Endeavour* shudders to a halt, Mary Agnes almost loses her footing. She is weak and unsteady. She chose not to have breakfast today so as not to appear ill going through interrogation and inspection. It will be fraught enough with worry without adding retching to it. The rumbling of the engines finally stops. Instead of constant engine noise, she now hears the squawk of seagulls hovering over the ship, loud voices from the shore, the din of anxious passengers. *New York.* She squeezes past families and jockeys for a position to offload, the sky threatening rain. Just before she debarks the ship, she hears an all-familiar voice.

"Best of luck to ya, Irish!" Jimmy waves from the top of the gangplank, and then, with a tip of his hat and that winning smile that's grown on her, she loses sight of him in the throng. She'll likely never see him again, him going to Boston and her to Chicago. She hadn't even given her true name if he ever writes. If he can write.

In a crush of human flesh, Mary Agnes presses between families and burly men and waif-like mothers, some no older than she, clinging babes to their breasts, all in such dreadful need of a bath she could gag. They are herded through the doors into a cavernous room, languages and cultures colliding. Three other ships have offloaded this morning, emigrants from Italy and Germany and another place with a language so guttural Mary Agnes thinks they must choke when they speak. She holds her satchel in front of her. A hand gropes her behind, but she doesn't turn to look.

It's a trick, she thinks, *to distract me. I can't be distracted now, not now, not after everything.*

She takes her place at the end of a long queue for processing in the octagonal building, the last hurdle before landing on the streets of New York. The stench of bodies presses close. She lifts her shawl to smell her underarms. Rank. She spits on her hand and rubs the downy-haired spot under her arms. Even though she needs to pass water, she doesn't dare leave her place in line. Besides, there is no one to save a spot for her. The family in front of her must be German; she can make out one or two words, *ein* and *ja* and the mention, over and over by the distraught mother, *Deutschland, Deutschland.* The couple behind speaks a language she's never heard. Even if she could, she cannot ask anyone to hold her place.

We are all on our own here.

At the two-hour mark, Mary Agnes's legs feel like deadweight, and she clamps her thighs together to refrain from urinating. She's shy of twenty more passengers now before it's her turn, so she prays for patience, a commodity God has gifted her in short supply. She's glad she's not ill. Stories of passengers being turned back once arriving shudder through her.

Finally, the gatekeeper of the queue, a stout man of indeterminate age, waves her to the next interrogation desk. There, a burly older matron, perhaps fifty or fifty-five, with weary lines at the corners of her mouth and eyes—and the dourest expression Mary Agnes has ever seen, even more dour than her mam, if that is possible—barrages her with questions.

"Name?"

"Mary Agnes Coyne, ma'am."

The matron ticks the application. "Age?"

"Fourteen at my next birthday. Unmarried, yes."

"Pauper? Diseased?"

"No and no, ma'am." Although she's down to less than a pound in her purse. *More than Jimmy has.*

Where is Jimmy? She is tempted to look around for him, but she dares not break her concentration. In the space of two minutes, she's battered with a litany of questions. She keeps her eyes focused on the woman's mouth, so as not to miss any inquiry in the cacophony that fills the great hall.

"Occupation?"

"Girl," she mutters.

"Speak up!"

Mary Agnes stares at the inspector and says with all the confidence of her ancestors bolstering her for this moment. "Pupil, ma'am."

"Final destination in America?"

"Chicago, ma'am."

"Who paid for your passage?"

"My grandfather," Mary Agnes says, and she adds for good luck, "I'm to stay with an uncle and aunt and cousin."

"Can you read and write?" The woman looks down her nose at Mary Agnes.

Of course, I can read and write. I'm going to university. But I must hold my tongue. My future is in the balance here.

"Excuse me, ma'am?" Mary Agnes moderates her anger at the woman's condescension. The stakes are too high.

"I said, can you read and write?" The matron enunciates the words as if Mary Agnes is deaf, or worse, dumb.

Mary Agnes nods.

"Read this."

Mary Agnes squints to read. *We hold these truths to be self-evident that all men are created equal . . .*

Her recitation seems to satisfy the matron, and the woman hands Mary Agnes the application. "Over there," she says, and waves to a station near the wall, where six partitions shield physical examinations from public view.

"I need to pass water," Mary Agnes says.

"You'll have to wait."

Mary Agnes walks to the station, her midsection bursting. Behind a faded curtain, an older nurse, wearing a starched uniform and hat, not unlike a nun, and as severe, pats Mary Agnes on the shoulders, chest, and waist. She parts the hair on Mary Agnes's scalp and runs a finger from the crown of her head to her prominent widow's peak, all the while grumbling. She yanks on Mary Agnes's hair so hard it hurts. "Lice," she spits. "You all have lice." She points to another station where a large man wields sharp scissors.

Mary Agnes walks tentatively toward the barber, skirting piles of hair on the ground. The large man has rounded, red cheeks and enormous hands. He stands with legs set apart and motions for Mary Agnes to a stool near the wall.

"Must you?" she asks. "Can't I wash them out?" She touches her hair.

He grunts as he lifts shears and makes a sweeping cut. Mary Agnes winces as waist length auburn hair falls in clumps to the floor. She holds back tears. *Now is not the time.* He then retrieves a blade and cuts her hair to the scalp. She stifles a cry. His large palm ruffles the stubble, and he thrusts his hand toward her.

He must be wanting coin.

But before Mary Agnes can reach into her purse, the man grabs her wrist and shoves her hand to his crotch. She squirms to get away, but his grasp is stronger. She feels his stiffness beneath his coarse wool trousers.

I can't scream. He'll turn me in.

"Next!" He drops her hand.

Mary Agnes's cheeks burn.

Does he do this to every girl? To see if she'll beg for mercy? Men are . . .

She stops at this thought. *Some men are good and kind. Other men are vile and awful. Men are . . .* she continues, *confusing.*

Wiping her hand on her dress, already three shades of foul after fourteen days at sea, Mary Agnes wants the man's touch, smell, gone.

I must keep my wits about me, she thinks to herself. *Especially now.* She does not look back as she touches her newly shorn scalp. Her heart drops. *All that lovely hair. What more must I do to pass inspection?*

She hands her application to a young man who eyes her suspiciously.

Not him, too, she thinks, *please, no.*

He holds her gaze longer than customary and then, with a *thump*, stamps her application. She murmurs her thanks and hustles past money changers and railway ticket offices and a post office to find a washroom. By now, she is sweating profusely. There will be plenty of time to part with the last of her money in New York; now is the time to straighten her dress and her thoughts.

After relieving herself, she heads with purpose toward the arched front doors of Castle Garden and then, *at blessed last*, past massive white columns and down a long pathway lined with bare trees. Clutches of immigrant families fall to their knees outside Castle Garden, some laughing, some crying, some kissing the ground. She hears what she thinks must be prayers offered up to many gods as families hug and wail.

Thank you, Blessed Mother, she prays.

All at once, Mary Agnes is on the rainy streets of New York with nothing to her name except meager belongings, a few coins, and the address, written in an uneven hand,

Church of the Transfiguration, Mott Street. There she will ask for a warm cup of soup, a crust of bread, and a bedroll before she heads to Chicago.

But how will she pay the fare? Will the church take care of her? Is that why Festus and Grace sent her to this particular church? To this particular priest? Have her people in Chicago sent the necessary funds to him and he is holding it for her?

That must be it, she thinks. *Gram said my people would take care of me. That they owed it to Mam. But why?*

Avoiding a raft of immigrant services lining the street corners, she hurries across Battery Place and ducks under the first awning she sees to escape now driving rain. Several others have huddled under the awning near her. The smell of unwashed bodies is somewhat mitigated by being outside.

Mary Agnes pulls her hat tight over her scalp and stands, shivering, as the world goes by in one city block, people of every color and manner of dress, dark trousers, vests, and jackets, colorful robes, long skirts under tunics, and every make of boot and hat.

Just then, Mary Agnes hears a shout, then a scream. Right in front of her, a mother in a knitted shawl and long dark skirt snatches her child just in time from being crushed by an oncoming dray.

"Move on, boyos!" A large policeman waves his stick at the crowd. "Nothing to see here."

Mary Agnes looks right and left in teeming rain as she avoids horse-drawn cabs and carriages. She crosses the cobblestone street and clings to her satchel, back hunched against the weather and rotting fish and coal smoke, manure and offal, not unlike Galway or Liverpool, but so much more crowded.

"Hot corn!" a street vendor yells. "Hot, sweet, buttered corn!"

If only she could afford to eat, but she only has English coin.

"Read all about it!" a newsboy hawks as he waves thick newspapers above his head: *The Tribune, The Sun, The Post.*

Statue of Liberty is Unveiled, she reads, then, *Liberty and Love: Frenchmen and Americans to Join Hands; Momentous Day for the World.*

Mary Agnes will try to read the daily papers, but how? How will she find a nickel every day for a paper and another the day after that?

ACUTELY HUNGRY DESPITE DISTASTEFUL SMELLS, Mary Agnes hurries up Pearl Street, wary of vendors and street urchins who swarm city sidewalks. She can't help stopping in front of shop windows: Delicatessens laden with rows upon rows of salamis, cheeses, and hams; bakeries offering an assortment of breads and sweets to fill a hundred baskets; fruit and vegetable grocers with items so colorful, so vibrant, one could feast for days, a fish market stuffed with more fish than must live in Ballynakill Harbour. She has seen more food in the last few blocks than she has seen in a lifetime. She reaches toward the glass. If only she could reach through it.

"Move on, boyo!" a shopkeeper yells, and so she does, again.

So this is New York. Move on, move on. Day I've had today.

On Water Street, Mary Agnes lingers in front of a storefront with a large blue sign: Rudolph's Grocery. It has been more than twelve hours since her last meal and she counts on the goodness of the grocer to take the last of her foreign currency.

"I'll have a bit of cheese," she says to the burly man behind the counter. *Please take my coin.*

"Out of Ireland, are you?"

"I am, sir. Arrived today."

"Is that so." He hands her two large slices of cheese. "On the house."

"Thank you, sir."

"Watch yourself, then," he says. "All the lads are looking for a piece of skirt fresh off the boat."

Mary Agnes reddens. "I'm not that kind of girl."

"That's what they all say at first. Here." He hands her a small apple. "You look like you could use it. Put some meat on your bones." He pats his paunch. "Be on your way now, Irish. It's almost dark."

Irish. It might as well be her name by now.

On the way out the door of the aroma-filled shop, Mary Agnes pinches a small loaf of bread from a shelf outside the doorway. *He won't miss just one, will he?* She knows she should pay for it, but her hands move faster than her brain and now the loaf is in her pocket and what should she do? Her mouth waters after living for the last few weeks on diseased potatoes and scraps of fish, weak broth and tea.

She waits for a strong arm on her neck, but nothing, and turns to see the grocer shaking his head.

"Sir?"

"I don't know why I bother with your kind. Worthless, every one of you. Don't come back!"

Worthless.

Her shame burns as she wanders through a maze of streets, Maiden Lane, Gold, Beekman, nibbling on apple and cheese. The bread sits untouched in her pocket.

Worthless.

Mary Agnes passes church after church. Our Lady of the Rosary. St. Anthony of Padua. Church of the Holy Sepulchre. She checks her granddad's note. She is looking for the Church of the Transfiguration. *Where is Mott Street? It can't be far now.*

So tired she is, it's tempting to sit on a bench or a stoop, just rest her legs, rest her mind. But it's getting dark now, and she doesn't want to spend her first night on the streets. Who knows who might approach her or accost her? Or what they might demand? The last of her coin? Her shawl? Her virtue? No, nothing good will come of spending the night alone on the streets of New York.

When she sees the sign for Park Row, she asks a tinware peddler for directions.

"Up Chatham, five, six blocks," he points.

At the corner of Park and Mott streets, Mary Agnes is close to tears. Ahead, she sees another spire. *Please, Holy Mother.* She hurries and squints to read the sign: Church of the Transfiguration.

She is finally here, after journeying from Dawrosbeg to Galway City to Liverpool to New York. Far from a city girl—*just a girl,* she thinks, *and only thirteen!*—she would have done what it takes, moved to Inishbofin or Galway—*or walked clear to France or Austria-Hungary or Siberia,* if that's what it took to get away from Fiach.

"AND YOU WOULD BE?" THE TALL PRIEST shuffles Mary Agnes into his cloistered office. It is after dark by now and the office is shadowed and musty. Behind him, the familiar crucifix, Jesus hanging sorrowfully on the cross, his head shrouded by thorns.

Mary Agnes exhales, and with it, relief. "Mary Agnes Coyne, Father."

"Sure as the sun rises, you'd be from Galway, yes?"

"Yes, Father. Near Letterfrack. You've heard of my grandfather? Captain Laffey?" She hands him the letter.

He rubs his forehead, opens the letter, and reads. "Laffey. Laffey. Ah, yes. I seem to recall a Laffey. Went west a few years back. Some sort of scandal."

A scandal?

"Those are my people," she says. "I am hoping you'll let me stay a day or two before I'm on my way."

"You're off the boat just today?"

Is it that obvious? "I am, Father."

"You'll be needing confession, then?"

Fiach. Noodling with Jonesy. Alone with Jimmy in Liverpool. Thinking ill thoughts of Mary Catherine on Endeavour. *And just today, touching a stranger's crotch and stealing bread.*

Too tired to say another word, she looks the priest in the eye. "I've nothing to confess, Father."

12

The Next Morning
Late October 1886
New York, New York

*A*fter a hard night on a hard bench in the priest's office, Mary Agnes tries to keep up with Father Benedict's housekeeper's long legs as they walk up Mott Street after tea and toast in the rectory kitchen. Stepping over refuse, Mary Agnes pulls her shawl close around her shoulders. The rain has stopped but still she's chilled. She will soon need a coat, it being October.

The housekeeper glances at a scrap of paper. "Here we are, number 67." Mary Agnes looks up at the massive brick building and counts the floors above street level: One, two, three, four, five, six. She mounts the steps and opens the door. Once inside, a strong smell of urine. She clutches her nose.

"They'll be on the third floor," the housekeeper says. "On the right. Up you go, now. Give them this." She hands Mary Agnes a large envelope addressed to a James Donnelly.

"And when will I be going to Chicago then? Tomorrow?"

"Aye, the good father will get you to the train." She clears her throat. "And this, for you, from the good father."

She hands Mary Agnes a small, beaded rosary. "Which is your favorite of the prayers?"

"Hail, Holy Queen."

"'To thee do we send up our sighs . . .'" the housekeeper begins.

"'. . . mourning and weeping in this valley of tears,'" Mary Agnes finishes.

The housekeeper is gone on her long legs before Mary Agnes can say a proper goodbye. She picks her way up the narrow central stairway to the third-floor landing and catches her breath. She could use a bath. There are two apartments to the left and two to the right, the doors to each worn and in need of repair. *On the right, the housekeeper said. But which one?* As she approaches the first door, she hears voices inside. *How many live here? Five? Nine?* She knocks. A young child, *perhaps six or seven*, she thinks, *like one of my brothers*, peeks out the door.

"It's the girl!" he yells.

This would be it, then.

"Aye, and!" the mother says, as she opens the door and ushers Mary Agnes in. Mrs. Donnelly is slightly taller than Mary Agnes, with an enormous bosom and beautiful dark hair framing a lovely Irish face. She takes the envelope from Mary Agnes's hands and rubs the dark stubble on Mary Agnes's scalp. "Just off the boat?"

Mary Agnes nods. She's heard that how many times in the last twenty-four hours?

And not a moment too soon.

"Don't worry, lass, yer hair will grow back in a pig's eye. And a beauty ya are, even without it."

Eight dark heads crowd the front room, all peering at her.

"This'll be our girl now," Mrs. Donnelly says to the children. "Mary, is it?"

"Mary Agnes, ma'am. I'll be off to Chicago soon."

"In time, lass."

"In time?"

"Didn't the good father tell ya?"

"Tell me what, exactly?"

Mrs. Donnelly pats Mary Agnes's shoulder. "Ah, it's better that he didn't then. A month's work and then we'll see ya off."

"A month?" It is all Mary Agnes can do not to break into tears in the Donnelly's front room. *But I thought . . .*

"Aye, the church will pay yer fare, after ya work for it, of course. Ya're not the first in Five Points to be beholden to the church."

"Five Points?"

"Used to be the best Irish neighborhood in all of New York. Right here. Not anymore. Crime, pimping. Too many . . . oh, never mind, ya'll see for yourself." Mrs. Donnelly blesses herself with the sign of the cross. "We're surrounded now, Italians and Poles. And Germans every-where. As soon as Himself can rouse the funds, we'll be off to Brooklyn. Best to stick with our own people."

I've heard that before, too.

A couch, two chairs, and low table crowd the front room, centered by a small coal stove. To the left, a large dining table sits on heavy mahogany feet with ten mismatched chairs packed around. A large picture of The Last Supper hangs on the yellowed far wall. A bedroom juts off the front room and a long hall beyond leads to what Mary Agnes assumes is the kitchen. She wonders how so many people can live in such a small apartment. *Where do they all sleep? Atop one another?*

Three of the Donnelly children, a boy and two girls, huddle under a blanket in front of the cold grate.

"That'd be Joseph, Anne, and Meg," Mrs. Donnelly says.

Mary Agnes winks at them.

"Joseph is the man of the house when his da's at work. Twelve, he is, on his next birthday."

"I'm ten," Anne says.

"And you?" Mary Agnes asks the other girl.

"She's our shy one, that Meg. She'd be eight."

"And here," pointing to four boys playing jacks in the corner, "John, James, Martin, and little Finnegan."

"Twins?"

"Yes, James and John, five they are now. Martin would be four, and Finn, two."

"And the wee one?" Mary Agnes asks, peering into a wooden crate on the low table.

"That'll be our Nell. She's three months on now."

"May I?" Mary Agnes asks, as she bends over the crate.

"Anytime, except as it's for feeding," Mrs. Donnelly laughs.

Mary Agnes picks up the tiny bundle and brings her to her chest. The baby mewls. "Shh, shh, now, wee one."

Mrs. Donnelly leads Mary Agnes through a narrow hallway to the cramped kitchen in the back of the apartment. One of the younger boys—*Finnegan, is it?*—crowds Mrs. Donnelly's skirts.

"We've our own kitchen," Mrs. Donnelly continues. "The bath is down the hall. Shared, it is, with the Mahoneys and Tooheys and Callaghans."

"I don't mind, ma'am. We didn't have a bath at home."

A wooden counter runs the length of the wall next to the coal stove. Dirty dishes pile in the chipped enamel sink and spill over on the counter.

"I was just getting to the washing up when ya arrived," Mrs. Donnelly says.

"I'm happy to help. Let me put the babe down."

Back in the kitchen, and through a smudged window, Mary Agnes sees the backs of the tenements that front

Mulberry Street, a block over. There, in the narrow gap between buildings, laundry hangs hodge-podge like sails between them—a ship without a sea—sheets and under-things flapping in late autumn wind. Even though each building has its peculiar traits (one dark brick, the next light; one with larger front windows and another, *to save cost*, she thinks, with much smaller windows), the buildings form a cohesive whole, five floors each above varied store-fronts, with wide stone steps up to each first floor.

With four apartments per floor up five storeys, and if each family is as big as the Donnellys . . . Mary Agnes taps her foot on the kitchen tile, as she calculates the number, hundreds per building. She cannot get over the fact she is to stay here, in New York, for a month before she goes to Chicago. But what is her choice? At least the floor seems sound, despite the number of people squeezed into the apartment.

"You've an extra dish towel, then?"

THAT NIGHT, SNUGGLED ON THE LUMPY sofa in the front room, Mary Agnes spies a shaft of moonlight coming down the hall. Unlike her future, she can count on the moon, like the seasons and the tides and the sun—and the grave, like her granddad said. But she doesn't want to dwell on the grave, so she watches the moonlight creep into the room until she falls asleep, day one in America come to a close.

November 1886
New York, New York

Mrs. Donnelly hands Mary Agnes a pencil, a scrap of paper, and a few coins. "Milk, bread, a dozen potatoes, and cabbage. That'll be all we can afford today. And butter, if Mr. O'Casey will add it to the tab."

Mary Agnes realized on the second day that Mrs. Donnelly can neither read nor write. What she lacks in schooling, she more than makes up for with talk. By now, Mary Agnes knows all about the Callaghans and Tooheys and the Mahoneys, some of whom she's met in the hall coming or going to the bath. She's glad she has an ample bladder. The door to the bath is rarely open.

But when it is free, she takes the time needed. An indoor commode! A sink! On Wednesday nights, after the children are read to and tucked in with nighttime prayers, she takes herself to the water closet and sponge bathes, taking care to scrub thoroughly and to wash her short hair twice, until it squeaks. She feels like a queen.

This morning, Mary Agnes gathers her green shawl and laces her boots. It's mild today, for which she's glad, the sun peeking through high clouds. Mrs. Donnelly only has one coat and Mary Agnes hasn't asked to borrow it yet, especially since she won't be able to afford one soon.

As soon as she steps out of the tenement building, Mary Agnes is accosted with sights and sounds and smells of the city. It never ceases to astound her how the city seems alive. Streets bustle with men and women and children and dogs. The clatter of horse hooves echoes as street urchins dart in and out of carts and wagons and merchants haggle with customers in unfamiliar languages.

In the shops along Mulberry Street, Mary Agnes drools over breads and sweets, poultry and fish. At the corner of Mulberry and Park, she counts out coin to the vegetable peddler and adds a head of cabbage and a dozen firm potatoes to her basket. She will get bread next and go to O'Casey's last because of the milk—and the butter, if he'll allow it on the tab.

As she stands in front of the bakery, she wishes she had enough extra coin for just one sweet. If she did, she would duck into the alleyway next door and take one taste and then bring the rest home to share, bite by bite, with all the Donnelly children in their crowded front room. But there is not enough coin for sweets.

She enters the small shop, bright with white walls and floors, and points to a heavy loaf on the shelf. The son of the German owners smiles at Mary Agnes as he hands her the wrapped loaf. "Danke," he says.

Mrs. Donnelly is right; the neighborhood is a stewpot of people, Germans who have spilled over to Five Points from nearby Kleindeutschland, and Italians from just north of Canal Street. Many of them are Catholic, like she is, except, of course, the Jews and the Chinese, who also make up the fabric of the neighborhood. There are dark-skinned people here, too, clustered in groups on stoops or in front of shops. She thinks it wonderful, all these people together, but when she mentions it to Mrs. Donnelly she is met with a scowl.

"Not our people," Mrs. Donnelly says. "There's Germans on the second floor now, and Italians on the fifth. All I smell is garlic." Mary Agnes holds her tongue after that, about that subject, anyway.

Mrs. Donnelly uses meager supplies to make supper: Cabbage and carrots, peas with potatoes, weak broth with vegetable scraps, hash. But there is always fish on Fridays and Irish Stew—rarely with meat, though—on Sundays. Mrs. Donnelly, ever merry, like her granddad Festus, teaches Mary Agnes how to make soda bread, a mixture of butter, buttermilk, egg, flour, sugar, and saleratus.

The children clamor about, all smiles, the two youngest sitting on the floor banging pot tops with wooden spoons. The three older children dash in and out of the kitchen with questions about maths or geography or how to pro-nounce a word. Mary Agnes bends down to help Anne with the word, "foreign."

Yes, everything is foreign here.

Mary Agnes finds herself dreaming of Ireland most nights. It's familiar in such an unfamiliar place.

"Out of the kitchen, now," Mrs. Donnelly says to the younger children.

"John, James, come help with the littles."

With so many people in such a small space, the kitchen window often fogs up and Mrs. Donnelly opens it and props it up with a yardstick folded in half. When she does this, she often lingers at the window. Mary Agnes wonders what Mrs. Donnelly is thinking.

By all accounts, Mrs. Donnelly is happy, especially when Mr. Donnelly comes home from work. He is broad in the shoulders and neck—*and uncommonly handsome*, Mary Agnes thinks. Although not much taller than Mrs. Donnelly, he gathers his wife up in his dirt-caked hands, sweaty after a long day as a laborer, and twirls her about like a schoolgirl.

"Be off with ya!" Mrs. Donnelly laughs.

After a quick wash up, Mr. Donnelly is lively at the table, entertaining everyone with stories of work as a ditch digger in Manhattan.

"Sand hogs, they call us." He snorts like a pig. The children laugh and then, all at once, the whole table is snorting. He gets up then and crawls around the parlor. Soon, all the children follow suit and crash into each other on the floor, still snorting like swine.

"Heavens!" Mrs Donnelly laughs. "What ever will I do with this man?"

Mary Agnes laughs so hard, tears run down her cheeks.

Later that evening, she hears the Donnellys in their bedroom. *The Tooleys must hear them, too*, she thinks, from her spot on the couch, *seeing as they are right next door and these walls are thin. Must married couples do this every night?* It reminds her of another reason she'll never marry. *But the Donnellys do seem happy, so there is that . . . maybe Mrs. Donnelly enjoys it? Is that possible?*

The next morning, Mary Agnes is tasked with finding a Mr. Rampelli, an Italian tailor near the East River who has come highly recommended. Mr. Donnelly's coat has a large gash under the left arm that's not easily mendable. Mrs. Donnelly has tried, but the fabric is too thick and too coarse and she broke three needles trying to mend it.

"It's no use," Mrs. Donnelly says, as she hands Mary Agnes the worn coat. Mary Agnes memorizes the address on East Seventh Street and sets out of Five Points, walking east toward the river in the morning chill through Tompkins Square, humming under her breath. She walks past Eidelman's Bakery, Maroni's Millinery, and Dowd's Trims, its dark, narrow aisles filled with every finery: lace, ribbons, furs. She won't mention it again to Mrs. Donnelly, but it is exciting to see so many people from so many places here in New York.

Mary Agnes can see the East River a few blocks ahead, tall masts docked to the quayside and a bustle of activity. She checks the address again and looks at the numbers over doors. She's jostled by a large man, and, at once, cornered by five burly men in work clothes.

"*Puttana!*" one spits. Mary Agnes doesn't know what "puttana" means, but the way he says it makes her stomach queasy. It sounds dirty. Another man scratches his underarms and mimics an ape. They all laugh. The largest man, the one who initially bumped into her, whispers in her ear, "Have you had five men at once?"

Her heart races, her body shakes. *Five men at once? Do I scream? Bite? Kick? Or will that make it worse?*

The men circle her, poking her shoulders and back as she's backed up against a brick building. She covers her breasts with Mr. Donnelly's coat. Her hands tremble. She has a vivid image of Fiach coming at her on the last night before she left Dawros and she feels sick.

"Come here, *piccolo*," the leader says. He grabs her elbow and leads her toward an alley. "We love Irish girls."

Mary Agnes is aware of a trickling of urine down her thighs into her boots.

Five men. Five Italian men. At once. Holy Mother of sweet divine suffering, like Jonesy would say.

She's shoved up against another brick building, men's hands fondling her breasts, her rear. She screams, dropping Mr. Donnelly's coat in the alley and batting at the men with her hands.

The ringleader rips her dress and exposes her camisole. He reaches for her breast, nothing between his large hand and her tender skin but a flimsy piece of muslin.

A loud whistle pierces the air. "Out of the way, you swine."

Through blurred vision, Mary Agnes sees a copper atop a large horse, his battering stick in the air. "Filthy pigs," he says. "Get outta here before I book all of ya."

The leader spits at Mary Agnes's feet. "Puttana," he says again and pinches her breast.

The policeman, clearly Irish, waves his hand. The men scatter.

"On your way now, lass," he says. "What are ya doing in this neighborhood in the first place? Go home to your mammy. I don't want to see ya here again. Let this be a warning."

Mary Agnes straightens her dress and turns back toward Mott Street, her gait fast and sure. She will not be going to the tailor today. She'll tell Mrs. Donnelly she couldn't find the address and offer to do the mending herself.

Are we really hated that much? By everyone? Or only some? Or does everyone hate everyone who's not like them?

She hurries back to Mott Street, avoiding stray dogs and other men. She stops into O'Casey's just to feel at home and places a jar of jam on the counter. "Men are pigs," she mutters under her breath.

"What's that, lass?"

"Nothing, excuse me, Mr. O'Casey."

"I suppose you'll be wanting to put this on Donnelly's tab again?" the shopkeeper asks. "This is the last time this month, lass. You can tell Himself the bill needs paying by week's end or there'll be no more credit." She nods and puts the jar in her basket. Her hands still shake. She tries to tell herself she's not as hungry as she was at home in Ireland, but that would be a lie. Yes, Mrs. Donnelly does her best with paltry groceries with so many mouths to feed.

But here there are so many temptations. Sweet rolls and sausages. Crisp apples and fried fish. Fresh milk. Baked goods filled with brown sugar and walnuts and butter.

Trying to put these enticements from her mind, she sits on the front stoop and opens the jam. In fingerfuls, she scoops it out. Savoring the sweetness to dull the sour feeling in her stomach, she digs it all out with sticky fingers until there is none left. She wipes her hand on her dress and takes the stairs up into the tenement building by twos and stops on the landing to slow her heart before bursting into the Donnelly's overcrowded apartment. She doesn't know how she'll explain the jam, or the tab, or not finding the tailor—and forgetting the butter—but she's safe, and that's all that matters.

"I'm home," she announces, and soon she is crowded by children, dark-haired and flushed, clamoring to hug her, shy Meg pulling at her skirt and Martin looking up at her with loving eyes. Their bright smiles and dirty hands produce a rush of love that fills her chest and she realizes for the first time in her almost fourteen years that family isn't necessarily blood, family is what you make it.

"RING-A-RING-A-ROSES!" THE CHILDREN chant as Mary Agnes helps Mrs. Donnelly with the washing up in the cramped stand-up kitchen. They've just had a supper of day-old haddock and poached egg, the best meal Mary Agnes can remember for weeks. Yesterday was payday.

"A pocket full of posies!" The children yell, their faces ruddy as they crescendo toward the end of the rhyme. "Hush! Hush! Hush! Hush! We're all tumbled down!" They erupt in laughter as they crash to the floor, skirts and dirty pant legs sprawled on the thin rug in a mass of sweaty black heads.

"Will ya all hush!" Mrs. Donnelly says with a smile as she bustles into the front room that serves as a parlor and a dining area. "Sure and the devil well knows Mrs. Kelleher downstairs will be pounding on the ceiling with her broom in less than—"

Bump bump reverberates through the floor from the flat below.

"She doesn't take kindly to the noise," Mrs. Donnelly whispers to Mary Agnes. She snickers. "But then, I can't blame her," she continues. "Poor woman lost her husband to the influenza and no one left to help. Her daughter comes by once a week, she's a janitress. Now, all of ya," she turns her attention to the children. "Time to wash up, girls first." The boys groan. "I said off with ya!"

Mrs. Donnelly pats Finn on the rear as he gets in line at the washbasin. "We could use help here, Mary A., if ya're thinking of staying in New York. I've talked it through with Mr. Donnelly. We couldn't pay proper wages, but ya'd have a bed of yer own and a bit to eat. We don't want to see ya end up in service or in the factories uptown, or worse yet, in Chicago."

Worse yet?

"If ya're lucky, ya might get on with a big house, otherwise it's only factories hiring on Irish. And it's still hard enough to get placement. Ya'd be safe here, with us."

A dirty tenement half a world away from home? And doing the same thing I'd've done if I never left?

"My people are expecting me," she says. "It wouldn't be right to disappoint them. Not that I don't want to stay." She cringes at the lie. "But it's been more than a month."

Mrs. Donnelly dries her hands on a faded tea towel that might have been green once. "Not that I blame ya, lass. I thought I'd see more of the world when I came over after the hard times. But love's got a way of changing yer plans."

She pats Mary Agnes's shoulder. "Just wanted to offer before Father Benedict takes ya to the station tomorrow."

Tomorrow? *Tomorrow!*

"Yes, he stopped by earlier. Said to be ready by ten. If ya hadn't changed yer mind."

Martin and Finn are back now, tugging at their mother's skirt.

"I can read to them if you'd like," Mary Agnes says. "One last time."

"All of ya!" Mrs. Donnelly says. "Mary A. here has a treat for ya."

"Lollies?" Joseph asks.

"Better than lollies," Mary Agnes answers. "A poem."

Mary Agnes roots around for her journal and gathers the children around her. "Come, Finn, close to me. You too, Martin." Meg scoots forward. "And you, Meg." John and James, the twins, sit to her right, and, to her left, Anne holds Nell. Joseph, being the oldest, is at the fringe of the circle.

She turns the book so the children can see illustrations she's made in her journal next to poems and reads upside down, although she knows all the poems by heart. She thinks of her brother Tommy and tries to see his eyes in the eyes of all the children clustered around her.

In winter I get up at night
And dress by yellow candlelight.

I'm going to Chicago tomorrow, she thinks. *Will it be better there?*

In summer, quite the other way,
I have to go to bed by day . . .

Mary Agnes's face grows dark. *Only time will tell of it.*

14

Late November 1886
Aboard the Pennsylvania Railroad
from New York to Chicago

The train clatters out of New York into the New Jersey farmlands in the late fall sun. *Clack clack a-lack* marks the miles, fields and barns and cattle, as the train devours the flat landscape. Mary Agnes sits by the window in a third-class car near the end of the train. In less than two days she will be in Chicago. First, Pennsylvania. Then Ohio and Indiana, with stops for water, coal, and crew changes. She rests her head against the dirtied pane and squints.

Everything is fuzzy, as usual.

In her bag, along with toilet items and one crisp American bill, she has a buttered bun that Mrs. Donnelly wrapped for her in brown paper. She will save it for as long as she can. Surely, she can afford a nickel for coffee or tea?

It was more tearful than she expected leaving the Donnelly family after a full month with them, although she knows it's for the best. Just before she left, she went from youngest to oldest, patting them on the head, bending for a kiss, shaking Joseph's hand, like a grown up. Meg was the last to let go of her skirt, and Mary Agnes wondered for a brief second if she should stay.

But she did her penance, as if the priest knew she should, especially as she never went to confession. Mary Agnes opens her bag to finger the rosary, and then recites the Apostles Creed and the Our Father and three Hail Marys and the Our Father again and is about to start the first decade of the rosary when a short, stout man of about twenty-five grazes her shoulder and she's brought back to the present.

"Don't mind me, miss." His accent is thick and clearly German.

Mary Agnes shrugs it off, but her hackles are up. Traveling alone brings wits to the fore, this she knows well already. *The barber at Castle Garden. The Italian men on East Seventh Street in New York.*

When the man returns to his seat from the water closet at the far end of the train carriage, he stops and stands at the empty seat beside her. "Pardon me for saying, miss, but aren't you too young to be traveling on your own? Perhaps I can be of some assistance."

"I think not." Mary Agnes is on high alert now. Didn't her gram warn her about fast lads? She tries to tamp down her anger, which rises from her sternum up her neck. Her shoulders tense, like they always did around Fiach, as if preparing for a blow.

"But a young girl, such as yourself—"

At the risk of creating a scene, she says, a bit louder now, "Has just traveled half the world alone and—"

"And has no need of your assistance, young man." An older woman of an indeterminate age bustles into the seat beside Mary Agnes. She is squat and compact, in a grey traveling suit. She wears a large, feathered hat and bandies about a large purse. Her boots, neatly polished, peek out from beneath her wide hem. "My niece here is under my charge." She moves into the seat next to Mary Agnes and displaces the young man.

Niece?

Mary Agnes plays along, harnessing her brogue. "Thank you, Aunt. As you can see, this masher was—" She has no need to finish the sentence—*rude as the barman's son*—because the rogue has beaten a hasty retreat, worn grip in hand. She stifles a laugh. "We made short work of him!"

The woman, clearly not Irish (*and probably not Catholic*, Mary Agnes observes from the woman's lack of brogue or gold cross on her large bosom), settles into the seat beside her and pats her knee. "That we did, didn't we?"

"Thank you so much, Mrs.—"

"Peirce. From Philadelphia."

Even though this woman is clearly not Catholic, Mary Agnes knows the woman has been sent by the Purple Mary herself to intervene. Her faith is that strong.

"I noticed you right off and have been keeping my eye on you. Remember that when you are old and crippled, like me." The woman relaxes into the cushioned seat and covers her mouth as she yawns. "We all have stories, and I've heard them all, most of them too sad for words. Family turns you out. Now you're on your own, traveling to cousins if you're lucky. Hoping for a position in a big house, like all the Irish lasses."

Or going to university, Mary Agnes longs to say, but doesn't want to sound presumptuous.

"No matter your story."

But that is my story.

"I'll be happy to keep you company until we reach Chicago," the woman continues. "Now. I'm in need of a nap, so don't mind me." She closes her eyes, and within a minute, gentle snores.

Mary Agnes relaxes now into her coach seat and tries to nap, but her mind races.

Do I have to be always on high guard? There won't be a Mrs. Peirce everywhere I go.

Ohio goes by in the dark. Mary Agnes spends the hours wondering about Mrs. Peirce's story, but it would be impertinent to ask. *A widow? A former nun? A madam?*

At midnight, her stomach grumbling loudly, she can hold out no longer and eats the bun Mrs. Donnelly packed for her.

The next day, Mrs. Peirce insists on buying Mary Agnes a sandwich and a coffee as Indiana lumbers by. "To put some meat on those skinny bones of yours." Before she knows it, *Fort Wayne, Warsaw, Plymouth, Valparaiso, Gary,* never-ending flat farmland without a mountain in sight, towns peppered in like an afterthought. As the train crosses the Indiana-Illinois line, she knows she's almost to Chicago. When she arrives, the city is blanketed with a foot of snow.

She thanks Mrs. Peirce and grasps her satchel tight as she exits the station. Wind whips snow into drifts and a howling wind greets her as she hails a cart.

Twenty minutes later, after shivering in only her dress and shawl in this blizzard—*and damn I don't have a coat (or stockings or new boots or . . . or . . . or . . .)*—the driver pulls up to a handsome row house on Monroe Street. After paying the driver with the last of her cash, she hurries up the walkway to the front door.

Only time will tell of it, she says again to herself.

The Same Day
Late November 1886
Chicago, Illinois

"Mary Agnes?" the girl says. "Is it really you? You look a fright! And no coat? I'm Helen."

No, no coat. No money. No family.

Helen stands the same height and build as Mary Agnes, as familiar as a cousin—*a sister almost*—freckles and a straight nose. *But more filled out*, Mary Agnes thinks, *and look at that fiery red hair!*

Helen ushers Mary Agnes into the richly decorated parlor calling, "Mother!" Taking Mary Agnes's arm, "Come in, by the fire," she says, leading Mary Agnes to a comfortable overstuffed chair. "We've been awaiting your arrival, checking off the days. Whatever took you so long? Tell me everything. About home. The passage. And New York! I have ever wanted to go to New York!"

Mary Agnes begins to thaw and she rubs her chapped hands together.

"Are you hungry? Thirsty? What can I get you?"

Mary Agnes nods, her teeth still chattering.

"Have you really no coat? In this weather? We will have to go shopping. Tomorrow!"

Does this girl ever stop talking?

A tall, elegant woman dressed in a pristine dark blue day dress enters the parlor with arms outstretched.

Did Mam ever greet me like this?

"Mary Agnes! At last!" She embraces Mary Agnes.

No, not like Mam at all.

"Helen! Have you offered Mary Agnes a cup of tea? A biscuit? A sandwich?"

"I would like very much to have a hot cup of tea," Mary Agnes says. "Thank you, ma'am."

"Not 'ma'am,' Mary Agnes. Aunt Margaret. Married to your mother's brother, Fiach."

Fiach. Color drains from Mary Agnes's face.

"Is everything a-rights, dear?"

Mary Agnes nods again. "'Tis nothing. Just a chill."

"Here, let me take your wrap." Aunt Margaret takes the shawl from Mary Agnes's shoulders. "And your hat."

When Mary Agnes removes her hat, both Aunt Margaret and Helen gasp.

"Your hair!" Helen says.

Aunt Margaret throws Helen a stern glare. "Helen, go see that the kettle is on and bring in some tea. We have much to catch up on. Fourteen years."

THE HOUSE IS AS GRAND AS ANY Mary Agnes has ever been in, complete with indoor water closets. Mary Agnes marvels over the smallest details: Fresh flowers in stately vases, crisp ironed napkins, matching bowls and plates and cups with an intricate pattern of birds and trees entwined with leaves and delicate nosegays, towels in every bedchamber, and none for sharing. And, most of all, food at every meal, prepared by a friendly Irish cook. *Whatever it is that Uncle Fiach does, it brings in more than a fisherman. To live in this kind of comfort . . .*

She remembers one of the Stevenson poems, the shortest one.

The world is so full of a number of things,
I'm sure we should all be as happy as kings!

"What is it that Uncle does?" Mary Agnes asks Helen that night, her curiosity getting the better of her. "A banker? A factory manager?"

Helen shrugs. "I haven't a clue. I don't even know if Mother knows. Something about politics. Now let's talk of something more interesting, like boys. I'm spoony over Paddy Kelleher. Do you have a sweetheart? Silly me, I shouldn't have asked that, you're just off the boat and if you left someone behind you're sure to be sorry over it. Is that it? Why you're teary?"

The next morning, after a fitful sleep and Helen's words reverberating in her head—*you're sure to be sorry over it*—*yes, I am*, she thinks, sorry about a lot of things. She dresses in her spare skirt and blouse and brushes her boy-cut hair. In the mirror, she sees her mother and prays right then and there not to have a sour outlook even though she is uneasy, everything new and unknown. She goes down to breakfast tentatively, not knowing what to expect. The sideboard in the Laffey's dining room is full. Eggs. Bacon. Sausage. Toast. Cheeses. Juices. Coffee. Mary Agnes stands in front of the buffet and wonders if it's a dream.

"Good morning, dear," Aunt Margaret says. "Please, help yourself."

Again, Mary Agnes could cry.

ASHLEY E. SWEENEY | 141

Later that morning, Mary Agnes boards the Madison Street trolley with her aunt and cousin. She cannot keep her eyes from wandering, right and left, as they pass stately homes, parks, and buildings. There is a sharp wind off the lake, raw, a chill that's hard to shake.

Chicago is as crowded and busy as New York. Mary Agnes tries to remember landmarks along the route, but Helen constantly distracts her, anecdotes of when she went to that spot and with whom, and soon they are in the heart of Chicago and Mary Agnes couldn't find her way back if she tried. She doesn't even remember the Laffey's exact address, she left it on a piece of paper at the house. It would be embarrassing to ask so she keeps an eye on Helen so as not to lose her as they disembark in front of the grand post office on Michigan and zigzag six short blocks south to Draper & Draper Drygoods on the corner of State and Van Buren.

When they enter the double doors of Draper & Draper, a small bell tinkles overhead. Three clerks nod to Aunt Margaret, the eldest of the three coming from behind the counter to greet her.

"Mrs. Laffey. Miss Laffey. And to what do we owe the pleasure today?" she asks.

"Miss Gooch. Let me introduce my niece, Mary Agnes. She has recently arrived from Galway."

Never has Mary Agnes seen such inventory, brocaded silk and woven wool gauze and glazed cotton. She stares at three levels crammed with bolt after bolt of fabric. She cannot imagine being measured and fitted for a new dress. The sacks her mother made for her and her poor attempt at the skirt and blouse she wears today are not worthy to be seen here in Chicago. She feels poor. And is sure the clerks notice. She tags behind her aunt and cousin and gazes at the surfeit of fabric. That there could be this much inventory in all the world, that's what she's thinking.

"This will make a fine day dress," Aunt Margaret says, pointing to a green glazed cotton. "And this, for another." She asks the clerk to pull a warm brown wool with cream stripes from the second tier of bolts.

"Two dresses, Aunt?" Mary Agnes asks. "I haven't—"

"You haven't a worry, Mary, dear. It's our welcoming gift to you, two dresses and a dinner gown."

A dinner gown! Mary Agnes draws in a deep breath. "For?"

"Sunday dinner, of course."

"What do you think of this one, Mary A.?" Helen points to a rich cream and gold embroidered silk. "It will be lovely with your hair. When it grows back."

Mary Agnes is keenly aware of her short hair, now grown past her ears, but not yet to her shoulders. She could plaster it back with hairpins if she had any. For now, it's an unruly mop she covers with her hat.

After undressing to her underclothes behind an opaque curtain in front of Miss Gooch, Mary Agnes is measured, neck, bust, waist, hips.

"You're a thin one," Miss Gooch says.

Because I haven't eaten in my whole life, nothing like what I had for breakfast this morning, Mary Agnes thinks, but she just smiles and hopes Miss Gooch doesn't make any more comments.

After being measured, she joins her aunt and cousin at the counter, where they are stacking various fabrics. The other clerks measure out the bolts, "isn't this the most sumptuous fabric you've ever seen," and "just in from London," and "won't this make the most appealing gown." Snip, snip, as sharp shears glide through fabric. Mary Agnes thinks it almost obscene. When the material is cut and folded and tagged, Miss Gooch presents a paper slip to Aunt Margaret, who pulls her pince nez down her nose to read the figures and nods.

"I'll pay you back," Mary Agnes says, as the clerk whisks the material away.

"Nonsense!" Aunt Margaret says. "When it's your turn to welcome your own nieces to America, you can repay me by splurging for them."

My nieces? The daughters of my brothers? That will be . . . she calculates many years from now. *If I ever see them again.*

"And now, tea." Aunt Margaret leads the way north on State Street, Mary Agnes and Helen trailing behind. Mary Agnes doesn't know if this is just a show of hospitality or a regular occurrence. She calculates that her aunt must be spending a near fortune today for dresses and vittles.

"Mother loves The English Tearoom," Helen continues. She has been talking, but Mary Agnes has not been paying attention. In twenty-four hours, she's deduced that, if anything, Helen is frivolous. Giddy. *Some might say silly. But I shouldn't judge so harshly. A sister, almost, Gram said.*

"All those little sandwiches and delicacies and the most sumptuous teas. Darjeeling, Ceylon, Congou . . ."

Mary Agnes feels suddenly faint. She takes Helen's arm.

"Are you ill?"

"No, it's just—" She falters for words. "So kind. So much. I am not used to such finery. Or such food."

"We will have to enjoy it while we can. Next week, I'm back at bookkeeping school. It's too bad you can't come along with me."

"To bookkeeping school? I'm very keen with numbers."

"It's not as simple as that, Mary A. I'm mid-semester already and even if that weren't so, you'd have to find a benefactor for tuition. Mother and Father have made it clear they are strapped providing for me. And I think they have other plans for you."

Strapped? A big house and dinner gowns and tea out?

Again, Mary Agnes blocks out Helen's insistent chatter.

Isn't that what Gram said? My people would take care of me?

Her mind is dulled. All she wants to do is burrow under the covers and have time to make sense of everything going on around her.

What am I to do then? If I'm not at school? A housemaid? A factory worker?

She shudders. *No, no.*

After tea service and small sandwiches, Mary Agnes and Helen board the streetcar for home, Aunt Margaret staying "in town" to meet Uncle Fiach for an engagement that evening. Helen pulls Mary Agnes to a seat near the front of the trolley. "Watch out for those lads." She cocks her head to a group of dark-haired young men standing in the rear. "Can't trust the Italians. Or the Poles, for that matter. And especially the Germans." She lowers her voice. "The city is 'overrun with Germans,' Father says. Taking jobs away from hard working Irish folks. It's almost impossible to get a position these days if you are not well connected. No one seems to like the Irish. Well, we don't like them, either."

Mary Agnes shivers, her suspicions substantiated. No one likes anyone who isn't like them. *Stick to your own kind, Irish.*

After returning home, the girls change into simple day dresses. Mary Agnes borrows one of Helen's, her clothes whisked away by the maid. When Helen suggests a nap in the parlor, Mary Agnes feigns sleep in one of the armchairs and then tiptoes to the bookcase. *Twenty Thousand Leagues Under the Sea. Around the World in Eighty Days. The Mystery of Edwin Drood.*

As she fingers leather spines of the books, her body tingles. *And more. Thomas Hardy! Victor Hugo! Mark Twain! Uncle must be a reader. Or, maybe,* she thinks, *just fills his bookcases for appearances.*

At supper, Mary Agnes doesn't get a word in as Helen fills in all the blanks of her own conversation, but Mary Agnes doesn't mind. Supper—roast pork, onions, and carrots smothered in gravy over rice—is delicious. Nor does she get a word in that night after she and Helen change into nightclothes. Again, Mary Agnes borrows one of Helen's. Helen prattles on about school and clothing and hats and boys. Mary Agnes doesn't know how to break in.

I'm tired, she'd like to say, but doesn't want to be rude on just her second night here in her new home.

"Let's have some pie," Helen says, and at the mention of "pie" Mary Agnes perks up. *Pie? There's pie?*

They scavenge in the kitchen and find a fresh mince-meat pie cooling in the pantry. With two forks, they demolish the whole pie, bite by bite. Mary Agnes has never eaten a whole pie before. Once a year at Christmas, she is lucky to have a small sliver. Today, she has had breakfast and tea and supper and pie.

The front door opens with a loud bang, and Mary Agnes throws a questioning glance to Helen.

"It's just Mother and Father."

Her heart drops. The name alone stings. *Fiach.*

"Come, meet Father."

"In my dressing gown?"

"We are family!"

Mary Agnes tails Helen to the front room, where Aunt Margaret sits on the same overstuffed chair Helen had napped on earlier in the day, her coat draped over the back. Her eyes are slightly glazed, as if she has imbibed. Mary Agnes knows the signs, she doesn't come from the west of Ireland without seeing her share of people who've enjoyed their drink. Some become boisterous and amorous, others retreat to a somnambulant state. Her aunt falls in the latter category.

Uncle Fiach pours an aperitif from a large mahogany bar on the far side of the parlor. Mary Agnes has never seen a likeness of Fiach (she didn't even know her mother had an older brother), but he looks so much like her half-brother, Mary Agnes feels palpably uncomfortable.

He turns. "Come here, lass!" He motions to Mary Agnes, who does as she's told. "Well, I never. If it isn't my dear sister, Anna, in the flesh!" He gathers her in a hug and pats her behind.

Mary Agnes turns to a pillar of stone, rigid and cold. *No. No. No.*

"Why, don't be like that. We are family!" He pats her behind again.

No, no, no.

"Speak up, Mary Agnes. Don't be rude to your mother's very own brother," Aunt Margaret says.

Fiach.

"Thank you for taking me in," Mary Agnes says, swallowing insecurity and fear. "Gram and Granda said I'd find a home here."

"As you will!" her uncle booms. "Welcome every Sunday to dine with us, like family."

Every Sunday?

"We promised your grandparents we'd look after you, so we'll help find you a position, won't we, dear?" He turns to Aunt Margaret.

"Of course, dear," she answers with a yawn. "A pretty face like Mary Agnes has here. She'll be hired before the week is out. And her people will appreciate the wages. I've circled all the adverts in the Tribune."

My people? My wages? She shakes her head to see if the words are only inside her head. They are not. *So I am to be hired out. Not going to school at all. No better than in New York. Or at home.*

No, I'm not sure it is better here, Granda. Not at all.

16

Early December 1886
Chicago, Illinois

Creeping up the back stairway just before dawn from her cramped and frigid room in the cellar, Mary Agnes steps on the third tread from the top, the one that squeaks. Her feet, still squeezed into last year's boots, press at her toes. Her black dress falls beneath her calves; she hopes the tear in her black stockings doesn't show, it being her first day at the big house.

It had been easy being hired out, much easier than Mary Agnes thought. With the newspaper in her hand, she walked for an hour east in bone-chilling wind, weaving through Chicago neighborhoods until she reached the Gold Coast to enquire about the first advert:

> *Sturdy young woman required for household service.*
> *Wages commensurate with experience. Enquire Monday,*
> *1236 N. Astor St.*

Just like Aunt Margaret said, Mary Agnes was hired on the spot. And at what a mansion! A sweeping curved staircase with polished bannisters lofts from the entry and disappears to the floor above. From what Mary Agnes can see, everything about the home is grand: its vaulted doorways; high ceilings; arched doorways; massive windows; parquet floors; floor-to-ceiling bookcases; heavy furniture; and thick draperies.

And the décor! Gilt framed mirrors. Portraits. Heavy tufted, brocaded settees. On every spare surface, assorted magazines, journals, newspapers. Doilies, urns, bronze statuettes. Chandeliers and sconces. Floral arrangements and fruit bowls. *Even a candy dish in the shape of a blue swan!*

It takes Mary Agnes's breath away. And then she thinks, practical as she is, *I must be careful not to break anything.* At home, the Coynes had one candlestick and nine chipped ceramic plates. Not even enough mugs to serve everyone at once. She scowls as she thinks of her mother but is quickly distracted as the *hiss* of the radiators comes on.

Imagine. Heat that comes from a radiator instead of a peat fire. Rooms upon rooms upon rooms fit for a queen. And enough food to feed all of Dawros!

There had been the bit about Sundays, Mary Agnes insisting she would need the full day off to attend Mass and then Sunday dinner at the Laffeys. The mistress of the house, Mrs. Rutherford, agreed, but there'd be no Thursday half-day off then. And only every other Sunday afternoon off. Room and board would be offered and fifty cents per day seeing as Mary Agnes had little experience, with a three-month trial period. So it is agreed upon across a chasm of class and culture and religion.

At least I'm on my own, Mary Agnes thinks. Helen has become tiresome, after less than a week. Aunt Margaret has far more questions than Mary Agnes is prepared to answer, most of them about her mother and Fiach.

And, as for Uncle Fiach, I am glad of it, to be here, away from him.

His nightly pats on her behind have turned to pinches and she fears what might be next. A brush on the breasts? Cold fingers on her neck? Footsteps outside her room? All at once, she is shocked with a thought.

Perhaps Fiach is the son of . . . not the innkeeper or a soldier. Maybe Mam's very own brother? The resemblance is uncanny.

She shakes her head at the thought of it, ties her crisp white apron tight around her waist over the black uniform, and swipes a stray hair behind her ear. Cook will remind her to do that many times today. But who can afford hair pins? She turns three times, an old Celtic ritual, and prays under her breath: *The love of the Father who made me; the love of the Son who died for me; the love of the Holy Ghost who dwells within me. Bless me and keep me, Amen. And you too, Blessed Mother, watch over me today.*

Into the kitchen she goes, hip first. All the morning smells greet her: Sizzling ham, fresh baked bread, coffee. "A nasty situation," is all Mary Agnes overheard as to why the previous housemaid was let go.

What could be nasty enough to get a housemaid fired? Theft? Deceit? A compromising situation?

There is no time to ponder at present. *I have to concentrate today,* she thinks. *No straying thoughts.*

The matronly cook grimaces, her floured hands pointing to the clock. "One minute past six; might as well be an hour."

Mary Agnes dips her head. "Won't happen again, Cook." She needs this job. Big house. Important family. Wages. She checks again to see that her hair is neat and dons a white cap. "Put me to work," she says.

Does Cook see my hands tremble? Or my heart?

The large, low-ceilinged kitchen spans half the length of the house on the first floor below stairs. A long window grazes the ceiling and allows light in from below street level.

A pock-marked table dominates the center of the room, with two cookstoves on the north wall and a huge sink under the windows on the east wall. Suspended from the ceiling, like so much hardware, a mélange of copper and cast-iron pots dangles from long copper hooks. A wiry black cat brushes her leg.

"That'd be Tom the Cat."

Mary Agnes reaches down to pat the cat. "Hello, Tom." It looks up with wide green eyes and purrs. Just the sound of the name, *Tom*, settles Mary Agnes's tight nerves. She thinks of her brother Tommy back at home and longs for him.

"Ya're allowed one cup of coffee, no cream, on a morning," Cook goes on. "And a piece of toast. Don't want ya fainting on yer first day. Ya'll start on the third-floor rooms first. Strip the beds, dust, polish, clean the grates, sweep. There's a mop in the closet at the top of the stairs. Rags, too. See to it there's no streaks."

"On the windows?"

"What do ya think, the backside of the queen? Of course, the windows. Are ya daft?"

"No, ma'am." Mary Agnes reaches for the butter knife and Cook swats her hand away. "Didn't say butter now, did I?"

Mary Agnes wolfs down the dry toast and black coffee, not daring to look at Cook.

"Get on with ya, then," Cook says. "Best have the third floor finished mid-morning. Check with me before ya start on the second floor. Mistress will be out today, lucky for ya. Oh, and this is Kathleen." She motions to a girl, a year or two older than Mary Agnes. "She's kitchen help. See to it ya mind her if I'm not about."

Mary Agnes nods to the girl, who nods back. The cook's assistant is dressed in black with a large white apron stained with grease. Her reddish-blonde hair is tied up on the top of her head like a knot, although wisps poke out beneath her ears and at the nape of her neck. She is uncommonly pretty with large blue eyes and only a smattering of freckles on the bridge of her nose, like Mary Agnes.

"What're ya staring at?" Cook asks Kathleen. "Get back to the pies. They don't bake themselves."

Mary Agnes looks at Kathleen, who rolls her eyes toward the ceiling.

"And what if I have to pass water?" Mary Agnes says as she approaches the back stairs. "Should I—"

Cook glares at her. "Well, aren't ya the impertinent one. No time for that. But if ya must . . ." She points down the stairs where Mary Agnes has just emerged. "There'll be stew for ya at the end of the day, six sharp, here." She points then to the large kitchen table. "Ya'll meet the rest of the help then."

Mary Agnes takes the back stairs to the top level of the house. She's fortunate to have gotten the position at all with no references and no experience, although she lied about that. Mrs. Rutherford needed the help, and that was that.

Mary Agnes fingers the ornate woodwork at the landing and her heart lurches. *What if I leave a fingerprint?*

She opens the closet to a rank smell. She knows what it is before she sees it, a dead rat. Rooting around with her foot, she kicks the rat aside with her boot and grabs the rags. The mop will wait. Three doors down, she cracks a bedroom door ajar. Never has she seen a room such as this. Bed, bedstead, chairs. And a dressing table strewn with handkerchiefs, face paint, perfume bottles. The bed linens look like someone had a wrestling match in the night.

"What are you standing there gawping at?"

A girl, not much older than Mary Agnes, comes up behind her, her long golden hair down. Wrapped in a plush dressing gown, she pushes into the doorway. If it weren't for the large dark mole above her lip, Mary Agnes would swear this girl was the prettiest she's ever seen.

"Excuse me, miss." Mary Agnes sidesteps the girl. "I'll go on to the next room."

"Theresa won't be up until noon," the girl says. "Wouldn't disturb her."

And how am I to be finished with this floor by mid-morning?

"The last room then?" Mary Agnes cocks her head toward the far bedroom.

"That'll do. Claire's already down with Mother. Wedding plans." The girl rolls her eyes.

Mary Agnes bobs and hurries to the far bedroom. "What's your name, then?" the girl asks after her. "We have so many housemaids I don't know why I bother."

"Mary Agnes, miss."

"Of course you're Mary. You all are. Just another worthless Irish bogger."

Worthless? Is that what everyone thinks?

"I'm Doria—Miss Rutherford to you. You'll meet the rest of them, Claire and Theresa and the twins, Ronald and Roland they're called," the girl says. She stops for a moment and leans against the door jamb. "A word of advice, bogger. Stay clear of the boys. They like Irish maids." The bedroom door closes behind her.

Mary Agnes tries to compose herself. It is not even seven in the morning.

Worthless Irish bogger? Didn't her gram say she was bold and independent? And her granda that she was, what? *A sight smarter—and prettier—than most?*

I'll show you what I'm made of, she thinks. *I'm headed to university. And you can bet I'll avoid the boys.*

If Mary Agnes thought Doria's room looked a fright, Claire's room looks like a tornado came through, and recently: Dresses, slips, stockings, and chemises, thrown helter-skelter on chair backs, bed, floor. Mary Agnes sweeps up garments in a heap and places them on the window seat. *Am I to fold them? Put them away? Wash them?*

She didn't get any instruction on this, and, of course, has not been a housemaid before, although she said she had been. She strips the bed linens as instructed and adds them to the pile, dusts the headboard and footboard and all the wooden surfaces in the room, careful to replace items where she found them, lamps, ribbons, figurines. The windows streak with rain and soot. It's spitting snow now. *Where to start? And where to get water?*

Doria's door remains closed as Mary Agnes heads to the water closet at the end of the hallway. She rinses rags under running water. Soot rings the enamel basin so she scrubs the sink until it shines and the water runs clear. Back in Claire's room, she wipes the window, up and down, mindful not to leave a streak. Back and forth she goes to the water closet to rinse the rags and wipe the sink. She must ask for a bucket. She then remakes Claire's bed with fresh linens and backs out of the room, her arms full of dirtied laundry and sheets, which she deposits down the laundry chute.

The coffee has by now run through her. *Do I dare use the water closet instead of going down four flights to the cellar? Who is to know?*

Checking again that there's no sound emanating from Theresa's room, and that Doria's door is still closed, she ducks into the privy to relieve herself. She knows she's breaking rules, and is as quiet as possible. As she pulls the chain and tidies up behind her, she listens for any sign of noise. None. She scurries to the kitchen then to report in to Cook before heading back up to the second floor. She is sure her toes are bleeding by now, and it's only not even ten in the morning.

AT HALF PAST SIX THAT EVENING, Mary Agnes limps down the stairs to her cellar room after a hearty bowl of beef stew with the house staff. Her first day is behind her. She falls onto the cot without lighting the lamp, still dressed.

How many times today was I scolded? The third-floor rooms not finished in time (*and whose fault was that?*), and no, Claire's dresses are not to be handled like dirty laundry, where did you learn housekeeping skills anyway? In a barn? Galway, ma'am. I'd have expected ya to know that, eejit. Sorry, ma'am. It won't happen again, ma'am.

And then there was the matter of passing water in the third-floor water closet. "Never again, girl," Cook said.

Who heard the chain pulled?

As Mary Agnes drifts to sleep, she remembers why she's here. And now she's got fifty cents on the ledger. Three months she has to prove herself. By then she will have earned thirty dollars, although she will have to send it home, it's expected, Uncle Fiach said. Maybe she can convince him that she should have half her wages anyway. She will have to figure out a way to present her case to him. *But not alone. Maybe I can enlist Aunt Margaret. Or, better yet, Helen.*

Mary Agnes wakes before dawn and rolls onto her back, her arms akimbo above her head. Her eyes adjust to the near light and she sees a water stain, its tributaries fingering out across the ceiling. In her fogginess and fatigue last night, she at least remembered to pull off her boots and stockings, but she is horrified to see she'd slept in her dress. How to get out all these wrinkles? *And did I even pray before I nodded off?*

She says a hasty prayer and springs up, her feet hitting the cold cement floor. Her heels are rubbed raw. A chill runs up her spine. She moves toward the radiator and spins slowly, not so much as to warm herself but to get the creases out of her uniform.

Two months ago, she left Ireland, not knowing what life in America would bring. Now she knows.

University? No. All the pretty Irish girls are housekeepers. You were right, Jimmy, my head was in the clouds.

17

Mid-December 1886
Chicago, Illinois

Mary Agnes's two-hour Sunday visits to her aunt and uncle's have provided a respite from what Helen calls "the ruthless Rutherfords." Mary Agnes thinks she may have overshared—*gossiped, really*—about the Rutherford clan, anxious Claire, bookworm Theresa, diva Doria, and the impossibly handsome twin boys who so far have not paid her a shred of attention. But she doesn't care. They are good fodder for conver—*gossip*.

And her new dresses have arrived! When she unwraps them, even the crinkly white tissue paper in which they're wrapped seems too precious. The green! And the rich brown and cream stripe! She smoothes the paper and folds it ever so carefully. She will reuse it for Christmas gifts next year when she can afford to buy them.

"Hurry up, slow poke," Helen says, as she whisks the dresses from her bed and holds them up for inspection. She hurries Mary Agnes into the dresses, and *oohs* and *ahhs* over Mary Agnes. "Will you look at this trim? Straight from Paris!"

Mary Agnes catches a glimpse of herself in the mirror in the fancier of the two dresses and her hand goes instinctively to her scalp. Her hair is approaching her ears, but she still looks more like a boy in a girl's dress.

"You'll be a beauty yet," Helen says.

Mary Agnes doubts it. *Not anytime soon. No boy will look at me, looking like this. But what a dress!* She runs her hand down the bodice to the waist and pauses there. She has had her monthly again, so there will not be a babe.

Two weeks into her position at the Rutherford's, Mary Agnes has memorized the family's schedule and plans her hours accordingly. If the talk isn't about Claire's upcoming wedding, it's about Chicago culture and news and politics. *More fodder for gossip next Sunday*, she thinks.

"Blast!" Mr. Rutherford exclaims so loudly it can be heard in the hall, where Mary Agnes has joined Kathleen for a quick cup of tea, the first raft of her jobs completed: opening draughts, putting on coal, airing the dining room, sweeping the front hall, dusting the bannisters, cleaning doorknobs, and shaking out rugs. And it's only 8:30 a.m.

"Damn that P.D. Armour!" Mr. Rutherford bellows. "There'll be no more ordered from that swine!"

"P.D. Armour?" Mary Agnes whispers to Kathleen.

"The meat marketer. We order all our meat from him."

From behind the dining room door that separates the Rutherford family at breakfast from the hall where the girls stand, they hear Mrs. Rutherford's high voice.

"Do you need your pills, dear? Or St. Jacob's Oil?"

Mary Agnes and Kathleen share a smirk. Kathleen mimics Mrs. Rutherford and mouths, "Do you need your pills, dear?"

The girls cover their mouths, move to the dining room door, and put their ears up to the wood.

"What can be done?" Mrs. Rutherford continues.

"What can be done?" Mr. Rutherford explodes.

Mary Agnes and Kathleen jump back from the door.

"All those boys maimed on the job, it's criminal," he says.

There is a long silence and then Mrs. Rutherford speaks up, her voice tentative. "Shall we write a check to the Lost Boys Fund?"

"Or write a check to us," Mary Agnes whispers to Kathleen. "So we can buy new shoes and dresses and hats." *And eyeglasses.*

Mary Agnes scurries then to the upstairs rooms. She's learned Theresa lingers in the parlor practicing piano and doesn't return to her room until mid-morning. As soon as the music stops, that's Mary Agnes's signal to head to Claire's room. Will she be there today? Or out? Claire doesn't seem to have a schedule at all. Sometimes she is in her room all morning; other times she can be found in her mother's room weeping. When Claire is out shopping with her mother (and that one blessed day Theresa and Doria accompanied Claire and their mother to shop), Mary Agnes has ample time to straighten the elder girl's room. As she dusts and straightens, she sings, sometimes old familiar tunes and sometimes ditties she makes up.

The next day, Claire rushes into the bedroom with her arms filled with packages and throws them on the bed. "Can a girl be as slow as you?"

Mary Agnes stands there, her song unfinished and the tune lingering in her head.

"Did you hear me? Move along!" Claire pokes her head out of the bedroom door. "Mother! The Irish girl is still in my room! And she's singing again!"

Mary Agnes doesn't want another tongue lashing from Cook for "bothering Claire at this time." *What time? Monday? Tuesday? Or doesn't it matter at all, anytime?*

The closer it gets to Claire's wedding, the more Mary Agnes avoids her. She cannot imagine how unstable the elder Rutherford daughter will become by February, two months away. It will be a lavish affair at the house after the ceremony, all the plans set in motion. In the meantime, it's *yes, miss, of course, miss, right away, miss*, bob, smile, and be on her way. Claire's mood doesn't match the scenario. *A girl should look forward to her marriage day, shouldn't she? Maybe she knows what she's in for.* Mary Agnes wonders why girls want to be married at all.

"Why is it that Claire is so cross?" Mary Agnes asks during supper. "I'm on eggshells all day."

"You and everyone else," Kathleen says. "But would you want to marry a man a full twenty years your senior?" Kathleen asks.

"But richer than Croesus!" Cook pipes in. "Wouldn't I like to marry the likes of him!" She sashays around the kitchen in a rare show of humor.

"But truly, Cook, would you want to marry an old man?"

"I'd marry the fishmonger, if he asked. What I'd do to cook for just one man."

"Yes, but there's more to marriage than cooking," Kathleen says, hiding a smile.

Cook bats at Kathleen with a spoon. "And how would ya know?"

Mary Agnes bursts with laughter. "I'm never getting married."

"We'll see how that turns out," Kathleen says. "One day you'll meet a handsome Irish lad. At Mass, I'll wager."

"Out of the kitchen, all of ya!" Cook barks, back to her usual surliness. "Except for Kathleen. We've got pies to bake."

"How many pies can one family eat?" Kathleen whispers to Mary Agnes.

"And they don't bake themselves!" Cook yells.

Mary Agnes wishes Cook would bake just one pie for the staff. Just one. Maybe one a week, or even one a month.

She remembers eating the whole pie with Helen as she trudges up the back stairs. *Cherry would be nice. Or peach. Even apple.* But she doesn't begrudge meals. She's eating.

After straightening up Doria's ever-messy room, Mary Agnes lingers at Theresa's door to see if she is in. *Has anyone read as many books?* Henry James and Mark Twain and Emilie Zola. Fyodor Dostoevsky. William Dean Howells. E. W. Howe. When Theresa is out—*which isn't much*, Mary Agnes has ascertained—she weasels precious minutes thumbing through Theresa's copy of Henry James's *The Bostonians* on her bedstand. Reading only snippets at a time, she wonders if Verena will ever marry Basil Ransom at this rate.

Mary Agnes hears a cough—Theresa always has a cough—and moves toward Claire's room. As she rounds the corner into the room, she trips on a loose rug and sprawls on Claire's bedroom floor. *If it isn't loose rugs, it's wet floors*, she thinks. As she gets up, she almost knocks a large blue and yellow chinoiserie vase off a side table. *Or china.* With shaking hands, she steadies the vase and waits for a moment to see if it is stable. *Damn my eyesight*, she thinks. *I can't be making mistakes here.*

When she knocks an urn off a ledge in the mistress's bedroom the next day, she is not as lucky. She watches in horror as the vase shatters into thousands of bits on the wooden floor. And the noise! Someone is sure to have heard. Mary Agnes freezes. So far, no one is running toward the mistress's bedchamber. All Mary Agnes can think is if the mistress will finger her and how soon she will be sacked.

She quickly sweeps the shards into a pile with her bare hands and looks around the room. *Where can I hide it?* Looking over her shoulder to be sure the mistress hasn't come up yet from breakfast, she pulls a fresh pillow sleeve from the closet and shoves the remains of the vase inside. Two of her fingers are bleeding now, tiny shards embedded in her skin. She picks out small shavings and stanches blood with the pillow sleeve. Her fingers throb. Pulling up her skirt, she jams the pillow sleeve into her waistband under the skirt. She will have to be very careful now.

Stealing down the back stairs to avoid the kitchen, Mary Agnes hurries to her cellar bedroom and stuffs the sack under her bed. She will have to dispose of it on Sunday, her afternoon off. *But where to get rid of it?* Certainly not the trash bin in the alley behind the Rutherford house. No, she will have to walk to an adjacent neighborhood, tuck into an alley, and dispose of the shards there. Without anyone noticing. *But surely the mistress will notice it's gone?*

Mary Agnes sits on the bed to control her shaking. *Maybe I should go to Mrs. Rutherford straight away. Confess.* But no, that would have her sacked immediately. Better to hope the mistress doesn't notice with all the décor in her boudoir. This Mary Agnes banks on.

THREE DAYS PASS AND NO MENTION of the vase. Mary Agnes feels a rush of relief. But she is wary of Doria. She is the only one who could have ratted on her that first day when she used the third-floor privy. *Maybe she heard? And is waiting to use it against her?*

Mary Agnes doesn't understand Doria. How could a girl be as different from her? In every way? Magazines are stacked on Doria's window seat: *Godey's Lady's Book* and *Peterson's* and *Harper's Bazaar*, with far more issues of the latter showcasing frivolous fashions replete with ruffles, flounces, ribbons, and lace.

Someday, Mary Agnes might be able to afford shoes like that. Or a hat with feathers. Or porcelain dolls. But she likely wouldn't buy any of those things. She would buy books, shelves and shelves of them like Theresa or her uncle. And she would read them all, cover to cover. She almost has enough saved up for new boots, if she can keep half her wages, that is, but first, eyeglasses. Then books.

"Did you ever see so many shoes?" Mary Agnes whispers to Kathleen at supper one particularly dreary night when the food was equally dreary.

"I don't get above stairs."

"Never? Not even to peek?"

"I couldn't, I'm only a kitchen maid. And, besides, I don't get a moment's rest. Most days, I wish I could trade positions with you, Mary A." Kathleen cocks her head toward Cook and rolls her eyes. "In a snit today, that one."

"Whatever about?"

"Mistress didn't take to the change in menu tonight. As if it's Cook's fault that the pork roast she ordered never arrived."

"I thought the duck smelled heavenly."

"Herself disagreed." Kathleen pulls a long face. "Cook had a talking to, according to him over there." She tilts her head toward the butler, Mr. Higgins. "Cook wouldn't dream of letting on, although it reflects badly on me as well. I'll remember from now on: No duck. Well, what we got isn't half as good as what they complained about above stairs tonight. Can you imagine? Complaining about duck?"

"Well, you should see Doria's room, the lucky duck. She has more pairs than a shoe merchant," Mary Agnes whispers. "I tried a pair on—"

"You didn't!"

"I did, and I'm not ashamed to say it. I traipsed about her bedroom with a bedsheet tossed over my shoulder and did I feel like money!"

"That will be the day heaven sinks to hell," Kathleen laughs.

"Watch me!" Mary Agnes laughs, and kicks Kathleen's foot under the table.

"If I were to sneak a peek into any room, it would be the missus's."

"The missus is very kind. Her room is something out of a ladies' magazine."

Mrs. Rutherford is indeed kind to Mary Agnes, a blessing Mary Agnes doesn't diminish when she prays at night. *Can you pray for non-Catholics?* she wonders. She does anyway, even for Doria.

Why does Mrs. Rutherford treat me with respect? Even if none of her daughters do? Was she a housemaid once? Not likely. No. She is probably afraid of losing another housemaid to another nasty situation.

Mary Agnes places mistress's comb and brush just so. Always curtsies. Folds undergarments discreetly away and arranges the mistress's dresses by color and season. Starches and presses the curtains and valances more often than they need attention, so that Mrs. Rutherford's boudoir is inviting and spotless, giving the mistress more time to work for temperance causes or moral reform or foreign missions or whatever it is Protestant women do, other than take morning naps, write letters, or plan for weddings. But it's as much for herself as Mrs. Rutherford. Mary Agnes can't afford to be sacked, maybe even more than Mrs. Rutherford can afford to lose another housemaid.

She moves through her days as if invisible, tending to the room each morning as Mrs. Rutherford takes breakfast. She comes in on soft feet, does her work, and leaves before Mrs. Rutherford returns. She hopes the mistress will never miss the chinoiserie vase.

If only I had so many beautiful items that I didn't miss one. Mary Agnes rebukes herself for her pride. *Why do I wish for things I cannot have? A blanket? A cloak? A home? I will have to go to confession.*

One morning close to Christmas, the house in a flurry and decorations adorning every mantel, door, and doorknob, Mary Agnes is just finishing up the mistress's chamber when she spies a note on the vanity. She picks it up and holds it close to her face to read. The note is in Mrs. Rutherford's fine hand.

My dearest Doria—

Sometimes words are best set to paper. When you told me of your young man's intentions, I couldn't find adequate words to respond.

My thoughts are three-fold. First, we cannot entertain any such talk with your sister Claire's upcoming nuptials. And what would Theresa think? She, without yet a suitor and older than you? But the third reason is the most important. You are too young to be contemplating marriage. There is much you do not know of the duties. I am afraid I must tamp down my happiness on your behalf and demand you put an end to this frivolous arrangement . . .

Mrs. Rutherford rushes in, pale as snow, clutching at the hems of her tea gown.

Mary Agnes places the note on the vanity and continues, as if dusting. "How may I help you, ma'am?" *Did she see me? Reading the letter?*

"I need to lie down."

Mary Agnes helps Mrs. Rutherford with her shawl and plumps up the pillows. "May I?" She bends to pull the coverlet down, helps her mistress into the wide bed, and removes the mistress's slippers. *Has she had another fainting spell?*

Mary Agnes wonders if the woman ever eats, so thin she is, like a slender reed. Or if her corset is too tight to harness her waistline into that impossibly small size.

"Thank you, Margaret."

"It's Mary, ma'am. Mary Agnes."

"Oh, please forgive me. I'm not quite used to Margaret being gone."

"Do you miss her?" Mary Agnes bites her tongue. *Have I said too much?*

"I do, but it couldn't be helped."

Mary Agnes sighs. She doesn't want to offend her mistress, but her tongue often moves faster than her brain. *What couldn't be helped?* But no, she won't ask. She has to watch herself even more now that she harbors a secret. She glances over to the ledge where the vase was. It is empty. Mary Agnes replays the memory of the vase *falling falling falling* and crashing onto the floor, red and green and black shards covering the mistress's bedroom like sharp confetti.

"It's usually the plain ones that find themselves taken by a dapper fellow," the woman continues. She stares at Mary Agnes. "You're quite a beauty, Mary, is it?"

She nods. "Mary Agnes."

"Still, you must watch yourself at every turn. I say the same to my own girls, although I doubt Doria pays me any mind. I worry after her."

"My gram said the same to me," Mary Agnes says. "But I've no time for a lad." *And didn't Doria warn me about her own brothers? Is that why Margaret and other maids have had to leave service?*

"You get Sunday mornings. And every other Sunday afternoon."

"Yes, and thank you for that, ma'am." Mary Agnes smiles. *It's allowed to smile at the mistress, isn't it?*

"After Mass, I go to my people for Sunday dinner. You must know them, the Laffeys?"

The woman shakes her head.

"After all the food and the talk and the laughing, that's enough for a day." *And I'm careful not to be alone with Uncle Fiach, even if it means listening to Helen gabber on.*

"And I've been meaning to say"—here, she holds her breath to steady her guilty heart—"I appreciate you taking me on, ma'am. I'm ever so grateful."

Mrs. Rutherford's eyes close. "I don't know what I'm going to do with Doria."

Did mistress hear a word I said? Or does what I say not even matter? I could probably scream, and no one would notice.

DORIA.

Mary Agnes has her suspicions. The unlatched window, the unmistakable imprint of a man's boot on the parquet, mussed sheets. *What is that girl up to? Has she received her mother's letter yet? Or doesn't she care?*

Mary Agnes leans out the window as she shakes out a rug. Coal dust flutters in the air like black snow.

Does he scale a ladder? Climb a drainpipe? Or has he bribed the cook and takes the back stairs at night?

Late the next evening, Mary Agnes pads up to the kitchen to root around for tea. Her monthlies leave her cramped and irritable. Tea always helps. As she rummages in the pantry—*it's here somewhere, I know it is*—the door to the kitchen creaks open.

She peers out the pantry door to see a tall young man enter the kitchen and close the door quietly behind him.

Isn't he the looker!

The lad nicks a piece of pie crust on the counter and steals up the back stairs. She follows after she's counted to ten. If it's an intruder, she'll scream to alert the Rutherfords. But she knows right away it's not a break in, her suspicions are confirmed. When she reaches the landing, she sees the tail end of a dark coat embracing Doria in her bedroom doorway. She ducks her head back into the stairwell until the door closes and then tiptoes to the door to listen. Hushed voices lead to hushed moans. No wonder Mrs. Rutherford has her suspicions. *Doria is entertaining a young man in her own house!*

The next day, up to elbows in suds, Mary Agnes forms a plan. Her birthday came and went without so much as a greeting, but she has one wish: To go to university. So no, she will not squeal. As much as she believes in being fair, she knows her place in the household order. It would be her word against Doria's and who would believe a poor Irish housemaid? It is better to forget it and press on. Let Mrs. Rutherford find out another way. And Doria?

She can stumble over her own discretions and see if I care one whit.

Mary Agnes cannot afford to be sacked, and now less than a month to Christmas. She needs to save up to go to university, to buy gifts, to get eyeglasses. And she cannot go back to her aunt and uncle to stay for fear of what might transpire there, her uncle's roving hands making her more uncomfortable every Sunday. The facts are plain. She must keep her head down and mouth shut. Work hard. Submit to the mistress, no matter what. It's hard to swallow the inevitable, but swallow she does, resignedly: There will be Dorias at any house she works in, and the Dorias will always win.

18

Christmas 1886
Chicago, Illinois

"Happy Christmas, Mary Agnes." Aunt Margaret hands her a letter. "From your people."

Mary Agnes perches on a settee in the parlor, dressed in her best green dress and new boots, her first purchase in America. She borrowed two dollars from Helen for boots after hers wore straight through the sole, promising to pay Helen back when she got her wages. She still does not have eyeglasses, the boots more dire. Her hair, which is now approaching her ears, is topped with a green ribbon tied in a bow at her neck and cascading half-way down her back.

And what a treat today is! She can hardly wait for Christmas dinner, roast goose and all the trimmings. She thinks of her gram and granddad at home, lucky to have a piece of salted fish today.

Everyone—top to bottom—has the day off from the Rutherford house, even Cook. It's the one day of the year Mrs. Rutherford and the girls take over the kitchen as if they deserve a prize. But Mary Agnes doesn't begrudge a day off. And it's a Saturday. She's to have tomorrow off, too, a whole Sunday, before she heads back to the big house tomorrow night.

Mary Agnes turns the letter over in her hand and wishes for eyeglasses. *Soon I will have enough saved up for them, too.* She opens the letter carefully and squints to read.

Shame on your head forever—

Shame? But why? Forever? She checks the envelope again to see if it is indeed her mother's spidery hand. It is, misspellings and all.

My fears were well-fownded. Ya've not only ~~ruwined~~ ruined our family name, but yer gross ~~immortality~~ immorality has now cawsed your dear grandmother to enter her Eternal Reward far too soon. When she ~~heerd~~ heard the news, it was the ~~deth~~ death of her. May God have ~~marcy~~ mercy on ya. Ya don't deserve it.

Anna Coyne

Mary Agnes's hands feel clammy. Her heart races and vision blurs. She struggles to find a breath.

"What ails you, lass?" Aunt Margaret asks.

Mary Agnes wordlessly hands the letter to her aunt. *Gram.*

"God bless her soul." Her aunt hands the letter to Helen, who skims it, her lips moving wordlessly.

"Whatever does she mean?" Helen asks.

"It were nothing," Mary Agnes answers. "My half-brother came at me one night and my mam said it was my doing. It wasn't! I swear!"

Aunt Margaret bristles. "Did he—"

"No! Nothing of the sort. I clobbered him on the arm right away, I did. He didn't touch me again." *Lie.*

"But did he—"

"No, he didn't sully me, if that's what you're after. Got a handful of . . ." She touches her chest.

"Good heavens!" she says. "Your very own brother."

Mary Agnes notices a curtness in her aunt's voice. *Am I right about Uncle Fiach? That he fathered his sister's child? Is that why he left Ireland all those years ago? Does Aunt Margaret know? Suspect?*

"Half-brother, Aunt." *And I wish he were dead, forgive me, Father.*

"Speak up, girl. I can't hardly hear you."

"I said, I'm glad to be thousands of miles away from him now. Although I do miss Tommy and the other boys." She thinks then of her dear gram, her keen eyes and gnarled hands, and the shawl that must have been painstaking to make. *Dear Gram.*

In a rush of thought, Mary Agnes tries to piece together the puzzle of why this news—*and false!*—would have been the undoing of her gram but it doesn't all fit. Her gram knew right away that Fiach accosted her in the lane.

Whatever can Mam mean that I ruined the family name? If anyone ruined the family name, it was Mam. Gram would never blame me.

Aunt Margaret punctures Mary Agnes's thoughts. "I thought today would bring happy news. Your mother and father coming to Chicago. With all the boys."

Mary Agnes chokes on a cough.

"Are you ill?" her aunt asks.

Mary Agnes shakes her head. "No, ma'am. My family? Coming to America?"

"I was saving the news for Christmas," she says. "I thought you would be pleased."

Not Mam. Not Da. Not Fiach.

"Will Granda come, too, do you think? Now that Gram is gone?"

"I think not. He would never leave Ireland."

Gram. Gone. Mary Agnes shakes her head to clear it. *But Tommy! In Chicago! Won't he love the streetcars! And Sean, the imp. I'll save up jokes for him. We can go, all of us, Ferris and Eamon, too, to the park and fly kites . . .* Her mind spins as she thinks of all her brothers, all except Fiach, that is. "When will they arrive?"

"You'll be the first to know," Aunt Margaret says. "Although for now, we should pray for your gram's eternal rest."

And that Fiach stays behind.

January 1887
Chicago, Illinois

"I've had a letter from my mam," Mary Agnes confides to Kathleen. "She says it's because of me my gram has passed on." She bites her lip. *Gram. Was it because of Mam? Fiach coming at me reminded her of Mam's shame? And that was too much for her? Or was it the lump? It had to be the lump.*

Kathleen stops kneading flour and lard on the worn kitchen table and looks up. She sweeps a mass of red hair from her brow. "Why would she say such a thing as that?"

"It's a lie, all of it."

"All of what?"

"My mam thinks it's my fault my half-brother approached me."

"Did he now?"

"Well, he didn't get far, if that's what you're after. Came at me in my bed."

"Who came at who in whose bed?" Doria bites into an apple as she rounds the corner into the kitchen.

Mary Agnes freezes. *How much did she hear?*

"A man in your bed?" Doria says. "Tart."

"I'm no such thing." Mary Agnes's face blazes. *The kettle calling the pot black, you mean.*

"Talking back, are you?" Doria sneers at Mary Agnes and rushes out of the kitchen. "Mother!" she calls.

Mary Agnes turns to her friend. "What am I to do?"

"I can't say rightly, but my guess is you'll be sacked within the hour. The mistress don't have your kind here." She shakes her head. "Anyone who can't keep her drawers on—"

"I didn't let anyone in my draw—"

Doria, triumphant, rounds the corner into the kitchen again. "Mother will see you in the parlor."

"'Who came at who in whose bed?'" Mary Agnes's face burns, her high cheeks tinged red. "Don't think I don't know what you've been up to with that suitor of yours."

Doria reaches out and slaps Mary Agnes on the face.

Holding her cheek, Mary Agnes walks to the parlor like a prisoner awaiting a sentence. She will never give in to Doria. And if Doria ever thought Mary Agnes would cover for her, those days are over. She will speak her mind. Even if it costs her the job.

Mrs. Rutherford, ashen, sits in an overstuffed chair near the fireplace. She doesn't look up when Mary Agnes enters the room.

"Ma'am?"

"That will be all, Mary. Pack your things."

"Can I—"

"I said pack your things. Doria told me what transpired. A man in your bed, in my house."

"There was no man in my bed, but there was a man—"

"Now!" She looks up and glares at Mary Agnes.

Mary Agnes doesn't move. If this were a chessboard, she would be backed into a corner. *There must be something I can say? Something I can do?*

"My wages, ma'am?"

"There won't be any wages. That was stated clearly in the contract. Three months probation. Go. Now!" Mrs. Rutherford barks.

No wages? Mary Agnes has never heard the mistress raise her voice but she stands her ground. "I understand that, ma'am, but nowhere did it say I wouldn't receive any wages, just no wages until . . ."

"Did you hear me? I said go. Now." She worries her hands. "If there are to be wages, I will have Mr. Rutherford send them to your sponsor."

Not to Uncle Fiach. He will send it all back to Ireland.

Doria, her back against the parlor door, stifles a smile. "Good riddance," she mutters under her breath as Mary Agnes leaves the parlor. "Worthless Irish bogger."

THE LETTER SITS CRUMPLED IN HER LAP. After she reads the news, she balls the letter into her fist and cries out. Her grandfather gone, too? So soon after her gram?

It can't be, Mary Agnes thinks. She uncrumples the paper, smooths it out, and reads again. Maybe this time the news will be different.

Dearest Margaret—

It is with great sadness that I rite now of the ~~pasing~~ passing of my dear Father, Festus. It has been a season of ~~sorruw~~ sorrow for all of us.

When he lost his men in a storm off Inis Bo Finne last ~~mouth~~ month, that was the last he spoke, except in the old langwitch. Into the nite, and in all weathers, he paced the shore here at Dawros. ~~Reeving~~ Raving mad, he was by then. He must have cawt his death of cold becawse the old innkeeper found him there on the strand. We buried him with all the others at the cemetery at Ballynakill.

I will rite again as soon as I have news of our travels to Amerika.

Give my regards to Fiach and Helen.

Your sister-in-law,
Anna Coyne

Dear Granda? Gone raving mad? Dead and buried?
"No," she wails. "Noooooo."

IN AND OUT OF CONSCIOUSNESS she goes, boundaries between wakefulness and dreaming blurred. The world is distant and muffled and hazy, thoughts disjointed and fragmented, time distorted. At times, Mary Agnes is almost lucid, and just as fast, she's plunged into disturbing thoughts and she's running, *they're after me, Granda*, she screams, and she reaches the end of the alley, *help me, help me*, and no one is there.

On another night, she finds herself on the floor, shivering although she burns with fever, but she doesn't have the energy to get up and trembles on the floor until early morning, when Helen finds her and urges her to return to bed. Helen tucks the sheets and blankets around Mary Agnes and calls for her mother.

Exhaustion, her aunt calls it, but anyone would know it is something else, something deeper. The loss of her granddad was the final straw.

"Get away!" she screams as the devil himself rouses Mary Agnes from sleep, his fingers clenching her head so tightly that she cannot escape the headaches. *Granda!* she calls out again. But again, he isn't there. She's tempted to give up completely. It would be so easy. Take a tablespoon of lye. But then she remembers all the Irish have been through in their long, bloody history. Celts and Vikings and Gauls. English occupation. Penal laws. Famine and starvation. Then she slaps herself into reality. *I can weather this. I have to weather this.*

And then, one morning, she doesn't know how many days or weeks later, she swims up through the fog and opens her eyes.

"Here, take some tea," Helen says. She is sitting beside Mary Agnes in a flouncy cream dress, her hair piled on top of her head.

Mary Agnes reaches for the tea with unsteady hands and nods her thanks. She hasn't spoken since the letter arrived.

"What day is it?" Mary Agnes asks.

"You speak!" Helen squeezes her cousin's hand. "It's Tuesday. January the 25th."

"That long? Three weeks?"

Helen nods, yes.

"Hazy . . . It has been very hazy," Mary Agnes says. "Like time went away and I was trapped somewhere. The last I knew we were reading the letter . . ."

"You were gone from us for a while," Helen says. "But now you are back. I'll fetch Mother."

"Not yet. Can you tell me what I've missed?"

"Missed? Not much. I suppose the biggest news is Mother and I went to a fabulous sale at Davis and Morse. Linens, towels, blankets."

That is not what I meant, Helen. I meant what did I miss in the world? In the country? In Chicago?

"But look at this!" Helen shuffles the newspaper. "'Wanted—Female Help. A young lady as bookkeeper.

Must thoroughly understand bookkeeping, reasonable salary.' And it doesn't say, 'Irish Need Not Apply.' I think I will do just that. Apply. As soon as I graduate."

"That sounds wonderful, Helen." Mary Agnes tries not to feel a stab of jealousy, Helen finishing bookkeeping school and she still a housemaid. *I could be sitting in a great hall reading Latin. Studying maps of all the continents. Writing poetry . . .*

"It's hard to land any position in this town, Mary A. Every ad says, 'German or Scandinavian girl.' Nothing for the likes of us. Still."

"Unless you work for another Irish family or an Irish business."

"Or they're desperate."

The barb stings.

Helen prattles on, seemingly unaware she has wounded Mary Agnes yet again. "Oh, look! Richard Mansfield is playing Prince Karl at the Columbia this weekend."

I can't afford to go to the Columbia or anywhere now that I don't have a position. And I don't want to go. To be entertained. To laugh.

Mary Agnes asks for the newspaper to shield herself from Helen. *If I need anything, it's eyeglasses.* She skims ads. "'Eyes skillfully fitted free of charge using the best of scientific instruments.' Prices $1.50-$2.50. And just over on Madison in the *Tribune* building. I think I'll save up for eyeglasses instead."

"You're no fun." Helen makes a face at Mary Agnes.

Fun? Gram gone and now Granda, too. It's too much. Can't Helen see? Can't anyone see? I don't know what fun is anymore.

THE DAY MARY AGNES STARTS HER new position in the kitchen of a wealthy Irish family in another parish, she is well, and outfitted with snug spectacles, thanks to Aunt Margaret entreating Uncle Fiach for two dollars of Mary Agnes's wages, "so the girl can see, for heaven's sake." He handed over two dollars reluctantly, the rest of her wages sent back home. She still owes Helen two dollars for her boots, a debt that hangs over her head.

This position will be different, Mary Agnes thinks. *I just know it.* The O'Sullivans live on the corner of Washington and Page, a stately home with a sweeping porch facing south just blocks from Union Park. *And*, she thinks, *what a relief they're Catholic.*

She's got Sundays off, and half-day Thursday, too, and is making seventy-five cents per day. Three days turn to three weeks turn to three months and she receives her first wages. She dutifully sends half of the money home without a note and deposits the rest into a new savings account at First Chicago Savings and Loan. She confesses to Father Gannon at St. Mel's and says three Hail Marys as penance.

When one of the six O'Sullivan girls marries—and with much less fanfare than Claire Rutherford would have—Mary Agnes and other maids fill the back pews. It's a gorgeous spring day, fit for a bride. *And isn't she lovely in that trim black gown, and that veil! And what a handsome pair they make.*

Mary Agnes's mind wanders as it's wont to. She can't help seeing the image of Fiach coming at her at night and again on the lane. The burly man who sheared off her hair at Castle Garden. The Italian gang in the alley in New York. Her Uncle Fiach fondling her rear.

No, she reminds herself. *I'll never marry. This is my life. A big house. Good wages. Enough food. I'll not complain of tired feet or aching hands, scalded wrists or scabs. I'll rise up and above it all, yes ma'am, of course ma'am, at your service ma'am, smile. Watch me, I say. I'll run a big house someday and won't I show them all, the Dorias of the world.*

Two Years Later
July 1889
Chicago, Illinois

The long light blue and green brocade dress hugs Mary Agnes in all the right places, its starched white collar ringed with gold trim. The dress falls below her ankles in small pleats. She splurged on new stockings this week and hopes no one notices last year's boots. They won't. Not with this hairstyle. Pulled back in a low bun, her dark auburn hair contrasts with the collar. She wishes she could unbutton just the top button. Maybe she will, it's near eighty degrees already at midday, the humidity making the air close, the city steamy. She pins a silk flower to her breast and wishes for pearls.

As she catches a glance of herself in the mirror, she sees her mother, green eyes and dark hair and a nice bosom, but minus the stomach that inflated and sagged every two years. She raises her chin to admire herself, sixteen now, two years older and much wiser than when she first arrived.

In two years, Mary Agnes has risen to the top of the O'Sullivan household. Second to the head maid she is now, with two housemaids below her, one recently from Galway. She's got a bank account, new eyeglasses, and a closet full of dresses. It seems a long time since she boarded the ship at Galway City and headed for America. *If Doria could see me now*, she thinks. *Wouldn't she be surprised.* She gathers up a wrap and a parasol before she bounds down the stairs, her straw hat in her hand. Life couldn't be grander. Thomas Halligan is coming to call.

"Well, I never," Cook says. "I do believe we have a new boarder." She smiles and pats Mary Agnes on the arm. "A fellow can do that."

Mary Agnes has a rare Saturday afternoon off, it being the day before Independence Day. The O'Sullivans—including Mr. O'Sullivan and his sister and family, eleven in all—are spending the holiday at their lake home in Delavan, Wisconsin. Four of the household staff went along so Cook gave the remaining staff the day off.

"No tattling on me," Cook whispers with a wink. "I could use a day off myself."

When Mary Agnes sees Tom in the parlor, her heart skips a beat. He has a large bouquet of flowers and plucks one bloom out for Cook.

"For me?" Cook colors.

"For the best cook in Chicago."

"You're not going to get anywhere with me, young man." Cook stifles a smile.

"No?" Tom laughs.

"Save your sweet for your sweet," Cook says. "But when you come round again, I'll have an extra slice of pie for you."

Tom takes Cook's hand and pecks it. "Like I said, best cook in Chicago."

As soon as Mary Agnes spied the tall, slim man with a mop of unruly brown hair at St. Mel's one Sunday this past spring, she was drawn to his kind face. It was something about him that made her stomach flutter. *What is it? I have sworn off men.* For two Sundays she watched him during Mass, and by the third Sunday her mind was straying. The next week she decided to put herself in his way after Mass.

"Excuse me, but why haven't we met?" she says. Her hair is down around her shoulders and she wears one of her three going-to-church dresses, a high-necked dark heather green to compliment her eyes, framed with rimless eyeglasses. Her hat, a matching green with a pheasant feather, sits at a jaunty angle, a tad risqué for Mass, but Mary Agnes is not afraid to spit at custom. *Those mantillas are so . . . old-fashioned.*

The young man stutters. "Miss." He worries his hat. "Thomas Halligan is the name. And you would be?" His brogue is thick as butter.

"Mary Agnes Coyne. Some call me Irish."

"Wouldn't be the first," he laughs. "I've noticed you. In fact, I was going to make it my business to meet you today. You just beat me to it."

"Were you now?"

Right away, Mary Agnes is at ease. The way he touches her elbow, ever so gently, as they exit the church. The solicitousness in his voice and gestures. The compliments on her hair and dress. The twinkle in his eye when he calls her *Irish.* They meet now after Mass every week, their conversations longer and longer, until Tom gets up his nerve and asks her for an outing.

"I thought you would never ask," she says. "I was about to ask you myself."

"Next Saturday, then?"

"Sounds delightful. I'm off Saturday afternoons."

Today, Tom Halligan wears a natty pair of trousers, a crisp shirt, a dark vest, tie, and smart bowler. She notices his worn shoes and hopes he doesn't notice hers.

When they step off the streetcar near Lake Michigan, Tom takes Mary Agnes's elbow. She links her arm in his as they enter Lincoln Park, the green filled with families and children enjoying this beautiful July afternoon.

Two boys run by trying to launch a paper kite. They stumble over a root and the kite crashes to the ground.

"Here, let me help," Tom says. He dusts off the kite, untangles the line, and hands it back to the boys. With a nod, they're off. As Tom and Mary Agnes pass a row of stately elms, a gaggle of girls looks up at the pair from beneath a towering tree. Most of them are cradling dolls, although one has a small stuffed bear.

Mary Agnes bends down to see the bear. "What a handsome little fellow he is," she says.

The girl looks up at her and smiles. "Thank you, miss."

"Can I pet him?"

"Of course."

Mary Agnes strokes the bear's worn fur. "You take good care of this wee one. He's depending on you."

"I will, miss."

Mary Agnes and Tom skirt the Academy of Sciences and circle around formal gardens, stopping by a large lily pond surrounded by pink azaleas. Mary Agnes hasn't felt this comfortable with a young man since Jonesy. *Three long years ago.*

Mary Agnes reads the inscription aloud as they pause before a large bronze of Abraham Lincoln, who stands pensively, one arm behind his back and head tilted down, as if in deep thought: *A.D. MDCCCLXXXVIII, Augustus St. Gaudens.*

She runs her fingers over the Roman numerals: 1888. "What year was Lincoln assassinated?" she asks. "Wasn't it before the end of the war between the states?"

"Yes, spring of 1865," Tom says. "History will find he was the best president this country has ever had."

"And the colored peoples still not treated equally?"

"We're not treated equally, that's for certain. The newspapers parody us both, Irish and colored peoples alike. You're sure to have seen it."

"Aye. But apes? As if we are nothing better than animals?" Mary Agnes scowls, for the first time today.

"Bigotry crosses many lines," Tom says.

Too many lines. She clasps Tom's arm tighter. *Stick to your own kind, Irish.*

When they reach the wide expanse on the shores of the lake, she focuses on families enjoying the picnic grounds. A large family—mother, father, eight children—occupies a blanket nearby, their congeniality familiar, yet unfamiliar. She will never know that harmony with her own family, in this life, anyway.

"Why, I should have packed a hamper," Mary Agnes says. She's mortified she didn't think of it.

"Next week." He winks. "Today, we'll go to the tea house."

Next week. He said next week. Am I changing my mind? No? Yes?

After a lunch of toasted cheese sandwiches and pickles washed down with cool tea, Tom and Mary Agnes stroll the promenade along the lake. She breathes in the scent of him. *Citrus.*

Discreetly, and turned slightly away from Tom, she unbuttons the top button on her collar. She instantly feels cooler. Her mind strays, thinking of his collar. His shoulders. His trim waist. The thoughts surprise her. She swore she'd never marry, and here she is, on a first date with a lovely bachelor, one she sought out.

"Tell me about your people," she says as she adjusts her straw hat.

"It's not very interesting fodder. 'Irish family emigrates to America.'"

"Yes, I want to hear." She purses her lips and shakes her head. "I'm not one to ask twice."

"I see. A girl who knows her mind." He smiles. "If you're not careful, I might just fall in love with you."

"You do that. At your peril!"

"Are you really sure you want to hear my story?"

She bats at his arm. "Like I said . . ."

He pauses. "We came from Monaghan ten years back now, 1879, it was. Hard to leave my grands and my friends from school but it seems like eons ago now. I can hardly remember it. I do remember the sea voyage, though. It was horrid."

"Aye." *So many died on the Endeavour from Liverpool to New York, old men and women, mothers and children. And Mary Catherine.* Mary Agnes winces, trying to expunge the memory. "How old were you then, in 1879?" she asks.

"Twelve."

So he must be twenty-one now? Or twenty-two? To my sixteen?

"We came through New Orleans and up the Mississippi."

"Not through Castle Garden?"

"No. You?"

"Yes, but we're not talking about me now." *And I don't want to talk about it, ever.*

"At first we stayed with kinfolk here, in Chicago. A few months later, my da got a job in Peoria. It wasn't easy on us boys. In Chicago we could disappear amongst all the Irish, but in Peoria, the boys at school treated us like we were from another place and time altogether."

"You, your brothers? Sisters?"

"Three brothers, all younger. It must have been our boots. Or maybe our trousers."

Or maybe your brogue. I've not heard one so thick since I left home.

"I was always in schoolyard scrapes. Trying to protect them." Tom's face goes dark. "I got a hiding from my da after every fight. 'You've got to fit in, Tommy,' he'd say. 'This is our home now.'"

"So, no sisters?"

Tom shakes his head.

"Me, neither. But I do have six brothers." She thinks of Tommy. "They're still in Galway."

"You came alone?" His eyes widen.

"I did. My grands couldn't take care of me any longer after—"

"After what?"

Mary Agnes has practiced this all week, knowing she would be asked. "Let's just say my mam and I didn't see eye to eye. She turned me out, sent me to my grands."

"But why did she turn you out?"

I don't want to say the real reason. "Too many mouths to feed. And me, a girl." The lie stings.

"I would have adored a sister," Tom says.

As would I. But I have Helen now, almost as good as a sister, even if she talks my ear off.

A warm breeze ruffles Mary Agnes's hair and sun glints off the lake. "You can't see to the other side," she says, changing the subject. She doesn't want to talk about her family anymore. "It's almost like an ocean."

"'Tis. One of the biggest lakes in all North America, after Superior and Huron."

"And you know this, how?"

"Working the railroad, you've got to know your geography. You can quiz me anytime. Now tell me more about you," Tom says. "I'm thinking you must be nineteen?"

"Seventeen in November."

"I would have never guessed."

"I'm good at it by now. Fooling people. No one needs to know, except of course I'm not sorry if you do. I'm thinking of applying for a position at The Grand."

"The Grand Pacific Hotel?" He whistles through his teeth. "Would think you'd need to be at least eighteen to work there."

"I've got credentials now. And like I say, no one needs to know. I got my first position at fourteen, told them I was sixteen. It would be steady work, but I'd have to find new lodging. I've been boarding at big houses since soon after I arrived, and I think it's time for a change." She straightens her skirt. "A little more freedom." She turns to Tom. "Wish me luck!"

A sudden crack of lightning forces them under one of the elms. Mary Agnes holds out her parasol. "I thought I'd be needing this for the sun, not for the rain." She huddles closer to Tom.

He holds her gaze and takes her hand. "Ready for anything, I see."

"I have to be ready, Tom." A brief flash of Fiach's face. A clench in her stomach. Her hand in a fist. "You don't have six brothers and find yourself lacking."

"Amen. I admire you, Mary Agnes Coyne, coming alone from Ireland and working your way up. If I'm lucky, and I am, I think, you'll agree to see me again. Sure if I'm not falling for you, Irish."

Falling for me?

Staccato pulses throb in her head. Is it guilt or trepidation? Or both? She looks away—*will he notice?*—and feels a fraud, sullied by her half-brother. It's something she cannot bear to say to anyone, even the priest. But she'll have to face it tonight or tomorrow or before she sees Tom again: *Do I deserve him? After Fiach?*

November 1889
Chicago, Illinois

"'Irish Courting,' they call it," Aunt Margaret says. "Meeting a man and walking down the aisle before the year is out." The train had to be mended in two places where moths had made a bed, but other than that, Aunt Margaret's black wedding gown fits Mary Agnes like a glove. She wears pearl earrings and pearl hairpins Tom gave her just last night and adjusts the black veil.

Her aunt circles her and clucks. "The dress will bring you luck. It has, me."

Of all the times Mary Agnes has been in her aunt's—dare she say, excessive—bedroom, all the chintz and frou-frous, pillows and throws, dressing table filled with every new potion, this is by far the happiest occasion. She puts out of her mind any resentment she felt for her aunt and uncle sending her into service and juts her chin and gazes in the full-length looking glass. It is as if her mother is staring back at her, but her mother is thousands of miles away and doesn't even know her daughter is marrying today. It isn't right, Mary Agnes acknowledges, but, in truth, she doesn't want her mother here to spoil her perfect day.

"I believe in luck," she says. "Don't we all?" No, there couldn't be a nicer dress. *And I'm the lucky one today. Marrying Tom Halligan.*

"Mark my words, by this time next year, you'll have a babe to call your own," Aunt Margaret says.

"Mother!" Helen laughs. "Not what Mary A. is thinking of today, a houseful of young ones. She's only sixteen."

"Seventeen next week," Mary Agnes says. She thinks then of all the Donnelly children in New York, her own brothers, Irish families in Dawros, and on the ship, and here in Chicago. That Helen is an only child is unusual for an Irish family. It raises questions.

"Maybe, in time, we'll have a houseful," she says.

"Always wishing for what you don't yet have," Helen says.

No, Mary Agnes has never been known for patience, and it was tried heartily last weekend. While the O'Sullivans were out at another one of Chicago's posh parties, and Cook gone home for the night, Mary Agnes stole down the backstairs and unlocked the kitchen door. She rooted in the pantry for tea and a biscuit and watched for Tom's shadow at the door. When he rapped on the window, she let him in and ushered him up to her garret room.

"Are you sure?" he asked.

"I am. As sure as anything."

They lay together in her narrow bed on the top floor of the grand house, but nothing more. It had been fraught enough to talk Tom into coming to the O'Sullivan's in the first place, but she had already given notice, so what if she were to be found out? She'd had insinuations before about her character, all of them false, first her mother's bitterness over Fiach's attack and then Doria's false charge that she had had a gentlemen caller at the Rutherford house. This time their insinuations would hold, and she didn't care. She will never work in a big house again.

But Tom was insistent. They would wait until their wedding night. He left her in the still, dark hours of night, with a kiss so fervent she thought she might melt. In the peachy dust of dawn, Mary Agnes wept, but not because of sadness. How was it that she could be so lucky? With such a good man? And how soon could the wedding day come? Like Mrs. Donnelly said when Mary Agnes first arrived in New York, love changes everything, although there will be one secret—she will never tell Tom about Fiach violating her.

Today, she can't wait to be in Tom's arms again, but first, the ceremony and the lunch afterward, and the cake Helen spent all day yesterday perfecting. *The afternoon will go on forever!*

For November in Chicago, they have surely lucked out: Sunny and chilly, *and no rain.* It is a small affair in a side chapel at St. Mel's with her aunt, uncle, and Helen in attendance.

But who is not here today? Her grandparents, long gone now. Her parents, still not arrived from Ireland. Her brothers. *Jonesy.* As she approaches the altar, Mary Agnes trains her eyes on Tom. Gone is everything before today, she looks now to a bright future ahead.

The way the sun glints into the chapel reminds her distinctly of the day the Blessed Virgin first spoke to her in the chapel at Ballynakill. *Come, take my hand,* the Purple Mary said.

Thank you for leading me here, Mary Agnes whispers.

AFTER GENTLE COUPLING IN THE LARGE feather bed at the Union Hotel, an expense Mary Agnes thought much too dear, she turns to Tom. "You know, I said I'd never marry."

He looks at her quizzedly. "To whom did you say that to?"

"My tutor." Mary Agnes remembers saying it like it was yesterday. *And now I'm a married woman.*

"And I'm finding this out just now?" he says playfully, twirling her hair.

Married. The realization hits her. Married women don't work outside the home. *Tom can work as a dispatcher, or at any job he chooses. What am I to do all the day?* She wonders if she rushed into this. *But no,* she chides herself. *I love this man, I do.* She turns and kisses him deeply. As for the rest of the night, Mary Agnes's patience proves well worth the wait.

They leave the hotel reluctantly the next morning and take the streetcar to their lodgings on Monroe Street. As they walk over the threshold, Tom turns to kiss her. "New beginnings," he says. "I hope we have sixty more years of new beginnings."

Their narrow apartment shares the first and second floor of a three-level brick building in a predominantly Irish neighborhood not far from the Laffeys. The entire block looks the same; Mary Agnes checks as she's mounting her steps by glancing at the number above the door: 4314. The adjacent apartment is occupied by an elderly Irish couple who keep to themselves, Barry and Anne McSweeney their names. The third-floor apartment above the McSweeney's is to let. The apartment above Mary Agnes and Tom's rooms is rented by a young bachelor who works nights as a janitor at a meat-packing plant. They hear him descend the back stairs just as they get into bed at night and see him trudge back up the stairs as they take breakfast in the kitchen.

"What a horrid place to work," Mary Agnes says. "A meat-packing plant."

"It's work," Tom replies. "Irish can't be too picky."

Tom and Mary Agnes learn a contented, steady rhythm of getting to know one another more intimately. That Mary

Agnes would enjoy congress so much, especially after her horrid assault from Fiach, shocks her. She thought she would cringe at the act of coupling, but no, Tom is gentle and kind and brings her pleasure. She colors thinking about it. Fiach fades from memory every day. *New beginnings.*

Why she wondered what she would do all day makes her laugh now. She is busy morning to night. Breakfast has never been an issue; Mary Agnes has been making breakfast since she was a young girl. She packs Tom's dinner pail he takes to the railroad office every day, in it, tinned meats, bread, and fruit. Then there is laundry, done by hand in the kitchen sink and hung to dry in the back alley, or, if it's too cold, strung across the small kitchen. And ironing, warming the iron on the wood stove and pressing shirts and trousers and drawers. The biggest decision is what to make each night on a meager budget. In Ireland, it was potatoes every night with mutton once a month. Surely, Tom expects more than potatoes.

After burning a piece of fish the first Friday after their marriage, Mary Agnes purchases Mrs. F. L. Gillette's *The American Cookbook*, published just this fall in Chicago. *I have to learn to cook. Really cook.*

Flipping through the pages, Mary Agnes can't imagine ever making Tenderloin of Beef (*To dress it whole, proceed as follows: Washing the piece well, put it in an oven; add about a pint of water, and chop up a good handful of each of the following vegetables as an ingredient in the dish,* viz., *Irish potatoes, carrots, turnips, and large bunch of celery . . .*) or Stewed Steak with Oysters (*Two pounds of rump steak, one pint of oysters, one tablespoon of lemon juice, three of butter, one of flour, salt, pepper, one cupful of water . . .*).

On Tom's wages, it is all they can afford to get fish on Fridays. She best not burn it next time. She pages to the fish section and peruses recipes for sole and cod.

A loud call outside her back door interrupts her reading.

"Fresh vegetables today! Carrots, onions, potatoes!"

Mary Agnes takes a few coins from her purse and opens the door into the alley.

"Festus!" She always thinks of her granddad, Festus Laffey, when the vegetable peddler comes around. In addition to Festus—a striking lad from Donegal, always cheery, like her granddad was, before he went mad, that is, a thought Mary Agnes has never been able to reconcile— the alley is filled with an array of other cart merchants. Voices cling and clang, the deep-throated voice of the knife sharpener, the shrill call of the ice man.

"Wait! Festus!" *How I love that name.* "I'll take two onions and a handful of carrots," Mary Agnes says. *Maybe we'll name a wee one Festus . . .*

"No potatoes today, Mrs. Halligan?"

It's a joke between them.

"I've had my fill of potatoes to last a thousand lifetimes, Festus." She returns to the kitchen and the cookbook. At four, after a sponge bath and a rest, Mary Agnes takes to the kitchen. Tom will be home in an hour and a half, a blessed Friday. *I will not burn supper tonight.* And then she thinks of the old story her granddad used to tell her about the boy and the magic salmon. *When he burned the fish, he got all the knowledge in the world. All I got was a burnt thumb and a burnt pan.*

Tom comes up the back stoop whistling. "How's my missus today?" he asks, as he kisses Mary Agnes's cheek. She's in her green apron with her hair piled on top of her head as she bends over the stove, where onions sizzle in a cast iron pan and carrots come to a boil. Soon, the pan will be hot enough for the fish. She turns her head and kisses him on the mouth, dropping her wooden spoon into the pan.

"I'm guessing not every lad at the yard will get a greeting half as nice as this," he says. He turns to the stove. "And what have we here?" He didn't even complain when she burned the fish last week. "Ah," he says, as he sees the small filet. "My favorite. Cod."

Mary Agnes increases her repertoire week by week, filling in the weekdays with soups and stews and homemade bread. Now she's experimenting with pies, not that she'll ever hope to best the pies made by Cook at the Rutherford's. Not that she ever got any. She thinks how curious it is that she lives in the same city as her former employer and never once has seen them or any of the help. She thinks briefly of Claire and wonders if she's happy in her marriage, and then of Theresa and her books. She doesn't dwell on Doria. *She called me a liar. She was the liar, and she knows it. She'll have to live with that.*

On Mary Agnes's birthday, she spends the day making an ice box cake.

....

ICE BOX CAKE
1 c. butter, warmed to room temperature
2 c. sugar
3 c. flour
4 eggs

Cream butter and sugar. In separate bowl, whisk eggs. Add to butter/sugar mixture. Add the flour one-half cup at a time. Batter will be thick. Spoon into greased cake pan and bake until golden. Top with white icing and store in ice box.

....

When Tom arrives home, he sweeps Mary Agnes into his arms. "How is the birthday queen today?"

Mary Agnes wears a new red and tan striped dress with a high neckline trimmed with lace. It has taken her all week to finish it by hand. "Better now that you are home."

"Well, will you look at you. The best-looking woman in all of Chicago."

She smiles.

"What are we having to celebrate your seventeenth?" Tom asks.

"An ice box cake."

Neither of them comments there is no supper. The four eggs that Mary Agnes used in the cake would have made a nice omelet. But some days are for celebrating.

On the first Friday in December, just a week after her birthday, Tom comes home looking peaked.

"What's wrong, love?" Mary Agnes asks. She ushers him to the kitchen table and takes his hat. His handkerchief is stained with blood.

"It's nothing," he says. "Must be the change in weather."

"Here, let me take your coat," she says. "And take off those wet shoes. You'll catch your death of cold." *Please Jesus Mary and Joseph, not like Granda.*

"Shall I fetch a doctor?" Mary Agnes knows the answer before he speaks. How would they pay for one? Tom rests all weekend, rousing himself only for Mass on Sunday. They decline their weekly dinner at the Laffeys and he sleeps all Sunday afternoon. That night, despite his weakness, he takes Mary Agnes in his arms and snuggles his head in her breasts.

"How am I so lucky?" he says.

Mary Agnes strokes his head. "I'm the lucky one, Mr. Halligan. You'll never know how lucky."

22

Three Months Later
March 1890
Chicago, Illinois

espite Tom's insistence that nothing is wrong, Mary Agnes finally prevails. He has an appointment on Wednesday afternoon at four. Tom leaves work an hour early—Mary Agnes doesn't press him for the excuse he gave—and she meets him downtown at the doctor's office off Madison on La Salle.

"Fatigue? Night sweats?" the doctor asks. "Cough? Phlegm."

Mary Agnes nods.

Motioning Tom to the examination table, he listens to Tom's lungs with a black stethoscope. "Deep breath."

Tom struggles to take in a breath.

The doctor puts the stethoscope down, removes his eyeglasses, and turns to Tom. "Consumption," he says, one word to change a life.

Mary Agnes and Tom look at each other. There are no words, the diagnosis flattening.

Since then, Mary Agnes has read everything she can about the disease. A bad cough. Pain in the upper chest. Bloody sputum. All of these symptoms present and yet she still hopes.

Tom no longer goes to the rail office. His last day was the twenty-eighth of February, just past his twenty-third birthday. He wanders the house during the day, hollow-eyed and deathly thin. Mary Agnes encourages him to eat, drink water, rest. He sleeps on the parlor couch now that he labors to take the stairs, but Mary Agnes can't sleep herself, so she checks on him several times each night, helps him to sit when he coughs, wipes him down when he sweats.

When she catches a glimpse of herself in the hall mirror one night—is it two a.m.? Or closer to three?—she gasps. She looks a fright. From somewhere deep within her gut, she feels rage rising. She pounds the wall next to mirror so hard, the mirror shakes. She throws herself on the bed then and pounds the pillow, as if beating a feather pillow will change anything. The sobs begin then, first dry heaves and then gasping breaths between sobs.

"Mary A.?" Tom is at the bedroom door.

"Tom!" Mary Agnes sits up, swipes her eyes, straightens her hair. "What are you doing upstairs?"

"I heard you crying." He comes to the bed and climbs in next to her.

She lies in his arms as the tears come again.

He holds her close, strokes her hair, whispers. "Shh, now, Mary A. I couldn't ask for a dearer woman at my side."

"It's so unfair," she says, between sobs. "C-c-consumption. You're only twenty-three." And then another raft of sobs.

"We can beat this, Mary A. Together."

She doesn't answer and he doesn't elaborate.

"How?" she asks.

He cups her face and bends to kiss her forehead. "The fellows at work told me about a place, Colorado Springs. It's said to be the best environment for consumptives."

Consumptives. I hate that word.

"Pure air, clear water," he continues. "We should think on it."

"Colorado Springs? In—"

"Colorado. I know it's not what we hoped, staying here, having a family. But it's worth a try."

A try? Is that all we can hope for, a try? Mary Agnes, face tear-stained and heart drumming, sinks into half-sleep.

Tom stays up and tends to her this once, humming an Irish tune and stroking her arms, her shoulders, until, at last, she succumbs to sleep.

"IT'S FOR THE BEST," HELEN SAYS, closing Mary Agnes's suitcase with a sharp *snap*. Mary Agnes's and Tom's meager apartment on Monroe Street is now empty except for the spare furniture that came with the rent.

"That's what my gram said to me when I came to America," Mary Agnes says. "And see where that's gotten me."

"It's gotten you a good husband and a good friend."

"One of whom is not long for this world and the other who is saying goodbye to me. I am tired of other people making decisions for me." Mary Agnes shakes her head. "I should be making my own decisions. Or at least be in concert with my husband on this."

"Chin up, Mary A. You need to be strong for Tom's sake. And then for you. After."

"I refuse to think about 'after.' He's only twenty-three."

"Colorado Springs is known for the cure," Helen says.

"Why not here? There are doctors, sanitariums, even. Colorado Springs is a thousand miles from here."

"Rock Island will take care of him. Best job in all Chicago. Men are dying to get a job with the Chicago-Rock Island Line."

"I don't think 'dying to get a job' is the best way of phrasing it."

Helen colors. "Oh, I'm sorry, Mary A. I didn't mean it that way . . ."

"I know you didn't." She pats her cousin on the shoulder. "You've been so good to me, Helen. Even if you never let me get a word in sideways."

"Oh, pah," Helen says. "You're right handy with words yourself."

"Even if I didn't go to university." *Literature. Poetry. Writing* . . . When is the last time she wrote anything other than a grocery list?

"Who needs to go to university?" Helen says. "There's a whole world out there." She takes the two small suitcases from the bottom of the stairs and places them by the front door. "You'll have to write me from Colorado. Just think, the mountains, the clean air . . ." Helen chats on and then checks her pocket watch. "I'll get these to the curb before Tom gets back from the bank." She hefts the suitcases to the porch. "Don't want him to strain himself before he even leaves Monroe Street."

Is it that obvious?

"I'd like a moment, Helen. For remembering. Oh, but before I go . . ."

Helen turns, a quizzical look on her face.

Mary Agnes hands Helen two dollars. ". . . Here's the money I borrowed from you when I first got to Chicago."

"I've forgotten about that."

"I never forget."

After Helen takes the satchels outside, Mary Agnes walks slowly from room to room, fingering the wallpaper, the woodwork, the door handles, simple things one takes for granted in a home.

In the entry, she hears the echo of Tom's laughter as he comes in from work, hanging his grey coat on the brass hook and sweeping her into a kiss, every night, the same. Although the parlor was already furnished, Mary Agnes did what she could to make it feel homier. The coal fireplace is cold now, and her decorations—the framed picture of their wedding day, the bits of lace she saved up, a single brass candlestick—are packed.

She lingers in the kitchen—*I spent most of my waking hours here, sometimes with little more than pennies and love*. She runs her hands over the backs of the two chairs scooted up to the table where she and Tom ate each night, the dining table too large for just two. *Memories.*

As she goes upstairs, Mary Agnes fingers the banister, its whorled woodwork soft beneath her fingers. At the bedroom door, she stops, surprised how emotional she feels. The wallpaper in the bedroom she loves, a green and cream stripe. When she couldn't sleep at night for all the worrying, she would count the stripes on the near wall, the counting alone blurring the burning fear of Tom's illness and the thrumming in her head, *I cannot be a widow. Not yet.* She remembers many grieving widows at wakes in Dawrosbeg. Most of them were aged, although some of them were younger, with children. But none were under eighteen, none.

Mary Agnes hears Tom coughing in the entry. She hurries downstairs and takes his arm as they stand in the parlor one last time. It looks smaller and shabbier than when they first arrived, but maybe they didn't notice then, being newlyweds with other things on their minds.

"We've been happy here," Tom says. "Except for—"

"Except for nothing. I will always remember this place, my love. Our first home."

Helen waves to Mary Agnes, and shouts, "Hurry, we don't want to be late for the train."

"Come now, Tom," Mary Agnes says.

Tom walks out the front door without looking back and uses the iron rail for balance. Mary Agnes lingers in the doorway for just a second more, *one one-thousand, two one-thousand, three one-thousand*, like she's done so many times before in so many situations to stave off leaving, leaving, leaving—*Am I leaving again?*—before she pulls the door closed behind her.

23

May 1890
Aboard the Chicago, Rock Island and
Pacific Railway from Chicago to Colorado

The whistle wakes her with a start. Mary Agnes glances out the smudged window to see acres of flat prairie spool out toward the horizon. It will be twenty-some hours before they reach Colorado Springs, her neck already kinked. Juddering to a halt at a short platform, the train's brakes squeal. Mary Agnes squints to read the sign: *Centerville*. Rifling through her satchel, she pulls out the schedule for the Great Rock Island Route and runs her finger down the timetable. Within the hour, they'll cross the Iowa-Missouri line.

Tom stirs and Mary Agnes pats his leg. "Did you sleep? A wink?"

Tom smiles, his eyes still closed. "Not a wink, but rested, all the same."

At Altamount, the train takes on coal and water, a half-hour's stop. Passengers debark in search of coffee or to stretch their legs. After a hasty cup of coffee in the depot's cramped café, Mary Agnes and Tom walk the length of the platform twice before Tom's coughing stops them. He reaches for a hanky and covers his mouth. The bleeding hasn't stopped.

"All aboard!" the new conductor barks. Mary Agnes takes Tom's elbow and sweeps up her traveling skirt with her other hand as they make their way to their coach, a "solid vestibule" car with plush maroon velvet seats, heavily polished paneled walls, and its own water closet. Oil lamps suspend from the ceiling down the center of the railcar and afford good light. Heavy, brocaded drapes with thick tassels frame large picture windows adorned with intricate molding. Small reading lamps affixed to the wall above each row of seats emit a soft glow.

Within minutes, Tom's eyes close again. If she could read on a train, she'd have several days to settle in with her very own copy of Henry James's *The Bostonians*, bought before they left Chicago. She won't have to read it in bits and pieces like when she was at the Rutherford's. She's up to the part where Verena moves in with Olive, and wonders at Olive's intentions. *Does Olive have designs on the girl? Or are her motives laudatory?* Mary Agnes doubts that. It's Henry James, after all.

Mary Agnes clasps the book in her lap, rubbing the rich green leather cover. *Oh, does it ever feel grand to have a few dollars to our name*, she thinks, thanks to Tom's father who, because of Tom's condition, gifted his son his inheritance early. All at once, she regrets her initial glee at the bequest. *What did Tom's father know? That Tom isn't long for this world?*

Mary Agnes's stomach heaves. It would anyway if she reads underway, so she leans back in the reclining seat and watches as *Winston, Clarks, Cameron, Lathrop, Holt, Liberty* pass by in a blur, every mile further away from Chicago and everything they know.

The train *clacks* along, Kansas City next with a full hour's stop. Almost halfway. Colorado Springs will loom larger with every mile after this.

Will Colorado Springs live up to its reputation? Cure for the invalid? New lease on life? Please, Mary Agnes entreats Mary and all the saints for the hundredth—or is it the thousandth—time? *Tom cannot die.*

JUST BEFORE THE SUN RISES ON THE second day, Tom and Mary Agnes change trains in Limon just shy of Denver to take the spur line to Colorado Springs. Tom nods off but Mary Agnes stays wide awake. As they pass through Mattison and Ramah, Calhan and Peyton, she sighs. *Only two more stops* according to her now-worn schedule: *Falcon. Roswell.* She puts her head to the glass and watches as the eastern slope of the Rocky Mountains comes clearer into view. They are by now a mile higher than sea level and she feels she could reach out beyond the glass to touch the mountains. What they called mountains in County Galway are mere hills compared to these.

She peruses a brochure she picked up in Limon when they changed trains.

COLORADO SPRINGS, COLO.
THE CITY OF SUNSHINE

IS THE IDEAL ALL-THE-YEAR-ROUND
HEALTH AND PLEASURE RESORT

This unique City of Sunshine, nestled at the threshold of the Rocky Mountains, has the international reputation of being one of the greatest health and pleasure resorts in the world.
Why?

Mary Agnes looks at Tom, dozing beside her. Yes, why? She wants it proved now. Prayers alone are not guaranteeing Tom's return to health. It's up to Colorado Springs now.

> The atmosphere is absolutely aseptic and free from all germ life.
> Epidemics of such diseases as Scarlet Fever, Diptheria, Typhoid, etc. are unknown.
> There have been more permanent recoveries from Pulmonary complaints than in any other climate in the world.

She scans the rest of the brochure, amazed by the benefits touted by the Chamber of Commerce.

> All the year round one may indulge in such sports as golf (two courses), polo, cricket, tennis, hunt clubs, and riding.

Tom can't walk more than twenty steps, she thinks. *I don't think he'll be riding or playing at any games . . .*
The next line catches her eye, in bold print and all capital letters:

THE AVERAGE DAYS OF SUNSHINE IN A YEAR ARE 310.

"That will be a wonder," she says aloud.
Tom stirs. "What's that, Mary A.? What's a wonder? Other than you."
"Always the rogue." She bats at him good-naturedly. "Look," she says as she waves the brochure, "Colorado Springs has sunshine *every* day. Or nearly every day." She thinks back to the cottage in Dawrosbeg. *Did it ever stop raining there?*

"Let me see," Tom says. He skims the brochure. "I feel better already."

At 7:20 a.m., the Halligans step off the train at their destination, forty-eight hours and more than a thousand miles behind them. It has been eighty-eight whistle stops since Chicago. Their belongings fit in two bags, Mary Agnes's satchel and a battered suitcase of Tom's; in their pockets, $485 of the $500 they began their journey with.

When the train pulls out of Colorado Springs, they breathe in brisk mountain air, puckeringly dry. A gnawing in Mary Agnes's stomach reminds her they haven't yet had breakfast. She thought she'd never be hungry again after last night's meal in the sumptuous dining car: Pork loin with roasted potatoes, julienned carrots, and applesauce, and finished off with coffee and chocolate torte. But, fickle is life, and she's hungry again.

She touches Tom's arm. "Shall we hire a rig?"

"Let's walk."

"Is it wise?"

Tom consults a ticket agent.

"Nevada and St. Vrain?" the agent says. "A short walk, unless—"

"We could use a walk," Tom says matter-of-factly. "If it's not too far, as you say."

The ticket agent points northeast from the station and tips his hat to Mary Agnes. His mouth is set in a fine line as he nods to her. Mary Agnes wonders how many people have come through this station, exactly like Tom. *And how many never leave to go home again, wherever it is they come from?* She pulls her hat down low on her brow to avoid intense sun. Her skirt, crinkled after two days on the train, falls to her ankles. She can't wait to settle into their new lodgings and draw a bath.

"Come now," she says to Tom, flashing a winning smile. *I have to be strong for him. For me.* They walk up East Platte two blocks in bright sunshine to North Nevada and stand at the corner for Tom to catch his breath. There they turn north two more blocks until they reach a handsome boardinghouse on the corner of Nevada and St. Vrain. "We'd be here," Mary Agnes says. A freshly painted sign hangs above the door: *Colorado Springs Inn*. She raps on the door.

A tall, buxom woman with long, light-colored hair swept up into a bun answers the door. She wears a blue dress and an apron. "Ah, you must be the Chicagoans. I'm Tilly VanRy, owner. Come in, come in." She opens the screen door. "Here, put your bags down. You haven't eaten, no? You must be starving, come, come." She leads the way through a large parlor to a kitchen in the rear of the house. "Sit, sit. We are like family here," she says, the "w" sounding like a "v".

Several minutes later, Tilly serves up two plates heaped with thick bread, butter and jam, and a cup of coffee each. As Mary Agnes and Tom eat, Tilly finishes with washing up.

"Come now," the landlady says, when both Mary Agnes and Tom have drained their cups. "Your rooms are ready. Six dollars per week, paid in advance." She hefts their bags and leads up the carpeted stairs. *So strong she is*, Mary Agnes thinks, *she could carry four bags or more, and I'm grateful for the help*. She doesn't want to embarrass Tom trying to lug bags up the stairs himself, which he would do, ever the gentleman despite his infirmity.

At the second-floor landing, Tilly points two doors down to the left. "The washroom is at the end of the hall," she says. "You'll share with Mr. French"—she motions to the first door to the left—"and the Smith sisters."

A stout, well-dressed gentleman of about forty or forty-five opens the first door. "What have we here? The Chicagoans? I'm from Chicago myself, via—"

Tom sticks out his hand. "Tom Halligan." He nods to Mary Agnes. "And my wife, Mrs. Halligan."

"A pleasure, Mrs. Halligan." The man bows and holds her gaze longer than fitting upon a first meeting. His accent is clearly German, not French.

The door at the far end of the hall on the right opens a crack.

"There will be time to make your acquaintances at dinner, Miss Smith." Tilly turns to Tom and Mary Agnes. "Breakfast at seven, dinner at twelve sharp, supper at six, except on Sundays. That's my evening off. But for now, it looks as if you two are in need of a bath and a rest. Would you excuse us, Mr. French, Miss Smith?"

Tilly opens the door to their lodgings and steps inside. Their "rooms" are one room, separated by a folding screen between the "bedroom" and the "sitting room" by the window. The yellow and cream striped wallpapered room is furnished with a bedstead, bedside tables and lamps, a small writing desk, and a large heavy wooden armoire on the far wall. Beyond the screen, two comfortable red damask chairs face a bay window with a view of the Rocky Mountains. Other than a small looking glass next to the armoire, there is no other artwork in the room. Not even a crucifix. Except for the time she worked at the Rutherford house, never has Mary Agnes slept in a bed without a crucifix hanging above it. Not in Ireland or New York or Chicago.

"It's lovely," Mary Agnes says. "Isn't it, Tom?" *Where to find a crucifix? In Colorado Springs?*

Tom coughs into his hanky and quickly puts it back in his trouser pocket. Mary Agnes hopes the landlady hasn't noticed. She extracts six dollars from her purse and hands it to Tilly.

Tilly hauls the bags into the room. "Please to excuse Mr. French. He is a meddler, *always* in your business. As for the misses Smith, they keep to themselves. *Ve haff* another boarder across the hall, a teacher at the normal school. You *von't* meet her until supper, along *vit* the others. But here I am, going on and on and you needing to settle in. Until dinner, then." She turns to leave.

"Thank you, Mrs. VanRy."

Tilly laughs. "Just Tilly."

Mary Agnes closes the door. Thoughts flood her mind, and she tries to still them. She must be strong for Tom's sake, that's what Helen said. She hugs Tom and lingers in the embrace. Then she takes his hand as they dance a few steps around the small room. She looks up at the face she has grown to love more than any other.

"Welcome home, my love." She pronounces "love" like Seamus Bourke instructed her, not like a girl from a Connemara farm but like a girl from America, no hint of brogue. She knows this is not home, just a stopping off place, but home, nonetheless, while it lasts. Will she ever have a home of her own? One that she lives in for more than a few months at a stretch? She's not past dreaming of it, the way the curtains will hang just so. And a bed-sized quilt. A kitchen filled with crockery and glassware. And out the back kitchen door, a riot of flowers . . .

Early June 1890
Colorado Springs, Colorado

Colorado Springs is gorged with color, heritage plants brought across the plains wrapped in petticoats or newspapers as settlers opened the West: Fragrant violet lilacs; brilliant orange Oriental poppies; ruffled German iris dense with purple, white, and yellow blossoms; and multi-layered peonies in pinks and crimsons and soft whites. The mercury tops eighty by day and dips no lower than fifty at night.

Mary Agnes is glad she packed a white dress, all the women in Colorado Springs wear white in June. She adjusts her straw hat and follows a map as she gets to know the city, laid out in a neat grid bounded by North Cascade to the west, North Wasatch to the east, San Rafael to the north by the new college, and East Fountain to the south. Most of the businesses, butchers and grocers, milliners and druggists, are found on North Tejon and North Nevada between East Pike's Peak and East Bijou.

"What makes Colorado Springs different from Denver?" Mary Agnes asks the newsagent when she picks up her newspaper.

"You can thank General William Palmer for that."

"And he is?"

"Far-sighted," the newsagent says. "Creating a family town, schools, hospitals, churches."

Not my church, she thinks. Colorado Springs is bursting with churches: First United Methodist Church, Presbyterian, Congregational, Episcopalian, even a group of Quakers—but no home for her. She walked the streets up and down not thinking that a city of any size would not have a Catholic church. But no, although there are plans for one in the next year. In the meantime, Mary Agnes cannot bring herself to attend services at any other house of worship, it would be close to blasphemy. At least, grossly irreverent.

"Near ten thousand souls here now," the newsagent says. "Good for business!"

"Until next week," Mary Agnes says. "I'll be back for next week's edition."

Dear Helen—

Life at a boardinghouse is never dull!

We have settled into a routine here at The Colorado Springs Inn (never assume to use the washroom at 6 a.m. when the schoolteacher gets up or at any time between 2 and 4 p.m. when the misses Smith bathe. I will tell you more about the misses Smith later in this letter).

Our neighbor on the second floor, Mr. French—who isn't French at all, but German as it turns out—speaks three languages: German, English, Dutch, having grown up in New Guinea with his missionary parents, a reference he works into every conversation. Tilly, our landlady, and Miss Huizenga (she's the schoolteacher) converse almost exclusively in Dutch, with Mr. French joining in, particularly when Tilly's brother Pieter visits for Sunday dinner. He works at a ranch not far from here, as handsome as they come, although I shouldn't comment on that now, should I? The sisters Smith, both short and stocky, turn up their noses as soon as any of the other boarders begin to speak in any language other than English and raise their voices to an ear-splitting level, talking ceaselessly about gardens they visited while in Coventry.

"That again?!" Tom whispers to me every time they bring up Coventry. "I've never been there," he says, "but I feel as I have been. Many times over!"

"'The roses!'" I always mimic, holding my hand out as if I'm smelling a rose.

"Don't mind if I do," he always says, as he plucks the imaginary rose from the air and offers it to me. You should hear him, Helen! Ever since my lessons with my tutor, I have tried consciously to tame my brogue, unless it serves me. But it's hopeless with Tom, you could cut his brogue with a kitchen knife and have knifefuls left to spare.

Have I mentioned how noisy it is at mealtime? And who can forget to mention the portly college instructor who lives on the first floor, who isn't hesitant to correct anyone on, well, anything? He sits in the parlor reading in the evenings, so it is impossible to avoid him or his comments after supper. I am plumb worn out with talking most days. You, however, would probably talk them all under the table!

Tom and I have our own secret code and take turns covering our mouths as we listen to the circus around us. We often laugh late into the night mimicking the others. Once, the professor banged on the ceiling with his cane when we were laughing too loud, which just set us to laughing even more.

It is beautiful here, Helen. I walk every day in the clear mountain air. You must visit us sometime as we aim to stay here. Tom is doing as well as can be expected.

Send my regards to Aunt Margaret.

Until next week,
Mary A.

P.S. Any gentleman callers?????

P.P.S. Please send a crucifix. I have enclosed one dollar to cover cost and postage.

"I'VE COME FOR MORE POWDERS," Mary Agnes says to the druggist one hot late June afternoon. Even with the fine mountain air, hearty food at Tilly's, and a daily consti-tutional around Acacia Place, Tom is losing weight. His breath, tight and ragged, keeps him up at night, which means Mary Agnes tosses and turns most of the night. Not that she says anything, she doesn't. She wishes she could afford different powders, ones to cover dark circles under her eyes.

"Roger's Tonic Powders, please, Mr. Walker," she says to the druggist. "I do believe they're helping." She counts out twenty-five cents and hands the coins to Walker. Anything to help Tom ease into sleep and sleep soundly. Mary Agnes doesn't know if she believes the powders are helping or if she just wants to believe it.

"Have you tried Ardle's Potion yet?" Mr. Walker says, holding up a blue and yellow box. "Can't keep it in stock, said to be even more potent than Roger's."

"How much for Ardle's?"

"Another twenty-five cents. You can mix the two. Your husband will sleep soundly, mark my words."

Armed with two packages, and minus fifty cents, Mary Agnes puts her hopes in the unknown. Anything will be better than hearing Tom gasping for breath at night.

She gazes at the shop windows at Hibbard's Department Store and stops for a cold lemonade at Pickford's Fountain before she walks the three short blocks home. She's grown fond of lemonade here in Colorado Springs and makes it a habit to stop at the fountain when she's out on errands. It's five cents of bliss, the way the ice-cold lemonade slides down her parched throat.

As she sits on a high leather stool at the counter, she assesses herself in the large mirror behind. She looks hale and fit. *Unlike Tom.* He is sleeping in past breakfast most mornings now and she doesn't have the heart to wake him after he finally succumbs to sleep. *I never thought it would be like this.* The last few days he hasn't been hungry at supper either. That leaves just one meal a day, *at least it's the main meal*, which Mary Agnes makes sure he finishes. She coaxes him with her eyes and touches his arm to goad him along. Bite by bite. He can't live on sleeping potions alone.

A lazy fan rotates overhead from the embossed tin ceiling, its *whirr* like a kitten's purr. Mary Agnes remembers Tom the Cat from the Rutherford's. Blocking out any recollections of Doria, she thinks how far she's come since that first day as a housemaid. In the past few years, she's learned to keep house and cook. And have even more of a mind of her own—*if that could be possible*, she laughs—and the confidence to say it aloud.

Mary Agnes checks her pocket watch. She cannot linger. When Tilly sprained her ankle in the kitchen yesterday, Mary Agnes offered to bake two pies for today's supper as a favor to Tilly. It's the least she can do. As long as Tom doesn't need her.

When Mary Agnes returns to the boardinghouse, a package is waiting for her. She checks the return address: Chicago. *The crucifix!* She opens the wrapping and holds the cross tight to her chest as she mounts the stairs to their room. Pushing the door ajar, she sees Tom is still asleep, so she leaves the crucifix on the bedside table and tiptoes from their room back down to the kitchen.

Supper tonight will be cold slices of roast, boiled potatoes, and cranberry aspic. And pie. She borrows one of Tilly's aprons and takes to cutting rhubarb, their entrails falling into a pail. She deftly slices the firm fruit, places it in a deep bowl, and coats the fruit with a tablespoon of flour and a cup of sugar. She tosses it together until the rhubarb is covered with the crumbly mixture and sets to making crusts. Her gram's secret was to double the pie crust recipe to make it thick and add a quarter cup of fresh cream to the rhubarb mix before baking, if cream could be found. Cream is plentiful in Colorado Springs, so Mary Agnes sets a quarter cup out on the counter to reach room temperature.

Mary Agnes hums while she works, songs her granddad used to sing, although she's heard you're hexed if you sing a sea shanty off the water. *Well, there's no salt water for a thousand miles, so I don't think I'm in any danger of hexing.*

She opens the lip of the oven door to slide the pies in to bake. While she waits—*pies don't bake themselves*, like Cook used to say—she tidies up the kitchen, singing now, this one, one of her granddad's favorites, *Whiskey in the Jar*. She wipes her forehead with her sleeve and laughs to herself. *I've just gotten the crucifix and I'm singing about whiskey.*

She sets the tables in the dining room, careful to follow Tilly's example (the Dutch are very precise, she has learned). By now, the pies are out to cool.

Will Tom eat any of it?

She nicks a piece of crust and licks her fingers before getting to the rest of supper. Pulling her now long-again auburn hair high on her head, she secures it in a knot. She realizes for the first time in a long time, *I'm not hungry!* She wonders if Tommy is still hungry, or any of her other brothers. *Have they come to America yet? Will I know? Sean is sure to find me.*

Later that night, Mary Agnes shakes her husband awake. *Is he breathing?* His nighttime breathing is always heavily labored, but just now, she thought he stopped breathing at all.

"I'm fine, Mary A."

Mary Agnes begs to differ, but she holds her tongue. "Roll over, then." She reaches for a glass of water and hands it to Tom. His hand trembles.

"You're my angel." He offers a weak smile.

How I love this man. "A good helpmate, maybe."

"Not maybe. I couldn't take my eyes off you when you first walked into St. Mel's." He coughs deeply, bringing up red sputum.

"Enough of that now. It was me not being able to take my eyes off you. I almost had to go to confession right then and there."

216 | THE IRISH GIRL

"We're quite the pair."

"That we are."

Mary Agnes rubs Tom's shoulder and traces a three-inch gash there. She has never asked about it before. But if time is getting scarce, she needs to know everything about him before it's too late to ask.

"How—?"

"Silly, really. I was climbing an old oak in the yard and fell. My shoulder grazed the fence."

"How old were you?"

"Seven, maybe eight. You say you were fishing by then."

"Aye, I was." Her eyes well up. *Granda. Gram.*

Tom touches Mary Agnes's shoulder.

"Ah . . ." she says. "Like we were saying. Best looking couple in all of Chicago."

"Or Colorado Springs," he says. "Or anywhere."

"Don't go getting your pride so swelled up you'd be lying," she laughs. "I'll settle for Colorado Springs."

"I'm thinking we should stay here, Mary A."

"Do you?"

"And, when the time comes . . ."

Mary Agnes bristles, a chill up her back. "That's a conversation for when we're seventy or eighty, Tom. Not today."

No, not today, she thinks. *Or tomorrow. Or—please Jesus Mary and Joseph—not anytime soon. I'm not even eighteen, much too young to be a widow.*

Late June 1890
Colorado Springs, Colorado

"It must be the powders. I'm thinking we could take a trip to Manitou Springs." Tom is dressed, sitting in one of the red armchairs by the window.

Mary Agnes walks to the chair and puts her hands on his shoulders. She feels the outline of his collarbone, so thin he's become she wonders if he'll break. "You're up for a trip? That far?"

"It's just a short ride on the trolley. Let's see what all the fuss is about."

The day could not be more perfect—bright blue skies, no clouds, and a balmy seventy degrees. Mary Agnes and Tom board the trolley downtown and travel west through Colorado City toward the spa town at the foot of Pike's Peak, and they're not the only ones who thought today ideal for an outing. There's hardly a seat open on the train. Mary Agnes scoots closer to Tom to allow another passenger to sit. By the time they reach the outskirts of Manitou Springs, it's standing room only and Mary Agnes is doubly glad Tom got a seat.

"Let me catch my breath," he says, after walking the first block. They find a bench and sit, facing away from the sun. When Tom says he's ready, they stroll past several natural mineral springs, marveling at the wonder of nature.

Tom's breathing is taut, as if he can't get enough air.

"Shall we sit again?" Mary Agnes asks.

Tom points to a large hotel a block away. "As good a place as any."

Slowly, Mary Agnes holding Tom's elbow and stopping every few steps, they wend their way up Cañon Avenue toward The Cliff House. A resplendent structure it is, the hotel's wide covered porch offering shade and refreshment, with sturdy tables and chairs lined against decorated railing. Up the spacious stairs they go, one step at a time, Mary Agnes patient with Tom as his breathing labors. They sit at a table for two overlooking the expansive lawn, the town, the mountains beyond. A waiter, replete in black trousers, crisp white shirt, and black tie, hands them oversized menus. On the list, pickled eggs, toast points, and champagne.

"Why not?" Tom says.

"But the cost . . ."

"Why not celebrate this beautiful day. This beautiful place. My beautiful wife."

Not a worthless Irish bogger! Damn you, Doria, for trying to take away that one thing I believed about myself, that I am worthy just as I am.

"Mary A.?"

"Oh, forgive me, Tom. My mind was wandering. It's nothing." Mary Agnes looks out over Manitou Springs toward the looming mountains. "How ever did we land in such a beautiful place?" But then she remembers why and doesn't say anything more.

Two champagne flutes arrive at their table and Mary Agnes takes a sip, bubbles tingling as they slide down her throat. "I do believe I might have champagne every day." They linger on the porch, watching other couples come and go. *If only we could be like other couples with a whole life ahead of us . . .*

But Mary Agnes knows better. Tom's eyes close and she watches him as he dozes. She has memorized every feature of his face, the sharp nose, the trim eyebrows, the cleft chin. She loves to touch him there.

When he rouses, he excuses himself to use the facilities and settle the bill.

"Shall we take a stroll?" he asks.

Mary Agnes thinks it best to head back before he tires himself out. But she sees that familiar spark in his eyes and can't deny him this moment of happiness. "Are you sure you're up to it?"

He nods. So instead of making a triangle loop back to the trolley, they walk up Ruxton Street, slowly, slowly, sitting twice on benches to watch other spa goers and Saturday visitors. When Tom is ready again, they walk again.

Is that . . . ? Mary Agnes's heart bounces. She squints to read the sign: *Our Lady of Perpetual Help.*

"At last!" Mary Agnes says. *This has to be a sign, a Catholic church.*

Tom is perspiring heavily as they enter the small church, hushed in contrast to the general ruckus outside. Genuflecting at the front pew, Mary Agnes sinks to her knees and focuses on the crucifix, surrounded by the familiar smell of incense. She doesn't forget she promised to follow Jesus when she was thirteen. She begins with the Apostles Creed and the Our Father and then begins, *Hail Mary, full of grace . . .* She then prays earnestly for Tom. That he will improve. Have strength. Be healed, *please Mary, Mother of God.* She's lost in prayer until Tom's coughing ratchets up and she thinks it best to head back from Manitou Springs to Colorado Springs.

On Monday, Mary Agnes buys more powders. There is a dance next weekend at The Antlers and she is itching to go, even if she and Tom have to sit on the edge of the dance floor and watch. Anything to make their lives seem ordinary, even just once a week. The flyer promised a cure. She is waiting. And he made it to Manitou Springs and back, although he was bedridden the next day. *With almost a full week's rest, and a double dose of powders—the Roger's and the Ardle's—is it possible he can rouse himself to go out again?*

By the next Saturday morning, Tom goes down for both breakfast and dinner. Mary Agnes holds her breath as they mount the stairs for his afternoon nap. Before he lies down, he takes the coffee can from its place in the armoire and hands it to Mary Agnes. "A dollar apiece for admission and another dollar for refreshments."

"You are up to it?"

"Wouldn't miss it. And I know how much you want to go."

They skip supper and dress after careful loving. Mary Agnes wears the red and cream dress that Tom loves, the one she wore for her birthday. Tom wears trousers, vest, and shirt and dons his bowler. "Don't you look the picture. Ready, Mrs. Halligan?"

"I am always ready."

"Another thing I love about you."

The Antlers is filled with music as they enter the ballroom at half past eight. The room is vast, its high cream walls soaring to the tin ceiling. Chandeliers in the shape of antlers cast warm light throughout the ballroom. Chairs and tables line the sides of the room to make way for the wide, parqueted dance floor. In the far corner, a large bar is set up, a long line already formed.

"Have you ever seen so many people squeezed into one room?" Tom asks.

"I don't believe I have." Then Mary Agnes remembers

Castle Garden, but she doesn't mention it. It seems a long time ago. And far away.

Tom and Mary Agnes garner a small circular table near the refreshments, two tables back from the dance floor. Mary Agnes spies Tilly's brother Pieter and Mr. French across the hall. She and Tom listen and watch as dancers take to the floor, dancing to August Junker's *I Was Dreaming* and *Star of the East* and then to the lovely *Passing By*. Mary Agnes taps her foot. "I love that one. Edward Purcell."

"Go ahead, dance with Pieter," Tom says, motioning to the other side of the hall. "I don't have the stamina. But I'd love to watch you."

"Are you sure?" Her eyes dart around the hall. *I would love to dance.*

"Of course, I'm sure. Fella doesn't have a date and you're a keen dancer. He would never impose by asking you. And it would save him from talking another minute to that intolerable Mr. French. It would make me happy, Mary A."

"I will then, if it makes you happy. And to save him from Mr. French."

Mary Agnes crosses the floor in between songs. "Care to dance?" she asks Pieter. She ignores Mr. French.

Pieter colors. "It's my honor," he says. "You look lovely tonight."

"Oh, posh. I'm the one who loves dancing. You're doing me the favor."

"In that case, Mrs. Halligan . . ." He leads her toward the crowded dance floor.

"Please call me Mary Agnes. Or Mary A."

"I don't think it's proper, using your first name." He glances at Tom.

"How about Irish, then?" she says. She thinks of Jimmy Scanlon and hopes he's found his way in Boston.

"Well then, Irish. Let's dance, shall we? And please, call me Dutch, everyone does. Except Tilly. She insists on calling me Pieter. I hate it."

"Yes, let's, Dutch."

Mary Agnes accepts Dutch's hand as they move out into the throng of dancers. She throws a wave over her shoulder at Tom. He nods, smiles, then coughs into a handkerchief.

"How did you learn to dance like this?" Dutch asks. "You're so light on your feet. Like dancing with a feather."

A tap on Dutch's shoulder indicates Mr. French is cutting in.

"May I?" he asks.

Mary Agnes looks at Dutch and he lowers his hands, resigning the dance to their acquaintance from the boardinghouse.

Mr. French holds Mary Agnes a little too tightly as they finish the dance. "You are absolutely *herrlich*," he whispers with a thick German accent. "Ravishing."

Flushed, Mary Agnes returns to the table.

"You dance like an angel," Tom says. "And you look like one, too."

Mary Agnes waves her hand in the air. "If I get any more compliments tonight, my feet aren't going to touch the floor."

He coughs violently. "I do believe I'll have to be going now."

"I'll get my wrap."

"I wish you'd stay. Dance some more."

"I couldn't."

"Let me have a word with Pieter." He motions for Dutch across the hall. The two confer, and it's settled. Mary Agnes will stay.

"But—" Mary Agnes says.

"But nothing," Tom answers. "You deserve a fun night out and here I go ruining it."

She walks him to the door. "Are you sure?"

"As sure as anything, as you like to say. Enjoy the evening, the dancing, all of it. I'll be fine."

At eleven o'clock, the band winds down with a slow waltz. Dutch takes Mary Agnes's hand and they take to the dance floor until the lights dim and the emcee thanks everyone for coming. She's glad Mr. French didn't cut in this time.

Once outside, Mary Agnes refuses Mr. French's offer of an arm and instead takes Dutch's arm as they walk the four short blocks back to the boardinghouse. There is something about Mr. French that raises her hackles. She can't quite put her finger on it, but she trusts her gut.

August 1890
Colorado Springs, Colorado

"Here, love, have another glass of milk." Mary Agnes hands Tom a tall glass. "The sisters say it's the best thing for you."

Tom sits in a reclining chair at St. Francis Hospital, third in a long line of men who sit along the open-windowed west wall facing the sun.

Mary Agnes knew it was inevitable, from the first day. She had hoped against hope, but when Tom awoke one morning covered with blood, they both knew. He would have to go to the sanitarium.

In addition to other tubercular patients, the wards are filled with injured railroad workers from the Midland; Denver and Rio Grande; Atchison, Topeka, and Santa Fe; and Chicago-Rock Island lines.

"So many accidents," Sister Mary Hermana confided to Mary Agnes when Tom was admitted. "And so many more with the great white plague."

"Do you think—"

"I do not think, Mrs. Halligan. I do. That is my calling."

"What I mean to ask is, do patients ever recover? From consumption?"

"There is always the possibility of a miracle. In the meantime, I have written to the diocese in Indiana for more help. We are only five of us here now."

Today, Tom is dressed in the same trousers, shirt, and vest he wore to The Antlers, with his bowler in his lap. His white cot sits across the wide walkway, made with crisp white sheets and two folded grey blankets at the foot of the bed.

Mary Agnes wipes his forehead. "You're so cold."

He shakes his head and shivers. "Am I?"

She takes one of the blankets from the end of Tom's cot and drapes it over his shoulders. "Better?"

He smiles wanly. "Everything's better when you're in the room. The sisters can't leave me alone. Milk at six. Sponge bath at seven. Raw eggs and rare beef at eight. And more milk at nine. I can't wait for you to get here." He checks his watch. "And we have exactly how long?"

"Ten minutes. But I'll be back tonight."

"It's a long walk up the hill for a ten-minute visit."

"Never too long to see you." She kisses his forehead.

That evening, Tom is already dozing in his cot when she arrives. It is only 6:45 p.m., a full three-quarters of an hour before lights out. She sits by his bed and waits for him to stir.

A young nun walks the length of the walkway carrying a tray of milk glasses. She stops at his cot. "Mr. Halligan!"

"Again?" he asks, opening his eyes.

She smiles. "It is time," she says in a thick German accent as she hands him the tall glass.

"Thank you, Sister—"

Mary Agnes has not seen this young nun before. *It is sure to be Mary, though, like Sister Mary Notberga, Sister Mary Kunigunda, Sister Mary Silveria . . .*

"Mary Roberta, ma'am."

Ma'am? We are likely the same age.

"From Indiana?" Mary Agnes asks. "Like the others?"

"Yes, from St. Francis of Perpetual Adoration. And from Germany before that."

Mary Agnes nods her thanks. She thinks of what Helen said, that Germans are taking over Chicago. *They are in charge here,* she thinks, and she is glad of it.

Tom takes a sip and shivers again. "How is Tilly? Pieter? The rest of—?"

"They send their best."

"Tell them I'll be back before you know it." He starts a bout of coughing.

Mary Agnes knows there will be no "before you know it." Tom has wasted away to bone and skin, cheeks gaunt and ribs showing. He coughs incessantly, and his handkerchief is bloodied. He must know it, too. Soon he will have to move to one of the ranch tents on the outskirts of the property. Marriage is a long lane with no turning, her Gram used to say. *We're at a sharp turn here,* she thinks. *Is it the last?*

"I—" Mary Agnes falters.

"Shush now, Mary A." He finishes the milk and hands her the glass. "There's something we need to discuss . . ."

"Please, don't, Tom."

"I'd like to be buried here, in Colorado Springs."

Mary Agnes looks down. This is not the conversation she wants to be having, not now, not ever. She is only yet seventeen. "Not Chicago?"

"No," he says, waving his arm toward the west, Pike's Peak in full view at sunset. "I want to have a view like this for eternity."

Eternity. The verse that springs to mind, drilled into her since her catechism: *And this is the promise that he hath promised us, even eternal life.* What does Mary Agnes know about eternity, other than it is forever? *How unfair! We will never have a proper home or family or long life together, not in this world anyway.* It is hard not to begrudge it, in a long list of things to begrudge.

After Tom nods off again, Mary Agnes tucks the blanket around him and scurries down the hill at dusk. She walks north on North Wasatch toward the boardinghouse, it's faster this way. Back at Tilly's, she fits her key in the front door lock and closes the door softly behind her. Thank goodness the verbose university professor has retired for the night. She is not in any mood for conversation and she wants to get a letter off to Helen in tomorrow's post.

When she reaches her door on the second floor, she sees a shadow. Mr. French is at once beside her, his breath thick with beer.

"How is *Mrs. Halligan* tonight?"

Mary Agnes bristles. "Well, thank you." She fumbles with her key. *Please please please.*

"Here, allow me," Mr. French says. He wrests the key from Mary Agnes.

"I'm obliged, Mr. French." *Hail Mary, full of grace, the Lord is with thee.* He opens the door and she hurries in, pushing it closed behind her and breathing a sigh of deep relief. *Blessed art thou amongst women—*

Mr. French circles her waist from behind.

"How?!" *Was his foot wedged on the threshold?* "Please, Mr. French." She tries to pull away. *Please, Jesus Mary and Joseph.*

"Please, you say? I am happy to oblige *you.*" He pushes Mary Agnes against the now-closed door.

"Mr. French!" She raises her voice.

"Shh, *der leibling.*" He bends to kiss her. "You must be very lonely, a beautiful woman on her own."

Mary Agnes raises her hand and slaps Mr. French on the cheek. This only heightens his ardor. She feels him harden against her.

"I will scream if you don't leave this instant." She stamps on his foot with her boot.

"Little hussy." He pulls off his tie and in a swift movement circles her head with it, gagging her. She tries to scream but it is muffled. No one will hear at this hour. The Smith sisters retire just after supper and Miss Huizenga is gone for the school holiday. She kicks at his shins and beats at his arms.

"I haven't come to hurt you, *der leibling.* I just want to gaze upon you. You have bewitched me since you first arrived. Since you do not return my intentions, I will not force myself upon you."

Thank you, Jesus Mary and Joseph. Mary Agnes lets out a deep breath.

"I only ask you to undress."

Mary Agnes pales and doesn't move.

"If you will not do so yourself, I am happy to assist you."

Mary Agnes realizes in a swift moment she has two choices, fight and be hurt—or worse, maybe strangled—or give in and only be shamed. No one needs to know. She can do this. *As long as he doesn't touch me.* She fingers the top button on her blouse.

"Go on."

With fingers trembling, she slowly unbuttons her blouse and lets it slip to the floor. *Forgive me, Father.*

"Ah, that's a good girl." Mr. French pulls up a chair and sits. He crosses his legs and strokes his moustache.

She hesitates before unbuttoning her chemise. Soon she will be naked in front of a man she loathes. *Can't he see enough?* Her face is warm and she fights back tears. *It can't be as bad as the night with Fiach*, she tells herself. *At least, he won't touch me.*

He motions for her to remove the chemise.

Mary Agnes removes the garment and quickly covers her breasts with her arms. *What would Tom think? He would bash Mr. French's head in with a hammer, if he could.*

Mr. French rises from the chair.

She snarls through the gag as he reaches for her. "No," she seethes.

"I am only going to look."

"Then sit." Mary Agnes waits until he is back in the chair and lowers her arms. Her nipples harden in the night air.

"Ah, lovely." He nods his head. "Take down your hair."

This, too? She reaches above her head and removes her hair pins. Long auburn hair falls over her shoulders and breasts. She thinks to untie the gag and scream now but then it would bring attention to her nakedness. That she cannot do.

He sighs. "And now the skirt."

Mary Agnes hesitates, but when he rises from the chair again, she fends him off with arms in front of her. "I will do it," she says. "Sit." Her eyes are like darts. She loosens the skirt and it puddles to the floor. She is now in only stockings and boots, her neck, torso, and dark pubic hair completely exposed.

Mr. French smiles and rocks back in forth in the chair, his hand at his crotch.

To her horror, Mary Agnes realizes he is pleasuring himself. He doesn't take his eyes from her, but she refuses to meet his gaze, focusing on the window beyond instead.

Time is suspended, then, as if she is not really in the room, she is somewhere else, anywhere else, away from Mr. French. Her mind rattles off a prayer she learned in catechism: *Remember, O most gracious Virgin Mary, that never was it known that anyone who fled to thy protection, implored thy help, or sought thy intercession was left unaided . . .*

In less than a minute, Mr. French groans, sits back, and yawns, his hands stretched high above his head.

Mary Agnes exhales and glares at the man sitting in front of her, his trousers damp.

He smirks. "That, *der leibling*, is what I have dreamed about these many nights when you were next door with that invalid husband of yours."

How dare he! Mary Agnes inches away from Mr. French, her rumpled skirt still puddled at her feet. She unties the gag and spits on the floor. "You will never come to my rooms again," she says. "Or I will make your life very difficult."

"I got what I was after," he says. He is now standing. He brushes against her, his breath sour. "I will see you now every night in my dreams."

She pushes him away, grabs her robe from a hook next to the door, and covers herself. "Get out."

October 1890
Colorado Springs, Colorado

Blood. Cough. Diarrhea. Tom has declined so rapidly he is now confined to one of the tent houses reserved for the gravely ill that dot the perimeter of St. Francis's high on the hill overlooking Colorado Springs. Mary Agnes is not allowed inside.

When the doctor said Tom's time was near—*please*, she pleads again, *not yet*—she spent an additional five dollars per week to secure him a place in one of the coveted octagonal canvas-sided huts in addition to the original five dollars per week she had paid for months now for his care and a never-ending supply of milk, eggs, and beef. He is forced now to drink a gallon of milk per day and swallow twelve raw eggs. He can no longer stomach beef.

Mary Agnes stands by the screened door of Section House F and calls Tom's name. She has not told Tom about her encounter with Mr. French. It would upset him, and he has hardly the energy to breathe. Nor has she told Tilly or anyone else, although she avoids Mr. French, daggers for eyes when she cannot dodge him.

"That you, Mary A.?"

"'Tis, Tom." She places her hand on the screen as if by doing so the screen will burn away and she can touch her husband. Ten feet has never seemed so far.

"The stool still out there?"

"Yes." She lowers herself on a three-legged stool beside the door and removes her hat.

"Well, if it isn't the prettiest woman in all Colorado Springs."

"Pah. You probably say that to all the nurses." *Humor is the only way*, she thinks. *The only way I can get through this.*

"I might . . ." He laughs and then begins to cough. He's propped up on a cot to the left side of the hut. A bedside table, washbasin, chest of drawers, stove, and open closet fill out the rest of the room. His reclining invalid's chair has been moved out as he is confined to bed now.

"It wouldn't surprise me."

"I wish it were you bringing me milk, rubbing my shoulders, putting me to bed, though." He drops his hanky on the floor. "Drat." He stretches one arm off the side of the bed but cannot reach it.

"I could come in."

"You know what the doctor said."

"I don't care what he said." She opens the screen door and closes it softly behind her. "No one will know."

She scoops up the hanky, throws it in the hamper, and opens the top dresser drawer. "Here." She hands Tom a fresh hanky and sits on the edge of his bed, taking his weak hand in hers. She bends to kiss his cheek.

"This is not what I had in mind," he says. He looks past Mary Agnes toward the screen door. "I pictured a houseful of youngsters and Sunday dinners and—"

"Today is not a day for words," she says. She lowers herself into Tom's thin arms and rests her head on his sunken chest. His heart beats hollowly, and slow.

One by one people leave, *or die*, she thinks, all of Ireland it seems, until there is no one left except the few, the stubborn, the ill, the poor, always the poor. Those left behind feel the absence of those gone on ahead, wherever it is they are going. And now she fears she must let the dearest to her go.

Dear Helen,

It is with great sadness that I tell you Tom has passed on.

Mary Agnes stops and lowers her head to the writing desk. She tries to imagine the scene, but no matter how many times she envisions it, she knows she'll never really know. She wasn't there. The nuns told her Tom just stopped breathing—no warning, no struggle. By the time Sister Mary Hermana called for Last Rites, he was gone. Because of tuberculosis, his body had to be cremated immediately.

I held onto hope that he would be cured. I had to, didn't I? That is why we came to Colorado Springs. But his luck didn't hold now, did it? All I do is cry, day and night. I cannot eat or think. To add to my grief, I haven't his body. They cremated him, Helen. Cremated him! I didn't even get to say goodbye! All I have left is one picture and my ring. I feel I am held together by bones alone.

Mary A.

The day bruises from blue to black. Mary Agnes sits in Tom's chair late into the night, devoid of feeling, yet filled with grief, if such a thing is possible, to be empty and full at the same time.

ON SATURDAY, MARY AGNES DRAGS herself out to pick up *The Weekly Gazette*. She hasn't been to dinner all week; Tilly knocks and leaves her a covered dish outside her door just before noon each day. The first day there was a small rose, the last of the season, and a note in Tilly's neat hand: "To cheer you on this dark day."

The air has a tinge of fall in it as Mary Agnes nods to the newsagent. She is dressed in black. He declines payment as if he knows, here is another widow. She carries the paper like deadweight from the newsagent's shop back to her room and sits in Tom's red chair in front of the window. She cannot bring herself to open the paper yet and wills her mind to think of Tom when they first met, so handsome and solicitous and funny.

Wasn't it he who said, "new beginnings?" Mary Agnes cannot think of life without him beside her. She recited her vows just a scant two years ago, with a lifetime of ahead of them, until death us do part *part part part*.

She picks up the paper and scans the first page. "Railroad Wrecks" is the lead headline, a litany of rail accidents this past week in Missouri and Alabama and Illinois. Ohio and New York. And then pages of politics, strikes, investigations. *Where is it?* Pages four, five, six, seven. Words, words, and more words. *No Tom.* She wants him to be everywhere, on the train, drinking champagne at the hotel, here in the chair next to her, not in a death notice.

And there, finally, on page eight, squeezed between an advertisement for Perkins and Holbrook and another for

Bijou Jewelers: *Notice of Death*, a whole life whittled down to fifty-eight words:

> Thomas J. Halligan died Monday at St. Francis Hospital after a lengthy illness. Born February 24, 1867 in County Monaghan, Ireland, Halligan's family settled in Peoria, Illinois. He worked as a dispatcher for Chicago-Rock Island Railway. He is survived by his wife, Mary Agnes (nee Coyne) of Colorado Springs, and his parents and brothers, all of Peoria.

Mary Agnes cannot contain her tears and sits, the paper open on her lap, until the sun is long past the day. She fills the hours with every memory she has of Tom, right up until the end. "See you tomorrow, my love" was the last thing he said to her, but she knows now that will never happen. Near midnight, she folds the newspaper and goes to bed without changing. Nothing will be the same ever again.

There being no church in town to offer a Mass of the dead, *at least no church I'll set foot in*, Mary Agnes veils herself in black and takes the trolley to Manitou Springs on Monday to attend weekday Mass at Our Lady of Perpetual Help. She dissolves into the Mass and offers a prayer for the repose of Tom's soul. The language is comforting, and Jesus is here. He is always here. *And Mary, Blessed Mother, you are always with me.* Long after Mass is over she sits, as close to the church of her ancestors as she will ever be in Colorado, until she risks missing the last trolley back.

She returns to the boardinghouse long after supper and swipes a biscuit and an apple from the pantry before stealing up to her room. She is in no mood to encounter the Smith sisters or Mr. French. Especially Mr. French.

Taking the coffee can from its place on the shelf inside the armoire, she does what she's dreaded to do these last few weeks: Count out their—*my*—dwindling savings. Bills and coins fall onto the coverlet, far fewer than the bankroll they arrived with. Placing the treasury notes in order, fifties, twenties, tens, fives, twos, and ones (she doesn't bother with the hill of change), she counts out $149.

Her board is twenty-four dollars a month, meals included. If she doesn't spend a penny more, she can stay here for almost half a year. But she knows that's unrealistic. She and Tom were spending ten dollars a month on other expenses, medicines and clothing and newspapers and dances, even before he went to St. Francis. Even without the medicines, that would cut her time in Colorado Springs to far less than half a year.

A pang hits her midsection. *I have only enough then for a couple of months. November, December . . . and in this climate I will need a new winter coat. Ten more dollars!* With these calculations, she has three months of funds left, at the outside. That brings her to January, and she'll need train fare to go back to . . . *to where?*

Mary Agnes stuffs the bills and coins back into the coffee can, slicing her thumb on the rim. She stanches blood with her other sleeve and holds it there until the blood subsides. *And now I'll have to launder the bedding.* She crumples over, holds her torso, rocks. *Tom. Tom. Tom.*

"I'M NEEDING HELP IN THE KITCHEN," Tilly says after supper the next week. "Would you consider it? Everyone loves your pies." It sounds like, *Vood* you consider it?

"Are you a mind reader?"

"No, *vie?*"

"I haven't enough to stay much longer, Tilly. I'm going to have to work, here or somewhere. Maybe The Antlers?"

Tilly whistles. "I can't pay *vages* like The Antlers, but I can slice your rent in half."

"That buys me time." *What will I do without Tom?*

"Have you decided . . ."

"No. Tom wanted to be buried here. And now there won't even be a burial. I don't know as I can leave him, though, even if he is not here." *They cremated him, Helen*, she had written. *Cremated him!*

Tilly tosses the dish rag into the sink and puts her arm around Mary Agnes.

"The *vay* I see it," she begins, "you have two choices. You can wallow in your grief or continue to live. It is up to you to decide."

"But I have just lost my husband!'"

"*Ja, ja,* you have every right to be angry. Sad. But it doesn't change anything, Mary A. Tom is gone now. And you have the choice."

For the next six months, Mary Agnes works herself to the bone, *Tom is gone, Tom is gone,* to the point that Tilly must remind her to eat. She is now down to one hundred ten pounds and has had to take her skirt in twice. It is a painful reminder to wear black every day. She misses every little aspect of Tom, his smile, his hand on her elbow, his tender lovemaking. She has no energy for anything, to write Helen, to take a walk. She avoids Mr. French at every turn, and stares blankly at him when he calls her name or winks while she serves up dinner.

She is tempted to tell Tilly about her horrid encounter with Mr. French, but she knows Tilly needs the room and board now that the Smith sisters have found alternate lodging, their rooms empty for several months now with no new boarders. One couple did inquire about rooms just yesterday but left in a hurry when a mouse scampered across the parlor floor just as Tilly was about to take them upstairs.

Helen has written Mary Agnes, though, more than once. The last letter is open on Mary Agnes's dresser. The last paragraph gnaws at her.

Now that I am graduating from bookkeeping school, I am thinking of moving out on my own to one of the new boarding houses for young women here in the city. Think of the freedom! Shopping and dances and stepping out with young men. How can I persuade you to come back to Chicago? Please?

Should I go back to Chicago? Mary Agnes puts the thought out of her mind for now. It is too soon to be making any decisions, her husband just deceased. She longs to have a gravesite to visit, but there is no headstone. Regardless, she walks the long tree-lined rows at Evergreen Cemetery every Saturday afternoon in any and all weather, reading headstones and wondering why no one else is there today talking to their loved ones. *Because it's raining, you ninny.* The next Saturday, she finds a stately oak at the far end of the grounds and sits under its canopy. There, she talks freely to Tom, what she has been doing and thinking and feeling that week. Under that tree, she feels closer to him than anywhere else, for he is here—or should be here—among the dead. One might think she would spiral deeper into sadness doing this—a reminder that he was cremated—but the opposite is true. She knows his spirit is with her, around her in some intangible way. That keeps her to rights.

She starts, shyly at first, to look forward to small things then, lemonade on a hot day, napping, Sunday dinners. Sunday dinners are the highlight of the week, especially when Tilly's brother Dutch comes down from the ranch where he works. Mary Agnes has taken to sitting with Tilly and Dutch on Sundays, any excuse to avoid Mr. French, especially now that the Smith sisters have gone.

"Tell me about ranch life," Mary Agnes asks one particularly warm spring day in May when Dutch has come for Sunday dinner. She is wading into conversation, one sentence at a time. It is a long penance, to grieve the dead. She wonders if she will ever laugh again or love again. But joining in with the living is a start. Only a few more months and she will be able to shed her black, and next spring, she can wear white again, sing again.

"What is it I don't do!" he laughs.

"It must be heaven to have the mountains and grasslands and creeks as companions," she continues, "and no one to answer to."

"Except Henry."

"Henry?"

"Henry Hansen, the ranch owner. Best in the district."

"And you're not partial?"

"I'm not. Talk to anyone on the ridge."

"The ridge?"

"There's a divide between here and Denver. We call it the ridge."

"Tell me more."

"Depending on where you stand," Dutch continues, "you can look north or south or west or east and not see anything made by man. No houses, fences, barns. The grass grows tall away from the creeks. Mighty cold, the creeks, even on the hottest summer day. You can sit there, surrounded by aspens and willows to escape the heat. The cattle do, don't let anyone tell you they're not smart. There's always wind, though. Sometimes I think it's alive."

"Hmmm." She closes her eyes. It helps to picture serene scenes, the plains, the mountains, the streams, anything to get the image of Tom wasting away far from her consciousness, *my husband, dead at twenty-three.* Today, she concentrates on the scene Dutch is painting with words.

After a half minute, Mary Agnes opens her eyes and looks to Dutch. "All that land, the creeks, the wind even. I can picture it. Thank you."

"We're getting to our busy season. Cattle drives upping. Won't be by for dinner for a while, maybe not until the fall." He turns to his sister. "And I'll miss your cooking, Tilly. It's *niet goed* at the ranch."

The next week, Dutch isn't there. When she helps Tilly with washing up, Mary Agnes realizes she misses his company. The following week, Dutch shows up for dinner. She is surprised and happy and a bit giddy. The dinner conversation intrigues her, life at the ranch. *And he is so alive.*

"Do you have a moment?" Dutch asks after dinner, pulling Mary Agnes aside. He steers her to the back porch, where they stand along the porch rail in the mid-afternoon sun, another gorgeous day in Colorado Springs. She is aware of his presence, and that they are alone. She hasn't stood this close to any man since Tom died.

"We're needing help on the ranch," Dutch says. "Our cook up and left and we're in a bit of a pickle, with me cooking. It was bad enough before, but now it won't be long before I've poisoned everyone."

Mary Agnes laughs. *Did I just laugh?* "I couldn't. What would Tilly do? She depends on me here."

"I talked it over with Tilly before I approached you, Mrs. Halligan. She agrees. We can double your wages at the ranch. But there will be more responsibility."

"How far . . . and please, call me Irish."

"Just over the rise, ten or twelve miles. Don't worry, you'd have lodgings at the ranch house and we'll come for dinner Sundays here to Tilly's when we can get away. At least every other week in the fall and winter and spring.

Can't guarantee summers, though. That's our busiest time."

Tilly swings the porch door open, drying her hands on her apron. "You'd be a fool not to take Pieter up on this offer," she says. "There isn't a finer rancher in all the area than Henry Hansen, and my brother here can watch out for you. I can do just fine on my own. And we'll see you on Sundays. You can help me with washing up. And maybe bring a pie."

Mr. French pokes his head out the back door. "I can't help overhearing. I wonder if I might have a word with Mrs. Halligan. I have an offer for her as well . . ."

Never. Mary Agnes's skin crawls with invisible ants as she makes a snap decision. It might be too soon to make a change, but, as Tom would say, new beginnings.

"Yes, Dutch. Give me a few minutes and I'll have my things ready. Tilly, would you mind coming upstairs to help me pack?"

28

May 1891
Larkspur, Colorado

Mary Agnes runs her fingers over knobby white aspen bark as she walks through budding bluestem toward the creek bottom. It's certainly not summer yet here. She's been at Double H Ranch for two weeks now, settled into duties and an empty bed. She still wears black, seven months now since Tom has passed. She gets teary most nights, but never lets anyone else see. Nothing she can do will bring Tom back.

It's the first day she's been out alone with Clara, a gorgeous mare, Henry Hansen's gift to her when she arrived at the ranch.

"You'll be needing a mare," he said when he handed her the reins the first day.

"A mare? I'm afraid I don't ride."

Henry laughed. "We'll remedy that in no time. I'll have Dutch teach you. He's the best horseman I have. But I must warn you, we don't have a sidesaddle."

That night, she snips one of her older black skirts and refashions it into a split skirt, keeping the extra fabric for rags.

The next afternoon, after completing Henry's list of duties, and not without a tremble in her stomach, Mary Agnes walks to the barn for her first lesson. The split skirt rubs her thighs.

"A first time for everything," Dutch says as he opens a stall where a medium-sized sorrel munches hay. "You need to learn together. How to handle each other."

Mary Agnes enters the stall tentatively, nervous but excited. The mare, much bigger than her granddad's donkey, looks at her with soft eyes, her copper-reddish mane framing a beautiful face.

"Go on, touch her neck, gently," Dutch says. "That's good. Now pat her, say a few words."

"Hello, girl."

Dutch grabs a halter. He gently tacks the horse: Halter, saddle, bridle, girth, explaining how each is used.

"You lead her," Dutch says. "I'll be right here beside you."

With her stomach a-flux, Mary Agnes walks the mare from the barn, talking to her with every step.

Once in the ring, Dutch takes the reins. He places a mounting block to Clara's left and pats her. The horse stands still. Mary Agnes steps up on the mounting block and gathers the reins with her left hand.

"Not too tight," Dutch says.

He takes her right hand and places it farther back on the seat.

"Ready?"

She nods.

"Bend your left leg and put it in the stirrup," he says. "I'll hold you under your knee and help you up and over with my other hand."

Mary Agnes's hands shake.

"You'll be fine," he says. "On my three."

She bounces, and on the count of "three," Dutch lifts Mary Agnes's left leg and guides her right leg over. She is now astride the mare. The seat is deep and secure, made for a man. She fits her boots firmly in right stirrup and rearranges her split skirt, legs now against a leather fender.

"Alright?" he asks.

"I think so."

"Easy as you go," he says. "Soft hands on the reins. I'll lead you around the ring now. Try to keep your body straight and heels down."

"Heels down?"

"Like this." He grasps her ankle and moves her heel lower than her toes. He moves his hand up her leg to her calves.

She feels a stretch there.

"Good, very good, Irish. Now take the reins and pull gently."

Mary Agnes squeezes her legs against the mare's flanks and Clara moves quicker than she anticipates.

"Whoa, girl." Dutch looks up at Mary Agnes. "Keep your legs quiet," he says. "When you squeeze her flanks, that's a signal for her to quicken her pace." Again, he puts his hand on her leg. It is warm and large and comforting.

"There's so much to learn." Mary Agnes is overwhelmed with the smell of the mare, her inexperience riding, Dutch.

"Soon, it will be second nature to you. Take it slow and easy."

The first lesson makes way for the second and third and fourth, and, *more a credit to Clara than me*, Mary Agnes thinks, she is trotting, Dutch watching from the edge of the ring.

Two weeks later, Dutch suggests an evening ride.

"Out of the ring?"

"Like I say, there's a first time for everything."

They ride for a half hour toward the western edge of Henry's property, the vast, open landscape covered with low grasses. Mary Agnes follows Dutch at an unhurried pace, clucking and talking to Clara as they climb a low knoll and dip into a verdant valley. She trusts Clara but is glad Dutch is nearby. Pronghorn antelope dash across the valley beyond, their white rumps bounding. Overhead, a red-tailed hawk, its hoarse, piercing *kee-kee-arrrr* a warning to rabbits and rodents. The sun is not yet set, but the sky takes on its evening dress: *orange pink purple* above the Rocky Mountains.

When they reach the western boundary, Dutch pulls his horse to a halt and waits for Mary Agnes to come alongside.

"You're a right horsewoman now."

"You're too kind."

"I'll follow you back," he says. "If you're as good as I think you are, you'll be able to take Clara out on your own from now on."

Today, out on her own, Mary Agnes rides through rolling, grassy hillocks bathed in every shade of green. She clucks as she guides Clara through rock outcroppings that line the foothills of the Front Range. A lazy creek meanders through hills and swales, taking its own time. Cattle graze along aspen-lined creek bottoms, sheltered from the sun. Keeping her distance from the cattle—"Be slow and gentle around them," Dutch says—Mary Agnes dismounts, removes her hat, and pegs Clara to a tree. She wipes her forehead with a kerchief and sits under a clutch of aspens, her back against bark and skirt pulled up to her knees, tracing the sun as it filters through branches and fluttering leaves. She's aware of all her senses, the warm breeze, the trill of birdcall—*a finch?*—and the strong, earthy scent of the ground beneath her. If there is another place as beautiful as this, it can only be at Dawrosbeg, she thinks. A sharp pang hits her midsection. They've come more regularly now, the pangs, every time she thinks of something she wishes to ask Tom but there's no Tom to ask. What did his home look like in Monaghan? Landlocked northwest of Dublin? She cannot imagine not growing up near salt water. If she lived in Monaghan, she thinks, she would burst across county boundaries and run for the shore. But here she is, nowhere near the sea, and too far to run.

Maybe she will stay in Colorado, like Tom had wished, tend for Henry Hansen, cook for cowhands, sell pies to neighbors. Or maybe she will return to Chicago, to Helen and family. Or maybe she will go home to Ireland. *But what is home if no one you love is there?*

A sickly greenish-yellow cloud covers the sun. *Is this one of those tornadoes Dutch told me about? That can touch down anytime here in higher altitudes?* "If you see what looks like an elephant trunk dangling from beneath the clouds," he said, "it's time to be up and moving."

How long has she been resting here? Three-quarters of an hour? More? Weather comes on fast here on the eastern slope of the Rocky Mountains, and it behooves her to turn back now. The slightest downspout confirms her decision. If she's learned anything since living in Colorado, it's that the weather is always one step ahead.

"Come now," Mary Agnes says to the mare, coaxing her away from her spot under a tree. "We best be back now." Clara whinnies, as if she knows, too.

Instead of riding—she doesn't want the mare spooked by a tornado, she's spooked enough herself—Mary Agnes walks two miles back to the ranch, just beating rain. As she comes around the corner of the barn, Clara in tow, she almost bumps into Dutch. He stands well over six feet tall with wide shoulders, as if he could carry an ox. His worn farm clothes need washing, but he is adamant about doing his own laundry. His blond bangs hang low on his face, in desperate need of a haircut. Maybe she can offer to give him one soon.

"Here, let me," he says, and takes the mare's reins. A jet-black cat brushes against his leg. "Shoo!" he says, but the cat doesn't budge. "Mind of her own," he says.

"What do you call her? Snowball?"

He laughs. "Mind of your own, too, I see. Midnight's her name."

Mary Agnes removes her hat and swipes at her face with her kerchief. A ring of sweat circles her underarms and drips of perspiration run down her cheeks. She is in need of a sponge bath.

"Not exactly ready for a dance," he says.

She tries not to smile, but it escapes her. "Not today."

"We had a grand time that night at The Antlers."

Mary Agnes bites the inside of her lip. "That was the last night we"—she checks herself here before she continues. "What I mean to say is that is the last night Tom and I went out." But it isn't Tom she's thinking about at this moment. She can still feel Dutch's large hands circling her waist as they danced and how strong his arms felt around her. How she misses a man she could love.

Dutch lowers his head. "I'm right sorry for bringing it up." He clears his throat. "See the bulls?"

"Did. Under the aspens by the creek."

"They should be alright there. I'll ride out in the morning."

Mary Agnes looks at the threatening clouds, ready to burst. "If we're not under water by then."

"Henry's gone to Denver overnight, told me to tell you. Cattleman's meeting."

"Well, that lightens my load."

"A night off."

"Off? I've got to have a bite myself. Supper'll be on within the hour. Come in at seven. We'll eat in the kitchen."

Dutch tips his hat and dips into the barn with her mare. Mary Agnes opens the kitchen door and hears the familiar squeak. She goes down the dark hallway to her room and splashes water on her face and underarms, changes her shirtwaist, and scrubs her hands. The crucifix is mounted above her bed. She had asked for a hammer and nail. With evening coming on fast, she lights the oil lamp in the kitchen and sets out to fix supper.

Henry's list of duties for Mary Agnes (written out in his spidery hand and still tacked to the kitchen wall, as if she might forget): Meals, housekeeping, laundry, chickens. *Oh yes! The chickens!* She asked Henry for permission to have a small kitchen garden, and he agreed, so for the last few days, she's been digging and tilling a garden plot not far from the kitchen door. In it, she'll plant lettuces and carrots and onions and herbs. The next time she's in Colorado Springs, she'll get seeds and seedlings to plant.

It suits her, the ranch life. There's no civic club or general store or grange or school nearby, so she doesn't need to dress for town, although she misses attending Mass, as sparsely as she did in Manitou Springs. There is finally going to be a church erected in the next year in Colorado Springs itself, St. Mary's, downtown on Kiowa, but it's too far for her to attend regularly. Dutch says a traveling priest comes once every couple of months to Larkspur to offer Mass to neighboring Catholics. She will mark her calendar and save up her sins.

Tonight, there's leftover stew and biscuits so all she needs to do is get coffee on and whip up an applesauce cake with preserves she found in the cupboard. Mary Agnes hums as she works and wonders why Henry, kind, soft-spoken, never assuming, never found a wife. But she dares not ask. His clothes—trousers, shirts, vests—are always clean and pressed, the mark of a man who is used to keeping house for himself, long past sixty years of age by now.

And tidy, she thinks, not just generally, but down to kitchen shelves and pantry. *And probably his dresser drawers, not that I'll ever have a look.* As she prepares supper, she can't help but think that maybe Henry had a sweetheart once who broke his heart, and that is why he is still unmarried. Or was it he who broke her heart?

When the cake is in the oven, she takes the batter-crusted spoon and curtsies to it.

"I'd be delighted," she says. She licks the wooden spoon, clasps it to her chest, and waltzes around the kitchen by herself, humming one of the popular tunes she heard that night at The Antlers.

A knock startles her. "Come in, come in," she says. Her face is flushed. "You caught me—"

"I know. I saw."

After supper, eaten mostly in silence, only interrupted with shy glances, first from Dutch and then from her, she clears the dishes away. Something has changed between them, it's palpable. *You need to learn together. How to handle each other, he said. Did he mean me and the mare? Or me and him?*

The thought excites her. But she's at once confused by her feelings. Her husband of two years is dead. She hopes for a long life—and maybe someone to love again—but this is too soon. She will have to temper her desire, it's not appropriate.

When Dutch gets up to leave, she motions for him to stay. *I will think of him like a brother*, she thinks. *That will serve.* "Five more minutes. You're needing a haircut." With that, she retrieves sharp shears and ties one of her aprons around his neck.

Dutch looks up. "Have you done this before?"

"And is the sky blue? I have six brothers." She flexes her hands to keep them from shaking. "Sit still now."

He looks straight ahead as she lops off several inches of thick blond hair.

What is he thinking?

Aware of his smell—a mixture of hay and sweat and something else she can't put her finger on—she clucks and fusses to fill the silence, the kitchen clock the only other sound. She has not been this close to him except when they shared that one dance a year ago, and he was shined up that night.

What am I thinking? I was married then. And not thinking the thoughts I'm thinking now.

Mary Agnes tries to clear her head, but all she can think of is running her hands through Dutch's mussed hair. *And then down his chest. And then . . .* She snaps back and finishes clipping his blond sideburns. *A brother, a brother, I must think of him only as a brother.* She stands back then and hands him a looking glass. Their fingers brush.

"Fine job," he says, and gets up to leave. "'Til the morning then."

Mary Agnes finishes the washing up and turns down the lamp. The room seems so empty. She undresses in the dark, pulls down the covers, and slips in between the sheets. Her mind races—his hands, his smile, his hair, his . . .

She tries to still her mind, first reciting the Hail Mary three times and then going through the alphabet A to Z, praying for Helen and her aunt, her brothers and the repose of Tom's soul. She hums a shanty. Starts a poem. But Dutch is there, luring in her mind. *It's no use,* she thinks, and pictures his rough fingers touching hers, the deep, weathered lines around his eyes, that sunburnt smile to light up a room. And his laugh.

What is it that Tilly said? You can wallow in your grief or continue to live. It is up to you to decide.

She runs her fingers around her nipples and then tentatively down her thin torso until she reaches the dark mass of hair between her thighs. With a deep breath, and a prayer of forgiveness, she takes her hand to herself in the dim moonlit room. It is not the first time since Tom has been gone that she has done this, and it will not be the last. If she's saving her sins up, she may as well have a long list when that traveling priest arrives.

29

June 1891
Larkspur, Colorado

The trail stretches long and flat in front of them, rutted and dry. The mules' hooves pound dirt as Mary Agnes steers the chuckwagon toward the far reaches of Double H Ranch. After the morning fog lifts, the sky opens in pure golds and oranges tinged with red. It's not long past dawn and there's a slight chill.

Dutch rides ahead in a cloud of dust, his long brown riding coat flapping behind. He wears heavy canvas pants and a flannel shirt, a dirty cattleman's hat and boots, and a red plaid kerchief at his neck. A long gun hangs in a scabbard affixed to his saddle. His cow horse trots at a good pace, its head high.

Mary Agnes wears a black day dress, shawl, and boots as she sits on the buckboard of the chuckwagon, clucking at the mules. Her hat is two townships wide and keeps the relentless sun from browning her already freckled face. Soon, *by eleven maybe?* she will not need the shawl. She clicks her tongue to keep the mules moving. Dust billows around her and she covers her mouth with a kerchief.

She readjusts her bottom on the hard seat and takes in the view. How is it that she landed in this seat? Fortune? Misfortune? She is thousands of miles from home without a husband and pinch-penny poor. Why is it her brothers could choose to be a village schoolteacher or go into the priesthood? It was Mrs. Kerrigan's greatest joy back in Dawrosmore that her Michael followed the call to the priesthood. Father Kerrigan went to Sligo at first, home for a week come summers. For days after his visits, all the boys would talk of going into the priesthood, until they started fishing again or going around to the pub or stepping out with local girls. Then it was a subject lost to reason until the next summer came around.

Boys have all the choices, she thinks. *They can join the bar, go to sea. Be a shopkeeper. Run a farm.* Mary Agnes doesn't have these options. But she does know how to cook. And men are always hungry.

The chuckwagon brims with cookware, foodstuffs, medicines, water, and everything Mary Agnes can think of that might be needed on the trail: Knives, matches, coils of rope, a long gun. And plenty of ammunition. One cannot be too careful on a ranch.

A drive is due to Double H tonight at the halfway point of the old Goodnight-Loving Trail. These days, drives end at Larkspur, where cowmen load trail-weary cattle onto the rails headed for Denver after a few days of fattening, them and the cattle.

To the south, through a gash in the hills, Pike's Peak—Sun Mountain, the Utes call it—juts into the thin Colorado air, rising more than fourteen-thousand feet to pierce the clouds. She squints through smudged eyeglasses and wonders if she'll ever see a peak as high. The hills around Dawrosbeg—Bengoora and Benbaun and the others she thought as a child were the tallest mountains in the world—are dwarves compared to Sun Mountain.

One of the mules stumbles and Mary Agnes loosens her rein. "There, now, Betty." Betty's ears flare back, as if she's embarrassed. "Walk on, now. You too, Bill." The other mule wheezes, his brand of answering.

As she sets up the chuckwagon, a dizzily fast humming-bird nosedives to attract a mate. From Mexico they come, she's heard. On those tiny wings! The male flutters, dives, arcs again, the *whirr* of its wings beating faster than its heart. She reaches out, not to touch the tiny bird's iridescent wings or bejeweled head, its elongated bill or quivering tail, but to touch something out of reach.

What does this little bird teach us? she thinks. It doesn't take but a second for an answer. *Even though the journey is long, never give up. Never.* She smiles. *It might as well be tattooed on my heart by now. Never give up.*

She tosses together beef stew, cornbread, and dried apple cake, and puts coffee on to boil. There is never enough coffee for ranch hands. She'll have her share of compliments tonight, too. Not only because the cowhands have reached their destination, many weeks into the drive. Or that they'll enjoy a home cooked meal. Yes, that. She also knows she's a pretty face, something they haven't seen much of on the trail. She'll take all the compliments, but that's all. Her heart is tender, but she can't let anyone see, least of all a handsome herdsman. She misses Tom in every way, more so in her empty bed. But it's only been eight months now since his spirit left the world. A year in mourning will never be long enough. Or any cowhand more winsome, in every way it can be measured in a woman's heart.

Or am I fooling myself? Am I falling for Dutch?

Every time she passes him, her heart races. At night, she thinks of him. She quietly takes her hand to herself like she does almost every night now. She no longer fools herself. She lusts after Dutch—his hands, his mouth, his body. *But he is not one of us. Not Irish. Not Catholic.* Because he is forbidden, she lusts all the more. She is careful to be quiet; Dutch is sleeping not ten yards away by the fire. *Why did you have to die, Tom? And why can't I be with you, Dutch?*

Stars dot the night sky, constellation to constellation. Mary Agnes remembers Mary Catherine, her bunkmate on the ship carrying them to America, and learning about the zodiac. "Scorpio," she whispers. "Secret bearer."

The second night, hot and dusty and a bit crochety, Mary Agnes makes blanket steak with tomato rice and dumplings, one of Dutch's favorite dishes. He thanks her with his eyes. She nods her thanks back. *Is this how we will communicate from now on? Just nods? As if we don't know what to say to one another? Like strangers?*

After washing up, Mary Agnes climbs under the chuck-wagon and settles on the rough tick pallet, an old quilt covering her. It is darn cold again, the ground seeping dampness. She is tempted tonight to sleep in the cooney, a low-slung hammock under the wagon, but it's filled with supplies. In the middle of the night, she gets up to pass water on the far side of the wagon and sees the glow of the night herder's cigarette thirty yards off. He's getting even less sleep than she is. She wonders where Dutch is. He isn't in his bedroll by the fire. Mary Agnes stays awake for most of the night, wondering, but he never returns. She is uneasy, used to his company and near to panic that he might be gone.

The next day is transport day, a haze of dust and lowing, shouts and whips, as the cowmen prod cattle through the long wooden chute to the loading dock in Greenland on the old Denver and Rio Grande route up to Denver. When the train pulls in, its wheels squeaking, the cattle begin to bellow, a deep keening that rattles Mary Agnes. Like they know. She spends another restless night under the chuck-wagon, her heart fileted like cattle.

On the final morning, the night herder is the first in line, eyes rimmed red. He nods, "Ma'am." She sets the coffee pot down on the table that extends from the rear of the chuckwagon. She hasn't yet pulled out the canvas cover, but today is closing up shop day, so likely she won't bother. The other cowmen have had an extra two hours of sleep today, now that the cattle are gone. Soon they'll be lined up waiting for grub, as if it magically cooks itself.

The sun creeps over the hills as Mary Agnes reaches for a long stick. She stokes the fire under the cast-iron pot and lifts the lid at an angle to avoid dirt and ashes from getting into the hash. Gathering baking supplies from the cupboard, Mary Agnes sets to mix up biscuit dough. The larder is almost bare after three days here on the range, rice and beans gone, lick, too, and flour and sugar short. It's been a blur of men and cattle and horses and dogs. She's still got some air-tights, so today's eggs will be flavored with canned tomatoes. Dried fruit she has abundantly, so she softens apples in water to serve with the biscuits.

"Grub's on!" she yells, as she clangs two Dutch oven lids together, like a cymbal. Slowly, one by one, cowmen line up for breakfast, dirty and unshaven, Whip-O-Will and Old Dan, Brownie and Texas Jack, "a mean sumbitch," Dutch says.

"Move along, Brownie," Texas Jack prods. "You, too, Whip, Dan. Don't care for God or the devil, or any of you." He cuffs Whip on the side of the head.

"Quit it, T.J.," Whip yells. "We've a lady present."

Immediately Janus-faced, Texas Jack tips his hat toward Mary Agnes. He reeks of man sweat and horse sweat and clothes that haven't been washed for a month. "Pardon me for saying, ma'am. But," he continues sweetly, with a wink, "I never said anything about not caring for the ladies."

"Plainly," Mary Agnes says, as she slops hash and bacon and eggs onto his plate. He holds out his plate as if wanting more. She waves her spoon at him. "You got your vittles. Now move along before I cuff *you*."

He arches his eyebrows and dips in a mock bow, the plate still proffered in front of him.

"No one tangles with a skunk, a mean horse, or a cook," she says, as she shoos him away. "Haven't you learned that yet, greenhorn?"

Mary Agnes shakes her head while others stifle laughs. Being called a greenhorn is the deepest cut to any cowman, and Mary Agnes just made her point. Texas Jack slinks away to eat his fill on the far side of the encampment, muttering under his breath.

"See what I mean? Meanest cowboy I've ever encountered," Dutch says, as he grabs a tin plate. He is last in line this morning, but Mary Agnes has saved him a thick slab of bacon.

"I do." The last time she said those words were on the altar at St. Mel's.

I do, Dutch. I do lust after you. I do want to be with you, damn convention.. I do want to run my hands through your hair and down your chest . . .

She hands Dutch coffee. He reaches for the mug and she doesn't let go. She meets his eyes and doesn't let go there, either.

"Thank you, Irish."

After breakfast, the crew readies for the trip south, this year's cattle shipped to market. Cowhands roll up bedding and stuff extra clothes into grain sacks. From the sides of their saddles, they hang lariats and scabbards, and tuck oilskins and bedrolls behind. Mounting, they slide firearms across their laps and tip their hats.

Thank you, ma'am; Best vittles this side of the Rockies; Hope you'll wait for me.

"Pah," she says and waves them off with a laugh. "Don't fall off your saddles, boys."

And then they're off in clouds of red dirt. If they're lucky, they'll make Pueblo by nightfall. Now to washing up and packing up and heading back to the ranch. *With Dutch.*

As Dutch packs up his kit and bedroll, he glances at Mary Agnes. *Is he biting back a smile?* She nods and secures the wagon. There's been no rain for days so the trail should be smooth, and, forgoing any breakdown, they'll be back at Double H before supper. *Home.*

It's not a life she thinks she would have chosen, a young widow alone in Colorado cooking on a chuckwagon, but here she is in God's High Heaven Country, and she bites back a smile herself. *I'm right where I need to be. Where I want to be. Thank you, Mary, for leading me here.*

Mary Agnes offers up a short prayer to the Purple Mary. Then she pipes up. "Dutch!" she yells. "Daylight's burning! Let's get moving on."

AFTER SLEEPING LIKE THE DEAD, Mary Agnes wakes to a stain of dawn bleeding through her window. She dresses in half-dark. In the draughty kitchen, she sets to breakfast. It's not long past dawn now, when the day's spindly fingers reach deep into the kitchen. She primes the wood stove and replaces the coffee pot on one of the two burners. Henry has been up already and made his first pot. She takes another cast iron pot from its hook above the stove and places it on the second, larger, burner to warm. To her left, kitchen implements sit on a small table wedged in the corner; dangling from a shelf above, a sifter, wooden spoons, spatula.

Next to the table, a ceiling-high hutch grazes low, rough-hewn rafters. Where glass fronts once had been, Henry replaced glass with old newspaper to keep dust from settling on dishes and stemware. A pail of clear water sits to the left of the hutch, and above it, Henry's holstered pistol, saw, oilcloth coat, and canvas canteen. His hat is missing from its peg; a signal he's out in the barn already.

Two small chairs and two short wooden benches surround a large table in the middle of the room. She bustles to set the table for three. They only eat breakfast in the kitchen; dinner is always served in the dining room. Henry isn't much for conversation, but he loosens up some nights.

"If that kitchen table could tell stories," Henry says, "it's a good thing no woman lives within fifty miles, pardon me for saying, Mrs. Halligan." Every time he says her name, it digs deeper. If he knew, he wouldn't hurt her intentionally, this she knows. But what else would he call her? Irish, like everyone else? Maybe she will go back to Coyne, her birth name. *But how would Tom feel about that? Or maybe Mary Agnes Laffey*, she thinks. *Gram and Granda's girl.*

Henry and Dutch talk of the seasons of a cowman's work, riding bog and cleaning out water holes in spring, breaking horses and roundup in summer, herding the last of the cattle to market in fall. Winter is for "old hands," Henry says one night when it's long past shut-eye. But the light lingers, so she and Henry and Dutch sit at the table sipping coffee as one tale spins into another.

"There's enough to do, cutting ice, feeding bulls, gathering firewood, riding line," Henry says. "Dutch here is the best there is."

"Don't go puffing up my head," Dutch says. "It's you that taught me. Remember that good-for-nothing, Spike What-Was-His-Name?"

"Don't recall," Henry says. "There've been too many to count. Good-for-nothings, that is."

Dutch slurps coffee and leans back on his chair. "I'll never forget him, though, even if I can't dredge up his surname. We were working up north of Salida and would likely have forded the Big Bend that time of year, the riverbed's wide enough there, less deep and less dangerous to swim the cattle across. But the weather was coming on fast and we had to ford the Arkansas instead, the river angry and little time to get herd across before nightfall, and he says 'Why risk the Ar-Kansas River?'"

Henry snickers.

"With the straightest face I say to him, 'It's Ar-Kan-Saw, you *idioot*. And if we don't ford now, we're going to be up a crick.' And he comes swinging for me, from the saddle, and falls right down, *kerplunk*."

Mary Agnes laughs, picturing the cowhand in the raging river.

"When he finally gets himself up, wet from hat to boots, his horse has taken off across that 'Ar-Kansas' and he's left to ford it himself," Dutch says. "He was none too happy, you might say. All hat and no horse!" He slaps his thigh and laughter fills the room.

Mary Agnes realizes she's happy, for the first time in more than a year or maybe longer. *Count the days, girl,* she thinks, *the days you are happy to bursting.* Because any manner of heartache will mar them, dash them, bury them six feet deep, this she knows.

She wonders if Dutch can read her thoughts like her mother used to do when her mind strayed at church, but then she doesn't care if he can, and almost hopes that he does. *If wishes were horses, beggars would ride*, her gram used to say. She knows what she's thinking. *Is it what he is thinking, too? That we could fall into bed together, today?*

Days turn to weeks and Dutch plies on compliments about her progress with Clara, her new garden, her green apron—"a change from the black," he says. *He notices.*

And food, he always compliments her on food. After

scrambled eggs, hashbrowns with bacon gravy, and pancakes, "Another fine breakfast, Irish." After short ribs, buttermilk biscuits, and dried cranberry pie, "Mmm, I'll have more if you've got more to spare." *Oh, I have plenty to share.*

She daydreams about Dutch all through the day, regardless the task. She could be washing up when she thinks of him coming up behind her and wrapping his large arms around her. Or pegging sheets out on the line, thinking of what Dutch could do to her in bed.

At night, the cooling time, she darns socks, knits neck warmers and mittens, and sews flannel skirts for the long winter ahead. *If I had Dutch in my bed, I wouldn't be so cold.* She tingles then and checks the clock—it won't be long until Henry and Dutch are back from out riding lines.

She spreads fabric on the table, using a pattern for an apron she found in an old ladies' magazine in the parlor. She wonders who left it there. Maybe the last cook. Maybe a woman visitor. She'll never know, but it doesn't matter. She has read it three times, every word, recipes, articles, even the classifieds, one advertising for a cook on another Colorado ranch, up in Golden. She pictures a young woman reading the magazine in New York or Pennsylvania or Ohio and writing back, yes, I'd like to apply, and *waiting waiting waiting* for an answer before riding the rails to this new life. *And how many cooks end up as wives?* she wonders.

With sharp shears, she makes cuts and pins right sides together. Close to the lamplight, she weaves her needle through cotton lawn with even stitches. That makes three new aprons now: The green with small sprigs of dainty flowers that Dutch commented on, a solid blue she sewed together a few nights ago, and, tonight, a red stripe, a bold choice when custom dictates she should still only wear black. She holds the apron up and loops it over her neck.

It falls below her knees. She feels suddenly . . . desirable. Pretty. Young. Wistful. *Am I climbing out of my grief?*

Tying the loops of the apron behind, Mary Agnes cuts off excess fabric on the back ties. This she will use to bind summer flowers that she plans to plant beside the kitchen door, tall off-white hollyhock and fragile blue delphinium and a riot of pink and purple foxglove, if they will survive in this climate. Already, the Copper Queen roses outside the door are beginning to bud. *That Henry thought to plant roses around the house*, she sighs. *Making a house a home. And what about Dutch? Where would he like to call home?*

Mary Agnes checks the clock and peers out the kitchen window. The moon is full —she knows this, it's circled in black on the calendar—so Henry and Dutch will be out riding late tonight. She thinks of them up at the perimeters of the ranch and wonders how long it will be before she can take Clara that far at night, either with Henry or Dutch *or on my own.* Then she thinks of the moon, and how it's shining everywhere she loves—especially Dawrosbeg—and how her granddad said you can count on the moon.

Granda, I miss you.

As she puts her sewing things away, she conjures up scene after scene of her childhood fishing with Festus off Dawrosbeg. The currach. The cold Atlantic. Cod and hake. Frozen hands, frozen feet. But such a happy heart. And so many stories. *So long ago, another life.*

She hangs her new apron by the cookstove for tomorrow, *ah, tomorrow. More cooking and baking and cleaning and gardening. What is that old wives' tale about being a wife? Washing, Ironing, Feeding, Etc.?*

As she walks down the dark hall to her bedroom, her mind wanders brazenly. It's the *etcetera* she's thinking about tonight. *It's not too bold to think about a new life, is it? At only eighteen? Might I be a wife again? To Dutch?*

Mary Agnes undresses in the dark as the moonlight climbs through the window and makes whitish-yellow slits across the wooden floor. She pictures working hard beside a man she loves, pulling weeds and tending horses, riding lines and rescuing cattle, weathering tornados and thunderstorms and snow, and growing through the seasons with him, many meals and aprons—and maybe children—later.

And then her mind explodes with images, more immediate, Dutch coming in after a full day's work and taking her into his arms, the shaft of the full moon the only thing between them as they come together. So real the images are, Mary Agnes can *feel* them, the way their loving would blur out all the stars, every one of them.

August 1891
Larkspur, Colorado

From a thick stand of aspens, Mary Agnes hears a mock-ingbird chitter its *cheh cheh cheh ah-ooo*. Drowsy clouds range high in the expansive Colorado sky, skirting the sun. The rest of the sky is charged with the bluest of blue, the air bone dry. An unexpected late cattle drive arrived the day before yesterday, and she and Dutch are back on the range for the last time this season.

It's a measly bunch, only a dozen cowhands and less-than-market-worthy cattle. The drive had been halted at Raton Pass during a nasty skirmish and had to detour, costing them almost a month. The trail boss is out of sorts, and the cowmen look like they'd rather be anywhere than within spitting distance of him. Mary Agnes has plied her charm—that's when her brogue is the thickest, and she's learned to use it to her advantage, whatever her tutor Seamus Bourke had said.

"And you're doing what, exactly, Irish?" Dutch taps her on the shoulder.

Startled, Mary Agnes turns toward her crew boss. Her heart quickens. She's taken to picturing Dutch in bed next to her. *Stop*, Mary Agnes, she tells herself. *Stop.*

"Same as yesterday, Dutch. Getting to supper." She hefts the blackened pot from its hook and scrapes it onto the stove. In it, beans and pork and the last of the carrots. Flour is low, too. It's a good thing they're nearing the end of the season. Talk is, it's the end of the line for the cattle drives. Barbed wire. Lack of grass. The railroad. But today, there are twelve hungry cowhands due in by nightfall.

Mary Agnes squints. Just yesterday, she misplaced her eyeglasses. "Can't see my way," she said, when she told Dutch.

"Do the best you can," he said.

She stirs the chili and reaches for the cornbread pan. The western sky bleeds red above the mountains, the eastern sky tinged with an echo of it. Beyond the ruddy sky, the weathered grassland, the teeming cities, the black ocean even, she sees a green place, a winding lane flush with wild strawberries. She follows the lane to where it veers left at the Jones's crooked turnstile. It's a familiar sight, and one she returns to often in her daydreams.

It is then she spies the corner of the cottage. Hurrying, her skirt whipping against bare legs, she stops at the edge of the snug house to inhale its stone face, weeping with moss. Even before she rounds the corner, she hears their voices. She knows without a doubt the door is open.

Maybe, she thinks, *the ending will be different this time.*

"Today, Irish?"

Mary Agnes snaps back. Ireland is far, far away and the chili is boiling over.

"Yes, Dutch. Give me ten minutes and you'll think you were sitting at The Empire Grill in Denver."

Dutch pulls his hat over his mop of hair. "It's a date, you and me at The Empire."

Mary Agnes colors and turns her head away. *A date. Can I really love another? After Tom?* She looks at Dutch. *I think I can.*

Dutch clears his throat, dips his head. "I'd better get cleaned up then."

She stirs the chili, then, and burns a finger. She swears, sucks it dry. She recalls the story her granddad told her about the boy who caught the magic salmon and then knew everything, past, present, and future.

Mary Agnes can see the past, and clear enough for the present. But damn if she can't see the future with or without glasses.

After supper, Dutch lights a cigarette and settles back against the wagon on a three-legged stool, long legs splayed in front of him. Mary Agnes sits next to him as the sky bleeds to black.

"I've decided to go to Santa Fe," he says.

Santa Fe? Santa Fe?

Caught off guard, Mary Agnes's pulse races. *Slow down, girl, slow that heart of yours. What does he mean? He's leaving? Leaving?* "D-d-do you have family there?"

"No. I'll be ranching."

"But what about Henry?" It's all she can say.

What about me? is what she thinks.

"Time comes, a man's got to strike out on his own."

Her heart hasn't slowed. She doesn't even know where Santa Fe is on a map or how long it takes to get there. She wants to scream, "When?!" or "Why?!" but asks instead, "Santa Fe?"

Dutch settles back, takes a long drag on his smoke, holds it, and blows out rings. "Don't know where to start, Irish. It's got a grip on me, like a woman."

Like a woman.

"And you'll tell me more?" *Please tell me more. And tell me you're not really leaving.*

"It's hard to put to words. Up Guadalupe from the depot, there's a maze of crooked, narrow streets, two-storey buildings built Spanish style. You can lose yourself there." His hands weave through the air.

"Spanish style?"

"Adobe, tile roofs, wide porches, murals around the plaza. She's mysterious, Santa Fe, filled with all kinds of people—Indians and Mexicanos and Black—people with secrets who've come from somewhere else and chosen Santa Fe to start over with."

Can I start over with you? Mary Agnes longs to say it aloud.

"The air, it's clear and dry, at seven thousand feet," he continues. "And the sunsets, they come quickly, like snuffing a candle." He blows out another waft of smoke. It's as if he's somewhere else, his eyes focused on the horizon. "And then the lip of the moonrise over the Sangre de Cristo Mountains . . ." His hands outspread against the night sky.

Mary Agnes holds her breath, mesmerized, and watches his large hands backlit by the moon.

The moon scrambles higher and higher in the sky and stars begin to speck the night sky, the tail of Scorpius curling around toward Antares and then forking out like fangs.

"It sounds lovely, all of it," Mary Agnes says. *He's thinking of leaving?* "But it's lovely here, too."

Dutch takes a long, last drag on the smoke and then crushes the butt beneath his heel. "Oh, I haven't scratched the surface, Irish."

"Like the food?"

"I thought you'd never ask." He elbows her. "Roasted chiles, barbecued meats, frying bread. You can almost taste it."

They sit in silence.

"I can almost hear it," he says.

"Hear what?" *Coyotes? Dogs? Owls?*

"The bells, the way they peal from the basilica. It's a wild, beautiful tangle of noise, it is, ringing and clashing and full." He turns to look at her. "I'm in love with Santa Fe."

WHEN MARY AGNES WAKES AT DAWN the day after they've returned from the range, she's acutely aware of silence although she can't get last night's conversation out of her mind. *He's really going to Santa Fe?* She pulls up the covers and looks at the ceiling.

What am I to do? Stay here? Go back to Colorado Springs? Chicago? Ireland? Eenie, meenie, miney, moe. Do I list the reasons or just decide? Follow head or heart?

By this time, Henry is usually clattering around the kitchen, getting coffee on. "No one makes coffee better, so why not do it myself?" he had chided her the first morning she arrived. "Not that I can cook like I've heard you can, young lady." She hadn't seen him last night, either, when she and Dutch got back late. His door was closed and she didn't want to disturb him.

She slips on her black day dress and slippers and pads down the hallway. "Henry?"

Henry's bedroom door is ajar and bed empty. He must be out already as she doesn't hear his usual rattling around the kitchen. As she rounds the corner, she grabs her apron from a peg on the wall. Midnight rubs up against her leg.

"What are you doing inside, little one? You know Henry won't stand for that." She reaches down to scratch the cat's jet-black head. It's then she sees Henry slumped at the kitchen table, his mug on its side, coffee dripping from the lip of the table onto the floor drop by drop. The door is ajar.

"Henry!" She calls his name again, but he doesn't answer. She tugs at his shoulder, but he doesn't move. No one needs to tell her he's dead. She's seen more dead bodies than most girls her age—in Ireland, on the ship to America, in Colorado Springs. She races out the open door in the dry morning to Dutch's shed and bangs on the door. "Dutch! You awake?"

Dutch opens the door, hoisting suspenders over his shoulder. He wears a union suit under his trousers, hasn't had time yet to put on a shirt. "What's the fuss?"

He runs a hand through his hair.

"It's Henry. He's left us."

"Left us? What in—" Dutch looks at Mary Agnes. "You mean—?"

She nods.

"I'll be less than a minute."

Mary Agnes peers inside Dutch's shed. She's never been inside. Next to his mussed bed, a bedstand, and on it, a lamp and a framed picture. She can't see whose image appears. A clothes tree holds all his familiar garb: Wool shirts, rough trousers, hat. Less than a minute later, like he said, Dutch flies out the shed door, brushing past her.

In the kitchen, with the cat now underfoot, Mary Agnes and Dutch lift the dead man and carry him back to his bed. The room is, as to be expected, very orderly. Bed, bedstand, dresser. A large armoire and looking glass. A large rocker draped with a fringed ivory shawl. *His mother's? Sister's? Lover's?*

Mary Agnes straightens the sheets and combs Henry's hair back from his face. There's an intimacy with the dead. She would never find herself in Henry's room for any reason, and would never think of touching him, not even a handshake. She steps back and Dutch steadies her. She turns and buries her face in his chest. He waits a moment before encircling her with hairy arms.

"Shhh," he says.

She sobs, all the grief held in since Tom died spilling out in wracking jerks. He holds her there until she pulls away. "I'm sorry, Dutch, I don't know—"

"It's alright, Mary A." He's never used her given name before.

They sit at the foot of Henry's bed. Dutch puts his head in his hands. Small shudders rise from his shoulders.

Is he about to cry, too?

He raises his head after a minute, his eyes red and moist. "Been with Henry since the time I was first shaving."

"Shaving?"

"A long time. Years. He saved my life, you might say."

"We can talk of that over coffee." She rises from the chair.

"Sit down, Irish. It's early yet, no one else will be up for an hour yet. We can stay here with Henry until then. Isn't right to leave the dead alone, at least that's what my *moeder* said. Coffee can wait."

Mary Agnes sits again and Midnight hops onto her lap.

"Here, here," she says, as she strokes the cat's sleek, black fur. Midnight looks up at her, yawns, and curls up, head disappearing into fur near her tail, a perfect circle of black, as if she hasn't slept in years and isn't wasting the chance.

"THERE WERE EIGHT OF US: ME, MATHILDE—that's Tilly—Lena, Dirk, the twins, Atje and Anje, and two others who died, one a boy who died young—*Moeder* felt that was God's will, although I have my own thoughts on that—and another, a girl, who died at birth. Moeder never got over that. She left us a year after she lost the child, God rest her soul, and *Vader* couldn't care for us. Tilly and I tried to step in, but we were poor substitutes for a mother. We were ten and nine at the time."

Dutch rubs his hands together.

"Shall I put coffee on now?" Mary Agnes asks. She rustles Midnight, who issues a huge yawn and then settles back on her lap.

He shakes his head. "Everything can wait." He looks at Henry and pauses the story. He reaches to touch the blanket, his fingers lingering there. Clearing his throat, he continues. "By this time, it was clear our father had found another woman to take Moeder's place. She was the daughter of our neighbors in Ontario, the VanVliets. Tess was her name, a very comely girl. She wasn't more than eighteen, though, and by that time, my father was forty."

Dutch must be thirty-two or thirty-three by now, almost twice my age.

"Did they marry?"

"Less than a month after Moeder died. Tess moved in and it wasn't a week before she said she couldn't care for all of us. But she loved the twins, she said. She could care for them." His face darkens.

"My father was faced with an unenviable choice then— honor his new wife's wishes or she threatened to go back to her family. We all heard the argument; it was hard not to hear in such a *klein huis*. No man should have to make that decision, but he did. That left Tilly, Lena, Dirk, and me, farmed out first to two different families, Lena and Dirk to the local preacher and his wife, who had no children, and Tilly and me to relatives back home."

"The Netherlands?"

"Yes, he sent us off. Tilly got a pat on the shoulder. I got a handshake, although he didn't meet my eye. That is the last time I saw him." Dutch lowers his head into his hands again.

"We lasted there less than year," he says, softly now. "Beaten one too many times. I could take it, but I couldn't bear to see Tilly ill-used. I stole money from our uncle and took Tilly with me. We lived on stale bread and pigeons on the way to Rotterdam and stowed away on a merchant ship to New York. We weren't found out until five days at sea, and the captain was kindly, although I don't know if he would have been if it hadn't been for Tilly. No one dislikes her, as you know. The captain took a shine to her, but to my knowledge, she was not mistreated."

"That's horrid what your father did. And your uncle!" Her face darkens. "I had a beastly time at home myself."

"Which was where?"

"County Galway. But this is not a time to speak of that. They are all dead, too. At least to me. Please, go on."

"This is surely boring you."

"You are most certainly not. Please, go on."

Dutch wrings his hands, right, then left.

She waits, silent as Henry.

He begins again, at first haltingly. "In New York, I went to work as a butcher's assistant. We boarded at a rooming house run by the Dutch Reformed Church. They were severe, but not unkind. Tilly began cooking there, feeding hungry mouths morning, noon, and evening. It broke my heart to see her, maybe twelve she was by this time, with burns on her arms and bloody feet." His face contorts and he presses his eyes. "We couldn't afford boots then." He scuffs his boot on the floor.

"How did you end up in Colorado?"

"Like I said, Henry Hansen saved me."

"In New York?"

"No, I headed west and told Tilly I would send for her. Which I did, several years later. When I got off the train in Colorado Springs, I went straight to a butcher and offered my services. Henry here"—he reaches toward the man on the bed—"was in the shop just at that time. 'A strapping young man like you? I'll best any wages Fred Feigl here can offer.' He winked at me and shook the butcher's hand. 'Came in for the best steak in the state and came away with a new cowhand.' He shook my hand then. 'Got an opening at Double H Ranch, half-a-day's ride north of here, if you're interested.' I said I was, and that afternoon I sat on the wagon seat next to Henry and have been here ever since. But now I've got no reason not to go to Santa Fe before fall."

Mary Agnes's eyes are moist. Dutch stands and offers Mary Agnes a hand. She rises, tentatively, and doesn't let go.

"Here," he says, and envelops her in a hug again.

Oh, how she wants to melt into him, right here, take his hand and lead him to her bed and let him undress her slowly. But it wouldn't be right. She is caught between longing and propriety. After a few awkward seconds, she pulls away. "I'll get coffee on."

31

The Next Week
August 1891
Larkspur, Colorado

*A*t the crest of the hill, the men remove their hats. The weather is dubious today, clouds banked up against the mountains looking to open into a downpour at any moment. There are more than thirty here, neighboring ranch owners and their wives, cowmen, and townsfolk. A delegation from the cattleman's association is here too, from Denver. And Henry's executor.

The Presbyterian minister, who arrived last night from Colorado Springs and slept in Henry's newly tidied room, offers words for Henry's repose. Under her breath, Mary Agnes recites the words from *Exsequiarum Ordo*, the rite of Catholic burial, followed by Psalm 50: *Miserere mei, Deus, secundum magnam misericordiam tuam . . . Have mercy on me, O God, according to your great mercy . . .*

Mary Agnes slips away before the committal as she needs to get the last of the food prepped and on the table. She has never been to a Protestant funeral, but she knows

Catholic funerals—and Catholic appetites—so she's been cooking and baking for two days to be ready. There will be many hands to help at the clean-up later this afternoon, but the bulk of the work now is left to her alone.

Last night, she shined the table until it gleamed and set out plates, cutlery, and napkins. Today, she plates cold meats and cheeses and heaps biscuits into two baskets, placing them on the dining room table. Back and forth she goes to the ice box, hands chilled from carrying heavy bowls of cold potato salad and platters of sliced tomatoes and onions. *What have I forgotten?* She goes back to the kitchen to retrieve butter and nudges one of the baskets with her elbow to find room on the table for the crock. Four pies—two apple and two cherry—are already cooling on the buffet near the dining table. She adds two iced yellow cakes—Henry's favorite—to the sideboard and stands back to admire her work. Henry would be proud.

The buffet is a success by anyone's standards, the only thing receiving more praise than her pies is Henry himself. She is able to piece together his life from snippets of conversation. A Bostonian. Almost married to a cousin, who died tragically right before the wedding. *That settles that. The reason he never married. The ivory shawl.*

"That's when he headed west," one neighbor said. "With enough money and enough drive to tame all of Colorado."

Another neighbor cut in. "If it weren't for Henry's generosity, we wouldn't have gotten a start here." Others nod.

"Irrigation—"

"Easements—"

"Seed money—"

Mary Agnes steals away to the kitchen to refill trays. It is blasted hot. *There's no getting away from it, the heat. Or Dutch. He's everywhere. Around a corner. In my dreams.* She plunges her hands into ice water in the sink. She looks out the window to the expanse of the ranch, which will fall into new hands and carry on, another man, another woman, another generation.

Life is so fleeting, she thinks. *Why is it that people can't come to their own funerals? The dead might be surprised to hear the words spoken, after living a whole life where words were too few and grudges too great.*

As she's standing there catching a moment's rest, Dutch barges into the kitchen.

"They're asking after you."

"Me?"

He nods.

Mary Agnes follows Dutch into the parlor and stands at the edge of the crowd.

"And he's left the remainder of the estate to the cattleman's fund," the executor says. "For cowmen injured on the job." He turns to Mary Agnes and Dutch. "With a handsome amount put by for Dutch here. And a small allowance for Mrs. Halligan." He hands Mary Agnes an envelope.

She touches her chest. "For me?"

The executor nods and hands Dutch a larger envelope.

Mary Agnes's head swims. *An allowance?* Later, long after everyone has left and the washing up is done and she's collapsed in a bath and now languishes on her bed in fresh nightclothes, she opens the envelope in her room and gasps. Two hundred dollars. She counts again to make sure she has tallied right the first time.

"Thank you, Henry," she says to the air, as if he is in the room. "You've no idea how much this means to me. What I can do with it. Where I can go."

"WHY DON'T YOU COME TO SANTA FE?" Dutch picks at his fingernails. He doesn't make eye contact.

There is a long silence. They are sitting in the kitchen of Double H Ranch, their last night there. A buyer has just closed on the property, a Denver cattleman who'll bring all his own help in. Mary Agnes spent the last week scrubbing and dusting, more for Henry's sake than for the new owner; Henry would have wanted the place to shine. When she packed up Henry's belongings for the poor, she fingered the ivory fringed shawl and set it aside. No one needs to know.

"I'll be heading out at the end of the week," Dutch continues. He clasps his hands in front of him and looks toward Mary Agnes. "But that's not all. It sneaks up on you, Santa Fe. How much you miss it when you're not there. I know I tried to describe it to you. It's the most, I don't know how to say it in English, *magisch*. Maybe *magical*? Santa Fe is the most magical place I've ever been."

Dutch digs into the steak and kidney pie Mary Agnes prepared. "There are plenty of men begging for cooking like this." He wipes his chin with a cloth napkin. "And plenty of men there."

"Not looking to be a wife again. It hasn't even been a year . . ."

Dutch puts down his fork and knife. "Not talking of being a wife, Irish. A cook. At a restaurant, maybe your own one day."

"And where would I get the money for that, I ask you?" She is standing by the sink scrubbing a dish that is already clean, but it keeps her hands busy. She has exactly two-hundred seventy-five dollars to her name now, seventy-five saved up in addition to Henry's gift, but she won't be getting rich working on a ranch anywhere around Colorado Springs. *And if Dutch isn't here . . .*

"I've thought it through," she says. "It's best I go back to"—she remembers Helen's letter, *How can I persuade you to come back to Chicago? Please?*—"Chicago."

He lets out a whistle. "I thought you were going to say Ireland."

"I thought so, too, for a moment. But—"

"But, what?"

"But nothing. I fear there is nothing left for me in Ireland, although it pains me to say it."

"When will you go? To Chicago?" He hasn't picked up his fork again since this part of the conversation began. His dish must be cold by now.

"End of the week, same as you." Mary Agnes's voice catches on the words. She is making this up as she goes along. "Maybe we can ride up to Denver together." *Together.*

"But why Chicago? You don't seem so sure. Why not stay in Colorado Springs for now, until you make up your mind? I'm sure Tilly would love the help again."

I don't want to see Mr. French again, but I can't tell you that. If I did, I fear you'd squeeze the life right out of him like Tom would have done if he only knew. And what I wouldn't have minded doing . . .

"And I'd be up to visit next summer," he continues. "And, by then, maybe you'd have changed your mind and come to Santa Fe."

"Chicago is a life I know, Dutch. And Helen has been badgering me."

Dutch's eyes bore into hers. "I've not known you to run back to safety. You came all the way from Ireland alone, and then made your way to Chicago. Came west with Tom and then here, took a chance with Henry and me. I've got no claim to you or your thoughts, but the offer's open. Come to Santa Fe. You could make a new life there, a new adventure. A new beginning."

A new beginning? Like Tom used to say? She doesn't break eye contact. *Is he? Am I? No, I am reading too much into this offer, it's prideful thinking. But . . .*

"I've had enough adventure to last a lifetime, Dutch." *There.* She sits opposite him, her hands clasped in front of her. *But, home? After being tossed out of my own home and moving, moving . . . will I ever have a home? One I choose?*

"Never enough adventure. Wait until you see it. The skies alone, and the most spectacular sunsets you've ever seen. And the air, fresh, new, like it's never been breathed in before. And the food . . ." He stops, places his hands palm-side down on the table. "Well, I told you about the food. I'm going to make my home there, settle down, take up ranching. Rancho Vista, I'll call it. I can't put my finger on it, but it's like it's calling me."

Calling me. Settling down. Home. The words stop her.

"But if you want to know the real reason why I'd like you to come"—here he stammers, looks down, and then looks up again. He clears his throat and holds her gaze. "I've grown fond of your company, Irish." He reaches for her hand.

Their fingers touch, linger, but Mary Agnes pulls her hand away. It's been less than a year since Tom was lowered into the ground. Much too soon to consider loving again. She resolves then and there to put her mind first, heart second. And what has she been thinking? *A Dutchman? Not even a Catholic? Never.* She gets up abruptly and clears his supper plates.

If only . . . no. No. She thinks to speak, but holds her tongue, caught in a confusing web of custom and convention, reason and religion. What she would like to say is, *I've grown fond of your company, too, Dutch. No, that is a lie. You have captured my heart, filled a hole, made me want to live*

again and dance again and sing again. Of course, I will come to
Santa Fe with you.

Instead, she places the dishes in the sink and places a
dishtowel over them. Dries her hands. Leaves the room without daring to look back, for looking back would break her.

October 1891
Chicago, Illinois

"Mary Agnes!" Helen Laffey rushes toward her cousin on the crowded train platform at Chicago's ornate Grand Central Station. Helen clasps Mary Agnes tight. "You poor thing. Look at you," she says. "Brown as a gypsy. And what is that you are wearing? We will have to get to the dress-maker *today*."

Still the same Helen, Mary Agnes thinks.

Helen takes Mary Agnes's satchel from her and leads her through the cavernous station to the street outside. There is deep chill in the air, with a shrill wind coming off Lake Michigan.

Mary Agnes is glad she has a cloak this time as she arrives in Chicago, not like the first time, five years ago, when she arrived in The Windy City in a blizzard with little to her name. "Everything looks so—"

"Crowded," Helen interrupts. "Father says the city has exploded. Industries, streetcars, buildings. But it's also brought disease. Cholera, typhoid. And people, more than a million now."

"A million?" Mary Agnes thinks of the wide-open skies of Colorado, the way the sky bruised purple at the end of a day, so much her heart would ache. And no matter where she looked, east or west, south or north, there was never anyone in sight. The whole expanse of it: the Front Range, the air, the grasses, the sky, the creek bottoms. *Dutch.*

"When I got your letter, the one about Tom . . ." Helen trails off and hails a rig. When they are settled in, she takes Mary Agnes's hand. "But it's time to talk of other things now."

Like Dutch? With every mile behind her, Mary Agnes questioned herself. *Did I do the right thing? Or just the expected thing?* And then the devil taunts her and she thinks her thoughts obscene. *What was I thinking?* It might as well be her hymn to herself, to her life; she repeats the question over and over again. But she can't shake him, or thoughts of him. Every blond head she sees, she catches her breath. *Dutch.*

Mary Agnes moves in with Helen in a boardinghouse that caters to young, single Irish women on Halsted Street not far from Jane Addams' Hull House. Helen goes off to her position as a bookkeeper and Mary Agnes secures a position at The Tremont House, one of Chicago's most prominent downtown hotels. As she walks past the University of Chicago, she looks wistfully at the new buildings being constructed. Classes will begin within a year. *To think I thought I would go to university . . . but no.* Again she chides herself. *What was I thinking?*

Mary Agnes throws herself into work. Similar to big houses, she pays attention to detail in all her tasks: crisp linen sheets mitered at the corners, coverlets tucked neatly at the foot of the large beds, and pillows plumped; sumptuous towels stacked in tiled baths; fresh flowers on every entry table. And not a mote of dust, this she checks daily, floorboards, ledges, drapery rods. The clientele at the Tremont expects nothing less. Her rooms are not lacking.

Unlike big houses, where she was privy to family whims and secrets, she sees new patrons every day, although several male guests frequent the hotel, some with multiple "wives." She overhears lover's arguments. Sees men fondling each other in dim halls. Sweeps aways beribboned condoms under beds. Finds drained bottles of laudanum. All of this is overlooked; maids are only to go to management for brazenly illegal or suspicious activity.

Mary Agnes finishes making the large four-poster bed in the President Suite and begins her daily routine: Clear drawers and cabinets of items left behind, dust, sweep, mop on hands and knees. When she opens the top drawer of the bedstand, she gasps. *A revolver.* She looks behind to see if anyone is watching. No one is. With shaking hands, she lifts the revolver and wraps it in a towel. *Is it loaded?* This will have to be brought to the hotel manager's attention. When she finishes the room—and right tidy it is—she places the towel in a small basket and takes the back stairs to the ground floor.

"Sir?" Mary Agnes approaches the manager's secretary, a young man in his twenties in a dark suit.

"And you would be?"

"Miss Halligan, sir." She has taken to calling herself Miss Halligan instead of Mrs. Halligan. A widow would never be hired for a job like this. And she's only eighteen, nineteen next month, so she easily passes as unmarried. Tom's ring is hidden in her satchel at the boarding house, tied and wrapped in a handkerchief. Her finger feels bare; she often finds herself touching the spot to twirl the ring, but there is no ring to twirl.

"From what floor?" the young man asks.

"Eighth. I'd like to talk to Mr. Winters, if he is available."

"And why do you think Mr. Winters has time for you?"

"It's something I found, sir, in the President Suite."

The young man rises from his desk and comes around to the front of the desk. He looks at the basket. "In here?"

She nods and unwraps the towel and he peers inside.

"You found this where?"

"In the bedstand drawer, sir."

"One moment." He takes the revolver and disappears into Mr. Winters' office. Within minutes, the secretary ushers Mary Agnes into the manager's palatial office. Mahogany desk, leather chair, spittoon. Large red leather armchairs facing the desk and a full bar on the side wall. *And the paintings!* But what did she expect from one of Chicago's premier hotels?

She has only seen Mr. Winters from afar. In person, he is much more imposing: Tall, robust, balding, with a large, pointed nose. He wears an expensive dark suit with a small navy and white handkerchief in his chest pocket and a watch fob. A pince-nez sits low on his nose. His shoes are so polished, Mary Agnes thinks you could see your reflection in them.

He motions for Mary Agnes to sit. She doesn't know if she should curtsy. Or wait to be spoken to. But before she can form any thoughts or words, he thunders.

"And why, may I ask, did you remove this item from the President Suite?"

She freezes. "I thought . . ."

"What you thought? How dare you."

"But . . ."

His face reddens. "Mr. Price is one of our most valued guests."

Yes, he's here three nights every week. Or four. How many wives can one man have?

"We strive to put the guest first. Period. And to protect their privacy. I will be relieving you of your duties on the eighth floor, effective immediately."

Am I being dismissed? For following orders? To report suspicious activity to management?

"You can report to the second floor from now on." He puts the revolver on his desk. "That will be all."

It is with some relief that she hasn't been sacked, although the second floor is a blatant demotion. She swallows her bruised pride and reports to the second floor. When she hears through the hotel gossip chain that Mr. Price's bullet-riddled body was whisked out of the President Suite late at night the next week, Mary Agnes does not flinch. That things like this happen at the hotel are veiled in secrecy.

Now when she cleans rooms—many times after a rendezvous that looks more like a bacchanal than a hotel stay—she performs her duties without judgement and never goes to management again. Unlike other maids, so far she has not been propositioned or put in a compromised situation. She doesn't begrudge her luck. And she certainly doesn't want to endure Mr. Winters' wrath again.

Today, as she checks if fresh flowers have yet arrived in the largest suite on the second floor, she encounters another maid—*one not long for employ*, she thinks—engaged with a gentleman guest up against the polished closet door. She quickly exits the room and hurries to the women's changing room to dump her uniform into the hamper and change to her street clothes. No, she won't say a word.

Her education is growing in ways she would never learn at university, adultery and crime and sinfulness veiled in lavish surroundings. Her bank account is growing, too, as she's now on a salary, a full six dollars a week, and her pockets filled with extravagant tips.

She squirrels away enough for new eyeglasses and two new dresses, now that it's been a year since Tom died and she doesn't have to wear black. Helen goads her to the theatre, to shop, to buy magazines. Mary Agnes splurges on Thomas Hardy's long-awaited *Tess of the d'Urbervilles* after finishing Oscar Wilde's *The Picture of Dorian Gray*.

Mary Agnes stops sending wages back to Ireland. Never did she receive even a curt thank you from her mother. Now she could afford a dinner out once per week, although women don't dine out alone. She wonders what it would be like to go to the hotel dining room and order off the extensive menu, littleneck clams on the half-shell, lamb with mint sauce, mashed turnips and squash, and steamed apple dumpling with hard sauce. But she cannot complain, suppers at the boardinghouse are adequate, if not excessive. Boiled lake trout. Leg of chicken. Smoked beef tongue. Tonight, it smells like Irish Stew, one of her favorites. She always has enough to eat.

"Miss Halligan, is it?" A tall, striking woman Mary Agnes has not seen before approaches her at supper. "Eilene Osborne," the young woman says. She uses her given name and offers her hand like a man. Mary Agnes shakes it. "Mrs. O'Rourke says you're from Galway. I am, as well. Tuam."

"A pleasure," Mary Agnes says. "How long have you been in Chicago, Miss—?"

"Eilene, please. I just arrived. And you?"

"A few months, this time."

"And by that, you mean?"

Mary Agnes doesn't know how much to divulge. The boardinghouse is strictly for single women. But she feels a kindredness to this frank, forthcoming woman. "I was away in the West for a few years."

"Ah, the West. Now you intrigue me."

Mary Agnes tells Eilene about Colorado Springs and the ranch. She doesn't mention Tom—she cannot risk being found a widow—or Dutch, although she thinks of him every day, especially when she passes tall, blond Dutch-men or Scandinavians on Chicago's ever-crowded streets.

What does Dutch eat for breakfast now? Where does he work? How does he spend his time in that mysterious town he says he loves? Where has he made his home? What she never contemplates is another woman in his life. It might be selfish, but she cannot imagine him looking at another woman like he looked at her that last night at the ranch.

It's harmless thinking of him this way, more than a thousand miles away, isn't it?

May 1892
Chicago, Illinois

Mary Agnes lets go of Dutch one day at a time, but it hurts, the letting go, every thought of him a pinprick. Whenever he surfaces in her mind, she tamps thoughts down, *no, I can't think of him that way, not anymore.* It is getting easier to push him out of her memory the longer she is in Chicago as most of her waking time is spent working. It is tiresome work, long hours and hard labor. But you never know what a day will bring, what you will find, what you will see.

Today, Mary Agnes encounters two women together, naked in a bathtub, facing each another. She has never thought of being with another woman. *Is it immoral? Or not?* She excuses herself quickly and moves on to the next room, her head spinning. But all she can think about is being in a tub with Dutch and it takes her by surprise, the way he still holds sway, as if the harder she pushes him away the closer he gets. *I cannot think of him this way. No.* She shakes her head to set herself straight.

Both she and Helen have Saturday afternoons off now. When they are not shopping—Helen's favorite pastime, *other than gabbing about nothing*—they spend their time walking Chicago's posh neighborhoods and sometimes stopping for tea. It is pleasant out now, crocuses beginning to spring up and temperatures free of winter's grip. On a particularly beautiful afternoon, balmy for Chicago in May, a flyer catches their eye as they walk past St. Brendan's Hall on Randolph Street.

SPRING FLING
Saturday, May 16
8 p.m.—Midnight
St. Brendan's Hall

"Look, Helen." Mary Agnes points to the flyer. "A dance!"

Helen looks at her with incredulity. "What will people think? Tom dead not a year and a half?"

"'Tis a curse to worry about what other people think, Helen. Plus, I have a new dress, thanks to you, I might add. What would you have me do, play the widow for three years? Five? More? No, it's been eighteen months and you know how much I love to dance. It's been far too long. Tom wouldn't want me moping about." She remembers The Antlers, dancing with Dutch. *Dutch.* She shakes her head. *Why am I thinking of him? Still? I've got to shake him.*

IT'S SATURDAY NIGHT, AND WITH IT, crowds. A line has formed on the steps of St. Brendan's as young people jockey for a place. There are pockets of Irish and Italians and Poles. Mary Agnes runs her hands down her simple green dress. Maybe she should have worn the red and cream one? The one she wore for her birthday just before she and Tom left for Colorado? And the same one she wore to The Antlers? She wishes she had made a different choice, seeing all the elaborate dresses the young women wear tonight.

As they enter the crowded hall, Helen, in a much more provocative dress, leans in toward Mary Agnes. "Watch out for the Poles," she says. "Mix them up with our boys and we'll have quite the ballyhooly. Well, of course, there are our boys." She points to the bar. The air is stale, as if the hall hasn't been opened in months, or only to pensioners.

Mary Agnes checks her purse. The two dollars she stashed in there earlier this evening are folded in half. With any luck, she'll still have two dollars when she leaves with all these fellows here. She relaxes her shoulders.

It's about time I'm back out, no matter what Helen says. I want to have fun tonight. It's been far too long. Tonight, I will dance!

Young men and women hustle to find tables scattered around the wooden dance floor. Mary Agnes and Helen find a table near the bar, close to where a small band is setting up in the corner.

Helen nudges her. "See Paddy Kelleher over there?" she asks. "With those brothers of his?"

Mary Agnes strains to see the Kelleher brothers lined up at the bar, jostling and laughing. Helen has had her eye on Paddy Kelleher for months now at Mass, although Mary Agnes doesn't know how Helen can tell one brother apart from the next, all four of them like quadruplets. Or maybe she doesn't mind which of the four would pay her any mind, although she always uses Paddy's name.

"I could use a drink," Helen says. She positions herself so that any of the Kelleher boys might notice her.

And so they should, Mary Agnes thinks. *With that gorgeous flaming red hair and plentiful bosom. That beautiful smile and gift of gab. That spunk. It's a wonder all four of them haven't lined up yet and started a boxing match over her. They must be blind.*

The band warms up and starts in on a lively tune, one Mary Agnes recognizes from the dance at The Antlers. Before the first few bars have played, a handsome young man about her height dressed in a natty suit and tie with a handkerchief in his pocket approaches their table. He's got a swagger.

Mary Agnes feels an unfamiliar stirring and realizes she is eager to meet a young man. To have a conversation. To dance.

New beginnings, Tom would say. *But this one isn't headed for me. He is sure to be coming for Helen—bright face, beautiful hair, and that dress!*

The young man approaches Mary Agnes, his back to Helen. "Ronan Rooney," he says in a tamed brogue. "But everyone calls me Rooster."

"Irish." Mary Agnes extends her hand.

"*Irish?*"

"Too many Marys. And this is my cousin, Helen."

"Delighted," he says. He turns to Helen. "I hope you don't mind I'm asking your cousin here for a dance." He smiles to reveal slightly yellowed teeth. "Well, Irish, how's about it?"

Mary Agnes takes Rooster's outstretched hand, nods to Helen, and follows him to the dance floor. And still not a Kelleher brother in sight. They have disappeared from the bar. Mary Agnes can feel Helen pout without looking at her.

Rooster's trim hips sway as he turns and gathers Mary Agnes in his arms. He is a better dancer than Tom and Dutch and anyone else she has ever taken to a dance floor with. They do the two-step and the cakewalk, followed by a fast-paced waltz. By the time the third dance is over, she is glistening with perspiration.

"Thirsty?" he asks.

"I am, just."

"I'll go for punch. Wait here."

Mary Agnes sits at the now empty table and licks her lips. They're dry.

Where is Helen? She scans the dance floor and doesn't see her. When Rooster returns with punch, she gulps it. A tang burns at the back of her throat. She is sure it is spiked with alcohol. "That was just what I needed. Another?"

Rooster returns to the bar with a second cup of punch and she motions for him to sit. "Tell me about you," she says, leaning to hear above the din. "I already know you're a natty dresser and a fine dancer." Her attention is split between Rooster and wondering what has become of Helen. She is beginning to worry. *What if she has taken off with a fast lad?*

"What else do you need to know?" Rooster laughs. "Should I start at grammar school?"

She swats at his arm. "Aren't you the rogue."

"But if it's work you're talking about, I'm a company man. D.F. Willinger's Hardware Sales. You've heard of it? Over on Rucker and Frank? I'm head of accounts now and aim to go higher. One day I'll be sitting at that fine desk calling the shots. I can see it now." He spreads his hands wide. "Ronan P. Rooney, President."

"That's not far from my boardinghouse."

"Where?"

Shall I say? Or not? She gulps. "On Halstead."

"Don't tell me you're staying at that radical's? Hull House?"

"No, although you say that like Jane Addams is someone to avoid. I don't see it that way. She's doing more for young women in this city than anyone ever has."

"Are you a radical, too?"

"I suppose I am." *And glad of it. I'm not thirteen anymore. I work to support myself. And I can make my own decisions now.*

After the last dance, a much slower tune where Rooster worked his hand down from her waist to her buttocks, Rooster takes Mary Agnes's arm as they unfold into the cool, gas-lit street outside the church hall. Couples disperse into the night. She finally spots Helen on the arm of Paddy Kelleher.

See you back at the boardinghouse, Helen mouths to her.

Mary Agnes is unsteady. *Is it the heat? The alcohol?* Rooster steers her elbow through the crowd and they duck down an alley filled with rotting fish. He backs her against a brick building and pulls her into a deep kiss.

"That's my girl," he says.

"Your girl? Since when?" Mary Agnes looks up at Rooster. *I am Tom's girl. But, no . . . not anymore.*

"Since just now."

Rooster's girl? Is that what I want? No, just a bit of fun, to dance, nothing more.

"I need to get back, Mr. Rooney," Mary Agnes says. "Doors lock at twelve."

"I'll get you back," Rooster says. He bends to kiss her again, this time caressing her buttocks openly.

"I'll appeal to your gentlemanly behavior," she says, more sternly. "Please, I've got to get back."

As they exit the alley, Rooster guides Mary Agnes to the left toward North Clinton Street. She looks back over her shoulder. She's still unsteady and her head spins. "This isn't the way."

"I know a shortcut," he says. "Trust me."

Trust you? Trust you?

The Next Day
May 1892
Chicago, Illinois

Mary Agnes wakes with a pounding headache. She feels like her head is in a vise, a *thud thud thud* resonating in her head. She starts to get up but falls back on the pillow.

Where am I?

The cracked ceiling weeps with moisture; faded wallpaper peels from the seams. She bolts upright and her eyes sting. This is not her room.

And her dress! She gasps as she shimmies her stained dress to cover her behind. Where are her stockings? Her shoes? It comes to her in a rush, the dancing, *the drink*, the narrow alleyway, the kisses, the stairs. And then Rooster on top of her, heaving. What had he called her? *Rose?*

Mary Agnes moves to the edge of the bed and takes in the rest of the room. She feels ill. On the table, a note.

To my Irish Rose, thanks for a good time. R.

Her legs are sticky as she rushes to gather her ripped stockings and scuffed shoes. She forces the shoes onto her bare feet and balls the stockings.

Where is my purse?

She looks on the chair, beneath the table, and spies it on the doorknob. Opening it, her compact clatters to the floor. The two dollars she had stashed inside is gone. At least she is still wearing her pearl earrings. She feels for her hairpins, stuffs the stockings into the purse, and grabs her wrap. She only hopes she's remembered the streets in this neighborhood well enough to get back to the boardinghouse.

"LOOK AT THE SCRAPE YOU'VE GOTTEN INTO," Helen says. "Now what will people think?" They sit on narrow beds in the room they share at the boardinghouse.

"I told you, it's a waste of time to worry about what other people think," Mary Agnes says. *Do I believe that?* "I've got enough to worry about on my own." She runs her hand over her stomach. She missed her last monthly and her breasts are tender. It can only mean one thing, what her gram—and Mrs. Rutherford—warned her about: Fast lads. *However will I care for a child? Alone?*

As if Helen can read her mind, she says, "Maybe you should go to the good sisters. They'll take care of everything."

"Not a chance. I'd like to keep this a secret for as long as I can, Helen. The Coffey girl back home, the one I told you about, taken advantage of by boys in our town? Her parents sent her to the nunnery. They took the babe away from her, Helen. Took her away! I didn't come all this way to have that done to me. It may seem contrary to want a child under these circumstances, but I can't blame it on the child."

"You'll have to move."

"That I know." *However will I manage?*

Thankfully, she still has her job at Tremont House. But that won't last long, she's nauseous most mornings and feels sluggish. It won't be long before someone suspects that which will be evident very soon.

When she is called to Mr. Winters' office the following month, it can only mean one thing. She is not even ushered into the manager's office. The smug male secretary looks at her midsection and scoffs as he hands her an envelope. "That will be all, *Miss* Halligan." The word stings.

"Sacked?" Helen says.

Mary Agnes nods. "If the girls have noticed at the Tremont, they'll certainly notice here. I don't want that shame piled on top of the shame I already feel."

The next day, she walks for hours asking at different boardinghouses. No and no are the answers. She crosses into rougher territory, hoping to find lodging soon. It's snowing and the wind off Lake Michigan runs through her like a knife.

At a rundown tenement off South Robey—far worse than the tenement in New York—she sees a small sign: To Let. Mary Agnes knocks and an older Italian woman opens the door.

"You've a room, Mrs.—?"

"Spinnelli. You'd be Irish then? Are you Catholic? I only rent to Catholics."

Mary Agnes nods. The woman eyes her suspiciously, mumbles, and leads Mary Agnes up three flights of stairs to an unheated attic room, carrying under her arm a set of sheets. Mrs. Spinnelli opens the garret door and plops the sheets on a cot under a dormer window. Beyond the window, Mary Agnes sees rooftops and chimneys and smoke through the snow. It must be thirty degrees in the room, she can see her breath.

"Do you have a blanket?" she asks.

"That will be two dollars."

"For a blanket?"

"For the week. No charge for a blanket." Mrs. Spinnelli turns to leave.

"What is the address here?" Mary Agnes asks. "For my employer?" *Not that I have a job.*

"Just say Mrs. Spinnelli, Back of the Yards."

Mary Agnes counts herself lucky, cheap lodgings, no questions asked. She will have to watch herself here in this rough neighborhood and secure a new job within a week. She is in no danger of meeting anyone she knows in this part of town. Of course, she will miss the girls at the rooming house and especially Helen. In the meantime, Mrs. Spinnelli does not ask why Mary Agnes has come to her or is willing to pay for an unheated garret. It must be written all over her face.

"We'll have no male visitors here," Mrs. Spinnelli says sternly before she leaves the room, eyeing Mary Agnes's stomach beneath her cloak.

"There won't be," Mary Agnes replies. "I've no interest in male visitors. None at all."

August 1892
Chicago, Illinois

Seated at the worn table in her attic room, Mary Agnes stares at the blank sheet of paper. She doesn't know how to start or where to start, how much to say or not say. She made excuses in May as to why Rooster Rooney hadn't come round to the rooming house, but all the excuses in the world ran sour by June. Rooster Rooney never meant to call. He is the sort of man her gram warned her about, and all she has is a growing stomach to show for it.

Of course, she is going to have the child. It would be sin not to, although she's heard of a procedure that could remedy the situation. But the cost! She doesn't have nearly enough funds. And it could cost her her life as well. *Nothing is worth that risk.*

Yesterday, Mary Agnes worked up her guts and went to the hardware sales office to ask after Rooster. It was a bitterly cold day, made more uncomfortable without gloves. Snow drifts banked along buildings and she shuffled on a small pathway until she reached Willinger's.

A honorable man would surely offer to pay for confinement, at least, wouldn't he? She has no intention of accepting an offer of marriage. She will have the child on her own.

"Rooney, you say?" The foreman at Willinger's shook his head. "Never heard of a Ronan Rooney."

She didn't wait for the snickers that followed her out the door.

Now she puts pen to paper. She has no other choice. She will not go to the nuns.

Mother—

My shame comes before me. You were wrong about Fiach, but here I am, nevertheless, with child. I have been a blight to you for so long that I am now giving over to it. I have nowhere else to go. I will arrive in Galway late October and will send word as to the day and time.

Your daughter,
Mary Agnes

She mails the letter on a Friday. *How long should I wait for an answer?* She will go to Ireland regardless of one. By February, she will have a child, and she needs a home. She can't support a baby alone in Chicago, and going back to Aunt Margaret and Uncle Fiach is out of the question.

She finds part-time employment, Fridays and Saturdays only, at a seedy restaurant off South Robey, where she peels potatoes until her knuckles bleed. There is a rhythm to the boredom, the way the potato peels curl off the end of her knife and slop on the floor. It is getting more difficult to bend over to clean the mess at the end of her shift. Already, she cannot stand for long periods and asks for a stool.

The manager sneers. "You'll be wanting a bed next," he says, and laughs.

But it is not funny. Her usual wit escapes her and she takes the barb without a retort. She will now have a reputation she cannot escape, and her mother will be sure to remind her every day. *But where else can I go? Not to the nuns, no.*

The answer comes a month later (Mary Agnes's skirts straining at her stomach by now), not in the form of a letter, but in the form of her younger brother, Sean, waiting in the Laffey's parlor.

"Sean? It is you?"

"'Tis, Mary A. Bearer of sad news."

Whether or not he notices her condition is buried after hearing him out. She bursts out of her aunt and uncle's house, running now, tears blanketing her wind-chapped face, her heart beating to burst, crying blood. *It can't be true, can it?*

Early October 1892
Dawrosmore, County Galway, Western Ireland

Mary Agnes stumbles off the rat-infested ship in Galway. It has been a hellish two weeks aboard the steamship, sick every day. Now that she is back on Irish soil, there is no one to meet her. The same when she exits the bumpy coach in Letterfrack and makes her way toward Dawrosmore. *Do they hate me that much? My own family?*

It's October, the chilling month, six years to the week since she first left Ireland, thirteen and nearsighted and with more straying thoughts than a dictionary has words. Now she is nineteen, almost twenty, with more experience than girls twice her age. She passes the Jones's place, but she already knows there's something amiss. She can feel it, in her bones. *Or maybe I had a premonition?* As she rounds the corner, she sees the cottage, sad and familiar, her attic window dark.

Picking up her soiled hem, Mary Agnes walks the long, curvy lane toward her parents' cottage. It will be a difficult conversation. But home is where you go to sort everything out.

She hurries then, holding her middle. Her coat swishes behind her. Breathless, she reaches the cottage, her boots muddied and hem ruined. Wind blows the gate open and shut, open and shut. Everything is as she remembers it, farm implements, cart, a scant pile of peat. But there is no smoke curling up from the chimney, no boys in the yard.

Mary Agnes pushes the door open. It is unlatched, its creak familiar as family. At first glance, nothing is out of place, the kettle on the stove, tableware stacked next to the drying sink.

Everything is the same, as if someone has just stepped out. *Why has the fire gone cold?* She remembers the old adage that a soul flees from the people of a house once the fire goes out. She lays a peat fire and stands in front of the fireplace. Shivering, she turns slowly to warm herself, her mind racing. *Where can they be? Gone to a funeral?* She hasn't heard church bells tolling. *Perhaps to a neighbor's?*

When she warms, Mary Agnes removes her coat and hangs it on a peg. *Tea, I want tea.* She rummages through the pantry until she finds a bottomful of tea leaves and puts the kettle to boil over the fire. While she waits, she takes a cloth to the windows. It looks like no one has cleaned them for quite some time. Dust and grime muddy her cloth.

"Mary A? Is it really you?"

Mary Agnes turns to see Jonesy in the doorframe. "Jonesy!" She wants to rush into his arms, but her feet don't move.

"I thought I saw you c-c-coming up the lane, but at first, I thought my eyes deceived me. No one who goes to America c-c-comes back." He steps forward but then stops.

Mary Agnes flattens her skirt over her stomach and wonders if he's noticed. *Who couldn't?* But Jonesy doesn't say anything.

"Where's Da? Mam? The boys?"

"I thought they would have found you."

"Found me?"

"Fiach. The others. They left for America after your parents . . ."

"My parents?"

His eyes lower.

"When?" she asks.

"A year past, your pa and your ma both. We lost half the town, by my reckoning. Influenza."

Mary Agnes sits on a chair, her backside suddenly cold. She hesitates before asking, as if she doesn't want to know the answer. "And the boys?"

"All survived but one. Fiach took the others to New York. Said you have family there. I thought he would have tried to find you."

"I wasn't in New York. He knew that. Our family is in Chicago." She takes in a sharp breath. "And who was it who didn't survive?"

Jonesy looks at his hands. "Wee Thomas."

She gasps. "No!" She flies into Jonesy's arms and sobs. "Not Tommy."

He caresses her head. "Shh, shh, now. It'll be to rights soon enough." He holds her at an arm's length and looks at her from head to heel. "I know I said I'd follow you, find you. I'm sorry, Mary A. I c-c-couldn't leave."

"I looked for you on the boat, and on the street. But I knew in my heart you could never leave this place."

After a few moments, he guides her to the table and helps her to sit. He pulls up a chair close to her. "There's more, Mary A. A baby girl after you left. She's gone, too." He stumbles over the next words. "I see you're in a delicate way. Is there a—"

"No. No husband. There was one, but he's gone, too." She leaves out a bulk of the story. "Fiach hasn't sold off the farm, then?"

"No, he said to watch out for it until he returned. Four months, he said. Enough time to find homes for the boys. But it's been the best part of a year now. I would have thought he would be c-c-coming up the lane, not you."

"Well, I'll keep house until he returns, then." Mary Agnes looks past Jonesy to the yard. "If he returns."

"I'm farming alone now."

Mary Agnes feels a pang. She should have asked after Jonesy's mam and da already. "That will make two of us."

"I'm so glad to see you." Jonesy reaches a hand across the table. He kneads her hand.

Mary Agnes remembers back to the innocent days, Jonesy taking her hand as they crossed the creek looking for frogs. The stolen kisses behind the barn. His eyes before she left as they lay in the barn. *Maybe*, she thinks . . .

Jonesy scans the sky. "Milking time. I'll bring you some c-c-cream before supper."

"Can you spare any bread?"

After Jonesy leaves, Mary Agnes takes the worn broom from its place behind the door and sweeps the dirt floor. She rinses a cloth and works over the counters and table. The light fades, pooling in uneven splotches on the now clean floor. When her work is finished in the great room, she goes behind the curtain and gathers feather quilts. She balls them in her arms and strides to the threshold. One by one, she airs them out on the stoop, balloons of dust flitting off like dirty snow. She stacks them in a lumpy pile inside the doorway.

In the waning day, she looks west. She'll not cross that ocean again, even if Fiach comes back and throws her out on her head. But maybe he won't return, and the farm will be hers.

Her daughter—she's sure it's a girl—will grow up here, on Irish soil. *I'll call her Gracie, after Gram. She'll run in the fields and gather eggs, her hair flying behind her like sunlight trailing the day. Never will she know Chicago or men like Rooster or back alleyways filled with rotting fish and vegetables. I will never send her away for straying thoughts. No, I will never send the girl away for any reason.*

Especially at thirteen.

Mary Agnes rests on the doorjamb, breathing in the view that's been burned into her mind since memory first took it in. For every night she went to sleep crying for this place, poor as it is in *every way,* here she is again, on the stoop of the cottage, in a place so familiar—the barn, the fields, the ocean. *Home. Where the lane curls down to the sea. The greening hills and the rain, yes, even the rain.*

Thoughts jumble and reverberate, like a child splashing in a puddle, mesmerized, as the rings go out, out, out from the center, drumming the edge of the shallows and then rushing back again toward the core. *Would it have been better to stay, with a guarantee of nothing except a lifetime of joys and sorrows? Or was it better to go? Even with this as the ending?*

Mary Agnes picks her way down to the beach and stands there at the last breath of day. She looks west through the mist, as the dark Atlantic slaps the shore at Dawrosbeg, scattering pebbles and seaweed and lost pieces of line, seawater oozing into her black boots. She raises her face to all she does not yet know, the secrets and sorrows, the joys and jubilations, and, in that fine alto that has gotten her through a thousand wakes, she lifts her voice and sings down the day.

THROUGH A THIN SKIN OF SLEEP, Mary Agnes wakes, shivering. The morning has dawned grey and damp, not unlike the west of Ireland, windows leaking rain. But she is not in Ireland. She is in her attic room in the boardinghouse in Chicago. She closes her eyes to bring the dream back, back, back.

But she can't.

All at once, what comes back in a rush is what her brother Sean told her yesterday in the Laffey's formal parlor in Chicago.

"I'm here as ambassador of our family, now that Fiach is in prison—shouldn't have gotten himself mixed-up with the rebellion, serves him right. Mam and Da are following with all of the boys. Except for young Tommy. He caught the typhus. I'm sorry to be the one to tell ya. I know ya were fond of him."

"Tommy?" *Noooooo. Not Tommy.* She closes her eyes to fight back tears. *First Tom and now Tommy? Both gone?*

"And I'm sorry to tell ya Mam doesn't want to see ya, Mary A. She says you've brought enough shame and heartache to this family, so don't try to contact her once she's arrived. And especially now . . ." He looks at her burgeoning middle.

Mary Agnes can't help the tears now. She puts her head in her hands and sobs.

"Shush, now, mavoureen." Sean puts his arm around her. "I'll try to get news to ya when I can, but I have to eat. For a while, at least, I'll have to abide by Mam's rules, but it won't be forever, Mary A. I don't have anything against ya. It's Mam that does, like she can't rid herself of a grudge, blaming ya for Gram's passing. And Granda's, as well."

"It's not true, Sean. None of it. You of all people should see that. I loved Gram and Granda. They took me in, for God's sake, when Mam threw me out." Mary Agnes wipes her eyes and shakes her head. "And Jonesy?"

Sean looks at the floor. "Gone, too."

"As in left? To England? To America?" *I'll find ya, Mary A.* "Or gone, like Tommy?"

"Gone, like I said. The whole family. Typhus. It swept the whole village. Those who are left are making plans to leave. Soon, there won't be anyone left at Dawros. At least no one ya know."

Oh, Jonesy, Jonesy . . .

"Until they all arrive, I'm at O'Flaherty's rooming house over on Randolph and May. Ya can leave a message there, although I'll likely be out looking for work if ya come to call."

AFTER THE DREAM, AND WHEN SHE THINKS she has the strength to get up, Mary Agnes sits up in bed, head woozy. She feels a gush of blood on her mattress. She moves to the edge of the cot as blood pools down her legs and onto the floor. A sudden cramp seizes her abdomen. She has never been in this much pain, not even after days with no food when she was a child. She doubles over as a pain sears through her groin. It is then she feels a lump pass through her vulva and—*so tiny, so tiny she is*—a grey fetus slips to the ground, her face frozen in a grimace. Mary Agnes bends to clasp her—*Grace!*—but the baby slips through her hands and Mary Agnes clutches air, *no no no*, and pulls at her hair until it comes out in clumps. Is that her voice howling? To wake the dead?

Mrs. Spinnelli finds her later that day and takes Mary Agnes to her own room, where she sponge-bathes her and tucks her under a blanket on a worn divan covered with a hand-crocheted coverlet. When Mary Agnes wakes, it is dark, the oil lamps lit in the otherwise dim room. There is no sign of the fetus.

"You're to spend the night," Mrs. Spinnelli says, handing her a cup of warm broth and piece of bread. "To get up your strength."

"But the baby . . ."

"I've called the priest."

"And my job . . ."

"You'll be sacked for not showing, so not another thought about that. You'll get another job, *ragazza*. There are jobs to be had everywhere."

"I'm not ready." *Tommy. Jonesy. And now the baby, gone.*

"No, it will take time, pet. I've washed your linens and tidied your room, so as soon as you've got the strength, you'll be comfortable. I'll see to it you've got soup and bread in you and extra blankets. And I won't charge you these next two weeks."

"Why would you do that for me? You hardly know me."

"I was a ragazza—a girl—like you once, I know it's hard to imagine," Mrs. Spinnelli says, kneading her knuckles. "A stranger provided a kindness to me then and I've never forgotten."

"Where?"

"At home. Napoli."

Mary Agnes tears up. "I don't know that anyone has ever been so kind to me, except for my grandparents." She risks mentioning Tom, so she doesn't. "Or Jonesy."

"Jonesy?"

"A neighbor boy, sweet on me. But I didn't give him much thought after I left Ireland. And now he's gone."

"Ah." She pats Mary Agnes's shoulder. "I had a boy sweet on me once, back in Napoli—but, never mind, that was a hundred years ago." She pats Mary Agnes's arm. "Back to sleep now, ragazza. Takes away all the hurt."

Mid-October 1892
Chicago, Illinois

"They're here, Mary A. Arrived a week ago Friday. And I didn't waste a moment finding a house to rent not far from here. On Walnut Street." Sean leans across the table at the small café, his hands cupping a mug of tea.

Here? At last? Mary Agnes tries to picture Walnut Street. She must have passed it countless times although she can't place it. She'll have to consult a map. "What news have you of them? Mam? Da? The boys?"

"Not just boys, they've a wee girl, Mary Rose, close to three. And Jamie, six now. He was born not long after you left."

After I was sent away, you mean. She shakes her head. *That makes*—she calculates the ages of the boys here—*Sean, 17, Paddy, 16, and Ferris*—she counts on her fingers—*14. Imagine. And Eamon, 11, the age Sean was when I left. And Jamie, 6, and*— "A girl, you say?"

"It pains me to tell ya, Mary A., but mam says Mary Rose is perfect, 'not like Mary Agnes,' she says. I'd be a rich man if I saved a penny for every time she says it."

It's like a dagger pierces her stomach, the pang is that severe. Mary Agnes moans.

"Are ya a-right, sister?"

"No, Sean, I am not."

"Is it—"

"It's nothing I can explain in one word. Or one sentence. They threw me out, Sean. And now they don't want to see me? Ever again?"

"I thought maybe it were the babe . . ." His face reddens.

"There is no babe."

He looks at her blankly. "But . . ."

She shakes her head.

Sean comes around the table and hugs her. "I'll see ya when I can, Mary A."

Although she knows it will likely only bring her more heartache, Mary Agnes cannot help herself. She takes to trailing her mother on Chicago's streets. *Is that really Eamon? And Ferris, almost a man.* She must catch herself before she calls out. *Ferris! Eamon!*

Her dream was prescient; her mother does have another boy she doesn't recognize. *And a girl!* It stings in so many ways: No love of a mother, no sister to help raise, *no child of my own.* She is at war within herself, grieving the babe she lost, each day more painful than the one before, her womb empty, empty. Everywhere she looks, babies. More babies. It is hard not to resent women she passes on the street, even though she doesn't know them. *Why them? And not me?*

It's a risky game she plays—and not good for her state of mind, this she knows—but she berates herself for falling into Rooster Rooney's trap, following him, and not protesting— *but how could I protest when I was under the influence? I only remember bits and pieces and damn him! Damn him! I wish I had kicked him where it stings.* Still, she grieves the babe. *I know it was a girl.* And then it's a spiral of picturing her little one and how she grows and runs and laughs and smiles and then Mary Agnes is rendered to sobbing again.

She can't help tailing her mother from Walnut Street to the grocer, the baker, and the laundry in all weather to get a glimpse of little Mary Rose. *My sister.* Mary Agnes wears a hat pulled low and shrinks inside her cloak. She cannot be detected. But she longs to reach out to the little girl. Back and forth she hides behind the corners of buildings and weaves in-between wagons to get glimpses of them, her heart racing. Streets and buildings become blurred as she focuses on the hem of her mother's coat. *Right, left, over there . . .*

She panics when she thinks she's lost them, but then she spies her mam again. Up one street, down another she slinks. She knows she shouldn't encroach on her mam's privacy by tailing her but she's desperate to see her sister and her brothers.

It's my family, familiar as dirt.

Mary Agnes cannot go to St. Mel's anymore for all the obvious reasons. She hasn't been to Mass for more weeks than she can count now. And her sins so grave, they risk not being forgiven. But still, she is up early on Sunday mornings to glimpse her family going to Mass.

From her vantage point across the street from the church, Mary Agnes is shocked to see her father—*he has aged twenty years*, she thinks—as he mounts the church steps. *Is it really him?* She steps out from behind the lamp post to be sure. She doesn't know if she would even recognize him on a street, so thin he is, and stooped.

All that stands between them now is snow, time and distance forgotten.

It can all be forgiven.

But her father looks her way and then looks away just as quickly.

Did he see me? She wrestles with the thought. *He must have seen me.*

From somewhere deep inside, she growls. It comes out as half-snarl, half-scream. She stands there on the side of the street, open to the elements and anyone's glance. People skirt her as they pass. She continues howling.

They will never come for me. There will never be a knock or a familiar hello. They're as dead to me as I am to them.

MARY AGNES WIPES SWEAT FROM HER FOREHEAD. She has landed a position at nearby Union Stock Yard now after fudging on her previous employer. The large German forewoman must have been desperate for help because she obviously didn't check Mary Agnes's reference. If she had, she would have seen Mary Agnes was a fraud, her only letter a less-than-glowing account of part-time back of the kitchen help at a seedy restaurant in Back of the Yards. Henry Hansen is dead, and Dutch is in Santa Fe by now, so they can't attest to her cooking skills. She will have to prove it. What cannot be debated is that she is a hard worker, the only real reference needed in factory kitchens on the south side of Chicago in 1892.

The city is exploding in growth, with more than one million people: Irish, Italians, Poles. Germans, Swedes, Greeks. A thousand of them work at The Yards, which, according to the crew boss, "rivals any abattoir in Omaha, Kansas City, or Cincinnati." Mary Agnes has never heard of these places, and has to ask what "abattoir" means. *Knacker yard, is what it means.* Two thousand hog, cattle, and sheep are slaughtered per day here, he says, along a crude assembly line, "right rank, it is."

Mary Agnes holds her nose when she arrives each morning at six. The smell of blood and death pervades the whole building, you can't get away from it, so you breathe in and out and after an hour, or maybe two, you don't notice it as much. It's a good thing the kitchen is three buildings away from the main slaughterhouse.

She peels potatoes and carrots by the thousands to add to hearty beef stews. Mixes cornmeal and sugar and butter and flour and egg and loads pan after pan with cornbread batter. Hour after hour on her feet she disappears into what the newspapers call the "industrial complex." It's too complicated for her to understand, industry and finance, and truth be told, she doesn't care. She has a steady job with income coming in.

Workers amble into the cafeteria, their bloodied aprons left behind in the abattoir. Still, their faces are tired, grimed, as they grumble: long hours, low wages, accidents. But still they apply, every face from around the globe that has come to Chicago working together—and a steady stream of hungry workers. Mary Agnes puts on a cheery face at work and converses with Slavs and Poles and Italians, and, of course, Irish. None is familiar, which means no one she knows will find her here, somewhere in the neighborhood bordered by Halsted to the east and South Racine to the west between 39th and 47th streets. That is, if anyone is indeed looking, which, by now, she is convinced no one is. Not even Helen, so smitten she is with that beau of hers, Paddy Kelleher. Mary Agnes is as lost now as her tutor Seamus Bourke was in Dublin or her granddad on Inishbofin. Sometimes one wants to be lost, or, she thinks, *at least, not found. Now I know what Seamus meant back in Dawros. That someday I would understand.*

Back at the boardinghouse, she is alone, and most nights glad of it, when sobs overtake her and she pounds the pillow until it's flat, and nothing—nothing—takes the hurt away. Except for praying the rosary, *Blessed are thou amongst women, Mary.*

"MISS RUTHERFORD? IS THAT YOU?"

A young woman about her age looks up with dulled eyes. Her face is filthy, her coat three shades of disrepair. Ripped stockings give way to holey boots, one toe protruding. If it weren't for the prominent mole and long now-dull blonde hair, Mary Agnes probably wouldn't have addressed her, although she would have given her coin, she always does. There is not a woman, old or young, on the street she ignores, regardless of her meager income.

But yes, this is definitely Doria Rutherford, from the first big house Mary Agnes worked in when she first arrived in Chicago, the girl who got her fired.

"Miss Rutherford? Doria, is it?" Mary Agnes says again, this time squatting to see the girl eye to eye.

The young woman spits and clutches her baby closer to her chest.

Mary Agnes wipes the spit from her hand and holds her tongue. She reaches for the child, but Doria bats her away. "I mean you no harm," she says. "Here, let me help you with the child. It's cold."

Doria releases her grasp and hands the damp bundle to Mary Agnes. Mary Agnes opens the blanket and gasps. It is not a child at all, but one of Doria's dolls. "How? Why?" she begins.

Doria does not answer. She is crying now.

"Here, let me help," Mary Agnes says. She pulls Doria to her feet and puts her arm around her. "I live just a block from here. Let's get you cleaned up. And dry."

Once in the cramped apartment, Mary Agnes goes to work stripping the girl of her filthy clothing and giving her a sponge bath. Doria doesn't protest. So far, she has yet to say a word. Mary Agnes hums as she washes Doria's underarms, breasts, and stomach. She rinses the washcloth and hands the girl the damp rag to wash her private parts. After rinsing again, Mary Agnes runs the cloth down each of Doria's legs. When she gets to her feet, she holds her breath. It's no less than what Jesus would do. Or the Purple Mary.

"Now for your hair." Mary Agnes hands Doria a towel and leads her to the basin. Still Doria has not said a word. Mary Agnes lowers Doria's head toward the basin and pours warmed water over her once-beautiful hair. She works the lather in, still humming as she works. Once her hair is rinsed, Mary Agnes wraps a clean towel around Doria's head, leads her to her bed, and motions for her to sit. She helps her into a fresh nightdress.

"Shall I brush your hair now?"

Doria looks at Mary Agnes. "Why are you being so nice to me? After everything?"

"Because it is the right thing to do," is all Mary Agnes says. She takes the brush and attacks Doria's hair, now a mess of knots. "One, two, three," she says, as she works the brush through tangles. She brushes in silence, except for the counting. "Fifty-eight, fifty-nine." She counts all the way to one hundred. "There."

Next, she turns her attention to the doll, its stuffing poking out through ripped seams. After cleaning the doll gingerly and reattaching an arm that hangs by mere threads with a safety pin, Mary Agnes wraps the doll-baby in a fresh scrap of blanket. She will have to wash the doll's clothes along with Doria's rags tomorrow before she goes to work.

"For you," Mary Agnes says as she hands the doll back to Doria.

Doria sits and rocks the doll, tears flowing now. "It was a girl," she says.

Over the next hour, Doria spills the story. Her pregnancy. Being thrown out of the house by her father and brothers. Going to a home for unwed mothers. Having the baby taken away. Being back on the street, earning a living the only way she knew how. "My sister Claire wouldn't even take me in. As for Theresa . . ."

"What about your young man?"

"Never saw him after I told him. I thought better of him and now—"

"You can stay here, for a week or two, until you are on your feet again," Mary Agnes interrupts. "I don't think my landlady will mind. I can cover the rent. And I can put in a good word for you at The Yards. It's good wages. But for tonight, sleep." She pulls back the coverlet on the narrow cot and tucks Doria in with her broken heart and broken doll. "And remember, you can always go home."

Who am I fooling here? I can never go home. But Doria, on the other hand . . .

"But my father? My brothers?" Doria begins to sob again.

"Tell your mother what you just told me, Doria." *There. Maybe the truth will win.* "Your mother loves you."

"How can you be sure?"

Mary Agnes hesitates. By speaking out, she will admit she was a voyeur, reading a letter not intended for her. "I saw the letter your mother wrote you. When I was in service. Your mother—" here she chokes up. "Please, Doria. Go back home."

The next morning, Doria is gone, along with her dirty clothes. She did not take a thing, not a skirt or a blouse or a sweater, not stockings or boots. Mary Agnes sits on the bed and touches the place where Doria slept. It is stone cold, the lifeless doll staring back at her like from beyond the grave.

Late October 1892
Chicago, Illinois

"It's official," Helen says. "We're to wed on October the 26th."

"I couldn't be happier for you!" Mary Agnes embraces Helen. "I've been waiting ever so long for this day. Mrs. Patrick Kelleher."

Helen stumbles over the words. "That is what I've come to say—I'm afraid you won't be invited, Mary A. Mother has forbid it. Your mother and father will be there."

"What is it you're saying?" Mary Agnes feels a rush of anger rising from her chest. "My parents have chosen not to see me based on a lie, Helen, and you know it. A lie that Fiach spun from the beginning that has taken hold. Like a cancer." She tries to tamp down her rising anger. "And if what I think is true, about your father . . ."

"I won't have talk of that."

"You're blind, then, Helen! I've pieced together the puzzle. Your father came at my mother when she was just a girl, like my own brother Fiach came at me. Why else would my gram say your father owed it to my mother to take me in? Because it would be his penance."

"Or because that's what family does."

"But isn't it curious that Uncle left right away for Chicago after my mother was with child? And my grandparents sheltered my mother until she had the babe?"

"Why would your mother name her bastard child after her own brother then, if he violated her?"

"Maybe she thought it was her fault. Naming her child after her brother was like her penance. One she'd have to live with her whole life."

"And what if you're wrong?"

"I'm not wrong, Helen."

"Why didn't she side with you then, when your brother Fiach came at you?"

"Her shame. She would rather live in shame and penance. 'Sour as they come,' Granda always said. About his own daughter! I reminded my mam too much of herself, and that was the end of it. She sided with Fiach since the beginning and sides with him still. Let alone fraternizing with her brother. You would think she would never want to see him again. 'Tis more than troubling. 'Tis outrageous."

Helen touches Mary Agnes's arm. "Sorry, I am, Mary A. I hope you'll be happy for me."

"Of course, I am happy for you and Paddy. He's a lucky man."

Mary Agnes mulls all this over, what is family, what is home. She wonders what happened to that sense of calm she had in Colorado and second guesses coming back to Chicago. Maybe she will save up and go back. Get a good job. Start over. *I'm almost twenty! I can do whatever I want to do now.*

She is less than a block from her lodgings on payday, thinking of a present for Helen, something special for her wedding day. Somehow, she will afford it. Somehow, she will get the gift to her.

A large man—*is he Greek? Italian?*—bushy eyebrowed and weathered, with sagging jowls and strong forearms, pushes past Mary Agnes. He smells rank.

"Have you no manners?" she asks, throwing him an eye.

"Pardon, mavoureen, me nerves are up," he says. "Me woman is waiting at home and I've nothing for her." The man is not Italian nor Greek. It's an Irish brogue thicker than Tom's.

"Here," she says. "I'd best put my manners on." She opens her purse, peels out one of the six dollars she earned this week, and offers it to the man.

"I couldn't take wages from a lady. I'm knackered enough." He hangs his head.

Mary Agnes lets the bill flutter out of her hands and onto the ground. "Well, would you look there! A dollar for the taking!" She squeezes the man's arm. "Go ahead. On the pig's back, you are today."

Does it feel good to help another? *Yes,* she thinks. *Make the world a little kinder.* She dallies over coffee with Mrs. Spinelli, takes her weekly bath in her landlady's kitchen, and winds her way to her room, her hair wrapped in a towel. It's not freezing yet, and she has extra blankets now. She circles her shoulders with one of the blankets and sits at her desk, starting, stopping, starting again. In the end, the letter is only one line long. *It might never reach him, anyway.*

Mr. VanRy—

Trusting that Santa Fe is everything you hoped it would be.

Mary Agnes Coyne

Mary Agnes wakes with a start, sweating, not knowing if she should mail the letter or not. She pulls the pillow over her head. But it's dawn, no time to dwell on troubles, real or imagined. She makes her way to the stockyards, the letter in her coat pocket. Once at work, she changes into her uniform and doubles down to her tasks.

On the way home, before she changes her mind, Mary Agnes stops outside the mailroom at the stockyards. In it, the short note, and on the back of the envelope, her return address. She looks at the envelope one last time before she drops it in the slot:

Pieter VanRy
Rancho Vista
Santa Fe
New Mexico Territory

When she gets back to the boarding house, an envelope is tucked under her door with no note. The handwriting on the front of the envelope looks vaguely familiar, but she can't place it. Not Helen. Not her aunt. Not Mrs. O'Sullivan. Could it be Mrs. Rutherford?

"Mrs. Spinelli?" she calls. But her landlady is out. She wants to ask who left the envelope for her. A messenger? A stranger? Someone she knows?

As she takes the stairs to her room, she stops. *That's it,* she thinks, remembering the letter she saw on Mrs. Rutherford's vanity when she was in service there. Mary Agnes goes back and forth as she studies the handwriting. *Could it be? Maybe. Yes. Because Doria is the only one who knows where I live.* Mary Agnes opens the envelope carefully, not knowing what is inside.

What is this? Bills fall out into her hands, slipping through her fingers onto the stairway, like the dollar bill she gave to the Irishman an hour ago. She gathers the bills up and rushes to her room. Sitting on the bed with bills spread around her on the blanket, she counts them, twice. One hundred dollars. She cannot believe her luck.

Mary Agnes counts the bills a third time as she puts the story together, piece by piece. She has yet to take off her coat or her hat.

Doria must have gone back home . . . and Mrs. Rutherford repaid me for my kindness to her daughter.

After everything.

Now Mary Agnes really wishes Mrs. Spinnelli was in, in case she saw the messenger. *Did Mrs. Rutherford herself come by the boarding house? No, probably not. Nor Doria. But someone did. And now I have enough money to . . . do I dare?*

Mary Agnes gets up, hangs her coat on the door peg, leans against the door jamb, and pulls her long hair down, finger-combing the knots. *What is it that Mary Catherine told me on the ship to America?* She blesses herself with the sign of the cross to honor Mary Catherine's memory. *Think, think, think, Mary A.*

Take the risk, she said. Take the risk or lose the chance.

Late October 1892
Chicago, Illinois

*A*nother letter is in the mail. She gives it two weeks and then packs her bags. Her dresses fit again. Mary Agnes has invited Helen over, despite her disappointment over not being invited to her wedding.

But anger never serves, she thinks.

"Here I am again, leaving you," Mary Agnes says to Helen. She tucks the last of her garments and belongings into her satchel. A single letter, tied with a green ribbon, is already packed, under everything, not for Helen's eyes. How her heart jumped when she saw the letter on the front table, that unmistakable handwriting and news of his new ranch house, horses, cattle. The seasons. The skies. And food, he mentioned food. She remembers she hasn't eaten yet today, but she will. At the hotel.

"I'm sorry I haven't been the sister you always wanted," Helen says. She sits on the stripped bed and shakes her head. "I could have stood up to Mother. And your mother. But I didn't."

"You've been as good as any sister."

Although you got on my nerves.

"Honest and loyal."

Most of the time.

"You did what you thought you needed to do."

And you are going to have to live with them while I leave it all behind.

"I'm still sore at Mam about not having you at the wedding—"

"Old news," Mary Agnes says. "I have you here now, don't I?"

"And you'll keep the letters coming? From wherever it is you're going?"

"I don't know exactly where I'm headed," Mary Agnes lies.

She remembers her granddad's map spread out on the table in Dawrosbeg, his stubbed finger pointing out the continents and vast oceans. Yes, she could go to the Sandwich Islands or Canton or Bombay. The possibilities before her are as a banquet. *Jerusalem? Paris? Back to Ireland?* It is her choice this time. And she knows where she's headed.

"Last time it was me urging you to go," Helen says. "Today, it's you making the choice. Whatever will I do without you?"

"Oh, I've no doubt of that. With that fellow of yours, and the new exposition here in Chicago next spring, can you imagine? The whole world coming to Chicago? No, you'll have no time to think of me."

"You will write, won't you?"

"I will. From wherever I am. Like always."

Mary Agnes hugs Helen, and within the hour she takes a rig to the Tremont Hotel and checks in under an alias. In her palatial room on the sixth floor, similar to the ones she cleaned, she runs the tub. Off come her boots, her stockings,

324 | THE IRISH GIRL

her drawers. Skirt next, then blouse, and lastly, chemise in a rush of sweat and grime. Clothes pile on the floor like the mounds of laundry she would scoop off the floors at the Rutherford's or the O'Sullivan's. She pulls the combs out of her long hair, shakes her head, and stands next to the tub. When the water licks high on the sides, warm and frothy, Mary Agnes steps over the rim. As she lowers herself into an envelope of water, she exhales slowly.

What is it about luck? You have it or you don't? You chase it as it flies by, a finger out of reach, every time? Or maybe, you have it all along, but don't know it's luck at the time?

That's it, she thinks. *I've had it all along. With the Purple Mary leading me.*

She thinks then of people in her past. *Granda and Gram. Jimmy Scanlon from the ship to America. Father Benedict and Mrs. Donnelly in New York. Aunt Margaret and Helen. Mrs. O'Sullivan in the big, beautiful house. Tom. Lovely Tom.*

Even Doria, she thinks. *None of this would have unfolded the way it did if I didn't walk every step of this journey. And now Doria's mother, Mrs. Rutherford, with this gift!*

Mary Agnes splashes water over her skin and thinks of still others, Mrs. Spinnelli, her landlady, offering her unexpected kindness and understanding. And everyone in Colorado Springs. *Well, almost everyone.* Tilly. Henry. *Dutch.*

Her mind wanders recklessly as she pours cups and cups of warm water over every curve and dip of her body. *So*—she rinses her hair and nods—*it all unfolded the way it was supposed to, although it was a long and twisted road. Why did I ever doubt it?*

The next morning, Mary Agnes dresses in fashionable traveling clothes, leaves a ten note for the maid, and tosses Henry's fringed ivory shawl over her arm, the only thing she took from the ranch house. She takes the stairs to the elegant dining room and eats a sumptuous breakfast, Eggs

Benedict and Arabian coffee, for God's sake. She can hardly believe it's her voice as she orders. *When I grew up eating mussels and weak fish stew, lumps of potato and twice-over tea. Or some days, nothing at all.*

Donning her hat, she leaves her room key on the hotel desk and steps out into the brisk October air. Once in the carriage—*not even on the streetcar today*—she passes street after familiar street on her way to Chicago's Grand Central Station.

In the large depot waiting room, Mary Agnes adjusts her eyeglasses and marvels over the number of people milling about and queuing up to read the long rotating list of destinations on the schedule board: *New York. Milwaukee. St. Louis.*

So many names! But I know where I'm going. The die is cast, like Granda said. Only this time, it isn't chance. It's her choice. Her mind has changed. Her heart has changed. *And now,* she thinks, *the story can change, too.*

Mary Agnes advances to the ticket booth, one hand on her worn satchel, the same bag she left Dawrosbeg with six long years ago at age thirteen. It's one of the only things about her that hasn't changed. She's no longer a girl, has lost a homeland, a husband, a child. She has money in her pockets, and dresses, hats, boots, and a cloak. Eyeglasses. Books. Confidence. And every day, enough food. What she is still searching for is home, and the satchel reminds her she's still on the journey.

As the line snakes closer to the agent, she blots out the noise inside her head, the station around her, bodies pressing close against her, damp sweat under her arms. She feels a familiar fire in her belly and remembers what her granddad said, to lay claim to what is rightfully hers.

It's then she feels it, all of her ancestors in the room (they are always with us, you know, all who have gone on before).

We have never left ya, girl, they say. And we never will. Ya carry home with ya wherever ya go. Don't go forgetting it. Morning and night we watch over ya, in yer waking and in yer sleeping. Look for us in the clouds and the rain and the sunlight and the rainbow. And always, always, in the faint smell of the sea . . .

Finally, it is her turn. She breathes in, expectant, and holds it for as long as she is able. Then, with a long exhale, she lets go of miles and heartache and troubles and pain.

Taking eight bills from her purse, she spreads them on the worn wooden counter and passes them through the iron grille. Despite the wild beating of her heart, her voice is strong.

"One way to Santa Fe."

AFTERWORD

The Irish as a people have little written history, so I have relied extensively on oral history and family memorabilia gleaned from my grandmother, Grace Sweeney Tannehill, my late uncle, Robert E. Sweeney, my father, Gerald F. Sweeney, and other family members and extensive family research as I wrote this fictional version of my great-grandmother Mary Agnes's story.

Mary Anne Agnes Coyne Cleveland was born in Dawrosmore, County Galway, Ireland on November 18, 1872, and died in Chicago, Illinois on September 11, 1957. As a young girl she lived with her grandparents, Festus and Mary (who I call Grace in the novel) Laffey, at the end of the Dawros peninsula in northwest County Galway outside of Letterfrack in Connemara.

Mary Agnes traveled to America either alone (according to my grandmother) or with a Laffey cousin and his wife and child (according to other family members) in the mid-1880s to rejoin her parents who left her in Ireland as an infant. While in Chicago, she lived with Laffey relatives and worked in domestic service. She met and married Thomas Halligan of Peoria, Illinois, who, soon in the years afterward, developed tuberculosis. After traveling to Colorado Springs with him to chase "the cure," Tom Halligan died in El Paso, Texas. After Tom's death, and before Mary Agnes returned to Chicago to stay for the rest of her life, she worked as a cook on a chuckwagon somewhere along the cattle trail from El Paso to Denver.

I've chosen to play with family history here to serve the story (including moving up the date that St. Mel's Catholic Church opened in Chicago by several years).

My father's recollection of his gram, who went by Mary Agnes, and who raised him in the early 1930s in Chicago, is that she was feisty and fair and frugal, possessed a sizeable sense of humor, and had a great love of all things Western. My father remembers she had a large set of Zane Grey novels on her bedroom dresser and always talked fondly of El Paso. He clearly remembers sitting with her as she listened to Westerns on the radio. Mary Agnes ruled with a firm hand, a tight purse, and a great smile—and always served more than enough to eat. That would be fitting.

I have always thought of myself as a proud Irish American (now, more than thirty-six million people of Irish descent live in the United States, nearly nine times the population of Ireland, with large pockets of Irish still in Boston, Chicago, and New York). It's no secret that those of us of Irish descent are prone to story and exaggeration. These are gifts. I hope I've used them well here as I've spun Mary Agnes's story.

I hope I'm forgiven by Mary Agnes and other family members for taking liberties with her story. This is where creative license comes in. Much like Mary Agnes repairing nets, I am repairing her life and giving her an alternative ending, for reasons of my own. It's fiction, after all.

Mary Agnes Coyne Cleveland, circa 1930s, Chicago, Illinois

ACKNOWLEDGMENTS

For everyone who helped with research, reading, mentorship, editing, and friendship over the past two years, I offer my heartfelt thanks.

My greatest thanks go to my author father, Gerald F. Sweeney—and his long memory and unconditional support—and to my husband, D. Michael Barclay, for both standing beside me every step of this literary and life journey.

In addition, I would like to thank my critique partners, Shelley Blanton-Stroud, Gretchen Cherington, and Debra Thomas, and early readers Tim Forsythe, Gail Lascik, Cathy Markham, Tisha O'Neil Smith, and Tom Wolf.

On the editorial side, thanks to editor Marilyn Janson, peer readers Janis Robinson Daly and Susan J. Tweit, proofreader Nancy Söderlund Tupper, and mapmaker Janet S. Hamill. And a debt of gratitude to She Writes Press publisher, Brooke Warner, project manager Lauren Wise Wait, cover designer Julie Metz, and the whole team and sisterhood at SWP.

On the marketing side, a big shout out to Blue Cottage Agency's Krista Soukup, Janell Madison, and other Blue Cottage Agency authors. Also, a thousand thanks to my webmistress Anji Verlaque.

There are many other people to thank: Meg Hall of the Roman Catholic Archdiocese of Chicago, Russ Powers of the Colorado Railway Museum, and a host of others, in Ireland and the U.S.: Raffaelle Chiusano, Breda Donoghue, Kathleen Bradshaw Davis, Lawrence Coyne, Caroline Herriot, Barry Hopkins, Patricia Jacques, John and Barbara Joyce, Ruairi Keogh, Barry Moloney, Ellen Notbohm, Ann Pollington, Amanda Rogers, Bill Stringfellow, Oisin Sweeney, and Kevin Walsh.

References

Bright, Natalie. *Keep 'Em Full and Keep 'Em Rolling*. Lanham, MD: TwoDot, 2021.

Brown, Mark H. and Felton, W. R. *Before Barbed Wire*. New York: Henry Holt and Co., 1956.

Dolan, Dr. Terence Patrick. *The Dictionary of Hiberno-English*. Dublin: Gill Books, 2020.

Evans, E. Estyn. *Irish Folk Ways*. London: Routledge & Kegan Paul, 1957.

Furnas, J.C. *The Americans: A Social History of the United States 1587-1914*. New York: G. P Putnam's Sons, 1969.

Hirsch, Susan E. and Goler, Robert. I. *A City Comes of Age*. Chicago: Chicago Historical Society, 1990.

Johnston, Lucy. *19th Century Fashion in Detail*. London: Thames and Hudson, Ltd., 2020.

Lynch-Brennan, Margaret. *The Irish Bridget: Irish Immigrant Women in Domestic Service in America, 1840-1930*. Syracuse, N.Y.: University Press, 2009.

McCarthy, Timothy G. *The Catholic Tradition: Before and After Vatican II 1878-1993*. Chicago: Loyola University Press, 1994.

Robson, Pat. *The Celtic Liturgy. London:* Harper Collins, 2000.

Scanalain, Eibhlin Ni. *Land and People: Land Uses and Population Change in NorthWest Connemara in the 19th Century.* Galway, Ireland: The Heritage Service, 1999.

Schlereth, Thomas J. *Victorian America: Transformations in Everyday Life, 1876-1915.* New York: Harper Collins, 1992.

Stover, John F. *The Routledge Historical Atlas of the American Railroads. New York:* Routledge, 1999.

Trow's New York City Directory 1885-86, vol. XCIX. New York: The Trow New York City Directory Co. 1885.

Ward, Fay E. *The Cowboy at Work: All About His Job and How He Does It.* Norman, Oklahoma: University of Oklahoma Press, 1987.

QUESTIONS
FOR DISCUSSION

1. What do you think it would have been like to leave your homeland and travel alone to a new country and a new life in the late nineteenth century?

2. How do think Mary Agnes fared for a 13-year-old girl alone? What were some of her biggest challenges?

3. What choices that Mary Agnes made do you agree with? What choices do you disagree with?

4. Colorado in the late nineteenth century was a wild and untamed place. How do you think women survived on the frontier of the American West, with or without a man?

5. Men like Rooster will always take advantage of vulnerable young girls. In what ways do men take advantage of vulnerable girls and women today? What steps can be implemented to curb or stop this predatory behavior?

6. During the novel, Mary Agnes dreams of Ireland often. Is there a place you dream about, real or imagined?

7. If you were offered the choice to leave your home at age 13, where would you have gone at the time? Or nowhere at all? What about now?

8. Have you ever felt marginalized? If so, how? How can we affect change to marginalized peoples?

9. Women before 1920 in the U.S. didn't have much agency, i.e. no voting rights, no property rights, no family rights, no reproductive rights, etc. What agency did Mary Agnes have? How much more agency would she have today?

10. There's a line in the novel about grudges. *Why is it that people can't come to their own funerals? They might be surprised to hear the words spoken there, after a living a whole life where words were too few and grudges too great.* How do you deal with grudges?

11. What family member would you like to research? Why? And how would you go about starting this research? Would you write about it?

12. Put into words your thoughts to your 13-year-old self. What would you say to encourage her/him/them?

ABOUT THE AUTHOR

A native New Yorker, **ASHLEY E. SWEENEY** is the winner of the Nancy Pearl Book Award and more than a dozen other awards for her previous novels, *Hardland*, *Answer Creek*, and *Eliza Waite*. *The Irish Girl* is based on her paternal great-grandmother's story of coming alone from Ireland to America in the late 19th century. Sweeney lives and writes in the Pacific Northwest and Tucson.

Author photo © Justin Haugen

Looking for your next great read?

We can help!

Visit www.shewritespress.com/next-read
or scan the QR code below for a list
of our recommended titles.

She Writes Press is an award-winning
independent publishing company founded to
serve women writers everywhere.